Becoming St. Patrick

Becoming St. Patrick

His Slavery

ERIC FOSTER

Author Website
www.ericfoster101.co.uk

Matador
Unit E2 Airfield Business Park,
Harrison Road, Market Harborough,
Leicestershire. LE16 7UL
Tel: 0116 279 2299
Email: books@troubador.co.uk
Web: www.troubador.co.uk/matador
Twitter: @matadorbooks

ISBN 978 1803135 403

British Library Cataloguing in Publication Data.
A catalogue record for this book is available from the British Library.

Printed and bound in Great Britain by CMP UK
Typeset in 11pt Adobe Jenson Pro by Troubador Publishing Ltd, Leicester, UK

Matador is an imprint of Troubador Publishing Ltd

Dedicated to
Noel Woodfine

Author's Note

D. A. Binchy revealed in 1962 that almost every biography written on St. Patrick, from the sixth century to that date, was unreliable. Binchy discovered a foreword written by Muirchu, a seventh-century biographer, stating that his 'Life' of St. Patrick was based on dubious sources and written to please his king. We can sum up a second biographer of the period, Tirachan, in his 'Lives' with one brief example of his writing: 'Coroticus, on hearing Patrick's letter, turned into a fox and ran off, never to be seen again.'

Binchy found that the authors of the main biographies used varied sources but all of them traced back to Muirchu and Tirachan. Since this revelation, historians have kept to the limited, though authentic, information provided by Patrick himself in his 'Letter to Coroticus' and his 'Confession'.

There are many claims on Patrick's place of birth, death, the locations of his first and last church, but none of these claims can be verified. Where there are differing opinions amongst historians, I have chosen – for story-telling reasons – but not invented.

I list a few examples:

Year of Patrick's birth: AD 385–AD 400. Chose AD 385

Place of capture: Anywhere on Britain's west coast. Chose north-west

Possible places of his slavery: Slemish, Co. Antrim; Foghill,
                                    Co. Mayo. Chose Foghill

It has been necessary to cut a path through often inaccurate, conflicting, and unrealistic dates and timelines to plausibly present Patrick's lived experience.

For the gaps in recorded knowledge I have imagined, with credibility in mind. Patrick's writings give useful information on his outlook and attitudes, providing a base from which to build his fictional character.

Throughout the book the name 'Ireland' is used for convenience and to maintain Ireland's identity, but the word didn't exist in fifth century Irish vocabulary.

However, the setting of fifth century north-west Britain, Ireland and Gaul is filled with historic interest and challenge, which I have used in my endeavour to serve the reader and to do justice to Patrick's compelling story.

Glossary
Place Names

Autricum	Chartres
Bononia	Boulogne
Condate	Rennes
Deva	Chester
Dubrae	Dover
Eboracum	York
Luguvalium	Carlisle
Marsalla	Marseille
Mide	Meath
Mona	Anglesey
Pannonia	Hungary
Peninus	Pennines
Segedunum	Wallsend
Turonum	Tours
Voclut	Foghill

CHAPTER ONE
AD 400 Alauna – Britain

Patricius galloped his young black stallion along the Roman road
to Alauna Wicus, his blond, wavy locks bouncing on his collar to
the rhythm of the mount. He enjoyed the weekly ride, if not always
the meetings with his father. Patricius and Shadow slowed to a trot
as they passed by the Alauna Fort. A driver and cart, laden with
sacks of corn, was being waved through the guarded portcullis by an
armed soldier. Patricius recognised the strengthened cart cribs and
the bald-headed driver as his, and was displeased that the load was
not stacked higher. He galloped Shadow again for the remainder of
the journey, slowing to a walk when they arrived at the walls of the
town. Patricius spotted the Keeper of The Gate as he spied them
through a grilled peephole and opened.

'I bid you welcome, master,' he greeted cheerfully.

'Good day,' Patricius muttered, barely looking at the gatekeeper.
He entered and dismounted to lead his horse along crowded streets.
Forges and workshops displayed their goods on the roadside. The
sound of hammers striking red hot iron rang out and pungent
smells were airborne. Further along, gentler aromas of freshly sawn
birch and beech greeted them. Carpenters, visible through open
doors, worked at their benches. Customers browsed furniture on
show in the joinery shop, whilst timber delivery carts queued to be
unloaded.

Pedestrians tapped their forelocks as they passed Patricius; others bade him the time of day. He nodded his way down the cobbled street past the tailors and candlestick suppliers and the crush of people at the bakers, for freshly baked bread. Next were meat purveyors, alehouses, most with living accommodation above their businesses, evidenced by the open shutters with bedding thrown over the sills. Streets of houses branched off to the left and right. Ahead Patricius and Shadow entered a select parkland area, arriving at a prestigious and prominently positioned, single storey house, surrounded by beautiful gardens and a perimeter wall; high enough to ensure privacy whilst displaying the Roman architectural features. Masonry-built walls finished in white stucco, set off the brownish-red clay roof tiles.

The groom saw Patricius coming and opened the wrought iron gate.

'Good day, master. I'll take the horse. Madame Conchessa expects you.'

Why tell me I'm expected, Patricius puzzled, when this is a routine visit?

'Thank you, Wynnstan.'

Patricius stroked Shadow's neck and whispered in the horse's ear, 'You're a good horse, Shadow, and my best friend; I'll see you tomorrow.'

But before he reached the door, his mother, plainly dressed, her hair in a back bun, swept into the courtyard.

'Patricius,' she said warmly, giving him a hug. Her eyes flickered briefly downwards before engaging him. 'Calpurnius wants to see you in the library as a matter of urgency. Don't go to the baths. I've sent a pitcher of hot water to your room. Wash and dress and go directly to your father.'

'Very well, Mother. Do you know the matter?'

'Not specifically. A wicus official came to see Calpurnius last night. They talked at length. Whatever they discussed disturbed your father's sleep.'

Patricius stepped into the hall, his mother following.

Turning to her he said, 'Thank you, Mother. I'll prepare myself.'

Patricius worried as he quickly washed and changed. Could it be about our tenants' open meeting last night? Surely Father isn't concerned about the servants and slaves organising? They wield no power. Anyway, my rents are up to date, he reassured himself.

He knocked on the library door and entered. His father, a tall, lean man with a full head of grey hair and a smoothly shaven face, greeted him with a briefer than usual handshake; a ritual begun when Patricius chose to stay in Banna Venta, rather than move with his parents to the town-house.

'I'm pleased to see you, Patricius, but we have difficult matters to discuss today. Help yourself to refreshment.' Calpurnius gestured to a low table, set with ewe's milk, cow's milk, and juice of summer fruits, presented in beautiful Roman amphorae, alongside drinking horns and mugs. A basket of breads stood beside shallow dishes of Mediterranean oils. Patricius poured a mug of juice.

'Thank you, Father.' He took a seat and perched formally on the edge. His father remained standing, in front of shelves stacked with manuscripts, and began his address.

'Patricius, your initial work in managing family business affairs was impressive and the collection of rental income could not be better. Your work on the land yield audits was useful.' He paced towards an open door and looked out over the garden. 'As a result, we held successful meetings with the tax officials.' He turned to face his son. 'Which leads to the question: why have you stopped trying?'

'I don't understand, Father. I haven't stopped trying.'

'Then let me help you to understand,' his father asserted, pacing towards him with heavy strides. Patricius stiffened his resolve but stayed silent.

'On the subject of defences, I have asked you more than once to give me information. When I chase, you don't answer properly. I have my own opinion and sources, but we need to make use of all that is available to us.' His father turned away, facing the open door and the pleasant tranquillity of the walled garden, then turned back

3

to Patricius slowly. 'I have another worry: you. How is your opinion informed?'

Patricius felt his heart pumping and breathed deeply through flared nostrils. As his father paused, Patricius sat deeper in his seat to appear more self-assured and began his fight back.

'Father, the mile fortlets from Bowness to Alauna are a successful deterrent and the military fort is active. The coastline is dangerous for shipping. Why would raiders attack a well defended area where navigation is difficult and dangerous?'

'I know your view. I asked for the views of the people on the ground, our tenants, the farmers, craftsmen and tradesmen, their customers, the purveyors, the merchants. Amongst these people there is experience, useful opinion, new information; some travel and trade out of the province and gain wider knowledge.' His father stopped in front of Patricius and fixed him with eyes undimmed by age. 'What do they know? What do they think? I'd like to know. Is your opinion so astute that you have not the need to listen to others?' Calpurnius raised his voice somewhat, 'I tell you, son, if you behave like an ostrich one day you will be ridden like one.'

'Unfair, Father, you know yourself the effort I put in…' Patricius protested, feeling the heat of accusation burning on his brow.

His father held up a hand to stay his excuses.

'The Procurator decreed the work you speak of. He put a date to it, and he's backed up by armies. But, given a choice, Patricius, I think you are work-shy.' Calpurnius raised his palm again to Patricius, blocking another attempt to respond. 'Don't answer me with words. Let me continue. Last night there was a meeting of citizens with the wicus representative, in Banna Venta. The people arranged this meeting. I didn't know about it. Did you?'

Patricius cast his gaze to the flagstone floor.

'Yes, I did.'

'That's worse.' He slapped his own forehead in annoyance, demeaning Patricius in the process. 'Why didn't you attend?'

Forcing himself to meet his father's glowering stare, Patricius raised his head and replied, 'The representative was only preparing for next week's Council Meeting. All will be heard then. We have nothing to fear from the peasants and tenants.'

'Well, let me tell you, Patricius, and I dare say our emperor already knows; the subject was defences. These insignificant people you mention discussed the fact of an alarming increase in the number of Irish raids south of here. The representative will ask the Council how the arrival on our shores of a raiding party of ten or twelve boats, with twenty warriors per vessel, will be defended.'

'Father, you worry too much about defences. We are in a secure position between Luguvalium and Alauna Fort.'

'Patricius, the people of Banna Venta are nervous because of our lack of concern.' His father shook his head. 'You're almost sixteen; I expect better from you. We should have been leading the way months ago. It's time you learned to listen to the wind.' Calpurnius paused to take a sip of juice then continued. 'There is potentially a much larger worry on the minds of all the British Council leaders; if the Romans leave Britain our entire coastline would be undefended.' He shook his head gravely.

Patricius benefited from a moment's relief as his father's thoughts deflected to the national situation.

'Let us move on. The rents are always up to date, which worries me. I'd like you to think about there being bad news hidden by the good news. I must leave now, to prepare a private service. Oh, be sure to try the breads. Your mother baked them. It's her latest hobby. I'll see you at table.' His father left the room, closing the door carefully behind him.

Patricius breathed out forcibly, relieved that the roasting, for the moment at least, had subsided. After a period of stunned silence, he reclined and ate from the platter as he mulled things over. He'd had to work hard at the audit because of the level of official scrutiny, he knew this, but afterwards he'd made a deliberate decision to work leisurely when he could and toil only when he had to. He knew it was laziness but justified the decision internally as being clever, because everything still worked out. However, the comment about the views of the people on the ground rocked him. He'd missed this point entirely and realised that his attitude had closed his mind.

I should have questioned our people, especially the travellers; he chided himself. Returning to his room, Patrick puzzled over his father's meaning about hidden bad news.

A packed bag including sandals and toiletries awaited him. He picked it up, left the house, and, without a thank you or a goodbye to his mother, walked the half mile down to the bath house. This attractive facility was situated in a stone building, with a tiled and ventilated roof, and was set amongst cultured lawns and flower beds. Patricius followed the paved pathway and entered the building through an elegant portico into a reception area with clearly signed doors and corridors leading off. Heading towards the changing rooms a voice behind him called:

'Congratulations, Patricius. You made it to the finals this year.'

Patricius turned and looked up to his tall and muscular friend. 'Thank you, Elias. I did, and I need some practice. Fancy a knock?' Patricius was pleased that Elias, a tough competitor was willing. He would need to concentrate to beat him and could put his business worries, for a short while, to one side.

They entered the sports hall barefooted, wearing white robes. Soldiers were boxing, others wrestling, some were stick-fighting and Patricius and Elias were about to join them.

After stretching exercises, they chose their sticks from the wall-racks. Taking up their two-inch diameter, seven-foot-long poles, they found a pitch and began their contest. The objective was simple: a strike to the opponent's body scored two points; a prod scored one, and the first to score six points won the game.

They began slowly, testing each other. It was a game of concentration and speed, combined with strength. Patricius deceived his opponent; appearing to pull out of a strike he speedily changed and struck. Elias produced a swift prod which Patricius anticipated with speed and power to force the deflection. The pair sparred and struck, blocked, and defended their way to scoring. Patricius took the game by six points to three and finished breathless.

'You weren't at your best today, Elias; you didn't make me sweat.'

'I ran out of energy,' he gasped. 'Let's go to the baths. Sitting will be quite agreeable.'

They undressed in warm changing rooms where Patricius put on his purpose-made wooden-soled sandals.

'You're going to the steam rooms, I see,' said Elias, glancing at the sandals. The stone and mosaic floors there, directly above the furnace, were too hot for bare feet.

'Yes, are you?'

'I'm taking a sauna. Maybe see you later.'

Patricius entered the first steam bath and followed a sequence of three rooms, each hotter than the previous one, leading to cleaning, cooling, and relaxation areas. Assistants were on hand to towel down the bathers and cleanse their entire bodies.

Patricius opted for this anointing. A masseur applied the oil and gave Patricius a shoulder and back massage. Face down on the table Patricius cast his mind back to when he decided to take life leisurely. He never expected a comeback from this approach. I think I'll have to work harder, he thought, as the masseur completed the luxurious treatment and covered Patricius with a warm towel before moving to the customer on the next recliner.

An assistant arrived and, using a curved, hand-sized metal strigil, deftly removed the oil from Patricius's body with a scraping action, dipping and cleaning the blade frequently in a flowing hot water trough. Patricius followed the oil and scrape with a cold plunge bath, which made him gasp aloud. From there, he dried off in a private warm room then robed and rested his body on a wave-shaped stone recliner.

But he didn't rest; he directed his thoughts immediately to the issue of security. Finding himself in such disagreement with his father, Patricius reasoned he would be better supporting a security system that wasn't needed than continuing his current stance of opposing the need for action.

He returned to the changing room, dressed, and departed. As he walked, his friend Hermanus bounded down the path towards him.

'Good day to you, Hermanus. I'm late today, which makes you very late.'

'Greetings, Patricius. Yes. I've just left a meeting. Have you time to talk for a while?'

'Indeed, let's take a seat.'

They sat on a garden bench overlooking the valley, bathed in cool evening sunshine. The river meandered, effortlessly cutting a swathe through crop fields and on through coarse and rugged grazing lands. In the distance, twirls of smoke sifted through the cone-shaped roofs of family homes.

'Any development on your education plans, Hermanus?'

'It's why I'm late. I'm going to take instruction from Rhetor Pantheos for two years and thereafter, when I am eighteen, I am to attend a Catholic residential seminary in York.'

'Good news, Hermanus.' Patricius slapped his friend's shoulder in jubilation. Hermanus smiled, enjoying the camaraderie.

'My father is sending me to Pantheos too. I'll be studying Classics, Latin, Roman Law, and the History of Rome. I'm on the sunrise sessions, four hours a day.'

'We'll be on the same course, in the library rooms at the Town Hall. In my case I will receive an extra hour each day on Theology.'

'We'll have some great discussions, your news has lifted my spirits,' Patricius was racing ahead in his thoughts. Dropping his smile, he faced Hermanus saying, 'my father is worried about the security of our farmlands. Worse, he thinks we should prepare ourselves for life without the Romans. What does your father think?'

'He thinks serious change is coming, possibly British self-rule.'

Patricius, with furrowed brow, asked, 'Do you think the Romans might leave?'

'No, I don't. We have embraced Roman rule and are better off with it. That makes us easy to manage. I don't think there is a strong reason for Rome to leave the Britains. What do you think, Patricius?'

'Regarding our local defences, Alauna and the mile forts serve us well. But if Alauna closed suddenly, we could not defend ourselves. Our peasants have become domesticated with their security being someone else's responsibility. They are no longer aggressive. I'd like to discuss further with you, Hermanus, but I must go. I'm happy to be on the same course as you for our Classics. See you next week, Hermanus.'

Patricius stood up and, unusually, gave Hermanus a parting handshake.

'Goodbye, Patricius. Keep well.'

Donning a lightweight, cream-coloured pallium over his short, matching tunic, Patricius clipped a ruby-enamelled brooch at his left shoulder, set off by the burgundy crenellated border of the silk. With sandals laced, he combed his wavy locks and made his way past the corridor frescoes to the patio.

Double doors led into splendid looking gardens, with flowers in bloom bordering plush green lawns. Taking a juice from a serving table, he reclined on the cushions of a full-length chair, enjoying the warmth of the evening sun. Enclosed on three sides this Little Eden was sheltered from the coastal breezes and winds, which could quickly turn cold and harsh.

His father crossed the lawn to him. 'Good evening, Patricius. How was your visit to the bath house?' He poured a juice, took a swig, and leant against a solid stone pedestal.

'Enjoyable, but busy too. I saw Hermanus. He's going to study with Professor Pantheos; we'll be in the same group.'

'Excellent. His family are prominent. That's a great testimony to Rhetor Pantheos,' Calpurnius said with an air of grandeur that was mirrored by his outfit, a light blue tunic overlaid with a full-length, dark-blue cloak, open-fronted and clasped at the throat with a gold-coloured brooch. His sandals were light brown and strapped criss-cross fashion to just above the ankle. He went on, 'This rent situation. What do you see on your collection rounds?'

'I don't see anything, Father. I don't collect. They come to my office at the villa.'

His father raised neatly groomed eyebrows. 'When did this come about?'

'The last collection was the fourth time.' Patricius said.

'I wish you'd discussed this with me, Patricius. Anyway, it fits in with my suspicions.'

Patricius sat upright, 'And they are?'

'I suspect we are losing stock.'

'Isn't that a sweeping conclusion, Father?'

'I don't think so. All our tenants are up to date with their rent, all the time. That is suspicious, especially so soon after a rent increase. It should be hard toil for the tenants to cope. They're earning more than we know, Patricius.' Calpurnius shook his cup-holding hand at Patricius, spilling some of his juice. 'Paying at your office is a gift, son. I'll wager they want it to stay that way. They don't want you snooping around, seeing things that you shouldn't.'

Patricius understood now what the bad in the good was. He stood to reply.

'Our largest commodity is corn,' he said, thinking aloud. 'Where would I begin looking?'

'You need to go through the process from field to fort. Tighten up your systems. Look for clues; souterrains with worn paths, they could be hiding places. Grain spills where there shouldn't be, spare sacks in circulation, conspicuous wealth.' His father extended a finger for each step Patricius must take. 'Reward supervisors for cutting out waste and losses but be sure to have a way of checking out your supervisors.'

Shoulders slumped, Patricius risked a final question. 'If I find someone thieving, how should I deal with them?'

'Harshly; and it's when, not if.'

Their discussion was interrupted by the graceful sight of Conchessa gliding over to them in her ankle-length, cream-coloured stola. A red silk border matched the palla that draped from her left shoulder to right hip, which, secured with a gold enamelled brooch, gave a vivid splash of brilliance that drew their eyes. Her plaited hair was tightly formed into a high bun. Light brown, closed sandals peeped below the hem of her stola. The absence of earrings and a torca indicated to Patricius that the occasion was not too formal.

'Conchessa, how elegant you look.'

'Thank you, Calpus,' Conchessa responded warmly, using her husband's abbreviated name. She crossed to where her husband stood and rested a hand lightly on his arm for a moment.

'Yes, Mother, beautiful. Can I pour you a juice?'

'Thank you, Patricius. Plum juice please. It's our own fruit, picked today.'

Patricius took up the amphora, speaking as he poured. 'You've been busy, Mother. Which reminds me; I enjoyed the fresh and tasty breads.'

Conchessa smiled appreciatively. 'I'm glad you liked them. I baked them myself with a little help from Sylvia. How was your trip to the bath house, Patricius?'

His father, following the conversation, nodded slightly as Patricius commented on the breads. Patricius caught his mother's eyes scanning his face carefully. She's looking for clues to my feelings after a bruising meeting with Father.

'Interesting; there were more soldiers than usual today.'

'There would be, the fort is hosting a conference prior to the administrators' meeting in Luguvalium.'

'What is that about?' Patricius asked.

'It's about administrative efficiency in the province,' his mother replied.

'Are they thinking of more reductions?' Patricius asked with a hint of resignation in his voice.

'No. They're trying to increase the feeling of security through strengthening order.'

Patricius gaped at her, 'How do you know these things, Mother?'

'Ah, well, Patricius, I am a member of the Decurion Wives club. We like parties and we love gossip. Last week we had a long lunch, to discuss the fashion style of the Empress. That's why my back bun is now a top bun.'

Patricius smiled.

'Tell your mother the news from Hermanus,' his father prompted.

'Hermanus will study with Rhetor Pantheos. We'll be in the same group for two years. After that, Hermanus will be off to York to take his orders,' Patricius related.

'You get on well with Hermanus, don't you?' his mother remarked.

'Yes. We have great conversations and share our thoughts and opinions. He's good at games too, especially dice.'

'Excellent. I'm sure your friendship will help your studies. Your discussions will be like an extra tutorial. Enough.' His mother clapped her hands. 'It's time to go to the dining room. Sylvia will be ready to serve.'

They entered a gently fragranced room with a new, impressive floor mosaic portraying a heroic-looking man riding a leopard. A ceramic vine of luscious green grapes framed the picture.

'What do you think of the floor art?' Calpurnius asked Patricius, gesturing down with a grand sweep of his arm.

'Magnificent.'

'I'll tell you the story of the scene after dinner,' his father promised as they headed towards their seats.

Three full-length lounge chairs, with armrests at one end and a generous scattering of cushions, lined the floor on three sides. Calpurnius took position at the head of the room. Conchessa and Patricius reclined on opposite sides. Low tables, draped with cream-coloured linen, stood before each of the diners, set only with breads and dipping oils. An additional smaller table stood at Calpurnius's side, partly covering the hero's Staff of Majesty.

Sylvia, the kitchen slave, entered the room carrying a tray. She stopped and bowed graciously to Calpurnius, then marched over the leopard and hero to place wine amphorae and goblets on Calpurnius' side table.

'Please offer wines to Conchessa,' Calpurnius asked.

Sylvia nodded and turned to Conchessa. 'Madame, the master's choice is a sweet Italian white wine or a local, peppered-honey mead.'

'Italian white please.'

When all were served Calpurnius raised his glass saying, 'A blessing to the health of the family, please God.'

'Please God,' said Conchessa and Patricius in unison.

Sylvia and the house-slave, a boy of thirteen called Simon, returned with bowls of fish soup, placing these, along with spoons, knives, and spikes on each table. As the family enjoyed their soup, dishes of mussels, whelks, cockles and a fish-based liquamen sauce were served to the tables, followed by green salads and small jugs of honey. The family spiked and spooned their way leisurely through the starters and finished by adding a shot of honey to their wine, which they quaffed.

'How is life at the villa, Patricius?' his mother enquired.

'The servants are working well, and the bath and hot water are in good order. I like the villa bath.'

'How do you spend your evenings, Patricius?' his father asked.

'I ride Shadow almost every day. Then I use the bath before dinner. Most evenings I dine alone, and occasionally I eat at The Tavern. There is a new gaming house there where I play dice.'

'What class of people do you socialise with?' his father enquired.

'Mostly soldiers and farmers at The Tavern, and at the gaming house it's usually students, craftsmen, centurions and so.' His father's look gave no clues, which Patricius took as acceptance; disapproval was usually expressed forthrightly.

Conchessa nodded to Sylvia, who was watching from the corridor. Walking over the border of grapes, she and Simon brought dishes of haddock, sea bream and jugs of fish sauce to the table. Calpurnius gestured and Sylvia responded by refilling the wine glasses. Patricius was relieved that the interrogative conversation from his father had moved on.

'Conchessa, the fish sauce is delicious. How do you do it?' Calpurnius asked.

'Thank you, Calpus. It's a paste of sprats and anchovies mixed with honey, wine and wheat starch, which we spice with our own garden herbs.'

Patricius glanced across at his mother who was delighted with the attention her hobby was drawing.

Fish course over, Sylvia replaced every wine glass and brought an amphora of Mediterranean red wine. Walking over the leopard's body to the wine table she poured three glasses, served them, and returned quickly to the kitchen. She re-entered with three dishes of roasted cow-meat pieces and small jugs of meat liquamen. Simon followed, serving bowls of leeks and onions. The family, at leisure, ate their fill.

With tables cleared, Calpurnius took up a cane stick, crossed the floor and turned to face Conchessa and Patricius.

'Allow me to narrate the story in the mosaic: "The Triumph of Bacchus". In Greek mythology Bacchus was the son of Zeus, a god, and Semele, a mortal woman. You know the story of his birth and rebirth from the fresco in the corridor.' Patricius nodded. 'Bacchus was born the god of agriculture and liberation. As a youth he learned how to cultivate the vine and extract its special juice. A jealous Hera inflicted madness upon him and he became a wanderer through foreign lands. In Phrygia, the goddess Cybele cured him and taught him her religious rites. Bacchus then set out on a progress through Asia, teaching the people how to make wine, signified by this border of grapes,' said Calpurnius, pointing to the perimeter of the mosaic. Patricius was enjoying the story and looked forward to learning more of these from the rhetor.

'The leopard symbolises the power of Bacchus and reminds us of his travels in Asia. The spear is ornate, his robes are fine, and, sitting astride a mighty but obedient leopard, he shows his majesty.' Patricius saw his father looking around for approval and, with a flourish he concluded, 'Bacchus returns to his home and declares himself the god of wine.' Calpurnius resumed his seat.

Patricius and his mother clapped briefly.

'Let dessert be served,' Conchessa announced, giving a nod to her kitchen servant.

Sylvia immediately entered, serving fruit, cakes, bread, and honey. She filled the wine glasses and, as the family ate, she brought a stool to the spot vacated by Calpurnius.

A young woman came into the room holding a lyre. She bowed to the family who nodded back in courtesy whereupon she took her seat.

'Psalm 23, written by David,' she announced. Plucking a smooth and peaceful tune, she captured her audience and began to sing in mesmerising voice 'The Lord's my shepherd; I shall not want. He maketh me to lie down in green pastures...'

Patricius enjoyed the music. He knew of the psalm but, against his tutor's wishes, had not learned the words. The harpist's mastery of instrument and vocals induced in Patricius a desire to know the psalm himself. She finished, bowed, and left the room to warm applause.

'An excellent choice of psalm, Calpus,' said Conchessa.

'Thank you, Conchessa. Your choice of musician was inspired,' her husband responded.

'How did you find her, Mother?' Patricius asked.

'She played at a wives' lunch. I'm told she's a cousin of Hermanus.'

Patricius was confused by the happenings of the evening. The dinner was fine but not exceptional. The lyrist was fitting for a notable occasion, though clashing with the mood of the afternoon. Furthermore, his sixteenth birthday was three weeks away and would be a special family event, so why have another one so close?

'Father, Mother, thank you for this evening. We always have a fine dinner, but tonight has been particularly so. May I ask if there is a special reason?'

'Not really,' said Conchessa, at the same time as Calpurnius said, 'Well. Yes.'

They laughed and Calpurnius spoke.

'Patricius, we want to explain our thoughts for the future. Let me begin with some dreary, though relevant, background in relation to taxation. The procurator exempts decurions who are clergy from having to use their personal wealth to make good the shortfalls in municipal tax collection.'

Patricius raised his eyebrows at this news. He didn't know the position of decurion carried such risk.

15

'This is to enable clergy to concentrate on developing the spiritual well-being of Roman citizens. Our family enjoys this exemption. On the other hand, Catholic clergy, under authority from the Church of Rome, must divest themselves of their assets in order to maintain their membership of the priesthood. I have not done this. Instead, I made special arrangements with The Keeper of Registers. However, the Church allows their clergy to divest to a non-clerical, adult person, including sons or daughters. As it happens, a team of oxen couldn't pull you, Patricius, into the church.'

Patricius smiled coyly at the thought that one of his errant ways was of benefit to the family.

'Soon you will be sixteen. By the time you are eighteen, Patricius, we want you to be familiar with running the family business.' Patricius listened intently. 'When you are, we want to transfer the estate into your ownership.' Patricius puffed out his cheeks. 'Therefore, you should take more and more responsibility for running the family affairs before then. At the same time, you will begin your classical education and professional studies. It means you will have to apply yourself.' Calpurnius paused allowing Patricius to digest the information.

Ownership of the estate and hard work bounced around in Patricius's brain as his father continued.

'Patricius, our style of living does not just happen.' He took a sip of the imported wine. 'Over the next two years we want you to become the leader. Eventually you will take responsibility for the entire estate, the family well-being, the security of our employees and tenants, and contribute to the civic life of our locality.' Patricius was flushed in the face. 'Your mother and I believe you have the ability. However, it will require dedication and constant effort. Leisure and privilege may ensue. In this event, you will have earned it. Till now it has been a gift to you. We want your commitment, Patricius. Think this over carefully. Your answer next week will be soon enough.'

A stunned Patricius fumbled his words. 'Thank you. I can't... I don't... I'm not sure... I can't... I'm overwhelmed.'

'Good, Patricius. Responsibility ought to overwhelm you, even scare you. Shall we finish our wine and make to bed? Join me in the library to break-fast. We'll discuss villa matters before you go.'

Patricius knocked back his wine. 'Goodnight, Father. Goodnight, Mother,' he said and left the room in a blur, unaware his parents had said goodnight back to him.

Standing at a tall and slim circular table, Patricius and his father ate a quick break-fast of bread and fruit, washed down with fruit juice. His mother's habit of not eating break-fast meant she didn't join them.

'Patricius, the security of the settlement requires further thought,' his father cautioned. 'Banna Venta is more than an hour away from Alauna Fort. We can defend a large attack but are vulnerable to small and stealthy raids. Check the perimeter of the whole settlement, especially the coast. Analyse our weaknesses. Come a day early with your findings and some ideas. We'll prepare for the Council Meeting together; you should attend with me as an observer. Don't neglect the other matters either. Well, you've no time to waste, so I bid you farewell.' They shook hands.

In his room Patricius sat on the edge of his bed, puffed his cheeks, and blew out. His neck was hot. The task set by his father seemed daunting. He worked out his next actions, from leaving his parents' house, to working on the tasks, going home at works-end instead of days-end. By the time he'd planned the day, his mood had changed.

'I can do this,' he said aloud and packed his bag to leave.

He sent Sylvia with a message to the groom to prepare Shadow, then looked for his mother, finding her unexpectedly in the kitchen.

'Mother, I'm going now. I'd like to say thank you, for everything.'

'Patricius, it's a pleasure. You have much to think about. I hope you grasp the challenge with both hands.'

'Thank you, Mother, I have more to do than respond to the challenge; I have your trust to regain. I apologise for my previous behaviour.'

His mother's eyes widened, even sparkled. Patricius could see he'd taken his first step.

'See you next week.' He kissed his mother goodbye and made for the stables.

CHAPTER TWO
AD 400 Ailech Province – Ireland

Colm glanced to the sky, hoping that rain would stay away. The moon, a silvery orb, cast shadows over the woods. He lowered his gaze and glanced at the scene around him; his blue eyes missing no detail. The full moon shimmered with enough light to reveal the gathering people. Their colourful robes brought the clearing to life; a mythical, multi-coloured manifestation. He himself wore an impressive blue robe, befitting his position as son and appointed successor of the chieftain they were gathering to honour. His brother Conn, walking beside him, was dressed in a blue and green striped tunic which signified he too was the chieftain's son, but the green stripe told he was not destined to succeed his father's leadership of the clan. Colm and his brother stood out starkly against the other pall-bearers who wore red, the colour of warriors and guards representing the blood of battle. Stepping slowly in unison, led by a tall druid in his ceremonial, hooded white gown, they carried the cask along a cattle track, their way illuminated by straw ground-lights.

Colm's mother, Medb Kilmurrach walked behind the coffin, dressed in the deep blue robe of a chieftain's widow; on her right, the poet bard, his flowing white gown emblazoned with a golden, embroidered Celtic Wheel. King Niall followed, draped in a regal crimson tunic and cape, his queen by his side wearing a tightly fitted gown of magisterial purple. Colm, seeing his father's funeral procession was an impressive, almost royal sight, returned his gaze to the path before him.

Bearing the weight of the cask on his right shoulder, Colm looked ahead to the clearing. Flimsy enclosures of woven willow panels were formed in a semi-circle for the occupants to see the forthcoming rite. In one stood bare-legged slaves clad in their traditional, simple yellow tunics with horns and bronze cups hanging from their belts; followed by leather-shoed farmers, also in yellow tunics but with bright green edging. Identified by the colour of their garb and with an enclosure for each class of person, Colm saw a patchwork of people. Seen like this, the age-old custom looked ridiculous to him.

The procession drew near to an empty enclosure, reserved for the family and nobles; Colm knew it was time to concentrate. The next step could go wrong, which is why he had insisted on practices. The bearers stepped up to the altar frame, positioned the currach above it and, on Colm's nod, lowered the boat smoothly and accurately into place. His father had expressed a wish to be interred in a boat and, although the handling was more difficult, there must be no clumsiness at a Kilmurrach burial, not with the eyes of the clans upon them. He and Conn stepped back a couple of strides into the reserved area and the red-robed bearers took positions round the altar, symbolising observance of the Four Quarters.

Standing next to his mother, Colm gave her a reassuring glance. He looked further along. Uncle Eamonn's expression was grave; his sister, Breege, kept her head down. The king was impassive whilst Conn was composed. Colm thought back to the family vote when the king had elevated his father to chieftain. The Tanist system of hierarchy required the family to elect a successor to Aeden. However, working closely with a king brought great responsibility, and this didn't suit Conn's personality. Conn had been relieved to see his younger brother chosen. Colm, at the time a confident fifteen-year-old, had also thought the decision was correct; but he never expected to be attending his father's burial a mere four years later.

The tall druid quickly lit the ground-lights along the front of the cask, transforming the altar into a dazzling spectacle. Behind the altar an apparition of the high priest mixed murkily with the shadows. Suddenly he held aloft two flaming torches, illuminating his flowing white robe. Placing the torches in holders to the west and east of the Cauldron of Rebirth, he knelt behind the altar in prayer. A wolf howled eerily, breaking the silence, and creating shivers in the crowd. The high priest chanted himself into a trance and slowly his monotone faded, replaced again by silence.

During the lull, Colm thought of the affection of the people for his father. Although duty-bound to attend the burial of their chieftain, people would happily turn up just for the spit and ale; this time they came to honour the man. Poverty and fighting prevented most Irishmen from living to old age, but Aeden Kilmurrach, a defensive warrior and conciliator, had brought peace into this corner of Niall's kingdom. These clans were enjoying full bellies and happy hearts and for this reason, his father was loved by the gentle and simple.

The high priest lifted an ox-head from the cask, turned its glassy stare to the crowd, and raised his arms to the sky.

'Spirits of the East, Powers of Air, we call you. Bring us bright memories of our beloved Aeden. Blessed be. Spirits of the South, Powers of Fire, we call you. Keep the fires of our love for Aeden alive. Spirits of the West, Powers of Water, we call you. Remember Aeden Kilmurrach who loved the sea. Let our tears flow in love for Aeden and in healing for self. Blessed be.' The crowd nodded their approval and the high priest paused in recognition.

As the emotion strengthened, Colm gripped his mother's hand.

Raising his voice on the first word, the priest continued, 'Spirits of The North, Powers of Earth, we call on you. From you we come, to you return. Remember Aeden Kilmurrach to whom you gave strength and wisdom. Embrace him in his passing. Blessed be.'

The people cowered silently, scared of the Spirits of the North. With Aeden gone would the Powers of Earth call for their return too? As the dread sank in, the air turned cold and the high priest, maintaining the ox-head aloft, appealed to the gods:

'We pray to east, south, west and north for favourable acceptance of our offering.'

Slamming the ox-head onto a pike he placed it upright in a holder and torched it. The shaft, wrapped in oil-soaked cloth, flashed aflame from bottom to top like lightning returning to the sky, igniting the bovine skull in a massive ball of flame.

As the open-mouthed crowd absorbed the spectacle, shivering in the face of flames, the bard fired-up the incense holders encircling Aeden's corpse. Spiralling smoke connected earth to sky and the high priest swayed behind the thickening swirls and merged with darkness. The smoke scattered, revealing a harpist, seated where the priest had earlier stood. She plucked a tune and poet Bard Feenan, standing next to the currach, sang in psalm, his Elegy to Aeden:

'Dear, dear unto me, is his body in the winding sheet. Gigantic he was, yet active, alert and fleet. Aed Kilmurrach.' As the bard paused, Colm, with head down and eyes open, noticed the king lean forward and glance at the Kilmurrachs.

'Strong in frame, no mortal could resist his blows, he worked his skilful hands till death, with wood and glass and bellows. Aed Kilmurrach.'

After a verse for Aeden's every attribute, the elegy was completed, whereupon the harpist and the bard retreated.

Colm gave a nod to his mother and they stepped to the altar. He placed a finely crafted triple spiral charm into the currach, made himself as a boy under his father's watchful guidance. His father, like many, believed in the number three and the power of three.

The crowd strained to see the goods, whispering their findings to their neighbours. Colm looked across to his mother's offering; a deep-red enamelled brooch which Aeden had made and given her during their courtship. Colm saw the pride of sacrifice in his mother's eyes as she placed it next to Aeden. Then, Uncle Eamonn set down a small horn, labelled "Mead". He'd learned from Eamonn how to make mead, from hive to amphora. Conn's grave goods were a pelt knife and leather sheath, given to him by his father after he had successfully skinned his first deer. Finally, Breege placed a sprig of mistletoe in the currach, symbolising the gift of new life. Her father had shown her a dying oak, but when mistletoe grew upon it, he said, watch this tree recover. As a girl she observed the tree regain its strength over ten years.

The high priest glided back from the shadows as the moon hid behind a cloud. Placing the cauldron and blackened ox-skull in the cask next to Aeden's feet he solemnly reinstated the cover. As the lid fell into place, suddenly all thought of continuing his father's legacy left Colm. He felt desolate, as a massive empty space entered his life.

'Be with me Father,' he prayed, then took a firm grip of his emotions.

Four pall-bearers raised and turned the currach. Colm and Conn joined them, shouldering their share of the burden. The high priest, with inscribed fey in hand, walked ahead, accompanied by torch bearers. Everyone followed, jostling among themselves for a good position.

Arriving at the grave with the currach pointing east, the torchbearers stood to attention as the boat was lowered into its shallow grave. The priest pulled back the cover for final prayers and was surprised as the king stepped forward and knelt before the cask. King Niall beckoned the bereaved family to join him and, with both hands, he laid a brilliant white sash, the regalia of royalty, from Aeden's shoulder to hip. Colm heard his mother gasp at the gesture and a tear of appreciation trickled down Colm's cheek. They stood as the high priest delivered a graveside prayer.

'We gather here and now to bid farewell to Aeden Kilmurrach, who must travel far. Let the blessings of the Goddesses and Gods, of the Old Ones, and of friends and family, be with you as you travel beyond.' After pausing for private reflections, the high priest delivered a concluding prayer:

'Aeden Kilmurrach, may you move beyond form, flowing like water, feeding on sunlight and moonlight, sparkling as the stars in the night sky. Enter the dark without fear, let the wheel turn, returning you to the womb of life. Rest, heal, and grow young. Blessed be.' He returned the cover and a lid was placed over the currach.

Workers backfilled the grave and shaped a mound and a ring of white stones. The high priest held the fey high, displaying the Ogham script which no one could read except a few nobles. The epitaph said: "Here lies Aeden Kilmurrach."

The formalities ended and the priest announced, 'The Kilmurrach family invite all to the fallow field for ale and roasted pig.'

With horns dangling and copper mugs jangling, the crowd followed the whiff of the spits. The nobles walked solemnly, to join everyone for a drink, and were overtaken by the eager crowd.

The tempting aromas of pigs on roast and fresh bread, baking over open fires, had the crowds queueing down the left side of the field while, on the right, hidden behind the mayhem of jostling people, were the jugs of ale. The centre of the field, a square marked by four short posts in the ground, was reserved for the family and nobles. Servants brought drinks on trays to them. Here, the family received solemnities from friends and the clan.

As the funeral party withdrew, the people spontaneously formed a human funnel down which the nobles had to walk to exit the field. Medb held back for a second but Colm, seeing her hesitation, immediately calmed her.

'They're showing respect for you,' said Colm, spotting the king too was reassured.

Slaves and servants, farmers and fishermen, craftsmen, and contractors, stood in straggly lines, their heads bowed to the Kilmurrachs and King Niall as they paraded out of the field.

'This spectacle of appreciation has opened my eyes,' King Niall said to Colm, nodding back to the crowd with sincerity.

Colm, who understood how his father was seen by the people, bowed his head solemnly to the crowd, receiving their respects on behalf of his father, with dignity.

'My Lord, the people crave relief from their spiritless, poverty-stricken lives. With your support, my father gave them a small measure of their need.'

The nobles and family continued their walk to the bridge and the crannog, where a banquet awaited them in the Mead House. Colm, walking with a chieftain, a few paces ahead of King Niall and the poet bard, heard the king's voice. He twitched his ears, catching every word that followed.

'The family, I see were impressed with your elegy.'

'A successful outcome, I would say,' replied the bard.

'Bard Feenan, I know, and Aeden knew, the poetry of Memnon,' the king continued, 'you will do well to remember it is your duty to write original words. Your peers call you Freelips, a name that should shame you. Remember, your high position is reward for high standards.' The king strode forwards to engage with Colm, leaving Freelips to fret. The chieftain who was walking with Colm, diplomatically moved ahead to catch up with the others.

'Colm, I believe the ceremony was worthy of Aeden. And especially made so by the family,' the king remarked.

Colm studied the king's face in the moonlight, seeing the king was expressing a genuine thought. *He looks younger than my father too, yet they're the same age.*

'Thank you, my Lord. I was moved by your generosity to my father, especially laying on him a white sash,' Colm replied. The king merely nodded his head.

Together they were approaching the open crannog gates. The family and Bard Feenan were in front, with only a few local chieftains behind them.

'It was his due,' the king added. 'Colm, it is a difficult time, but before parting tomorrow, we should briefly mention the project.'

Colm wanted privacy. He caught the king's eye and nodded discreetly towards the chieftains as he stopped at the gate. The king stopped with him. Colm, facing the king, saw his physique was fit and strong. His pointed beard, dark and neatly trimmed, grew a few inches below his chin and gave him a studious appearance.

'I helped my father build these gates,' he said to Niall as the chieftains, in animated conversation, passed by, leaving Colm and the king to follow at a distance. With no chance of being overheard, Colm addressed King Niall on the serious issue of the project.

'My Lord, I will explain my feelings now. If it pleases you, my intention is to spend three days of mourning with the clan then return to the project.' Colm heard the squeak of the gates being closed. 'My father discussed all aspects with me; we made a trial of the operation together and I trained the warriors for him. Father trained me and the crew, in detail, for the landing and departure. This plan is bigger and better than all previous and I want to complete my father's work. My Lord, I can do it.' Colm stared earnestly at King Niall then, realising his boldness, he dropped his gaze and added, 'If it is your wish.'

Colm was aware of the king studying him, assessing the conviction in his plea. His father had been a man of exceptional ability, but Colm wished the king to see in him the same or, dare he hope, greater, potential. I want him to see Colm Kilmurrach, Colm thought earnestly.

'It is my wish,' the king answered, his voice heavy with sincerity. And for a second, Colm saw his father in the king.

Colm took a deep breath, his eyes glistening with pride as he stepped into his father's boots.

'Thank you, my Lord.'

He took another, deeper breath, bracing himself for the weight of the responsibility. Then with dry eyes he turned square on to the king and said, 'King Niall, your raid on Britain shall happen.'

CHAPTER THREE

Rising often to the trot, interspersed with walking breaks and short gallops, Patricius and Shadow arrived at Banna Venta exhilarated by their journey. He set to work immediately, touring the tenant farmers to lay down the law for the new payment arrangements. Spotting a souterrain with some evidence of old and trampled grain at the entrance, he dismounted to the drilling gaze of a dozen eyeballs scrutinising his actions whilst feigning to be occupied on work in the fields. The cavern was bare. He mounted and moved on, stopping occasionally to scratch notes with a graif on his wax tablet.

He observed the derelict mile-fortlet, reflecting that only two years ago this lookout post was manned day and night by three armed soldiers. Rome's need for more soldiers in Europe had led to the closure of alternate lookout posts in Britanniae, and the remaining ones were reduced from three to two soldiers. Perhaps Father is right; maybe a withdrawal is already happening.

His parents lived in the wicus, south of Alauna Fort, built above steep and rocky cliffs, overlooking a treacherous, protecting coastline. In Banna Venta the terrain was flatter and rocky with a few small beaches of sand and pebble. Stories of trading and raiding vessels and crews perishing on the rocky coast had passed down the generations, telling how attempts to navigate safe landings were defeated by gusting winds, deadly hidden rocks and contrary currents. How real were those stories, he wondered?

Patricius took in the tidal shore: the Solway estuary, with mountains on the northern Solway bank and Caledonian coast. The sun was high in the sky, the day, fresh and clear, the tide rushing out from the wet and salty strand to a distant mist, obscuring the view of the water's edge. Patricius tried to imagine an attack and realised he knew nothing. Did raids take place in daylight, perhaps, or at night; in good weather or bad; stealthily or by battle? Would battle make sense? Dead people don't make slaves. Injured captives wouldn't fetch a high price. There were people on the estate who would know. He regretted having made no effort to learn.

Huh! Father wants to endow me with his estate, but he's not sure he can trust me. He's right; but from today I begin proving him wrong.

Making his way to the trades and crafts area, he revisited the family stories of the trading settlement being formed historically around a small fort called Beckfoot, where his grandfather, Potitus, had owned some land of little worth. The Roman development of Alauna Fort to the south connecting with the Roman administrative town of Luguvalium to the north changed all this, and the land increased substantially in value.

His grandfather began building craft houses and, at times, provided the capital equipment for the tenants. This enterprising approach had secured the family's future and Patricius' father had continued the commercial development. When the Beckfoot fort closed, the settlement and commercial area declined for a short period but adapted and grew. Making products once imported, such as oil lamps, incense burners, glass and bone goods and quality leather wares flourished, helping the traditional trades and services to prosper as well.

Patricius vowed he would match or beat his father in developing the area.

He called on Elijah, the leather man, who made high-quality saddles and accessories for the Romans, large traders, and local nobility. He employed workers and occupied two buildings. Elijah, working outside in his display area, looked up as he saw Patricius approaching. Patricius knew the saddle on which he was sitting was Elijah's workmanship.

'Good day, Elijah. How are things?'

'All's well. What brings you to my door?'

Patricius studied the man's stature. He was short, with a full mop of hair. From earlier dealings Patricius knew Elijah to be talented in his craft, a confident man and pleasant in his nature.

'I'll be coming to your door regularly, starting next Friday. I'm going back to collecting the rents.'

Elijah raised his eyebrows. 'That's alright with me. It's one job less to do. How's your father?'

'He's well. I was with him this morning. I'd like to ask you a question.'

'Go on then.' Elijah laid down his leatherwork tools.

'Slave raiding is increasing down the west coast, I'm told. Do you hear much when you travel?'

'Yes, I do. What do you want to know?'

Patricius, still mounted, looked down on the leather man. 'How do they do it? The west coast is wild and the Roman military presence large.'

'Well, it's a long old coast.' Elijah shook his head. 'Not all of it is wild and I wouldn't say the military presence is large.'

'How do they find where to land?' Patrick gestured with palms up.

'Maybe they get a bit of help. There are Scoti settlements down there, you know.'

'We don't have Scoti here. But help from within our communities? Could that happen to us?'

'Well, we're under the sun, aren't we?'

Patricius, un-amused by the patronising answer, enquired further, 'When do they do it; at night-time, daytime, dusk, or dawn?'

'I've heard tell of one raid in early morning fog and mist; another one in daylight, when they took battle with the soldiers in a mile tower. Soldiers arrived and the raiders ran off. It was a decoy though. The real raid took place, without retaliation, further down the coast,' Elijah said, studying his inquisitor's reaction.

Patricius frowned at the news. The heathens had a strategy? And their plan drew in the Roman soldiers?

'Do you have information on the size of the raids? How many boats and how many raiders?'

'Sorry. I can't tell you, but the decoy raid captured more than forty men.'

'Your answers have been helpful,' Patricius acknowledged, carefully avoiding the words 'thank you' to those who didn't address him as master.

'No bother,' said Elijah going back to the saddle he was working on. 'So, taking a bit of interest then?'

Patricius gave him a sharp look. 'See you next Friday,' he said, sourly, kicking Shadow into a trot as he set off to complete his tour of the estate.

On arrival at the single storey villa, his groom hurried to open the gate.

'Good evening, master.'

'Good evening, Janus,' Patricius replied.

'How's Shadow?'

'In good fettle. He trotted from the Fort this morning and had a gentle day round the estate.'

'I'll take care of him. Will you be going out later?'

'Yes, but I'll be on foot,' Patricius replied as he entered the villa and was met by Mary, his house-slave.

'Good evening, master.'

'Good evening, Mary. I'd like to dine in an hour. In the meantime, I'll be in the bath room,' he said, kicking and tugging off his riding boots, which he left on the floor for Mary to clean and put away. Removing the writing equipment from his pockets, he took off his cloak and hung it in the riding cupboard. Placing his tablets on his office desk he paused a moment to decide if the room was warm enough and rang a bell. Mary arrived.

'Yes, master?'

'I'll be using the office later. Please see that it is heated.'

Patricius undressed in his bedroom and donned a robe from a selection that had been laid out on his bed. In the restroom, a tray of fresh fruit and juices awaited him. He made quick work of the snack and then took his Turkish bath.

Fully reclined on the tiles with head resting on a ceramic support, he gazed at the baubles of condensing steam on his body and planned the rest of the evening; dinner, wine, report writing. Then what? I'll snoop around after dark.

He finished in the steam room and washed himself down with a handcloth, in a warm-water bath. Returning to his bedroom he spotted Janus carrying a heated metal plate and knew his office would be comfortably warm by the time he'd finished dinner.

Reclined in the dining room, having changed into a dry robe, Patricius was served a two-course fish dinner by Mary. He washed down his meal with a horn of sweet white wine and as Mary cleared away the plates, Patricius said, 'That was a delicious meal. I'd like you to light the office for me and place the wine stand on the writing table.'

'Yes, master.'

Patricius moved from the dining room to his bedroom, changed into the casual dress of tunic and sandals then entered his office and prepared his desk. From his writing cupboard he chose a swan quill, suitable for his large style of writing, and a short horn of black ink. Selecting and placing two pieces of new parchment into a holder he was ready to write.

Occasionally he struggled to express himself in Latin. Phrases wouldn't always come readily to him. Sometimes, in order to progress, he would leave a sentence grammatically unfinished. Pleased he would soon receive tuition in classical Latin, he resolved to study this time and become as articulate in written Latin as he was in his native Gaelic. He used Gaelic with staff, servants and slaves; spoke competently in Latin, privately at home, as well as amongst his peers and elders. But he would need to be much more proficient in the ruling language for the life ahead of him.

Patricius laboured to finally complete his report and, using the flat end of his graif, he scraped away the wax inscriptions, returning the tablets to a smooth flat surface. Inserting his two leaves of parchment in a leather folder he placed his report proudly in his desk tray, ready for the Council Meeting discussion with his father. Satisfied, he rang a small bell and Mary came.

'Would you ask Janus to prepare a storm lamp for me?'

'Yes, master.'

Opening a large cupboard, he picked out two wooden keys marked 'T Barn upper' and 'T Barn lower' and pocketed them in his tunic. Returning to his bedroom he pulled on a pair of leather boots, buckled a sturdy, brown leather belt around his waist then carefully slid a small dagger with a sharpened blade into the attached sheath. He donned a cloak and made his way to the door.

Janus arrived with the lamp. 'Will an hour be sufficient, master?' he enquired.

'Yes, it will, Janus.'

Patricius took the lamp, stepped out of the villa and into the still, dark night. Closing the shutters on the lamp he directed the light to the ground; close to the hedgerows he reasoned the light would be unseen from the roundhouses. He climbed the incline towards the grey silhouette of the barn. The gable was a face; the thatch a scruffy, centre-parted hairstyle; the flaking daub, a wrinkled forehead and two slits the watchful eyes. All was quiet save for his stride and the gentle hoot of an owl. A few moments later, Patricius paused to listen and, hearing no voices, he turned the key, entered, and closed the door.

Opening the shutters of the lamp, he immediately illuminated the open space of the cleanly swept threshing floor. Holding the lamp high, he stepped into the centre and studied the layout of the barn. To the left sheaves covered the floor, stacked yet higher against the wall and on the right, tied bales of straw were piled high. In front and above was a hayloft; below it, more bales, three feet deep on the floor.

Patricius followed the perimeter wall, kicking away sheaves in search of hidden sacks of corn but he found nothing suspicious. He came to the back wall, stacked with newly filled corn sacks, and counted them. A wax scratchpad hung from a beam. Holding the lamp closely he saw the check marks. They tallied, twenty-five in all. Moving along, he found the bale area was densely packed and too difficult to check.

Scaling the vertical loft ladder, holding the lamp in his right hand, the darkness of his own shadow hid flails and brushes from sight on his left. On the upper level he made his way to the gable. From this side the barn's eyes were ventilation slits. He looked out and saw only blackness. Putting down the lamp he looked out again, allowing time for his eyes to adjust. This time he made out the track from the barn to his villa and cringed as he saw his doorway.

I can be watched. No, I am watched.

Continuing his search of the hay loft he tried to raise the bolt of the upper-level door. It didn't move. Taking the dagger in his right hand, he prised at the door. Nothing gave.

It's probably not been used for years.

Moving to the eyes of the opposite gable he looked out to the roundhouses. It's a perfect watchtower. Watch the master from one gable, signal to thieves from the other.

What a fool I've been. I could have realised this was a lookout sooner; he closed his eyes and shook his head. I chose to be casual.

Returning the dagger to its sheath, he made for the loft ladder but couldn't see it as the ladder didn't extend above the floor level. Directing his light to the edge of the loft he followed the line. Stopping at some bird feathers on the loft floor, he looked more closely, surprised to find that a bird had built a nest in less than six inches of straw. Just before the nest, the straw was parted, exposing the boards.

Had the bird scratched this away? Then he saw the loft ladder and moved on. Kneeling to get into position, he began his descent. The lamp, now in his left hand, illuminated the soles of sandals on feet, to the left of the ladder. His eye followed from the feet to a pair of white legs and thighs, leading to large undergarments. Patricius couldn't understand what he was looking at. He held the lamp nearer to see if this was real and saw inside-out skirts, ending with the peering, frightened eyes of a teenage girl. Startled, he gasped aloud and slipped off the rungs but held on with his right hand; regaining his foothold he scrambled down the ladder.

At ground level he held the lamp high again, to see what was going on, and found a girl hanging upside down, her ankle snagged in the leather loop of a flail, stored on a sturdy hook. Her foot was at the height of the loft floor and her head three feet above the bales of loose hay on the ground floor. Had she fallen off the edge of the loft? Was it her slip mark next to the bird's nest? What was she doing in the barn alone, at midnight in darkness black as India ink? Holding the lamp close to both their faces, he looked her in the upside-down eyes, as his mind tried to find a nose in her forehead.

'Why are you here?' Patricius asked, with disbelief in his voice.

She didn't respond but wriggled and writhed trying to release her ankle.

'You will answer me. Why are you here?'

She shook her head from left to right, lips pressed firmly shut.

'Who are you?'

She gave him the 'No' nod again.

'I have more time than you,' he said, crossing his arms.

No response.

'Let me hasten this conversation,' Patricius said, putting down the lamp and taking out his dagger. 'You really should take an interest.'

She curled her body to watch the dagger, its blade glinting in the subdued light of the lamp. Her eyes, alert and fearful, flashed to and from Patricius's face to the blade. He climbed the ladder, placed the dagger haft aside the leather strap and, with a slicing action, cut halfway across. The leather strained but held.

'I'm meeting a lover,' she blurted. 'Please. Please set me free.'

'Is your lover late?'

'He'll be here soon.'

'We'll wait for him.'

Patricius left her hanging, expecting she would talk. She looked his way and nodded a no. Her presence and non-response gave Patricius an idea, about corn stealing. He looked at the girl and said:

'Wriggle free if you can. I'll be back to ask more questions.'

Taking his lamp, he went outside, locking the door behind him. He examined the far gable and quickly found small but fresh spills of corn on the ground. Scrutinising the wall by lamplight he saw no further clues. Prodding with his dagger along the edge of a wall beam he prised, but nothing moved. He continued along the beam to no avail. He tried the next beam and this time there was movement. He levered away until a hatch tilted towards him revealing a hidden cavity. He lifted the lamp into the space; five sacks of corn were visible. Slide marks guided him further into the hiding place. Now inside, he spied another framed panel on the opposite wall. Putting down the lamp, he kicked the panel through and crawled back into the barn. Getting to his feet he brushed off the dust and straw and recovered his lamp.

Seeing his upside-down friend still squirming and twisting but making no progress, he walked towards her.

'I've found the hidden room, with five bags of corn in there; fresh slide marks on the floor and grain on the ground outside. If you won't speak, I shall: I've disturbed grain thieves at work, and you are the lookout. When you saw me coming you hooted like an owl as a signal. All your friends fled. You slipped and fell, rushing in the dark. Am I right?'

She didn't respond.

'There is no lover, only corn thieves. Tell me names.' She didn't speak. 'Tell me names or I'll punish everyone; croppers, carters, threshers and balers, carpenters.'

She still didn't speak.

Patricius wanted to catch the ringleaders but this stubborn servant girl was frustrating him. He needed to scare her.

'If I have to cut you free without the names, you and your family will pay the price.'

She shook her head defiantly.

'Think carefully before you shake your head. You and your family will become our slaves. We'll separate you and sell you to the Picts. You will be the property of tyrants for the rest of your lives; or you could just tell me names.'

She gave the threat no consideration and again nodded her defiance.

This stubborn girl was annoying him. He couldn't leave her hanging there all night, but the thought of having to hold her, bear her weight while she wriggled her foot free, was too much to take. I should be nice to her whilst she, a servant, and a thief, caught in the act, feels entitled to obstruct me. Me, her employer; the one she's stealing from. Suddenly, a face-saving way of freeing her occurred to him. He kicked the bales of hay; they were deep and soft. Now Patricius rushed up the ladder and, with one theatrical action, sliced the strap and freed her ankle. She cried out in surprise as the severed strap released her weight, then fell onto the bales, her outstretched arms touching the straw immediately. The back of her head landed softly pushing her chin into her chest. Her torso and legs followed, coiling her body tightly. The crack was sickening, stunning Patricius rigid.

As realisation sunk in, Patricius rushed down the rungs and ran to her; her eyes, the pupils already rolled back in her head, gave her an eerie stare. He pulled her forward carefully, uncoiling her body to a flat position. The girl's head flopped into line, confirming what he had heard: her neck was broken. Disturbed again by her egg-white gaze, he gently closed her eyelids with the pad of his thumb. Now he recognised her as the good-looking girl, the daughter of one of his tenant farmers. Patricius knew, before he tried, that there wouldn't be a pulse, but he felt her neck and confirmed the worst situation.

'No. No. It shouldn't have been like this,' he groaned aloud.

Why did I have a last-minute impulse? Why didn't she co-operate when she was caught in the act? He looked at her. She was peaceful. 'I meant you to have a soft landing. You did have a soft landing, but not a safe one. It was an accident.' He looked at her again, 'a tragic accident.'

Patricius was in turmoil. He paced aimlessly. Guilty thoughts bounced around in his mind. Justifications fought back. He consoled himself, it was an accident. I gave her chances, but she chose to be stubborn. Silly girl. She brought this on herself. He stood up and stiffened his spine. Deciding to put the incident behind him, he cast his mind to unfinished business. Patricius picked up his lamp and left, locking the barn door behind him. He returned to the gable where he replaced the panel perfectly. Then he walked home, blotting the girl from his mind, and thought about the morning.

Back at the villa Mary opened the door for him, took his lamp and quelled it.

'Can I get you anything, master?'

'Yes, Mary. Bring me some ale, fill a horn.'

Patricius put away the keys, the belt and dagger and removed his boots. He slipped into a pair of light sandals and reclined in the rest room. Mary brought his beverage.

'I'd like to break-fast well before sunrise,' he said, the sense of purpose in his voice lost amidst his leisurely demeanour.

'Would you like Janus to prepare your horse?'

'No. I'll be walking tomorrow.'

'Shall I prepare your sturdy boots and a warm tunic?'

'That will be perfect,' Patricius nodded agreeably.

After she retreated Patricius recapped his day; breakfast with his father seemed a long time ago. He'd reported a suggestion for sea defences and active lookout posts; raiders from the sea should be seen before landing and attacked in the water. His father's instincts were right, a little snooping uncovered thieving. Now it all looked obvious.

Patricius thought, if someone returns for the remaining bags of corn, they'll do it before sunrise. The thieves will look for the girl when she doesn't return home and see that she's fallen from the loft. They won't connect me to her death, and even if they did, it doesn't matter; I was helping her down. A magistrate would usually believe the lies of a noble before the truth from a servant; but in my case I wouldn't be lying, though she, however, and the gang she worked with, were guilty of a crime. They couldn't come back on me without revealing their own guilt. A wry smile crossed his face. Nothing of this will see the sunrise. I've got away with it. What a tragedy for the girl though. He felt a tinge of regret.

Patricius switched his thoughts to the progress of the day and felt empowered. He decided he would take control of his parents' estate with vigour and determination, being tougher than his father had been.

Through his smile he softly said, 'Mother, you need not worry. I'll regain your trust and my reformed ways will win your admiration too.'

CHAPTER FOUR
Mann

Dew-like baubles of sweat coated the muscular bodies of the Irish rowers. Hours of gutsy rhythm had propelled them against a headwind to the shores of a small island called Mann, where Colm was to meet King Lugadd. The sounds of water-splash and creaking oars were carried by a gentle breeze as a formation of currachs in four lines of five, reduced their rowing pace. Colm studied the horizon and caught a flicker. Averting his gaze slightly – a trick he learned from his father – his night vision sharpened, and two distant orange torches emerged in the silver light of a half-moon; King Lugadd's guiding lights.

Colm ordered the raising of a white flag, and his four neighbouring boats copied. In a calm sea on a clear night, the signal dominoed boat to boat, till all twenty flags were fluttering. The fleet sailed into a vast water-filled arena and the boats dropped anchor, except one, which lowered the flag and sailed north.

Colm reduced the oarsmen from eight pairs to four singles, freeing men to arm themselves with sword and dagger and to bring the stock of spears to the ready. The mission was friendly but arriving with a large fighting force was bound to create tensions. Nervousness and misunderstanding could accidentally trigger a fight. The crew dived into a large wooden chest at the foot of the mast and took up their weapons as Colm shepherded the leading boats into the formation of a five die, with his own currach the central dot.

They advanced slowly towards the sandy beach; and were surrounded by a group of ten boats, primed with catapults and smoking fire bales. The crews on both sides eyed each other defiantly. Colm gave the signal to light the tallow-soaked, hessian-wrapped spear shafts, before they entered the shallows, and in loud voice reminded his men, 'No action unless I instruct; if I give it, torch the enemy's bales faster than they can catapult them.'

Colm understood King Lugadd's precaution and if things went as planned; the flaming spears would be torches to brighten a special occasion.

Opening the eyeleted door of the specially made stern enclosure, Colm said, 'It's time to step out.'

She rose from the bench and patted her wavy red hair, then smoothed the creases of her dress.

'Are you ready, Brigit?' Colm asked, looking her in the eye, impressed by her composure.

She looked around at the tiny, basic room – her travelling clothes now hanging on a peg – doused the candle and turned to face her future.

'I'm ready, Colm,' she answered firmly.

He offered his hand and Brigit – a sixteen-year-old virgin, elegantly dressed for a festive occasion – accepted, as she stepped onto the open deck. Being out of place and uncommonly fair, her appearance triggered a murmur among the crew of all the nearby boats as the warriors fixed their eyes on the apparition. Standing out like a bright star against a dark night, Brigit provided a perfect release of tension. Colm guided her to the edge of the boat and two crew members eagerly followed.

'These men will carry you to the beach,' Colm said, hopping overboard. He waded through the shallows followed by two smiling warriors who carried their precious load in a sitting position, clear of the water, until they reached dry sand. Colm linked Brigit's arm, escorting her to a candle-lit dais, set for festivities. King Lugadd and his retinue awaited them. Colm and Brigit took one stride onto an elegantly decorated, gold-coloured rush mat.

Colm bowed before the king and said, 'King Lugadd, I bring you Brigit Agnes Kilmain.'

The king nodded gracefully, after which Colm stepped back. She stood alone before the king; her face serene. He inspected her, slowly, inscrutably, and finally smiled.

'Welcome, Brigit Agnes of the Kilmains. Please join me in our festivities for the occasion of your arrival.'

'Thank you, my lord,' she said.

The king walked her to a seat at a banqueting table. Nobles filled benches around a floor space for musicians and dancers. He called his servants to offer Brigit food and drink and then turned to his chieftain, saying, 'Start the fires,' he then faced Colm, 'Colm Kilmurrach, you may land your boats and then I invite you to join us for food and drink.'

'Thank you, my lord.' Colm turned and signalled his captain.

At intervals along the beach a spit for each boat was fired-up. Within the hour, nearly six hundred warriors were feasting on baked fish and bread, washed down with skins of ale. At the other end of the beach in the royal enclosure, Brigit, at the King's request, was singing to the harpist's tune.

After generous applause Lugadd asked her, 'Do you play the harp?'

'I do, my lord.'

'Then I'd like to hear you.' He gestured the harpist to retreat.

Brigit settled on the stool, familiarised herself with the harp, and announced, 'Green Pastures'.

She played the tune with aplomb and could see that King Lugadd's soul too was satisfied. As she finished, the king applauded and leant across the table towards Colm saying, 'You may advise Cousin Niall that he's fulfilled his agreement to send me a princess.' Switching his attention to Brigit he observed her wholesome smile. He paused, taking in the moment, and then continued, 'Indeed, I think he has sent me a queen.'

Colm observed Brigit maintaining her poise as she took in King Lugadd's words. She allowed her elegant smile to radiate delight. Colm looked at the king, who, a moment ago, thought he'd been sent a queen. The king beamed. He knew for sure now.

The royal party bade farewell and retired to a nearby hill fort residence.

Colm and his warriors settled down to sleep on scattered skins, under the shelter of propped and upturned currachs. While Colm slept soundly, Goddess Nehalennia entered his dreams, revealing the coming of a firm and favourable wind that would take them by sail to their destination.

'Trust me, Colm, as your father did,' she said.

The dream faded and he awoke. A strong wind was gathering from the west and the stars told him the night was still young. He rose and weighed the weather. If it held well, they could rest the oarsmen and sail to their destination, arriving early. Accepting the gift from Nehalennia, Colm mobilised his men.

Following the Caledonian coastline, the black silhouette of the hills showed well against the dark-grey sky. From practice runs, Colm recognised the Solway Estuary and turned south. He spotted a small lighted beacon slightly above sea level and despatched three boats to aim for the light, which would guide them to a pebble beach, where men from the night boat would meet them.

Colm was pleased his night boat and crew had succeeded so far.

Continuing in the dark along the coast, another guiding light greeted them. Colm despatched four boats towards the beacon. His heart pumped with excitement. The second tower was expectedly manned by two Roman soldiers; to see the torches burning meant his men had dealt successfully with the lookout guards. Sleeping or awake, they would have been no match for six Colm-trained warriors.

He thought of his father's words. 'If you want a campaign to succeed, get off to a good start.' Step at a time, things were going right. Colm was nervous though; one major aspect of the raid had never been tried before, even by his father; that was the use of stealth on a large scale. He would find out later if his men succeeded in taking the soldiers alive.

The next beacon shone. His men had delivered three successes out of three, and this beach was his base. Colm sent three boats to shore but pulled alongside one of the last eight to speak to his second in command.

'The next two beacons are markers for where not to land. Anchor four boats opposite each mile tower. The night boat and crew will guide your boats to a safe landing. Send a runner as soon as you land. I want to know the status of the manned mile tower, and the buoys. Good luck to you.'

Colm directed his own boat to the beach.

Teams had already left to guard the exit roads and adjacent fields to stop runners from alerting the soldiers, southbound and northbound. Each crew knew their tasks and their targets and were gathered in groups on the open beach. These well-trained, tough, and canny Celts surprised Colm with their nervous demeanour. Waiting didn't help though.

Perhaps I should have kept them in the boats for a while longer, he thought.

Two runners, one from the north and the other the south, came to Colm, confirming the exit guards and early-warning guards were in place. The eyes of his teams were all on him. He nodded and one hundred men dispersed quickly to do their jobs.

As the beach emptied, Colm strode out towards a settlement of roundhouses at the southern end. He squatted in the shadows and watched. Darkness was on them, but a glimmer of pre-dawn light was wicking into the sky above the horizon. He saw the faint silhouette of buildings and imagined the raiding methods used by most chieftains.

Smoke pellets would be forced through thatched roofs. Choking people would pour from the houses and men would rush out fighting vigorously with spears and daggers. Screaming and shouting would be deafening; some would dodge their attackers

43

and run off to warn others. At the end of the raid, warriors and potential captives would be dead or wounded and sometimes there would be fewer captives taken than warrior lives lost.

My father planned to do better. Can I make his audacious tactics succeed?

Colm crept close to the road, fascinated by the quality of the British tracks. The sound of footsteps on gravel alerted him. Scanning carefully from the track towards the settlement, he saw the silhouette of a tall man on the paved road, a bag on his shoulder as though he was a tradesman walking to his work. Two shadowy figures rose from the ditch and Colm inched nearer to watch his men at work. They quickly had their target tied, gagged, and hooded. Colm, pleased with what he'd seen, came out of the shadows. His men were taken aback to see their commander.

'Thirty-eight heartbeats,' Colm said to them, quietly, retreating and moving on.

The men looked at each other and smiled in relief. They'd been trained to do the job in forty.

Colm returned to the beach and the sight of the first boat arriving from the north, gladdened his heart. Thirty crew members seemed to cram the currach tight and the only space for captives was on the floor. The captain hand-signalled twelve captives on board and then turned, navigating his way through the buoys and markers, to the open sea. Colm raised his thumb, then, observing his counter notching the tally, he turned to face the fields; captives, yoked in sixes were being marched down through the dunes. Taking a deep breath through his nostrils, Colm was acutely aware of the danger posed by the location of their raid, situated between two operational Roman forts; Luguvalium fifteen thousand strides north and Alauna fort two thousand south.

He approached the first batch of yoked captives and to his men who were leading them, he put up his hand, palm first. They duly stopped. Colm took out his dagger and walked around the abducted, inspecting their bodies for wounds. He found none. With his own dagger he placed the flat of the blade under a captive's chin and pushed up to make him look skywards, then moved on to the next victim. Colm checked every chin and found one with a deep cut. His inspection was an examination of his own men's work and he was satisfied that these captives had been caught without vicious fighting. The one with the sharp but hidden knife wound in the soft flesh beneath his bottom jaw, a simple slice away from his jugular vein, had likely put up a fight and been subdued. Colm, mean-faced and earnest, looked the man in the eye and with the tip of his dagger sliced an X shaped incision on the skin of the man's bare chest, which became a red X as the blood came to the surface.

'Your name is trouble,' Colm said quietly. 'If we have problems in the boats with our captives' behaviour, we throw one into the sea, as an example to the others.' Fear swept across the captive's face. 'The method works well. You are marked as our example.' Colm turned and waved his men to continue to the boats.

Pleased the operation was running well so far, Colm headed towards the fields in the last of the darkness. He saw a stone-built house, with clay roof tiles, a wrought iron gate, a yard, and stables. The home of a chieftain or a lord he thought. Crouching low as he ran behind a long row of bushes, an old wooden barn came into sight on the opposite side of the track. It was the same shape as an Irish threshing barn. Two of his own men were hiding and waiting for their chance. They'd seen Colm coming. He patted them on their shoulders and continued stealthily along the hedgerow. A few strides later he found a caped young man hiding behind a bush, facing towards the barn with his back to the fields, unaware of what was happening around him. Colm tossed a pebble to his warriors, quietly calling their attention. They looked around, saw Colm beckoning, and came to him. He took the opportunity to show his men that the teacher could act as well as talk.

The man in the cape was leaning against a dense bush, his hands clasped casually behind his head. No chance of getting him in a headlock Colm thought, so he rabbit-punched his target and slammed his victim's face into the earth; then ripped his head up by the hair, and quickly, before the man could shout, put his arm around the captive's face, his bicep covering the victim's mouth and with the grip of a blacksmith's vice, held him face down on the ground. The second man fettered the victim's ankles but struggled to get hold of the man's wrists. He was lashing out with his arms, determined not to be tied. The victim punched upwards a few times with left and right fists. One landed in Colm's eye and was quickly followed by a second punch to his chin, before Colm could move his head away. Each warrior grabbed an arm and after some pushing and pulling, the victim's wrists were tied behind his back. A stone was forced into his mouth and he was gagged with a few winds of a woollen cloth strip. The target was pulled quickly to his feet and as Colm released the headlock, one of the warriors drew a hood over the victim's head. Colm immediately, through the hood, nipped the man's nose and as the captive could hardly breathe, his struggling came to a halt. Colm was relieved. For a moment he thought he was losing control. He whispered in the man's ear, the consequences of struggling and released the nose-nip to see if his victim was co-operating; relieved when he remained subdued.

'Walk,' Colm commanded.

His captive shuffled in comical short steps, restrained by his ankle bonds. Colm, accompanied by his two warriors, prodded and pushed his temporary charge to the yoking area.

'Stop,' he said, into the ear of his captive.

By this time Colm had learned that his captive was a fit and healthy young man, quick enough to punch him twice in the face. He was a noble and would be valuable. I know who'll pay a good price for you, he said to himself; then turned to his warriors.

'I slowed ye down,' he said, light-heartedly.

'You did well my lord. This one was feisty.'

Colm walked over to his yoking marshal. 'Boat thirteen for that one,' he said, pointing to the man in the cape and then he made for the centre of the beach.

The light of dawn was creeping in and a ground mist was swirling. He felt his eye which was swelling and laughed to himself; that young man in the cape planted a bruise on me, with three of us on him. Colm surveyed the beach activity. Five yokes of six men each were being prepared for the boats. He looked out to sea and saw a cluster of boats heading for home; in the distance two of the currachs had raised their sails; in the foreground the man in the cape was straining to look round.

Have a good look young man. You don't know it yet, but you'll spend the rest of your life in Ireland.

Colm needed twenty more minutes and wondered if he would get the time. He turned to the south; there was no sign of the currachs, but his counter was coming apace. Colm strode out towards him, halving the distance, nervous that the daylight was arriving before the sun. They met in the middle.

'What are the numbers?' Colm asked impatiently.

'Eleven at sea, three here on the beach, and we're waiting for six from the south.'

As he spoke, four currachs from the south came into view. Just then a messenger emerged from the fields, running hard. Gasping for breath he raced up to Colm.

'My lord, we've lost three men fighting six Roman soldiers. All six soldiers are dead.'

Colm's face turned deadly serious. 'When did this happen?' he urged.

'I came without delay. I've run ten thousand paces.'

'Good work. Quick, get into your boat.' Colm turned to his tallyman, 'Call the men,' he instructed, relieved to be bringing the raid to a close.

His counter took a ram's horn from his belt, blew out a long deep note and immediately raiders and guards came running onto the beach. The steady flow of returning warriors continued and they took up their jobs as crewmen. Colm wanted ninety men to return to the last three boats but now it was eighty-seven. Would it end that way?

Two more currachs from the south arrived, their captains all waves and smiles as they turned to the sea. Colm felt a shot of relief, but he knew they were not out of danger yet.

'Captains; move, move,' he shouted with urgency.

The warriors pushed the remaining three boats into the shallow water and boarded. Colm and his counter were the last two men on the last boat.

'Two hundred and twenty-eight captives, my lord,' he answered, as though reading Colm's mind, 'and twenty out of twenty currachs returning. All we must do now is get home safely.'

Colm's attention was transfixed on the beach, working out whether to return to land and fight, or fight in the water, as scores of Roman soldiers stomped through the dunes onto the pebble-strewn sand with more arriving all the time.

'How true your words,' he said to the counter, as he turned to the crews. 'Twenty-four oarsmen, row for your lives. Everybody else, grab your spears and all the oarsmen's spears,' Colm shouted as loud as he was able. The soldiers had arrived in time to destroy the last three boats.

'We've been caught. All we can do is go down fighting.' Colm raised his arm and his warriors knew they should wait for his command to throw the spears.

As twenty soldiers reached the water's edge Colm commanded, 'Throw, throw, throw.'

Eighteen spears in three pathetic volleys of six caused the soldiers to do something Colm had never seen. They formed a shield wall in front of them and above their heads.

'Throw, throw, throw,' he called again, and they all threw, harder to compensate for being further away. The oarsmen strained in unison and powered the shallow draught boats into deeper water. More soldiers arrived at the water's edge and they too formed a wall.

By now Colm was laughing. He boomed to the whole crew, 'They don't like wet feet. They're letting us go.'

There was a roar of jubilation from everyone. Colm allowed a few seconds of celebration then boomed, 'Navigators, concentrate. Guide us safely past the hidden rocks.'

CHAPTER FIVE

Long before sunrise Patricius was settled beneath a bush, next to the fields and out of sight. His view of the barn and approaching track was perfect. If thieves returned for the five remaining sacks of corn, he'd wait till they'd removed the outside wall-panel, taken a sack, and placed it in their cart, before confronting them. Patricius was confident he would recognise the thieves. They would be employees of his contract farmers or even his direct employees. His mind flashed to the lookout girl. Her parents and her community would know of her death by now. Such an unnecessary tragedy.

The scruffy face of the offending gable looked on. This time Patricius was watching too. Hearing a cart on the track, he parted the shrub slightly to get a better look. The morning mist clung to the contours of the ground, obscuring his view, clearing fleetingly to reveal two men pushing an empty handcart, before erasing them again. Patricius smiled with the satisfaction of a man in control. He sat on his stone, clasped his hands pompously behind his head and leant back against the dense hedgerow, like he was in his office savouring the afterglow of having disciplined a slave over a minor misdemeanour. His gamble was about to succeed.

The wheel noise stopped. A muted voice seemed to cut short. Whack. He felt a powerful blow to the back of his neck and as his face hit the damp turf he passed out. He came round to find that fusty peat had filled his nostrils and smeared his teeth and tongue. Patricius didn't know what was going on.

Something tugged at his ankles. Unable to see or hear anything Patricius was guessing at the nature of this attack. His head was viciously pulled back by the hair before a massive bicep sealed his mouth. Suddenly, he feared for his life; he thought the lookout girl's family were taking their revenge. A second pair of hands grabbed at his wrists, pulling them behind his back. Patricius fought vigorously with his fists clenched tight, punching air, lashing out, writhing, anything to keep his hands free. His arms were at the front now and although he couldn't see his attackers, he knew from the bicep in his mouth that one attacker's head was somewhere behind his own head. He punched backwards, left, and right, and felt his fist land in someone's face, and then he quickly landed a second hit, in the same place.

Both his arms were grabbed simultaneously and forced behind his back. Patricius now knew he was dealing with three assailants and then he felt his wrists being drawn together, adding to the realisation that he was being overwhelmed. The sweaty muscle gave way to a smooth stone the size of a small apple, which was forced into his mouth, bound tightly in place and the bonds tied in the nape of his neck. Two more wraparounds made screaming impossible.

Overpowered, unable to struggle free, Patricius became fearful, and then the head-grip was released, and a hood was pulled over his head. The hooded darkness induced despair and humiliation in Patricius and then his fate worsened. Someone nipped his nose and for Patricius, the difficulty in drawing breath slowly began to kill him. On the point of passing out, he heard heavily accented Gaelic words in his ear. Not in his mother tongue, Welsh Gaelic, but there was enough similarity to understand the meaning, 'Noisy people die. Silent people live.'

The only thought in Patricius's mind was how to suck air past the stone that was steadfastly blocking the back of his throat. Then the nose-nip was released allowing Patricius to sniff and snort air greedily and ponder on the consequences of being noisy.

'Walk,' said the voice.

Patricius stumbled, his stride restrained by the length of his ankle-tether. He'd seen nothing of the last twenty seconds except a glimpse of earth, sky, and flesh. Twenty strides later the voice said, 'Stop.'

Patricius stopped, relieved simply to be breathing. He caught the accent as being Irish, similar to his grandmother's lilt. Oh God no. Please God this isn't an Irish slave raid.

The Irish lilt continued, but this time speaking to those around him. 'I slowed ye down,' he said, light-heartedly.

Patricius couldn't stomach this casual chatter.

'You did well, my lord. This one was feisty.'

Patricius's mood turned angry. I need to see your face "my lord", and when I get free, I'll show you what feisty is, he snarled mutedly under his hood.

'Boat thirteen for that one,' said the lilt.

Patricius felt someone's fingers pressing around his shoulders and neck and then the hood was removed. Through gritty eyes Patricius made out the back of a man striding with purpose between the dunes towards the beach. As his eyes recovered, he took in his own situation; he was yoked, with a heavy plaited twine, to a man in front. Blinking frequently, he looked further ahead and saw four more. Turning his dizzy head around he learned he was the last in a chain of six. Looking back at the barn of misfortune he saw the thatched roof silhouetted against the orange glow of an imminent sunrise. To the right he could see the roof-top of his villa residence. He felt sick, recalling his parents' wish for him to live inside the town walls, for the improved security, and his own resistance to the idea.

Commanded to walk, Patricius followed the other yoked captives to the sea between the scrub and dunes, the throw of a stone from the unattended watch tower he'd observed the previous evening. He noticed a smouldering torch mounted on the observation deck. Scanning ahead he saw currachs aplenty at the water's edge, being filled with captives at spear point. Raising his eye further, the heads of men were visible, packed tight in bobbing boats, as they rowed rapidly towards the open sea. Further out, more boats with hoisted sails were fading from view. He knew what he was witnessing and desperately hoped it somehow wasn't true.

No. This can't be happening to me, he screamed internally with wasted indignation.

As he awaited the dreadful fate promised by the currachs, Patricius was already as powerless as the slaves and servants he so often despised, and the double dawning arrived. He was a slave now. He spluttered with painful, involuntary suppression, and his ears popped as his guts forced a violent spurting of undigested fruit juice through his nostrils and blocked mouth. Patricius fought for breath as the unpleasant-smelling slime, and the last breakfast of an era, dribbled down his face.

'Keep moving.'

The raiders prodded the captives with the butts of their spears.

Patricius's ankles, and those of the other captives on the yoke, had been tied with enough slack for half a normal stride. They tip-toed quickly, in short steps, hoping to avoid further prodding and bruising. Two raiders drove and hurried Patricius and the other five prisoners along a path that led to the sand and pebble beach, where the currachs awaited them. The smell of seaweed, caught on the jagged rocks, was strong in the air. Some was salty and fresh, brought in with the new tide; the rest was old and stinking.

The driver bruising Patricius was tall, barefooted, bare-legged and wore a matted and dirty woollen kilt. From his leather belt hung a dagger in a sheath, and he held a spear with a heavy wooden butt, designed to bruise and break bones. The other end, iron tipped, was made for killing. Patricius shuddered at the sight of it.

He looked for an opportunity to break free and make a dash for safety, but the chances were simply not there. Patricius scanned the beach and was shocked to see so many raiders. Some guarded the paths between the dunes, down which captives were being led. Others were guarding the southern side of the beach. A young man in the centre of the beach was talking to warriors and giving out instructions. Could he be "my lord?" The one who captured me?

Thud! Patricius stumbled as a heavy prodding to his back propelled him forwards.

'Keep moving,' said the Irish lilt.

Head down, he shuffled towards the boats, thinking how the raiders avoided commotion, speaking their instructions with calm authority.

Only five minutes ago, I was hiding in the bushes waiting to catch a corn thief red-handed, unaware that a raid was taking place.

They were close to the water's edge now and the tide was in. Did the raiders know the tides? Patricius wondered. By mid-morning the tide would be so far out a boat wouldn't get near the fields. Patricius, now wading shin deep towards a group of three dark-brown currachs, felt the sting of the cold water on his legs. The boats were oval shaped but tapered to a point at the bow and stern. Waxed animal hides fixed to a basket weave, formed the hull, which was reinforced with a wooden frame. Six pairs of long slim oars were mounted in their slots and the currachs faced seawards ready for departure. The reluctant passengers were pushed brutally into the boat. Patricius's heart thumped, so fearful was he of the flimsiness of the vessel; he turned to the captive beside him and shook his head in disbelief before the guards shoved him to the floor. He was manhandled until his feet had been lashed securely to a post and cross member, then his yoke was untied.

'Off with your cape,' the guard commanded.

Patricius tried to ask why? But he could only manage a nasal grunt.

'No talking,' said the guard wagging his finger at Patricius then, with a cruel laugh said, 'slaves don't wear capes where you are going.'

The guard opened the buckle and roughly removed the cape himself, then tying Patricius's wrists and looking him in the eye, he gave the knot an extra tight pull before lashing Patricius's hands to the boat frame. It was clear that the captive's place was on the floor of the boat. A crew member threw the cape into a wooden chest. Patricius's face saddened; he felt the chill of the air immediately but the stripping down of his status hurt the most.

Patricius counted thirty raiders in the boat. Two rowers for each oar sat side by side on built-in benches. There were six crewmen, two at the bow, two at the stern and two in the centre. A sturdy wooden mast and its sail lay down the centre of the boat extending over the stern of the currach, with captives squashed into the gaps around it. Another six captives were being unyoked and tied down wherever there was a space. Patricius, at the stern facing sideways could look left to the beach and right to the sea. Looking right, he saw six boats rowing speedily away. Studying his own boat, he noticed one of the crewmen in the centre, wore a kilt of higher quality than the other raiders. The purple and green colours of the woven wool were clearly visible. His youthful features were enhanced by a trimmed beard and moustache. Patricius watched the young crewman call the oarsmen into position – which established him as the captain – before looking to the beach, probably for a signal from the commander. Would the young commander know the dangers of this coastline? Patricius hoped that their boat would be ripped to pieces on the hidden rocks.

He looked back at the pebble beach, desperate to see Roman soldiers arriving just in time to save them. Instead, he saw a flock of seagulls descending on the disused lookout tower. This time he noticed side panels had been put in place to ensure the torchlight could only be seen from the sea. Patricius was sickened by this further evidence of detailed planning. With increasing resentment, he thought of the smugness of the Roman decurions who sat on the defence committees. Where do they get their information? They've underestimated these barbarians by a Roman mile.

Patricius could see the beach emptying and his boat was the first of the last three. He wondered why they were waiting but it gave him hope because there was more time for the soldiers to arrive. And then four currachs rowed into sight from the south and turned seaward ahead of boat thirteen, their warriors waving jubilantly to the crewmen on the last three vessels. Patricius looked to the commander on the beach and saw him gesture, with his hand to his mouth, and immediately one of his men blew a long loud call on a ram's horn. Individual runners, raiders and outlying sentries began arriving from all directions, responding to the signal. It appeared to Patricius as though the raid had been called to an early end; before captives for the last boat had arrived.

Patricius knew the southern boats would have been raiding in close proximity to the Alauna Fort. He guessed the raid commander had kept back ninety warriors on standby to help the raiders in the south in case they became embroiled with the Roman soldiers. But they hadn't. One hundred and twenty raiders in four boats had completed their tasks under the noses of the soldiers and were now rowing for home with, probably, forty-eight captives on board. Patricius's disillusionment grew.

The second boat of the last three was almost full of warriors and the captives were now out of Patricius's line of vision, him being tied to the floor. To torture Patricius further, two more boats from the south arrived and turned seaward and then Patricius's boat captain seemed to have received the nod he was waiting for, from the commander. He gave his own instruction and twenty-four burly men began rowing. Boat thirteen pulled slowly away and with every stroke, Patricius's hopes ebbed.

A collective, aggressive-sounding hum came from the gagged captives; probably a crude expression of despair, Patricius thought. The ones who could strain their leashes and look back to Banna Venta did so. Patricius looked back again for the hope of salvation and saw the raid commander board the last boat. And then his heart leapt as twenty-four Roman soldiers in three rows of eight strode in unison onto the beach, followed by many more, close behind. The sight of legionnaires with red shields, silver body armour and helmets, had never looked so good. A humming version of pandemonium broke loose as the captives' muted excitement rose. Some began banging their heads against fresh air. The five crew members watched the situation on the beach gravely, cursing their luck.

'Crew; grab your shields,' called the captain having seen the spears the soldiers were carrying.

They've arrived in time to save us, Patricius thought and the raid commander will be caught too.

Just then the raid commander bellowed an instruction, 'Twenty-four oarsmen, in all three boats, row for your lives.'

By now the first twenty-four soldiers were closing in on the water's edge, triggering the raid commander to call to his own boat crew, 'Throw, throw, throw.'

A volley of six spears, three times in succession, eighteen in total, spitted miserably down on the soldiers, Patricius laughed. The raiders' defence was puny. Their commander had decided they should row their way out of trouble. Patricius's hopes were lifted by that wrong decision. The Roman soldiers' response to the inadequate volley of spears, however, was baffling. Patricius could not believe what he saw. The first twenty-four soldiers formed a shield wall and a shield roof, like a tortoise and stood still on the beach, as the spears clattered into their shields. The second formation of forty joined in and shielded in a similar way although now, there was no volley of spears to protect against. Patricius wanted to scream. He wanted to run onto the beach and kick them into action, 'Move. Move. Charge the boats. You've three full minutes to take them. Pierce the hulls; slash the hides, quick, quick while the rowers are rowing. They've no fighting power when they are rowing. And if they stop rowing, they can't escape. Go to it. You can't fail.'

For some reason the soldiers never entered the water. Patricius looked for the leader. There were two centurions. Both leading eighty soldiers each and between them they did nothing. Patricius boiled over. His ranting was hardly heard, his gesticulating locked in his imagination, but the words, from a man who never swore were, 'You dogs, you sons of dogs; you're not soldiers and centurions, you're not even the crap of soldiers and centurions.'

Soon, only the last boat was reachable, but the soldiers stayed on the sand. While their boat was still within reach of the soldiers, the raid commander bellowed, 'They don't like wet feet. They're letting us go,' his voice was losing power as he laughed with incredulity.

The crew waved their arms wildly in relief and celebration. The rowers stayed their oars and jumped up and down, cheering and laughing themselves sore. While the merriment abounded, Patricius watched their captain go to the two crew members at the bows of the boat. 'Concentrate. Watch for the buoys, remember where the currents lurk and guide us safely past the hidden rocks,' he said and then called the rowers back to work.

Patricius thought of his own condescending words to his father, uttered only two days ago and they choked him as surely as the stone in his mouth was doing.

Why would raiders attack on a dangerous coastline, in the vicinity of a busy and active military fort? But they just had, and on a large scale too.

He thought of the words of the decurion who ran the defence committee, 'The barbarians were no match for the superior, highly trained, Roman soldiers.' Huh. That might be true if they turned up. His bitter thoughts were interrupted by a tugging at the nape of his neck as the nearest crew member removed the bandage and the stone from his mouth. Patricius was relieved but scared they would be punished cruelly for the dissent, even though it was muted. However, the crewman threw the binding and the stone into a tub and moved on to the next captive. Shouting was futile. They were already in waist-deep water and the last boat was pulling further away from the statuesque soldiers.

Patricius gulped air greedily through his mouth for a while and then settled into normal breathing. His tongue came back to life, and the foul taste of his earlier regurgitation appalled him. He needed a mouth rinse and wondered when he might next taste the flavours of fresh fruit juice. Patricius examined his bonds visually. They were too tight to loosen. He couldn't reach them anyway, not even with his teeth. He studied the situation of each captive that he could see, and none could work their knots loose. Patricius resigned himself to waiting for a better opportunity.

Watching the other captives as their gags were removed, he recognised one of them at the far end of the boat, a thresher who worked for a tenant farmer. Probably one of the pilferers, Patricius thought. The labourer wasted no time using his mouth. Immediately the stone was removed he was yelling. 'A pox on you, Patrissio, a pox on you,' he screamed, pointing two forefingers at Patricius with a poking and prodding action, articulated from his bound wrists. Then the screamer yelped as the back of his hand was rapped with a cane, wielded by one of the guards.

The captain, with a slow sweep of his arm, pointed at the captives. 'No talking, or next time we'll use a dagger.'

Patricius was thinking about the thresher's outburst. Patrissio was a derogatory way to say Patricius and used purposely to insult him. Was it prompted by the incident in the barn, or the inadequacy of the defences? The guard had made sure the captives couldn't get to their feet but Patricius caught the thresher's eye and gave him a threatening glare. The return stare was pure hatred. It didn't trouble Patricius but the anger in the man's face was strong and gave him the feeling that this man would be the cause of further trouble.

Their boat turned south, travelling almost parallel to the shore, prompted by the presence of a buoy. With that move, any remaining chance of the boats hitting rocks was dashed. Patricius realised the buoy must have been put in place by the raiders. They know so much. Have we been infiltrated? Is our Irish tenant farmer an inside man? Turning his head to the left, Patricius could see the whole of the Banna Venta coastline. He thought of his report, written last night, containing recommendations for the type of coastal defences required. He'd included a political strategy to persuade the Roman Administration locally to allow the defensive measures. Patricius was numb with regret and fear and he began to realise that he might never ever, see the life he'd been living again. His eyes moistened and though Patricius fought to deny his emotions, still a tear escaped.

He looked back at the villa; the roof outline more visible now than when he was closer. He thought of his father who might be standing in the house, right now. His father, whenever the soldiers were mobilised, was always informed of their activity. He would have called for his horse to be saddled, and ridden hard to the villa, to see if I was safe. Patricius imagined his father standing in the villa office with the report in his hand, reading the words "Patrol the coast at sea. Fight the raiders in the water." The torment would be too much. He'd throw the report down on the table and stride out of the house. Standing on the wall, he'd look out to sea at the dozens of little brown dots heading with determination for the horizon. Father would feel powerless and frustrated with the enemy in full sight and no means of pursuing them. And he might shed a tear for his lost son.

Patricius felt the boat tilting and he dropped his imagined villa scene to observe their captain change course to the west and give instructions for the mast and sail to be raised. This young captain, nay the whole flotilla, had successfully navigated around the strong currents and hidden rocks. Patricius's face wore a look of utter resignation. The last boat to leave the shore was now passing them, made possible, without captives, by their lighter weight, he guessed. The boat was too far away for Patricius to see faces, but he recognised the posture of the raid commander. Begrudgingly, Patricius was beginning to respect this young leader. He'd stood by the warriors raiding in the south. He'd called the raid off before filling the last boat with captives. Whatever his reason, the decision saved thirty warriors from being overrun by soldiers on the beach, and they'd escaped by the length of a boat.

The captain of Patricius's boat, boat thirteen, rested the oars as they progressed well under sail. Three crewmen dished out chicken pieces and cobs of bread to the crew, followed by skins of ale. Patricius couldn't have stomached food. He was sick in his heart and the motion of the boat was already making him sick in his belly too. This could be a problem, Patricius thought, as the sea was calm.

'Master, any food for us?' a captive called out. All eyes turned; crew included. Every captive strained to witness the consequences of the insubordination. The captain's deputy approached the enquirer, took out his dagger, felt the sharpness of the blade with his finger and brought the blade swiftly down onto the captive's hands. Stomachs turned and the sound of retching blurted loud in the stony silence. Not all could see that he'd sliced the man's bonds, not his flesh.

'Hold out your right hand.'

The captive, trembling, obeyed. He held out his hand with palm uppermost. The other captives breathed out, relieved to see he still had a hand.

'Face your palm down,' the deputy commanded.

Hesitantly, he turned his hand. Whack. The guard caned the captive's knuckles.

'Now your left hand.'

As a bruising blue line surfaced on the back of the captive's hands, a crew member retied the bonds of the inquisitive man. The deputy called out in a menacing tone, 'There will be no talking.'

Patricius didn't wish his noisy detractor to lose a hand but the rule of silence was to Patricius's liking. He turned and watched their route, following the Caledonian Hills and large estuaries west, pleased they were coast-hopping and not crossing the open sea to Ireland. Patricius had no faith in the currachs. To him, they were coastal fishing boats not seagoing vessels.

Their boat sailed and rowed on under a blue and partly cloudy sky, but the fresh air and gentle breeze was lost on the miserable souls who'd been plucked from their fields and were heading for a new plantation. Their only consolation was that they were worth more alive than dead.

A chilly wind from the north, set in, roughing the sea. A few captives threw up their break-fast but Patricius had already expelled his predawn fruit juice and, although feeling queasy, he had managed not to vomit. The wind blew stronger and the crew dropped the sail as the sea turned angry. Their boat seemed smaller now and the oversized wicker basket and flimsy wooden frame was already twisting and bending. We'll never survive a storm, Patricius thought. The swell became a curved mountain of water, dwarfing the currach and threatening at any moment to smother them entirely. Patricius was scared but smiled wryly to himself; at least I know that I don't want to die. But somehow the boat stayed on top of the waves. As the sea became a wild horse, bucking, jerking, and jolting to unseat the rider, the boat became a tick embedded in the horse's skin. The human cargo was tossed and shaken and, for a while, the captives occupied the best seats in the boat, low down and strapped tightly to the frame. The crew clung to the structure, holding on firmly and, eventually, the sea settled until merely choppy waters seemed like a gift.

Patricius had sore jaws from clenching his teeth and was relieved they'd seen the storm through. His faith in the basket design of the boat was increasing. He could see how a rigid boat could be smashed by a storm and would never have believed the resilience of woven willow if he hadn't experienced it.

The wind from the north prevailed and the captain ordered the sail be hoisted, setting them on a south-westerly course, heading for the east coast of Ireland. He relieved half of the oarsmen and they promptly relieved themselves, most over the side, but some emptied their bladders in the boat; the captives' best seats had abruptly been returned to their status quo. Thankfully, a huge impact from under the boat tipped the vessel sideways, pouring the offensive liquid into the sea. As the currach corrected and tilted the other way, it shipped on board a substantial slurp of seawater, which crew members hurriedly scooped up in leather buckets and poured overboard. Land to the west came into sight and the rowers were set to a southbound course, parallel to the Irish coastline. Patricius concentrated on listening to the captain's voice as he spoke lowly to the crew.

'Be ready to drop the sail and mast urgently if I instruct you.'

'Captain, we always row against headwinds in these parts. I never seen a north wind,' his deputy said. 'We might get home quicker.'

'We might. But if a south wind and north wind get up strong and meet head on, we're done for,' the captain said.

'Have you ever seen that, Captain?'

'I have. It's a fiercer enemy than the sea. We can be lifted out of the water.'

'What can we do if it happens?'

'Nothing. We should be out of the way before it happens.'

Patricius noted the young captain had experienced the danger. Had he learned the lesson, or would he be like the well-trained Roman soldiers who didn't know the difference between training and reality? Either way, Patricius shuddered at the thought, adding to the shaking of his already shivering body. Sitting in just his tunic, in cold seawater and the biting air, he resented the thought that his cape was merely six feet away in a cabinet, doing nothing.

The boat sailed closer to the Irish coast and, as the evening drew darker, the breeze from the north developed into a firm wind. The captain rested half the crew while progress under sail was good. The wind strengthened and the single sail was arched almost to a semi-circle. Now, all but a few rowers were idle as the boat swallowed the miles at three times their fastest rowing pace.

Patricius watched the captain's concerned face as he studied the sail. He called his deputy. 'Do you think our tailwind is slowing?' he asked.

'I think not, Captain.'

'Watch the sail. See the curve ebb and return. Is it variation in the tailwind, or is there a headwind creeping in?'

His deputy studied the wind for a few seconds. 'The tailwind is full.'

'I agree. Let's get off the water while we can. Drop the sail and mast,' he called.

Patricius saw how this young man consulted with someone he trusted. He thought of his own friend Hermanus and how their trust in each other had developed. Just then, as the crew were in position, a violent gust of wind turned the sail inside out.

'Hold,' the captain shouted. Then the sail corrected and filled with tailwind again. 'Drop sail,' he yelled. The crew succeeded with the sail, but the mast was held by the tailwind at 45 degrees. His crew were skilled, holding the ropes at one side to pull and at the other side to lower. Whichever way the wind turned, the crew had hold of the mast. As the tailwind dropped and the headwind strengthened, they lowered the mast. By now the captain had ordered the oarsmen to turn the boat round. They pivoted, one side rowing forward and the other side backward, and headed for a large bay and promontory which they had passed ten minutes ago. Rowing against the headwind was almost impossible.

The captain spurred the oarsmen on. 'Hold, then progress,' he encouraged.

Patricius watched the captain. He was clear thinking with urgency about him. His judgement, however, was still under trial. The oarsmen rowed their guts out to keep the boat at a standstill and made progress only when the headwind slackened, or the tailwind strengthened. An hour later they entered the large bay, passed a headland, and turned into a neck, sheltered by hills on three sides. As they rowed into a world without wind, they saw another of their fleet hiding from the windstorm.

The relieved captain said to his deputy, 'I was too late.'

'Just in time isn't too late, Captain. We're all safe now.'

Patricius agreed with the deputy, in the silence of his own thoughts. The young captain had saved the lives of everybody on board boat thirteen. He'd done so because he'd had the experience and then made an informed decision at the right time. He thought of the raid commander calling off the action a boat early, and by doing so he'd secured lives and the overall success of the mission.

His father's words, two days ago, 'You Patricius, how is your opinion informed?' rang in his ears. I'm more like the Roman soldiers than these skilled young commanders.

The captain ordered food to be passed round and this time the captives were included. Patricius took his portion, a large chunk of bread, and he was ready for it. Holding the food in the fingers of his tied hands, he bit into the bread and was surprised at how tasty it was. The guard handed a skin of water to each captive in turn and stood over them.

'Two glugs,' he said, and no one dared to cheat.

Patricius's turn came, which he welcomed. Despite the flavour of the bread there was still an unpleasant aftertaste in his mouth from

63

the earlier retching. He was thirsty too and didn't want to lose his ration, so he drank his first mouthful and kept back a small amount of the second, before handing the skin back to the guard, who moved on. Patricius sluiced the water around his mouth thoroughly and spat it out on the floor of the boat. He felt refreshed, though aware that his standards of etiquette had plunged.

The windstorm took an hour to die and they resumed their journey on oar alone, turning into a large estuary and finding their inlet landing as the sun rose. Their boat was the next to last arrival, and they joined a queue of four currachs waiting to be directed to their mooring. They were one of twenty currachs. Patricius recognised the young commander, organising things on the Irish shore as he did in Banna Venta. He looked to be four or five years older than himself. Patricius wondered where he would be himself in four years; a wealthy landowning businessman running a large estate? But those plans were disappearing as quickly as the morning mist.

The twenty boats under this man's command had all arrived in what Patricius assumed was Ireland. The arithmetic sickened him. Thirty warriors per vessel, meaning a raiding force of six hundred in total. With twelve captives in most of the boats, over two hundred and twenty people had been captured. What a crippling cost to our community he thought, and then his father's words returned to torment him. 'How will we defend ourselves from the arrival on our shores of ten or twelve boats, with twenty warriors per vessel?' My father voiced that concern three days ago and I rejected the idea as not feasible. Such firm opinions yet I knew nothing. And when the attack came it was six hundred raiders not two hundred and forty.

Their currach was called to land and Patricius, having resisted being sick on the roughest possible boat journey, was suddenly stricken with fear of his unknown future, and as he saw foreign soil for the first time in his life, he vomited over the side of the boat.

CHAPTER SIX

Boat thirteen was moored with a simple loop thrown over a wooden stump, set deep on a gently sloping sandy bay. After yoking the captives to each other they were untied from the boat. Patricius, once again was the end captive in a line of six. Guarded at spear point, the captives were ordered from the boat. Patricius's line clambered out first onto the wet sand and was met by two guards.

'Walk to those marshals,' a guard commanded, pointing to an area about ten paces up the bay that was busy with naked captives coming and going. 'You lead off.' He pointed to Patricius. They were escorted and prodded with the butts of spears and ten strides later, lined up in two rows of six, in front of a marshal.

He threw down a basket. 'Strip yourselves naked except for footwear, throw your clothes in there, then wash yourselves in the sea,' he bawled, to be heard above the confusion of noise from all the other boat crews.

Patricius didn't like the infringement of his privacy but, having no choice, he found himself amongst the milky-skinned men, sloshing around in the estuary, eagerly washing their hair, and rinsing the diluted sewage of the boat journey from their bodies. The crisp, freshness of the cold water did not appeal to Patricius. He thought of the long hot, enjoyable soaks in the Roman bath house and rued how far he had fallen.

It was tempting for the captives to think of escaping now that their hands and feet were free. A commotion at the far end of Patricius's yoke drew his attention. The captive last in line was on hands and knees trying to slice through his necktie on a jagged rock, set deep in the sand. He'd pulled the next man down without warning and his noisy protestations brought unwanted attention to the feeble attempt to cut free from his yoke. A guard was on him immediately.

What a stupid attempt, thought Patricius. When I try it will be a better effort than that.

'Stand up,' the guard commanded the would-be escaper.

Patricius held his breath, not daring to think what would follow. The man stood up, and faced the guard, shivering.

Was it with cold, or fear, Patricius wondered?

'Turn round,' the guard commanded.

He did so and received three of the finest strokes of a willow cane across his backside.

'Any more tricks and it'll be the front side.' The guard turned. 'Out of the water everybody.'

Not a moment too soon, thought Patricius, shivering like the lashed captive. Returning to the beach, their guard gave a large woollen towel to each yoke of captives. Patricius luckily received his yoke's first, being at the right end of the line. He dried himself on the clean towel, then, averting his eyes, quickly removed his boots, poured out the water and dried his feet; after a furtive look towards the guard, Patricius quickly wiped the inside of his boots, before passing the towel on.

Each captive was handed a pale-yellow tunic, loose enough to step into. Patricius noticed this detail and dressed while neck-yoked. Next, they had their wrists bound tight and were marched to the top of a grassy hill.

From the hilltop, Patricius took in the scene; the comings and goings of a thousand men or more in three distinct areas. The first contained rows of spaced-out posts with captives tied to them, clearly his own immediate destination. Further down there was an area filled with livestock, held in open pens; beyond was more activity which he couldn't see clearly. As Patricius wondered if there was a cattle market in progress, a gentle whiff of livestock and the smell of open fires carried to him on a fresh sea breeze.

'Keep moving,' the guards prompted, directing the captives to the posts.

An organiser approached their guard, 'Foreigners on the right-hand side,' he said, pointing.

Patricius and the other captives were fettered once again, with enough slack to allow short steps to the posts, where their bodies were bound to the uprights and the neck yokes removed.

Buyers walked slowly along the colonnade of captives, scrutinising the merchandise to the left then right, haggling at times with caped officials. That's why my cape was taken, Patricius thought. They couldn't have me looking like an official. Suddenly the captain of boat thirteen came into Patricius's sight. He was escorting a noble who was looking with interest at a captive. They parted and Patricius watched the captain continue down the colonnade as he headed, unaccompanied, for the officials' area.

He's going to pass me. This is my chance. The worst that can happen to me is a beating. Patricius knew what he wanted to say, but first he had to catch the captain's attention.

'M'lord,' Patricius called as the captain strode past him.

The captain stopped and looked around, probably expecting to see an official.

'M'lord, thank you,' Patricius said.

The captain stepped closer to Patricius.

'Thank you for what?' he asked.

'You saved my life, in the storm. I don't like my circumstances, M'lord, but being fair; you saved the life of everyone in the boat.'

'I did my job, but I accept your thanks,' he replied, about to turn.

'M'lord, would you consider buying me?'

The captain faced Patricius, impatiently. 'I'm a captain. I don't invest in slaves.'

'M'lord, I am from a noble farming and property-owning family. You know where I live. Purchase me and take me home. My family will buy me back from you for twenty cows, two boats and your expenses.' The captain's deadpan look loosened into a smile. Patricius could see the captain was intrigued and thinking.

'You are a persuasive man and your proposal has merit but also plentiful risk. However, for reasons unknown to you, the answer is no. But I don't think you will remain a slave too long, and when your time comes it will cost you less than ten cows to become a freeman. Good luck to you.' This time the captain made off with no turning back.

Patricius was disappointed. He hadn't expected the idea to work but as the captain had given him a good hearing, he'd raised his hopes. At least he hadn't been whipped for trying.

Those from the boats looked bedraggled and sickened by their journey. The green complexions and despairing eyes of the foreign slaves was noticeable, even to Patricius and yet the foreigners were attracting more attention than the Irish slaves. A tall, slim figure with a long grey beard, and an official looking man carrying a stylus and wax tablets, looked Patricius over, giving no clues regarding their level of interest. A sullen-faced Patricius, however, did not hide his own frame of mind. His eyes followed their movements as they made their way to some officials at a desk.

The young raid commander engaged them in discussion, at one point glancing towards Patricius.

Had a deal been struck, Patricius wondered as the men parted without a handshake?

At the opposite row of poles, Patricius had seen a caped individual removing a captive's boots. His curiosity was interrupted when a man stood squarely before him. Patricius guessed he was a noble as his white robe, beneath the cape, was made of a high-quality, finely spun yarn.

'Name?' the official asked.

'Patricius.'

'Is that a Roman name?'

'Yes.'

'Well, your Irish name is Patrick and you are now the property of King Miliucc; bad luck, young man,' he said, in a seemingly genuine tone.

'Why is it bad luck?' Patricius asked, wondering what the guard knew that he didn't.

'He's from Mayo.'

'Meaning?' Patricius asked matter-of-factly.

'Meaning there are many long, hard days of walking ahead of you.' The official scratched a note on his wax tablet as Patricius digested the information and had a thought.

'M'lord, would you cut my shackles please?' Patricius asked, finding his politeness.

'Miliucc's guards will do that.'

'Please, M'lord. Just my feet.'

The official looked down at Patricius's splendid leather boots and gave him a friendly wink, saying, 'Just your feet, son, and don't forget, you're Patrick now.'

That's what you think, Patricius thought. The bard sliced the twine with a short sharp blade and moved on. All on his side wore sandals, except Patricius, who stood out in his high-quality leather, Roman-style boots. The guard from opposite was now in front of Patricius's face.

'Kick off your boots, slave boy.'

Patricius didn't move.

'Kick off, your boots,' the guard snarled.

Again, Patricius didn't move. Smack! Patricius's lips and teeth were hammered into his mouth with the full force of a knuckle-fisted backhand.

'They're not my boots,' mumbled Patricius, defiantly, through thickening, bloodied lips; and was swiftly interrupted.

'You're right, slave boy. They're mine.'

As the guard bent down to take them, Patricius with no thought for caution, gave him a mighty kick in the face. Teeth flew out and blood splattered as the unsuspecting guard was knocked up and over, onto his back. He lay there stunned, fooled for believing Patricius's feet were tied.

'They're King Miliucc's boots,' said Patricius to the bewildered bully on the ground as two other guards, dressed in smart blue and green tunics, came along.

'Patrick?' one called out.

'It's Patricius,' he corrected.

'I've been told Patrick.'

'You've been told wrong,' Patricius replied, tartly.

'Young man, some masters don't call their slaves by name at all.'

'Well, my name is Patricius,' he said, not listening to the guard's words.

'Young man, your master wishes to address you by name. You should think about that. He has allowed you to keep your name; he just wants to pronounce it in Irish. And – Patrick – the sooner you fit in here, the better it will be for you.'

Patricius was stunned into thoughtful silence.

I've sharp-tongued the guard but he didn't take offence; he respectfully took the time to give me an explanation.

Patricius thought about the message, especially about the fitting in. I want to escape as soon as possible. Perhaps insisting on the name Patricius will be a constant reminder to those around me, that I'm a foreigner. It may serve me better if I don't stand out. He snapped out of his thoughts as the guards freed him from the pole, his hands still tied behind his back.

'Come with us, Patrick,' said the second guard. Patricius began to react, then took a deep breath and resignedly said to himself, I'll be Patrick, till I escape.

As they left, both of his guards laughed at the bully on the ground.

'Ah, Fichran, boots will be the death of you,' said Patrick's mentor.

They marched Patrick away, but he glanced back at the failed boot thief who was unsteadily returning to his feet. He scowled at Patrick, angry that his opportunity for revenge had passed. Patrick quickly looked around for the official who'd understood his request and freed his feet. Their eyes met and Patrick nodded a thank you.

The official, with a glint in his eye, returned the briefest of nods, before Patrick was pushed in the other direction.

As they passed through the calvary of captives, the air became heavy with the stench of livestock. Walking through the narrow passages between cattle pens, Patrick inhaled the steam gushing from the mouths and firmly open nostrils of exhausted bulls and cows.

I'm a noble, reduced overnight to sharing the breath of cattle.

On they marched into a field with a more agreeable aroma of pigs on roast, broth bubbling in pots and fresh bread baking over open fires. Nobles wearing travelling clothes, including knee-length trousers under their tunics, leg wraps and leather shoes, were gathered around the spits on one side of the field, enjoying their ale and roast. I belong on that side, Patrick thought, smarting at his predicament; but he was led to a food table at which a group of ten slaves were already seated. He was tied by the ankles, alongside the others. They sat on log seats as slave girls brought them bowls of broth and fresh bread, which they gobbled hungrily despite the awkwardness of tied wrists.

Patrick expected gruel, and was surprised to receive a meaty broth.

After noon, a procession pulled out of an adjacent field and onto a nearby cattle track that headed west. The formation was led by two guards on horseback followed by the tall figure with a long grey beard, and two mounted bards. Next, a pair of work horses with a servant holding the reins pulled a cart containing sows, boars and piglets. A two-horse passenger cart followed, driven by another servant, with two backward-facing guards seated on board. As the column stopped opposite the servants' table, a guard quickly took Patrick and chained him by the wrists to the last cart, alongside two other captives and removed the fetters of all three, allowing them to stride out. Two more guards on horseback took position behind the slaves, completing the column. With all assembled, one of the rear guards called readiness and the entourage moved out.

Walking gave the trio time to chat, albeit under the gaze of the two seated guards.

'I recognise you,' said Patrick to the youth on his right.

'I know you, master. Remember Elijah the saddle-maker?' he said with a smile.

'Remember. In truth I was speaking to Elijah on the eve of my capture.'

'Well, I'm Joshua, Elijah's son. Why are you here, master? You shouldn't be here.'

'Thank you, Joshua, but… drop the master and call me Patrick.'

'Patrick? Are you not Patricius?'

'We're in Ireland now, it's Patrick.' He lowered his voice. 'Joshua, it is better our connection isn't known.' Patrick felt humiliated by his fall and didn't wish the extent of it to be known to others.

They walked for a while in silence. The weather was dry and breezy. Patrick took in the surroundings. The tracks were narrow and rutted; wide enough for two carts to pass, but only just; and both sides were bounded by deep ditches. They skirted woods and farmlands but something was amiss. This was Ireland, a neighbouring country separated by a narrow stretch of water; but should it be so different to his home? There was something disturbing about the lie-of-the-land they walked through, mile after mile?

Finally, it struck him and he turned to his left in the hope that the other captive might be able to answer his question. He started by introducing himself.

'I'm Patrick, and you?'

'Owain.'

'Owain, in half a day of walking we've not seen a town. Where are the market towns?' Patrick said aloud.

'They don't have towns in Ireland,' said Owain.

Patrick glanced at Joshua, 'No towns?' Joshua repeated.

'It's all farming and fishing,' said Owain. 'The kings are farmers and some will have a market in their fields once a year.'

'How do you know this?' Patrick asked.

'My father is a farmer's merchant. He journeys here to buy horses.'

'How does he find his suppliers?' Patrick queried.

'He met an Irish king at a farmers' market in Wales. They talked business and agreed to exchange a boat load of herd dogs for three horses. You know they don't have money here?'

'No money?' Joshua parroted. 'How do they trade?'

'Like I said, by exchange of goods.'

Patrick was concentrating. 'So, your father's first trip was by invitation?' he asked.

'All of his trips are. He would not come here any other way. You need the escort and the protection; like we are part of now. A king wouldn't visit a customer or supplier in a neighbouring kingdom, on his own. He'd be killed for his horse. He would always travel with five or six guards,' said Owain.

Patrick was listening to every word, his mind soaking in the situation like the fine sand blotting the ink of his writing.

'Could your father search for you under the guise of a business trip?' Patrick asked.

'We talked about it, because of all the raids. Being caught in a raid was always a possibility. However, the idea is too risky.'

This news dismayed Patrick. Owain's father was experienced in coming to and going from Ireland, yet the possibility of rescuing his son was too risky. Trudging long into the evening until the daylight faded, the track took them closer to settlements, some surrounded by earthen mounds. The Miliucc retinue stopped outside the gates of a low-walled enclosure.

Bards dismounted, led their horses to the gate and were met by the hostelry owner who spoke briefly with them and opened the gates. Ostlers and servants hurried to attend to their guests and tend to the horses. The livestock cart was wheeled into a barn, while the king, his bards and guards were taken to an ale house. The three captives were un-tethered from the cart and taken into a cattle house, where each was chained by the ankle to a post. Their hands and one foot were free.

Shortly, a servant girl brought bowls of vegetable broth, along with wooden spoons and black bread, into the cattle house for them.

'Leave the bowls outside the door when you've finished. I'll collect them later,' she said barely looking at the three captives.

Patrick and the other slaves ate hungrily sitting on the straw-covered ground in a cow-house, dipping the dry and stale bread into the broth to make it palatable. A ragged slave, chewing the last of a crust with an open mouth, approached them carrying a jug of ale and three tin mugs.

'Ale for the travellers,' he announced. 'Where are you heading?'

'We don't know,' answered Patrick.

'Where are you from then?'

'From over the water,' said Patrick, nodding to the east.

Getting nowhere, the scruffy man cut the conversation short.

'Your beds are there.' He pointed to an untidy pile behind the stable door. 'Well, ye've got the warmest beds, I'd say,' he gestured to the cows. 'Put your empties outside. The girl will collect them. Sleep well,' he smirked and sloped off.

'What of that?' asked Owain?

'Shifty-eyed no-good,' muttered Patrick.

'Indeed. I think he'd like to steal from us,' said Owain.

Joshua had nothing to say but he glanced towards Patrick and Owain, following the conversation.

'But we have nothing. Only the clothes we wear,' said Patrick.

'Exactly that.' Owain pointed to Patrick's feet, 'he'll be back for your boots.'

Joshua yawned and pulled himself up to his feet, 'I could do with some sleep. Let's sort these beds out.'

Joshua dashed the straw off three woven birch mats, passing one each to Patrick and Owain. Patrick set down his mat with his feet towards the post. The chain was six feet long giving him room to move and turn in his sleep. While the other two were settling down, Patrick was thinking about his boots.

'I've got blisters and need these boots off. I should hide them in case Shifty visits us in the dark. Do you think he'll find my boots up there?' asked Patrick nodding to a beam about twelve feet above them.

'Sound idea,' said Owain.

Patrick removed his boots and tied the laces together. 'Owain, you're the tallest. I'll squat; you stand on my shoulders and see if you can reach.' Patrick passed him the boots and crouched down, steadying himself on the vertical post.

Owain, hesitating slightly, the boots in his hands, laughed, 'As you're on your knees I'll go along with you.'

Owain stepped onto Patrick's shoulders. As he stood up, he wobbled, and Joshua put his hands on Owain's hips to stabilise him. Owain reached the bottom of the beam and threw the boots over. A boot hung on each side joined by the thong, but the throwing action made him lose balance and he tumbled down taking Joshua with him, landing on top of Patrick in a heap on the floor. Joshua laughed and Owain mocked in good humour, 'Hell, Patrick, this is some fuss over a pair of boots. Can I get some sleep now?'

'Thanks, Owain, you can. By the way, they're not just boots, I love those boots; they're a quality gift from my mother.'

Joshua bursting with pride said, 'My father made them, and I helped him.' Owain raised both eyebrows, 'Special indeed, goodnight to you both.'

'Good night,' said Patrick.

'Sleep well,' said Joshua.

Two long days, a night without sleeping and eight hours of walking helped Patrick to sleep. It was a shallow slumber, his mind as busy as a corn exchange on market day.

In the darkest time of night Shifty glided around the sleeping trio, but Patrick was awake and watching. Shifty appeared to study Patrick's bare feet in the very dim light of a candle lamp, and, finding no boots he persevered, searching within the limits of the captives' chains. Finding the post, he examined it, probably for hooks. There were none. Placing the candle on the blind side of the post, he raised it aloft and saw the boots hanging, high above his head.

Patrick adjusted his posture slowly. Shifty lowered the light and placed it at the foot of the support. With both hands freed, he shinned up the post like it was a ladder. Owain and Joshua slept on. Shifty, hanging on the beam with both hands shuffled along with the ease of a monkey. Patrick was ready for Shifty, whether he dropped to the floor or returned to the post. Suddenly, Joshua lunged to pull Shifty down by his feet, but his chain rattled, giving the thief a brief warning. Patrick's opportunity had been thwarted by Joshua, but there was a chance Shifty had not seen Patrick.

Shifty dropped onto Joshua, knocking him to the floor, wriggled free of the tangle of limbs and was back on his feet in an instant. Taking a combative posture, Shifty took a vicious swipe at Joshua. His attack didn't land though, as Patrick powered a crippling boxer's punch into Shifty's side. Hurt, he let out a muted squeal and went down on one knee. Struggling to recover, Shifty gritted his teeth against the pain and dragged himself beyond the reach of the captives' chains, whilst clutching at his soreness. Joshua grabbed the candle lamp and raised the light. All could see a knife, held firmly in Shifty's grip, signalling he hadn't yet finished his business.

Owain was with them now. 'Pull back,' said Owain. 'Make him come to us.'

With those words, Shifty knew his moment had gone. Like a wounded animal he vanished into the shadows of the shippon.

'Thank you, Patrick. You saved me,' said Joshua.

'I owe you thanks. You saved my boots,' Patrick replied kindly, knowing that Joshua had almost ensured Shifty got away with them.

'Hey, Patrick,' said Owain, 'you're a fighter.'

'Not really. I have no instinct for fighting.'

'You gave him a powerful punch.'

'In truth I did, but he couldn't see me. He didn't know I was there.'

'If you're not instinctive, you learned somewhere.'

'I trained in boxing with Roman soldiers,' conceded Patrick, picking up the lamp. His boots were hanging low; disturbed by Shifty before he was pulled down. Patrick put down the lamp, jumped up and retrieved his boots.

'Let us pull straws for the lamp,' Patrick suggested.

'Count me out,' said Owain. 'I was sleeping.'

'You keep the lamp, Patrick, and don't argue,' said Joshua.

'How would I get flints?' asked Patrick.

'Here,' said Owain, taking the lamp and pulling down the bottom section. 'A lighting set. Patrick, have you never lit a lamp before?'

He hadn't. Neither had it ever crossed his mind. Patrick realised his privileged life had left him in ignorance about certain things.

'How did Shifty get in, or out? He didn't leave by this door,' Patrick said, dodging the question.

'There's a servant's door at the side,' Joshua contributed.

They sat and chatted till dawn, when the slave girl came with hot porridge, black bread, and a jug of water for them. On her retreat she opened the door to let in the daylight. Patrick drank the water and thought how he would be enjoying fruit juice if he was at home. As they ate, they were amused watching Shifty scowling as he carried water buckets to the livestock. The slave girl loaded skins of water, breads and cheeses onto the king's cart and the trio hoped this lunch included them. The retinue was ready to leave and as they crossed the yard, guards released the captive's chains and secured the three slaves to the end cart.

Shifty was opening the gates and as the procession passed through, Patrick said, 'Nice lamp, Shifty. Thank you.'

Shifty scowled viciously; he was raging.

'It's a coward who attacks a chained man,' added Joshua.

Shifty exploded and ran at Joshua with a pole. The two watchful guards sprang from the cart and floored him as the bards and King Miliucc stopped the procession.

'Bring him to me,' Miliucc commanded.

In the steely grip of the guards, Shifty was presented on his knees to King Miliucc.

'Why do you attack my people?' Miliucc asked.

Shifty nodded towards Joshua, 'He offended me with his tongue.'

'I heard the words, and you made truth of them,' said Miliucc. He looked to one of the bards, 'Bring me the keeper.'

The bard and keeper arrived and Miliucc spoke.

'King Niall pays you to serve your guests, but this man attacks them. What have you to say?'

The keeper was white-faced and fearful. He looked like a man who dared not fall from his king's grace.

'My lord, I will chain him immediately and put him on hidden duties. I will also make sure that he answers for his offences before a brehon. I regret, my lord, I didn't know his character. I received him recently in payment of a debt.'

'Do this and the matter is ended. Know, however, that my bard will check for the brehon's judgement. Fail to do this and Niall will get to know.' Miliucc turned his horse and joined the procession.

The guards pushed Shifty to the ground, leaving him in the charge of his owner, and took up their places as the column moved out.

The three slaves walked silently, deep in their thoughts. Patrick was surprised to hear that Shifty would be judged by a third party. No slave in Roman Britain would have access to a magistrate over such petty affairs.

As they walked to the gate Owain spoke, 'My father mentioned that on his trips to Ireland he never paid for his hospitality. He presumed it was paid for by his customer. The conversation between King Miliucc and the keeper suggests the kings provide the hospitality. That probably makes sense in a country that doesn't use money. How could a traveller pay his bill by exchange of goods? It wouldn't work.'

Patrick was thinking what this meant for his escape. He couldn't use an inn or hostel and pay with coin as in Britain. No one, it seemed could use a hostel anonymously, here in Ireland.

After they had walked for some distance, they entered a forest and one of the guards commanded, 'Jump on the cart.'

They did with pleasure and for the next ten miles the procession trotted along a smooth forest track.

'Shifty attacked you, Joshua. Why not ask the guard what will happen to him,' whispered Owain?

'Can a slave speak to a guard?' said Joshua.

'I don't know. It was you who was attacked. You benefited from the guard's intervention. Why not try it?'

Joshua thought about it for a while and took a chance. Catching the guard's eye, he said, 'Thank you, sir, for protecting me.'

'It is my duty,' the guard answered matter-of-factly.

'You did it well.'

The guard nodded without expression.

'What will happen to him?' Joshua asked, with a tremble in his voice.

'He will pay a fine for attempting to harm a person,' said the guard. Patrick was shocked at the leniency.

'Even though the person was a slave?' Joshua ventured with a little more firmness.

'It makes no difference, slave or noble. That is the law,' the guard snapped, then, with a raised hand said, 'Enough.'

Joshua, not daring to utter another word, just nodded his acknowledgement. Patrick was surprised to hear the law in Ireland protected a slave as well as a noble, from assault. He wasn't sure that was a good thing.

Coming out of the forest they shielded their eyes from the brightness. The easy ride ended, and the terrain became a long, tiring uphill foot-slog for the slaves and horses. Eventually it gave way to a lengthy undulating run and the slaves once again were passengers, much to Patrick's relief, as his blisters were paining him. He was more used to riding than walking and thought, sadly of Shadow, his beloved horse, who he might never ride again.

The party pulled off the track into a shaded area next to a ford, where the horses were fed and watered and the slaves too were given a meal of water, bread, and cheese, fulfilling their earlier hopes when the slave girl was loading the cart. The guards gathered around a fallen tree, and the trio ate in the cart. Out of earshot of the nobles and guards, they took their chance to speak quietly among themselves.

'Miliucc defends us as his own,' said Joshua. 'And lets us ride when the horses trot. He seems decent.'

'He defends us as his own because we are his own. He lets us ride because he plans the journey round his horses. On the hills we walk so the horses pull less weight. On the smooth tracks he trots the horses, but we can't keep pace, so he puts us in the cart. On tracks too rough for trotting, the horses walk, and we walk too, to spare the horses' energy,' said Owain.

'I agree,' said Patrick. 'The king wants to make the most progress he can in a day. Humans don't stop when they are tired. Horses do.'

'But the King does not treat us cruelly or badly,' said Joshua.

'Let's hope it is his true measure,' said Owain.

'I think it is,' said Joshua. 'He treated the keeper fairly. He let Shifty answer for himself. He could have told the guards to give him a beating.'

Patrick listened and pondered. Here, in a wild, barbarian nation, where people cannot read or write, he's discovered a slave has a right to a third-party judgement and, worse, the king and the keeper respected that right, over a small matter. Patrick could not imagine being beholden to a magistrate over the trivial rights of a slave. To Patrick – and a generation of Romano-British Patrick's, born into wealth – because the slave was legally the property of the owner, they believed day-to-day justice for a slave was in the hands of the owner too. Why should it be different, he thought, when, on bigger matters, accidents, culpability, manslaughter, murder; the word of a noble was worth more than the testament of a slave?

Having finished their meal, they resumed the track. Like yesterday they passed large cattle farms, dozens of small mixed farms with chickens and pigs, corn and spelt fields in the valleys, oxen and mules pulling carts, goat-like sheep grazing on the coarse hillsides and many workers in the fields. The countryside around them was like the farming areas of north-west Britain, though Patrick was discovering the ways of the country were very different. They continued walking and long after sundown, arrived at a hostel.

Their lodgings were based in a woodcraft village with thatched, oval-shaped wattle and daub buildings for workshops. Stocks of fenceposts, planks and heavy bridge beams were visible in the open-sided despatch building. Stables and roundhouses for guests were in a separate enclosure. The king, his bards and guards were shown to a large house into which hostel slaves were carrying tubs of water and towels, for the comfort of the nobles.

Patrick and his two companions were unchained from the cart and chained to each other, then, along with the servants who'd been holding rein, were shown to a roundhouse, smaller than the king's but next to it. The room reeked with the smell of the sweat of previous customers. Body odour went unnoticed, however odious, by the others and Patrick found himself craving for the bath house at home and a private bedroom.

'This is better than sleeping with cows,' said Joshua, as a Miliucc guard, the one he'd engaged in conversation, entered the room.

The guard stood the three new slaves in a line, 'Let me tell you what happens to a slave who runs away. It is against the law in Ireland for a slave to run away from his master, or for anyone to help him to run away. It is an offence to turn a blind eye if you think or know a slave is running away. In Ireland a man's identity is his name. He belongs to a clan. You cannot travel or find work or buy food if you do not belong to a clan.' Patrick listened with the face of a worried man. 'No one will help you. Everyone will be your enemy. A foreigner in Ireland cannot pass for belonging to a clan. He will be caught and punished. But as a slave you belong to your master and the law protects a slave as it protects a noble. You have seen that with your own eyes. Now you understand why no foreign slave ever escaped Ireland. And now you have been told, there is no more need for these,' the guard pointed at the chains and freed them.

Patrick felt numb. "No foreign slave ever escaped Ireland". When will my torment end? From what he'd seen of Ireland so far, the guard's words seemed to be true.

A servant girl entered the house carrying a large basket of clothing and sturdy bags with shoulder straps.

'Give one pile to each man,' the guard told her. She handed a set of clothing and a bag to Patrick, Owain and Joshua.

'These are your new clothes. Change now and come to the food hall. Throw your old clothes in the basket,' said the guard.

'What about shoes?' Owain asked.

'You can keep your shoes.' Patrick was relieved; his boots had survived a third hazard. 'Don't take long, the king wishes to inspect you. Should you need to address the king you can say King Miliucc, or M'lord.' The guard stomped out, carrying the chains.

They examined their clothing. Two of everything; vests, underwear, night vests, grey knee-length trousers, a light shirt, a heavy shirt, yellow tunics, plus a pair of sandals and a sturdy bag.

'It's like soldier's issue at Alauna fort,' said Patrick.

'Maybe it's special for the kings' slaves,' Joshua responded.

Owain was already on his way to the water tub. All were pleased to wash and get out of the clothes they'd worn for three nights and four days. They dressed identically, in the light shirt, trousers and tunic. Patrick, however, cleaned his boots with the wet towel and wore them, while Owain and Joshua put on the shoes. They were a new experience; oval-shaped leather soles, soft unshaped leather uppers with a thong to draw them tight around the ankles – a larger version of a Roman money purse. Patrick kept his new sandals in the bag and wore his boots, not trusting to leave them in the bed house.

They arrived at the food hall before the king's party. It was a round house with a large rectangular table set out for the king and his retinue. Horns on holders sat beside jugs of ale; platters of pork chunks, chicken legs, and baked bread-cakes were placed down the centre of the table along with cups of meat juice. At a smaller table for the servants and slaves there was hot broth and chunks of bread. A guard arrived and stood them in a line to receive King Miliucc. The cohorts gathered in a semi-circle behind their king, who stepped forward to inspect his slaves. He addressed all three.

'You have been issued with clothing. One set is a gift from me. The other set you will pay for out of your allowance. You will always wear yellow, which is the slave's colour and whenever you are to be in my presence you will dress properly and smartly for the circumstances.' King Miliucc then stood in front of Joshua.

'You are Joshua, the son of a leatherworker?' he enquired.

'Yes, M'lord,' Joshua replied, surprise on his face at the king's use of his name.

'At dawn you will be collected by Conn. He is a craftsman in leather and ceramics. You will work under his instruction, but you are my slave. You should be suited to this work.'

'Thank you, M'lord.'

King Miliucc stood in front of Owain.

'You are Owain?' he enquired.

'I am, M'lord.'

'Tomorrow, before sundown Kilcullen will meet us, to collect you. Kilcullen is a cattle farmer and a chieftain. You will take your instructions from him. I have hired your labour to Kilcullen for a year.'

'Thank you, M'lord.'

Miliucc stood before Patrick.

Joshua and Owain have been given employment that matches their trade. What will I be given?

'You are Patrick, a farm owner?'

'Yes M'lord.' Patrick thought it wasn't too bad a description.

'Tomorrow evening, we stay at a hostel. The following day we will arrive at Voclut where you will become a shepherd.' Miliucc gestured to the three of them and said, 'Have you any questions?'

'Yes, M'lord,' said Patrick. He was unhappy to be given a job of very low status but was aware that he was talking to his owner and a king. 'Is there a reason for employing me as a shepherd? I run a farm but have never been a shepherd.'

'I am a sheep farmer. I own some cattle ranches, but my kingdom's wealth is mostly based on sheep. Does that answer your question?'

'Yes M'lord.' Patrick breathed a sigh of relief. I think the king has told me if it's good enough for him it's good enough for me, and he hoped his unspoken, condescending thought, had not shown in his demeanour. Patrick also thought there might be a prospect of him one day running a large sheep farm.

King Miliucc paused briefly for questions from the other two then stepped back and gestured to the table.

'Enjoy your meal and return to your room, where you will find a jug of ale.'

The king and his men sat at their table and feasted as though no one else was there. The slaves and servants finished their broth quickly and took the bread, which was stale, to their room, where they sat in a circle on sheepskins, placed on a straw-covered floor. As they ate and drank, Patrick opened conversation with a statement.

'Tomorrow, we take separate paths.'

'Indeed, and I'm scared again, though the worst days of my life have been easier for meeting you two,' Joshua said.

Owain and Patrick nodded.

'At least you are to work in your profession,' Patrick said, trying to comfort Joshua. 'Imagine me as a shepherd; what do I know of sheep other than eating them?' He smiled and Joshua returned the expression, making Patrick believe he had offered some reassurance.

Owain smiled briefly too then turned to the two drivers who were sharing the roundhouse with the slaves for the night. They were huddled in their own corner, as if determined to keep their distance from Patrick, Owain and Joshua.

'What is your position? Are you two slaves?'

'We are servants,' said passenger-cart-driver.

'Is this different to slaves?' asked Owain, as Patrick listened intently.

'We're still slaves, but higher status. We get better treatment.'

'How do you get this?' asked Owain.

Pig-cart-driver chipped in, 'If you serve your master well, which means looking after his wealth, it will happen.'

'How do you mean?' asked Joshua.

'Let me tell you by story,' Pig-cart-driver began, as Patrick paid attention.

'I am a woodcutter. Time came when the king wanted repairs to his house and buildings. I worked on his property for three moons. His queen was pleased with my work and I was given fifty hens as extra. Today I have 150 hens from breeding and getting more extras. When I have enough livestock, I can ask to become a rent-paying farmer. For this the livestock must be cattle. If the bard agrees and makes it proper, it will make me a freeman.'

Passenger-cart-driver added, 'You should be of good character as well. Livestock alone is not enough.'

'Are you Irish?' asked Owain.

'We both are,' said pig-cart-driver.

'How did you become slaves?' Patrick listened carefully; keen on learning the ways to escape slavery.

'My father got into big debt and could not repay. When I was twelve years old, he repaid his debt by selling me as a slave,' said pig-cart-driver. Owain and Joshua shook their heads. Patrick was horrified to hear this. How could a father, even one in such straits, sell his own son?

'And you?' said Patrick to the other driver.

'I was born a slave.'

'Do many slaves become freemen?' asked Patrick.

'Most,' said passenger-cart-driver.

'How long does it take?'

'Most do it in ten years.'

Dejected at the thought that his freedom could be ten years away, he finished his ale and, with a heavy sigh said, 'I'm going to soak my blistered feet.'

Outside, he sat on a log with his feet submerged in a tub of cold water. Ten years. Ten years to work my way out of slavery. Then how many years to pay for a boat trip? After a soothing ten minutes on his feet and a miserable ten minutes on his mind, he returned to the bedroom, where Owain was talking to Joshua.

'Let me bid you farewell, Joshua. Time will be short at dawn.' They shook hands. 'Joshua, you must strive to become an expert craftsman. Believe me, the best craftsmen become nobles.'

Passenger-cart-driver nodded his support for Owain's advice.

'Thank you, Owain. Good luck yourself. Pray Kilcullen is a good boss.' Joshua then approached Patrick. He bowed his head and said, 'Goodbye, master.' Patrick flinched as he spotted the two drivers glancing at each other. 'Er... sorry, I mean Patrick. I hope things work out for you.'

'Thank you, Joshua. Farewell.'

Soon all were settled in their Miliucc-chosen night attire. Owain and Joshua seemed pleased to change out of their tunics. Patrick, however, squirmed, humiliated by the king's reach. He curled up and covered his head and body with sheepskins.

Owain takes all in his stride. Joshua is fearful, but he'll fit in. I, though, am porcelain, broken into small pieces. A half bag of tiles, never to be a mosaic. How will I ever be someone, again? Patrick fought to muffle the sobs that were rising within him, using the heavy, stinking sheepskin.

The rain next day drizzled, poured, then lashed as Patrick and Owain departed the hostelry, leaving Joshua behind to await collection by his new master. Patrick was soaked, cold and feeling miserable. And his blisters were hurting again. He wanted to protest, but who to and for what outcome?

At a crossing of tracks, the retinue – dripping like figurines in a fountain – moved onto dry gravel under the shelter of trees and waited.

A passenger cart arrived from the south, drawn by two oxen; a farmer and his official jumped down, shook the rain off their sturdy cloaks and strode up to Miliucc.

As the nobles and guards paid much attention to the visitor, Patrick took the weight off his blistered feet and sat on the back of the cart. Light rain persisted but the wind had calmed, allowing him to hear the conversations that took place.

'Kilcullen, it's a pleasure to meet you,' said Miliucc as they shook hands. 'Allow me to introduce Bard Matrix.'

'My pleasure, Bard Matrix.' They exchanged a nod of heads.

'Meet Bard Pantheos,' said Kilcullen. Miliucc and Bard Matrix nodded politely.

How does the Roman name Pantheos arrive in Ireland? He then rued the missing of his planned classical education.

At this point both bards produced parchment scrolls inscribed with Ogham markings in jet-black ink. Miliucc's bard opened his, ran his finger across the script to bring a detail to Kilcullen's attention then pointed fleetingly to Owain.

'I think my payment will be to your satisfaction.'

Kilcullen approached the slave and standing in front of Owain looked him up and down.

'Show me your hands.'

Owain obliged. Patrick looked over as Kilcullen glanced down at the large, firm fingers and muscled, leathery and chafed palms acquired from the regular pulling of teats.

'I can see these hands have milked cows,' Kilcullen remarked.

'Yes M'lord; herds of them.'

'Have you driven oxen?'

'No M'lord.'

'Then start now. Sit with the driver.'

Owain looked to King Miliucc who nodded his assent, then, with a final glance at Patrick, he jumped onto the cart and sat beside the driver. Bard Pantheos finished looking over the document and was satisfied. Bard Matrix took a small cloth-wrapped writing set from an inner pocket and placed it on the flat bed of the cart. Leaning over to protect his writing space from the occasional tree drip, he rolled out a grey piece of tightly woven wool cloth, on which he placed a small pot of black ink and a quill.

Seeing this preparation took Patrick's mind back to the evening before his capture when he used a similar writing set. He couldn't bear to think the subject of his report was security against slave raids.

When the preparations for pad and ink were complete, both bards opened their documents, quilled their insignia, and waited for the ink to dry before swapping scrolls. Miliucc's was a note from Kilcullen acknowledging receiving a slave's labour for a year, as payment of a debt. Kilcullen received a scroll from Miliucc proving and maintaining his ownership of Owain along with a note of transfer.

Kilcullen leant into Miliucc and said, 'Before we part, I wish you to know that I have bred a herd of excellent, pedigree bulls. They will be ready for sale by the Festival of Beltaine. Would a purchase of this kind interest you?'

'Indeed, it would' Miliucc answered. 'We are building our stock. I will look at them. And you might consider hiring stalls at my livestock fayre. The festival attracts many quality buyers. I will ask Bard Matrix to visit you in the weeks before Beltaine.'

'I hope we can do business again. Thank you and good day, Miliucc.'

'The chances are favourable. Good day to you, Kilcullen.' They shook hands and parted.

The guard beckoned Patrick off the cart. He slid to his feet quickly, in time to see Owain looking back at him.

'Farewell and good luck, Patrick,' he called.

'Fare you well, Owain,' Patrick replied.

He watched as Owain shrank from view, then, without realising, Patrick dropped his chin to his chest. His shoulders narrowed slightly and his back rounded. Patrick felt lonely. Talking with the two other slaves, who were in the same predicament, had offered some comfort. He knew this moment would arrive, that the journey was unreal and the brief friendships would end.

Unaware that he was standing still and staring at the ground, he heard a harsh voice shout out.

'Quickly.'

He looked up slowly and saw the guard gesturing impatiently for him to get moving. Walking sorely on bleeding feet, Patrick took up his place behind the cart.

Miliucc saw his limping and said quietly to his guard, 'After this hill, let Patrick onto the cart.'

Patrick heard the words and resented walking the hill on sore feet to spare the horse. However, he looked forward to the relief after the hill and his spirits lifted a little.

Two miles later Patrick was sitting on the back of the passenger cart, facing the rear guards. The rain drizzled on but he didn't care. The weight was off his feet.

For the next twelve miles they drove through hard rain and met no one on the track. As they passed farms, teams of men could be seen digging ditches, unperturbed by the pouring rain. Cows, however, grouped under trees for shelter, sheep gathered near walls and fences, women and children were out of sight. As the rain eased, they arrived at a hostel. Patrick hobbled into the yard where everyone was shown to their accommodation. He and the drivers were sharing with four others in a roundhouse large enough for ten.

A slave girl saw Patrick's difficulty and followed the new arrivals into the bed house.

'You're not walking too well,' she said to Patrick.

'I've got blisters,' he replied.

'Show me. I'll help you if I can.'

Patrick removed his boots. Both feet were bleeding and raw.

'Stay here. I'll return soon.'

She came back with a tub of cold water, bandages, and some ointment. As she bathed his feet Patrick enjoyed the coldness of the water and the gentle touch of her fingers on his sore and swollen skin. He imagined he was at home and Mary was tending to his ailment. After dabbing his feet dry, she lightly applied herbal ointment to his damaged skin. Patrick stifled a sharp intake of breath as the treatment stung his open wounds.

'On raw flesh it cannot be otherwise. But soothing will follow,' she said, and swaddled his feet carefully with cloth strips that were clean, but obviously cut from an old vest. 'How does that feel?' she asked.

'Much better,' said Patrick.

By now she was examining his boots.

'These boots need drying and softening. I'll bring them to you before you break your fast. Have you got sandals?'

'Yes.'

'Good. Now don't be working them feet. It's rest they need.'

Patrick pressed his lips and put on an obedient look. 'What's your name?' he enquired softly.

'Breege.'

'Thank you, Breege. Let me ask, why are you doing this?'

'You walked in here like a hen on stubbles, 'twas obvious you needed help.'

'But why did you help?'

'That's what slaves do. They help each other.'

'You knew that I was a slave?'

She tugged at his yellow tunic.

'Oh, yes,' he said, 'I keep forgetting.'

'You must be a new slave?' She watched his expression.

'Yes.'

'From where?' she asked with a pleasant twang, which Patrick found charming.

'I'm from Britain.'

'You were no slave over the water,' she laughed, 'I can tell by your feet.'

'That's the truth,' he said, blushing.

'I must away,' said Breege. 'I'll be back before sunrise. If you're asleep I'll stir you.' She gathered up her trappings and left with Patrick's boots.

Patrick changed into dry clothing, put on sandals, and walked with hardly a limp to the food hall, pondering on his way. He had a good feeling about Breege and believed she was genuine. He was confident she would return his boots. Inside the food hall Patrick took a seat at a bench table, directly opposite the drivers, and poured a mug of cow's milk. Pig-cart-driver spoke to him,

'The broth is over there, M'lord,' he said, lingering on the word lord.

Patrick pretended not to have noticed and fetched his dish. As he ate, the other driver quipped,

'You're in the wrong room, M'lord.'

'You should be eating with the king,' the first interjected.

Ignoring their sniggers Patrick ate his meal, as they continued their teasing. When a servant girl delivered some jugs of ale to the table, Patrick stood up and said to the drivers,

'You can have my ale; I'm going to drink wine with the king.'

Pig-cart-driver shot back, 'He's leaving early. I'll wager he's meeting the nurse.'

The other driver mocked, 'Nurse, please, I have an ache in my groin. Can you help?'

Patrick strode out holding his head high. He was the only person in the bed house as he sat on his mat for a while thinking over the mocking. Then he thought of Breege. She was a slave, like the drivers, and there the similarity ended. Breege was kind and his feet were already soothed as a result of her care. On that brighter thought he settled to sleep, exhaustion coming to his aid.

He awakened to a gentle tugging. Through sleepy eyes he made out Breege, putting down a dish of water and he shifted to a sitting position. She unwrapped his feet, bathed the sores and applied fresh ointment before swaddling his feet anew.

'Your feet are soft as lamb's wool, but they're healing. Now, put on your boots,' she said, handing them to him. They were thoroughly dry and supple. He smelled an agreeable aroma of wax which had soaked deeply into the leather. Expecting a tight fit, Patrick was surprised how easily the boots slipped on.

'See that,' she said, 'the swelling of your feet is down. Stand up and take a pace.'

Patrick had only taken one step when Breege started.

'Oh, mercy. Is it any wonder you have blisters? The boots are too big.' She dived into her solution box and came out with a couple of pieces of dried tree bark. 'Put these in your boot soles and take another pace.' Breege watched carefully as Patrick did as she said.

'I like them. The boots feel good.'

'Why wouldn't they, now they fit? Here, put these in your bag.' She handed him a small tub of ointment, two extra bark pads and a spare strip of swaddling cloth. 'You look a right sight in your boots and night gown. Now, get yourself ready and eat. Your king will be leaving soon. And good luck to you.'

'Breege, thank you,' said Patrick.

'Happy to help,' said Breege. 'Your king helped you too.'

'He did? When and how?'

'Last night when I went for the bandages, my master was talking to the king and called me over to give me a job. I asked if I could finish bandaging your feet first. He was pleased I was looking after the king's man and agreed. King Miliucc asked if your feet were bad.

I told him raw flesh on both feet. Your king bought the ointment from my master and told me to use it, and he thanked me. I could have only treated you with water and bandages.'

'I'm lucky to have met you.' Patrick reached out a hand to shake hers but she shied away.

'On yer way,' she said, refusing the compliment as she left.

Patrick dressed quickly, thinking, as he did, of King Miliucc and Joshua's assessment of his character. It seems Joshua was correct. Across from his sleeping place the two drivers snored on. Patrick smiled and left without waking them.

In the food hall he dined in peace with servants who didn't know him. Downing a bowl of hot porridge, a chunk of cheese and some dry bread, Patrick left and passed the two drivers rushing to the food hall, having overslept. No more than they deserve, he thought.

Patrick packed his bag and waited in readiness for the king's assembly. The sun rose warmly and gave hope of a better day as he took up position behind the passenger cart. Miliucc passed on horseback and spoke quietly to one of the guards. When the retinue was ready to leave a guard said to Patrick, with a deadpan look on his face, 'Today you can ride on the cart.'

Patrick took a seat opposite the guards. Happy that they discouraged conversation he comfortably avoided their eye and drifted into thought. Counting the days from capture, he should have been with his father today discussing coastal defences. Hilarious and tragic, he thought, shaking his head in regret. I was casual, lazy, and now I'm paying the price.

Patrick stared at his boots and thought of everything good about Breege. This slave girl helped a stranger in need and wanted nothing in return. Not even recognition beyond a polite thank you. Patrick felt grateful for the treatment to his feet, but she'd shown him compassion and, better still, opened his eyes to the meaning of compassion to the receiver. In his wretched state her kindness had lifted him. He felt humble. The occasion held a mirror to his own soul and suddenly he saw himself with clarity; for the first time in his memory, he felt inferior.

His mind moved to escape, then to the hopelessness of the idea.

Not one public road have I seen in four days. Each cattle track we travelled was on private land. Every hostel we used was contracted to a king. It looks impossible for a foreign slave to move around anonymously in Ireland. The guard's speech was no bluff. He thought of Joshua and Owain; Joshua is a craftsman, Owain is a farmer, but what am I? I am my own enemy. I am a manager, huh. I am a bad manager, personally and in business. The only things I am good at are boxing, stick-fighting, and horse riding. I don't have the skills to be someone. I am not educated, because, given the chance to learn I chose to be lazy. When I was someone, it was given to me. Now, I have nothing and, on my own I am nothing.

He was jolted from his thoughts.

'Look,' the driver shouted, pointing at the hills. 'See the sheep.' He turned to Patrick with a cruel smirk on his wide mouth, 'Soon you'll be their master.'

Patrick looked at an ugly and rugged landscape with bog and marshy reeds in the foreground against a backdrop of rough and rocky hillsides, dotted with scrawny brown sheep.

The retinue had reached its destination. Pig-cart-driver directed the work horses and the load of swine into an enclosure. The stink and the sties foretold it was a pig farm. Passenger-cart-driver continued further up the track. King Miliucc, remaining mounted, came over to the seated guards and spoke to one of them, as though Patrick wasn't there.

'Equip Patrick for his tasks, and then take him to Cormac.' He then turned to Patrick and addressed him directly, 'Your job is to care for my flock and make it grow. You will take orders and instructions from Cormac. You could not wish for a better teacher.' He then looked Patrick in the eye, 'I expect the best from you, Patrick.' He spurred his horse and led his mounted guards and bards to a guarded residence at the top of a winding track. Passenger-cart-driver took the seated guards and Patrick into the next farmstead.

A dozen roundhouses, sectioned off with birch fences, were the homes of families and labourers. The cart stopped to let the guards and Patrick get off. One guard said goodbye to the other and made his way to a roundhouse where a child rushed towards him with arms outstretched. The other took Patrick into a workshop where shepherding equipment and clothing was laid out on a bench top.

'Wear this now,' the guard said, passing a broad and sturdy leather belt to Patrick. He just managed to buckle up in time to receive the next item. 'Here is your rod,' the guard said, passing a heavy club, to Patrick.

'I didn't expect a rod to be bulbous. What do I do with it?' Patrick asked as he fixed the bulky item to his belt at the hip.

The guard took a deep breath, 'It's a weapon for fighting off predators. Imagine a wolf with his teeth stuck into a sheep; strike him with one good swing of this rod and he'll be off, with no thought of returning,' the guard said, with what Patrick thought was the certainty of experience. He passed a large canvass bag to Patrick saying, 'Put the things I give you in here,' and continued, 'your bucket,' the guard said, giving Patrick a folded and flattened piece of leather with two short planks attached.

Patrick looked bemused.

'I'll show you,' the guard snorted.

The planks were stacked on top of each other, with a short spindle joining them in the centre. He pulled the plank ends in the opposite direction, which formed them into an X shape, at which point the leather opened-up into the shape of a bucket. Patrick flattened it and placed it at the bottom of his necessarily large bag. And now the things came faster, each one named by the guard; 'sling, knife, mug, water skin, reed flute, sandals, head-wrap, fleece, mantel, strap, dishes, and one more thing, a bag of oats.' The food bag, woven in flat straw was the size of a corn sack.

'Last of all, here is your shepherd's crook.' Patrick took this in his hand.

By now Patrick had two large bags to carry, one for his clothing, and another for his shepherd's wares.

'Let's go to the hills and find Cormac,' the guard said.

'Can I leave my clothing bag where my bed is?' Patrick asked innocently, 'to avoid carrying more than necessary.'

The guard looked at him with wide, disbelieving eyes under high-arched brows.

Patrick read the expression. What naïveté have I exposed this time, he thought.

'Young man, your bed is in the hills, with the sheep.'

Patrick's mouth opened wide. His humiliation was complete.

As they strode out, Patrick, more heavily laden than a battle-ready Roman legionnaire, felt broken. Looking ahead he saw a coarse and bleak landscape. Walking into the hills, on ground thick with thistle and gorse, grey rocks emerged haphazardly, partially covered with lichen in a half-hearted colour of ditch-water green and dirty yellow. Golden whin bushes, which added sunshine from a distance, had lost their beauty close-up, and the furze had prickles. Patrick looked up the valley and saw scruffy, scrawny brown sheep, or maybe goats, grazing on intermittent tufts and tussocks of grass.

The weight of the bags was nothing to Patrick, but staring at his feet as he walked, his broken spirit hunched his shoulders.

The place looks uninhabitable. If this is my new home, I think I've reached the bottom.

CHAPTER SEVEN
Shepherd

'They are the Woods of Voclut, the southern boundary of your sheep range,' the guard pointed out.

Patrick and the guard jumped stones to cross a fast-flowing river. Patrick loved becks and brooks. The sight of this clear water stream and the sound of its rushing flow was a welcome contrast to the coarse surroundings. Scattered sheep grazed on both sides of the ravine, oblivious to a loud but distant hammering.

Where is the noise coming from? Patrick wondered. At least it's a sign of life. The guard and Patrick walked the length of the ravine, closing in on the source of the noise. They turned a corner in the dog-leg shaped valley and came across a sheep pen nestled in a natural cul-de-sac. A narrow gateway, built into a woven willow fence, led to an open fold behind which was a structure. Double walls of hill stones three feet high and two feet wide surrounded with dense thorn bushes, formed the perimeter walls of a covered shelter. A roof of thatch, high in the centre and sloping down to the walls, completed the building. Another narrow entrance was positioned centrally in the wall of the covered pen facing the fold.

'Cormac,' the guard called loudly.

A cloth-covered head with a smiling face appeared from behind the thatch. Ageing yellow teeth stood out against a long and full-faced white beard.

'Eamonn, how are you?' boomed Cormac, rushing to greet him with a handshake.

'I'm well, and I bring you Patrick.'

Cormac turned to Patrick and offered his hand, 'Welcome to the hills, Patrick.'

Patrick returned Cormac's warm and firm handshake, 'Pleased to meet you,' Patrick said with sincerity, pleased at the warmth of Cormac's welcome.

'Put down your things, Patrick, and get out your mug. Eamonn has brought us some juice,' Cormac replied, as Eamonn started unpacking the bag he carried. They sat on rocks in gentle breeze and pleasant sunshine.

'Here, I've brought fresh bread and fish paste too. Now, Cormac, I've been travelling, so I have not heard the news. Tell me how your year ended,' Eamonn enquired.

'In happiness; after renewing the flock, we were eighty lambs to the profit.'

'Excellent news,' Eamonn responded. Patrick saw the look of genuine delight on Eamonn's face.

'And how was your journey east, Eamonn?'

'It could not have been better. We made great progress driving the cattle. All arrived in healthy fettle.'

'So Miliucc is happy,' Cormac stated.

'He should be. He sold them for three slaves and a cart-load of swine.'

Patrick listened with interest, learning much about the king and the business, but surprised that Cormac and the guard would speak so openly in front of him.

'Excellent. A good trade makes for a happy king,' said Cormac.

'Have you heard of Colm, son of Aeden?' Eamonn asked.

'I've heard of Niall's man Aeden; do you mean his son?'

'That's him. Well, the son, Colm, is like the father. It was Niall's biggest raid and Colm's first, yet he lost no ships and few lives. He organises well.'

Patrick took a sip of juice and wished he wasn't privy to this conversation.

'He not only organised the raid well, but he categorised the captives and the spoils too, increasing their value to King Niall. Miliucc bought a young craftsman to train with Conn, and a young farmer who he's hired out to Kilcullen and Patrick here, is educated. You could make a good shepherd of him.' Patrick winced at hearing Eamonn speaking about the raid, the value of the slaves and Patrick's education, as though he wasn't there.

Eamonn was quick to finish his refreshment and stood up, 'That's enough craic. I'll be off now.'

Cormac passed him an empty skin which Eamonn took without reference. He shook Cormac's hand then turned to Patrick. 'Good luck young man. You have landed on your feet, though perhaps you don't know it yet.'

Cormac stood and watched him away. Patrick stood too and raised his hand modestly in a farewell gesture, masking his true reluctance. And then Cormac turned to Patrick.

'Sit down, Patrick. We should talk awhile before we get busy,' he said. 'Tell me a little about your background.' Patrick thought for a while and decided to give a brief, but true answer.

'I'm from Britain. My father owns farmlands and properties and is a town councillor. He's also a deacon in the Roman Catholic Church. I manage a small part of his business for him.'

'This is a shock for you, Patrick,' said Cormac.

'Yes. We knew of raids, but our own area seemed safe.' He shook his head and laughed. 'I was on the land early that day. I did not see it coming. When first I knew, it was already too late.'

'Your enemy was ahead of you, Patrick.'

'Yes. I know.'

'This lesson will help you as a shepherd, and in your life. Bring your things. I'll show you a place for them.'

They entered the covered pen. Against the outer wall were shelves, made from planks supported on stones, and wall-pegs behind a woven woollen curtain.

'Place your fleece and skin on the shelf, along with your bag of clothing.'

Patrick put his possessions away as directed.

'Master, I have a bag of oats, some bread, and a full water skin. Where shall I put them?' Patrick asked.

'Put them on the shelf till later. Wear your head-cloth and bring your rod, staff, knife, and reed pipe.'

Patrick had already examined Cormac's head-cloth. The wrapping and tying were neat and tidy with no knots or tails visible. All the clues were hidden.

'Can you show me how to tie it, please?'

Cormac smiled and patiently said, 'Watch me.'

He untied and slowly retied his own. It looked easier than Patrick expected. Two wraparounds and a firm knot, one more wraparound, first tail tucked tightly under the knot, second tail flattened and tucked top edge down and bottom edge up. Patrick tried. He felt the tying. It was neat but the knot wasn't firm. He undid it and started again. This time he increased the angle of the first wrap from nape to forehead. He could feel the firmness.

'How is that, master?'

Cormac felt the knot, the firmness of the wrap. 'It's enough. Let us go outside. I will speak about the work, and then we'll bring the sheep in.' Cormac pointed to the hills, 'These two mountains run north to south. We are looking at the east side. Round the north side is another mountain, out of view from here. It's called Topp Mountain and runs west to east. Bring your eye to here,' he said, pointing. 'We graze the sheep on the east and west of these mountains, and only the south side of Topp Mountain. Today the sheep are on both sides of the ravine, spread out over its length. To call them we must stand in a middle position. Would you point to where you think that is?'

Patrick indicated an area further south on the opposite side.

'Let us go there.'

They came upon the place Patrick judged to be central.

'Take up your flute, Patrick. I call the sheep with my voice, and they know my call, but now they must learn your call. If you play a tune each time I call, the sheep will respond to your tune when I am not here. Can you play the flute?'

'No master.'

'Do you know a tune?'

'Yes master,' Patrick answered, relieved to be able to say yes.

'Hum it to me.'

Patrick hummed "The Lord's my shepherd". The tune the harpist played on Patrick's last dinner with his parents. Cormac listened and played along as Patrick hummed, until he got the tune.

'Is this close enough, Patrick?' asked Cormac, as he played.

'Faithful indeed,' said Patrick, impressed by the skills of this old shepherd.

'Then play the notes like this.' Cormac demonstrated.

Patrick fumbled for a while, but his teacher was patient and Patrick was soon following Cormac's sheep call with Psalm 23. His crude melody mesmerised a flock of sheep as a skilled harpist could humans.

'It's a good choice of tune, Patrick. The sheep like it.'

Patrick smiled. It was the only tune that came to his mind.

The sheep followed lazily in a disorderly line, responding to their master's call, interspersed with a tune about an important shepherd. Patrick enjoyed the playful thought that Cormac knew no more about the existence of the words of the psalm than did the sheep. As they neared the top of the ravine, the sheep at the front recognised their fold and ran to it excitedly, stopping at the closed gate. The followers ran headlong into the standing bunch of woolly bleaters.

'Like they do every day,' Cormac said, until all were crying for the gate to be opened. 'We count the sheep now, Patrick. There should be 151. Watch how I do it.'

Cormac opened the gate, which was a tight fit for one sheep at a time. Immediately there was a scramble to get in. Cormac held his rod in one hand and when the first sheep passed through, he moved his thumb across the carved handle to the first notch on the first row and continued; sheep and notch. When he finished the first row, he moved to the second, third and fourth rows. When all thirty-six notches had been touched, he pushed a stick in the wall and went back to the first notch. After four sticks and six more notches, the sheep were in the pen. At this point a hound came bounding over to Cormac, who fussed him for a while and then the hound sat dutifully on guard at the closed gate.

'Soldier will be your guard dog, soon; you should make a friend of him,' Cormac advised.

Patrick knelt and stroked the dog's fur. 'Where have you been, Soldier? You seem to come from nowhere?'

Soldier wagged his tail, welcoming the stranger.

'He's been round and about. Soldier guards against predators, wolves mainly and humans with thieving intentions. Did you get the count?'

'No master, I tried but lost it.'

'That is why you need the notched rod. There are 150. We are one short. Are we missing a lamb or a sheep, Patrick? Is it possible to know?'

'I think it's a lamb, sir.'

'Why do think that?'

'The last sheep in kept back from the flock, reluctant to follow. That one,' he pointed. 'Even now it looks outwards. I think it is a ewe to a missing lamb.'

Cormac raised both his brows. Patrick caught his look. He is impressed that I recognised the last sheep in.

'You're right, Patrick. Can you tell the bleat is a distressed bleat?'

'They all sound distressed, master.'

'It is too early for you. Time will come though, when you know a sheep's bleat. Where should we start looking?'

'Perhaps start at the furthest point of the ravine, and walk the length of it. If we don't find it, then do the same on this side.'

'Not such a bad answer. Sometimes it will come to this. Let me explain some general facts first.' Cormac leant on his staff.

'The most common reason for a sheep not returning is that it is stuck in a hedge. The next reason is they are on the opposite bank of a river. Sheep fear flowing water. For tonight, we will head north for that hedgerow.' Cormac pointed, 'a sheep over there was slow to join the flock and turned often. I know this because when I start to call the sheep, I look around and observe their manner. Our missing lamb might not be there, but it is our best starting point. Before we start looking, let me explain something else. If I were alone, Patrick, I would leave the sheep in the pen with Soldier at the gate. With two experienced shepherds, one would search and take the dog and one would stay, but as you are learning, we'll go together and Soldier will stay.'

Patrick was surprised at the tone of Cormac. He was patient and helpful. He doesn't seem to see me as a slave.

After half a mile of walking, Cormac made his call, to no avail. He called again after a mile and this time a frail bleating sound carried down the ravine. They followed the source and found their lamb snarled up in thick gorse.

'Before we cut him out, Patrick, what are we to do with him when he's free?'

'I believe he will follow you.'

'Maybe, but the lamb is distressed. I would carry him in my arms for a short while, and then on my shoulders. But this evening that task is yours.'

Patrick enjoyed seeing the lamb's tail wagging excitedly as he was cut free. He carried the lamb in his arms, amazed at the heavy weight of the little thing. He found the lamb's wool pleasant to the touch and slightly oily. When the lamb had calmed, Patrick carried her on his shoulders. At the pen, when ewe and lamb were reunited, two tails wagged with enthusiasm and Patrick's ear learned the sound of joyous bleating.

'Bring your food now and we'll light a fire outside the gate.'

Patrick brought his provisions and dived into his bag for Shifty's lantern, anticipating Cormac's next question.

'You know how to start a fire?'

'Yes. I have a set in this lamp,' Patrick answered coolly, as though he'd known all his life.

'How came you by such a thing, so soon?'

'It's a story,' said Patrick.

'Then let me hear it,' Cormac said in a friendly voice.

'A nasty hostel worker wielding a knife tried to steal my boots during the night. We were three captives in chains but managed to overpower him. He left in a hurry, and my fellow slaves insisted I take the lamp.'

'Your boots are special, Patrick. It is well you've kept hold of them. Now, let's build the fire. You gather up tinder and kindling and I'll fetch sticks and logs.'

Patrick failed twice to get a light but succeeded on his third try. He was pleased Cormac didn't see him struggling. He knew he was a useless privileged boy, but didn't want others to see that. Before long they were sitting round a crackling campfire lit by Patrick, and despite his struggles he was proud of his achievement. Cormac brought a small gutted trout to the fire and with the skin of juice donated by Eamonn together with Patrick's bread, they enjoyed a tasty supper.

'Your first half day as a shepherd is nearly ended. Have you any questions?'

'Yes, master, a few. Where will I sleep tonight?'

'There is no need for titles with me, Patrick. Now, in answer to your question, you sleep here, on the ground outside the gate. When it is harsh weather, we sleep in the enclosures.'

'How long will we be in the hills?'

'Three cycles of the moon,' Cormac answered.

Patrick kept a straight face, but his heart sank at the thought of three months of sleeping outside.

'What happens then?' Patrick asked.

'We return to the farmstead for business. This is the time for selling old sheep, choosing lambs to replenish the flock, selling lambs for supplies, and purchasing rams.'

Patrick did not know the hill shepherd's calendar but could see in half a day there was more to it than he ever imagined.

'Seems a varied job,' Patrick said, looking for a positive response.

'Indeed,' Cormac replied.

'What do we eat when the bread is finished?' asked Patrick.

'Porridge; your bag of oats will feed you for a moon. The fish, however, is never finished, and occasionally Soldier brings a rabbit,' Cormac said to a look of shock on Patrick's face.

'You mean we live off the land?'

'I do, Patrick, exactly that. Don't look so worried. It hasn't killed me yet.' Patrick, taken aback, paused for a while, thinking the bottom just became a little further down, before returning to his questions.

'You said earlier, "enclosures" meaning more than one?'

'I did. We have three bases; a fold next to a few trees, with no enclosure, one next to a cave, and this.'

'So, it really is an outside life?' Patrick said, belying his true feelings. 'How long will we stay here?'

'Around fourteen nights; we graze the sheep in two locations from here, and eight pastures from the other two bases.'

'I've slept in a different place, every night for a week. Fourteen nights in one place is most welcome stability, especially as my heart is sore and my mind mixed.'

'Be a good shepherd, Patrick, and your soul shall be healed.'

'The lamb and ewe already said this to me,' Patrick replied.

Cormac smiled at Patrick, wistfully and a little surprised. They finished supper in contemplation, and as Patrick noticed the light fading and the sky begin to look menacing, Cormac broke the silence.

'Let us prepare our beds and, before you sleep, play your tune to the sheep. Be aware that as we sleep, we must listen and respond to intruders. Soldier scares most perils away, but his growling unsettles the sheep. Playing your tune will help to calm them.' Cormac then handed a wicker mat to Patrick. He placed it on the ground adjacent to the gate, and laid a skin on the mat, woolly side up. 'Your fleece and mantel are your bedding, but if it rains, take them off, keep them dry at all cost; wear extra clothing if you must. It is easier to dry clothing than a fleece.'

Patrick nodded his understanding and began to remove his boots and tunic.

Cormac interrupted, 'Night clothes are not suited to repelling intruders. Sleep in your tunic and mantel, Patrick, and change in the morning. Wear your sandals when you remove your boots.'

'Thank you, master. Good night. And thank you for... everything.'

'Everything?' Cormac said with a hint of mock surprise.

'For your kindness, master.'

'Could I care for sheep and not a man? Good night, Patrick, and no more master, from now, it's Cormac.'

Patrick pulled out his reed flute and played a soothing verse. Cormac and the sheep drifted into sleep. The tune transported Patrick to the last evening with his parents and he lived again the harpist's psalm. His thoughts wandered to the slave girl in the barn. The rescued lamb could have been the girl, the ewe her mother. But he hadn't saved the girl or informed her loved ones.

Patrick compared himself with some of the people he'd met in Ireland. King Miliucc had been noble in his handling of the hostel bust-up. He'd dealt fairly with the aggressive slave. Patrick thought of the Irish servant girl, Breege, who'd swaddled his feet when they badly needed care, and the king who'd provided ointment. Cormac today had treated him, a slave he'd just met, with dignity and respect. In this dangerous and impoverished land of barbarians, he'd seen evidence of decency in the high and low born. His thanks to Cormac had been sincere.

Moisture came to his eyes on realising that his thanks to his father, who he loved, had been insincere, mere manners. He'd ignored his father's advice, sneered at his opinions. He'd liked his own way and got it. This wasn't how to express love. Patrick felt embarrassed at the extent of his own arrogance. Now, feeling contrite, wanting to be humble, he resolved to build his life on a better foundation. But he harboured a fear, deeply rooted in his blindness to his own faults. Would more character flaws come to the surface? His last thought before he fell asleep was, please God, let that be all.

A desperate plea, but not yet a prayer; Patrick was still talking to himself.

He woke at sunrise to the smell of frying fish. The words of the psalm, repeated in his dreams, were still on his mind.

The Lord is my shepherd, I'll not want. He maketh me down to lie.

Patrick felt good this morning, for the first time since his capture. His blisters had calmed. Cormac was in action at the fire and the breaking of fast was sizzling. Dawn was refreshing and his feeling of humiliation receding a little.

I'll not want, he thought. And then it struck him: he maketh me down to lie.

It's God. It's God's retribution. I would not listen to his word. I turned my back on his ways. My father, a deacon, my grandfather a priest, yet I chose not to learn the word of God. It's all my own doing. My capture is God's punishment. The depth of my fall seems harsh, though. Oh no! Is it equal to the depth of my arrogance? Is it down to me again? Did I need to be broken-spirited for the compassion of Breege, the fairness of King Miliucc, the respect of Cormac, to reach me? He paused in thought before answering himself. I fear I did.

In supplication, he knelt, cowed and cowering, hands palm to palm, head down in submission. There were no words in him, but his silence prayed. Eventually words passed through his mind and lips. 'Forgive me, God, for my sins. I am the least of the most contemptible.'

By the time he opened his eyes, he had committed himself to praying for forgiveness twice a day for a year. Patrick had seen his past ways with the clarity of a bright lamp lighting a dark cave. He wanted to change and saw his new life as a chance to start afresh. He decided to throw off his past ways; to embrace a new life built on a proper foundation. I shall be Patrick in my heart as well as in my naming.

He became aware of Cormac standing at a polite distance and knew his praying had been heard and respected by the silent retreat of his new companion.

* * *

For three moons Cormac taught Patrick the ways of the shepherd and the sheep. Patrick learned how to use a sling, catch trout and occasionally salmon, and get Soldier to hunt rabbits. He learned to milk a ewe for his own sustenance.

Patrick realised he needed practice to be competent using a sling. It was no use to nearly deter a wolf, or sometimes chase one away. Patrick had to fight off predators, whether animal or human, successfully every time. He measured the distance Soldier covered when he ran at pace and used this as a guide to a wolf's pace. He practised slinging a shot at twenty yards until he gained accuracy. Next, he worked out how to get two shots off to an attacking wolf at ten strides. He honed his slinging of shot, twice every day and when he became skilled, he continued practising to remain sharp. He searched for balanced round stones and kept a supply on his person and at the folds.

The time came when the lambs were strong and healthy; Cormac, Patrick and Soldier led the flock to the farmstead in Voclut for business days at a summer fayre. On the journey, Cormac explained to Patrick his plans for after the fayre.

'When our business week is finished, I will help you to guide the flock back to the hills and thereafter you will shepherd the flock alone. I will visit you at intervals or when you call me. You are learning well and ready to learn the art of lone shepherding. It is part of your training, and indeed part of the job.'

Patrick nodded seriously. It was what he wanted, and now he contemplated silently as the meaning of the responsibility became real.

CHAPTER EIGHT

Patrick and Cormac were working in the pens next to the lush lowland pastures; a short journey to King Miliucc's residence and walking distance from Eamonn's workshop. Cormac lived in a two-bed roundhouse next to the meadows, folds, and pens. When the sun shone, as it did this day, the place was Eden. Soldier was outside guarding a vastly reduced range and if the wag of his tail was a guide, it seemed he too enjoyed the festival week.

Their workplace was inside a large oval structure, built with stone walls to shoulder height, which supported a high and steeply pitched thatch roof. Wooden enclosures formed the pens, accessed from a corridor running the full length of the building.

'Feel the lambs like this,' said Cormac.

Patrick pressed his finger and thumb, two inches apart, to the root of the wool and gently squeezed the lamb's skin.

'Remember how it feels and do it again on the next lamb,' said Cormac.

'This one is thinner,' Patrick said.

'Good. Now you know the difference, find me six plump lambs like the first one, and put them in that pen,' Cormac pointed.

When Patrick had completed his task Cormac commented, 'We need some younger rams for the mating season. If we find some at the fayre, we'll trade these healthier lambs for them. The next job is to segregate the weaklings.'

Cormac set Patrick to placing the weaker lambs in a separate pen. 'We'll graze these here, on the richer pastures until their strength improves. Then we'll return them to the hills,' said Cormac.

And so, Patrick's training continued. He was looking forward to working alone as a shepherd because it represented progression in his work, but he also felt a tinge of nervousness.

In the evenings the sheep were gathered quickly, at the farmstead, giving Patrick a few hours to mix with the farm workers. The Gaelic vernacular came to him naturally, as though he'd inherited an Irish language trait in his blood, from his maternal grandmother. He quickly discovered the Irish men were fiery tempered, drank ale in excess and were addicted to brawling and fighting.

Voclut, as far as he could make out, was a locality consisting of a small number of farmsteads, a wooded area south of the ravine, and the king's residence. The king's presence generated activity and wealth but the people barely subsisted. Wealth lay with the nobles. Unlike in Britain, where there were middle classes, Patrick saw a very large peasant class, small nobility and little in between other than a select class of artisans.

At this time of year preparations for the festival occupied the people of Voclut. As Patrick went about his daily work, he observed oxcarts coming and going, delivering posts, fences, rocks, stones, and provisions. Hardworking men, often stripped to the waist, repaired cow paths, and built fords, constructed enclosures and stalls for animals. Tables were erected to exhibit trade products and craft ware. Hutches for hens and chickens arrived, roundhouses for accommodation were built; sturdy enclosures for bulls and sties for pigs went up. Over the days, Patrick saw the skeleton of a small village market emerge from the rugged and bare common land. People, carts, livestock, and goods arrived from nearby farmsteads and adjacent kingdoms, to fill the spaces.

Patrick thought of Owain and his comment that there were no market towns in Ireland. He remembered hearing King Miliucc invite Owain's chieftain to his fayre. This was the fayre. They're building a market on common land on the Festival of Beltaine.

At last, the preparations were complete, and the great occasion dawned. Patrick and Cormac rose from their roundhouse in Voclut and after breaking fast, Cormac outlined his plans for the day.

'It's the first day of the festival,' said Cormac. 'I want to look for tups. You are to come with me. I've arranged for two farmhands to tend the sheep this afternoon.'

Patrick happily joined him, and they walked into Voclut. On arriving he saw some similarities with the British farmers' markets, but the trading by exchange of goods was new to him. Milk cows, meat cows, bulls, geese, rabbits, hens, chickens, piglets, fish, and more were stock for sale as well as stock for payment.

Cormac inspected some rams. He ran his thumb down their backbone, feeling their flesh. He checked their feet for strength and health and finally took a firm hold of their testicles. Not entirely convinced of their quality, Cormac said to Patrick, 'We'll come back tomorrow. Not all purveyors arrive on the first day.'

Patrick was amused. 'What put you off, Cormac, the feel of their privates?'

'Laugh if you like, Patrick, but you speak the truth. They were not as firm as I like them to be.'

'What does "firmness" indicate?' Patrick asked.

'Tupping stamina,' Cormac replied. 'For a good lambing season, we need every ewe to be tupped.'

Cormac was right; he found what he was looking for the next day. The seller brought the rams in an ox-drawn cart to the farmstead.

'Patrick, take this man to the fat lamb pen. Let him choose four.'

The farmer looked the lambs in the face. He studied their features and nipped their skin. He checked all six and made his choice of four.

'You have your deal,' called the farmer to Cormac who then moved the rams to a pen.

Patrick placed the chosen lambs in the cart. Cormac and his customer affected to be unhappy with the business. The posturing was obvious to Patrick, and entertaining, as both men played their part seriously; the buyer who had been persuaded to pay too much, and the seller who had sold too cheaply.

Later in the evening after gathering the sheep, Cormac said to Patrick, 'You should enjoy some roasted meat and ale at the fayre. I suggest you watch the show too. You will learn some Irish legend.'

'I'd like to go, but how will I pay?' Patrick asked.

'You don't need to pay. King Miliucc provides everything.'

Surprised that slaves were treated to evenings of enjoyment, Patrick thanked Cormac, changed into a clean tunic, and wore the Miliucc sandals. He asked Cormac if he should wear his head dress.

'Do you want to?' asked Cormac.

'If it says I'm a shepherd, I'll wear it proudly.'

'It's the garb of a shepherd,' said Cormac.

'That settles it,' said Patrick and proceeded to dress smartly, head-wrap included. It was his own desire, though he remembered the guard's advice when the Miliucc outfits were issued.

'How do I look, Cormac?' he enquired.

'Fit for a king, but why are you carrying sandals?'

'They're spare because I have my own boots. I might see something to buy.'

'Ah! That's the spirit of the Irish, Patrick.'

'I'm trying.'

'If you want to trade, ask what your sandals can buy, and know you can have the double,' said Cormac. 'Before you go, let me show you something.' Cormac loosened his own belt and removed a hanging pouch from inside his tunic. He gave it to Patrick and said, 'Your belt weaves in and out of your tunic's fabric. Hang this on the inside, near your hip and put your sandals in it.'

Patrick did so and stepped out for the markets, hands free. The mile-long walk was busy with people. Farmers and carts came towards him returning from the day's trading; others were on their way, the same as Patrick. Some faces were friendly and nodded good evening. Of course, no one touched their forelock to greet Patrick. Those days were truly gone.

He thought of his progression as a shepherd. He'd come a long way with Cormac and understood, now, the words from Eamonn about landing on his feet. Nervousness again crept into his mind about the lone shepherding role which was getting closer, and then the buzz of the fayre caught his attention. The festival thronged like a Roman vicus on market day. Patrick joined a small queue for a mug of juice and though it was watery, he was still intrigued that no coinage was asked for. Jugglers and jesters entertained the passers-by.

Patrick sipped his juice, as he nosed through the craft stalls. A section of black metalwork, copper and pewter held no interest for him, but he was more impressed by the items of clothing for sale. Woollen mittens, scarves, wraps and covers knitted with various Celtic patterns. He saw fabrics woven with colourful dyed yarns, wooden crafts, including elegantly carved spoons and bowls, platters engraved with Celtic wheels and knots and other symbols unknown to Patrick.

Then he spied a bright and colourful cornucopia of ceramics and glassware. He picked up and examined a striking emerald cut-glass jewel, centrally set in a cream-coloured ceramic brooch. Decorative Celtic curves kissed like mirror images releasing leaf and petal patterns. He almost missed hearing the woman saying, 'Very good quality; made in Britain.'

So, Britain has a reputation for quality, it seems.

Patrick turned the brooch around to study the clasp and laughed aloud. The ceramic workmanship was quality, but instead of a moving pin that located in a clasp, it was a solid piece of casting with the exact contours of a pin in a clasp. It could not be worn as intended.

Looking further he found a solitary scarf ring with the same cream and emerald colouring. In a band, the shape of an over-size finger ring, emerald glass jewels were set at intervals all around the ceramic-coated copper.

A perfect gift for Mother, he thought. Looking further he found an unusual brooch engraved with a Celtic rope pattern around the perimeter and an emerald stone in the centre. The idea was appealing but emerald wasn't his mother's colour. Most items were dull and made of pewter, but he came across a ceramic-coated version with a ruby-coloured jewel on a cream background. The contrast was attractive and suitable, Patrick thought, for his mother to wear with her stola. He pulled out his currency, new sandals, a gift from the king, and possibly duplicated by accident.

'What can I have for these?' he said trying to sound Irish.

'From here to here, one piece,' the woman replied. 'Very good quality from Britain. My price is good.' The range she offered excluded the ceramic brooch.

'I want this one.' Patrick pointed to the unusual brooch.

She shook her head. 'From here to here,' she repeated. 'Here, not enough,' she said pointing to the tray containing the brooch he wanted.

'Too much,' said Patrick and walked away, though pleased with the woman's unintended endorsement of his Irish accent.

He caught the whiff of roast and followed the aroma to a huge spit where he joined the queue. People ordered their choice of cut by pointing and when his turn came, he pointed at the topside of the roasting cow and said, 'From here please.'

The server laughed. 'When your tunic is yellow you choose from here.'

Patrick followed the indication to the poorer quality and saw that it included the rump.

'One from here, please,' he said.

'Ah! The rump. Now you know your place,' the carver joked.

'And maybe I know my meat,' quipped Patrick.

'I'll grant you that,' smiled the carver, handing Patrick a plate of chunky steak, boiled roots, and a spike which he stabbed upright into the meat. 'When you've eaten, return your plate and spike to that table,' he nodded.

Patrick stood to eat at a barrel table, opposite another slave. The man, a few years older than Patrick, spoke to him. 'You from round here?'

'Not exactly. I was brought up further afield, but I live here now,' Patrick answered, feeling a pang of homesickness.

'I never seen you before,' he said, as though he ought to have.

'I'm a shepherd out on the hills, and you?'

'I'm a driver.'

'Who do you work for?' asked Patrick.

'For a contract farmer, by the Conn. Do you know it?'

'I don't, but I'm interested to learn.'

'It's a big lough south of here.' The driver finished eating, took his plate and knife to the returns table and seemed to wander off. A few minutes later he was back with a jug of ale and two mugs. He poured two drinks and said, 'To freedom!'

I'll drink to that, thought Patrick. 'To freedom,' he enthused before continuing, 'Let me ask what brings you here?'

'Trade; the master wants a young ox. We've brought a cart of pigs to exchange. And you?'

'Same story,' said Patrick. 'Lambs for rams.'

They small-talked for a while and then the man from Conn knocked back his ale, saying, 'I'm on a break. I must be going, maybe see you next festival.' The driver began to collect his mug and the jug.

'Leave those. I'll take them back,' said Patrick, as they exchanged farewells.

At the returns table Patrick spotted Pig-cart-driver in the background, washing the plates and spikes. Patrick wasn't inclined to talk to him, but the driver, unaware of Patrick, turned his back and began talking to someone. At first Patrick could not see who, but as they moved position, he recognised Shifty, and they were talking furtively.

Momentarily shocked, Patrick stared briefly. Two foul eggs up to no good, he thought, but the sight of Shifty disturbed him. Why is he in these parts? How is he connected to King Miliucc's driver? Patrick moved from their sight and returned to the jewellery table, the woman already beckoning him.

He offered the sandals for the elaborate brooch. She refused but offered the scarf ring plus any pewter flat ring. Finally, Patrick had to walk away, disappointed that he was unable to buy the brooch he wanted. As he passed the next stall, he felt a tugging at his sleeve and turned. The woman from the craft stall had followed him.

'You want this?' she asked, showing him the brooch.

Patrick nodded.

'Special for you, I'll take the sandals,' and they completed their exchange.

Patrick made his way to the rear of a cattle stall to avoid prying eyes as he slipped the brooch out of his hidden pocket and proudly looked it over. He was pleased with the attractive ruby and ran his finger over the cream ceramic background, feeling the crevices of and the Celtic rope pattern. This would be an unusual feature in Banna Venta; to the delight of his mother.

While in the shadows, he saw a line of men further along, behind a pig sty wall. They too had found a little privacy. As they peed in the darkness, Patrick was reminded how far he had fallen from the civilised arrangements he enjoyed at home. He left quickly and returned to the fayre.

There was a show he wanted to watch, and the seats were filling up as poets told tales of old. Soon Patrick was watching actors playing out the story of the legendary Cuchulain, and how he received his name. They performed on a raised platform before an audience seated on benches arranged in straight lines. The shape of an amphitheatre had not reached Voclut, Patrick noted.

As the show progressed, he learned of a young boy named Setanta, born of his father Lugh, an immortal god, and his mortal mother Dechtire, sister of King Conchobar. A blacksmith by the name of Chulain was hosting a banquet for Conchobar and a number of nobles. Conchobar had invited Setanta to join them but forgot to inform the host. Chulain ordered the release of his guard dog to protect the premises as they dined. Setanta, who possessed special powers, arrived to find himself attacked by Chulain's hound; Setanta hurled a ball at the hound which smashed into his mouth with such force as to propel the dog backwards against a tree, whereupon he fell to the ground dead.

'It sounds like my dog is attacking an intruder,' Chulain

remarked. Conchobar, hearing the commotion, apologised to Chulain.

'I forgot to inform you; I invited my friend, Setanta.' Chulain became worried for Setanta and left the table to go outside. He soon became more distraught, however, on finding Setanta in good health and his hound dead. Setanta felt remorse over the unfortunate occurrence and offered to guard Chulain's house himself until a suitable hound could be raised and trained. Cu, meaning hound, gave rise to Setanta being named Cu Chulain, meaning Hound of Chulain. The local people were in admiration of Setanta's fair judgement in response to the tragedy and so King Conchobar decreed that from that day Setanta be called Cuchulain. Thereafter Cuchulain's fame spread over all Ireland.

The show ended and the audience dispersed quickly, the men to the alehouse and the women to home. Patrick returned to Cormac's roundhouse. He'd been thinking of the similarities of the story with Greek legend. As he entered the roundhouse, his musings were interrupted by a friendly voice.

'Ah, Patrick; it seems the alehouse did not tempt you?' said Cormac.

'I drank some ale and ate a rump end, but only after trying for the topside.'

'You like to eat like a noble, Patrick?'

'I certainly do,' Patrick replied, in a purposely noble tone. 'But rump is a perfectly respectable quality, for a mere slave.' He smiled at Cormac who returned his good-humoured look.

'Did you make a purchase?' Cormac asked.

'I did. I bought a brooch for my mother. Let me show you,' Patrick removed the jewellery from his hidden pocket.

'Very nice,' said Cormac. 'I think you traded well.'

'Good. The woman made me laugh. She didn't know I was British. "Very good quality. Made in Britain" she kept saying. The ceramic quality is good. They are copies of British jewellery, made here.' He told Cormac the pin and clasp story.

'We will get there,' Cormac said. His expression softened and showed pity. 'When were you thinking of giving this gift to your mother?'

'It is a contradiction, Cormac. I accept I am now a slave and that I cannot escape from Ireland. But I love my parents and miss them. Fathers and sons don't show outwardly, but mothers and sons do. Buying her a gift is a sacrifice for me and a testimony to the sincerity of my thoughts. It doesn't matter that I may never give it to her.' Patrick returned the gift to his pocket.

'Hefty thoughts, Patrick,' Cormac replied.

Patrick felt the weight of them in the back of his throat. He changed the subject.

'Cormac, I saw one of King Miliucc's drivers at the fayre. I think he was talking to the slave who tried to steal my boots. Could it be possible? The hostel was one night away from the slave market on the east coast.'

'I can't say, Patrick. Who did he work for?'

'The hostel owner was his master.'

'The hostel owner would not travel to this fayre. There are others nearer and the slave will not be here on his own account. Without knowing more, I would say it is unlikely.'

'I know some more about him. The owner had received Shifty, that's our name for him, in payment of a debt. He swore to Miliucc that he did not know the man or his character.'

'Why was Shifty, as you call him, the subject of a conversation between the king and the hospitaller?'

'He tried to strike one of Miliucc's servants over an insult, in the presence of the guards. King Miliucc questioned the owner for employing such a servant. The hostel owner vowed to make Shifty answer before a brehon. Miliucc accepted this course of action but promised to check its fulfilment. He said failure to do this would lead to King Niall getting to know; a thought that worried the hospitaller,' Patrick recounted.

'It is possible that Shifty was returned to his previous owner and the debt reinstated. If the previous owner was from a different kingdom, Shifty would be returned to that kingdom. Therefore, it is possible that he lives in a neighbouring kingdom. The brehon's judgement, if there was one, would need to be known. If Miliucc's bard verified this, the information would not be difficult to find,' said Cormac. 'By the way, did you watch the actors?'

'I did. They told the story of Setanta, and how he came to be called Cuchulain. There is a similar story in Greek legend. Have you heard of Achilles?' Patrick asked.

'I haven't, Patrick. The hills teach me much, but not foreign legend.'

'Achilles was son of an immortal nymph and a mortal father, who was a king. It's interesting, Cormac, that men from different countries with different ways and different languages have stories and heroes that are almost the same.'

'I'm not surprised. All men are alike underneath the skin.'

'The fayre surprised me. I never expected pig and bull roasts, ale and mead, music, dancers, jesters, singers, poets, jugglers, actors, in addition to the food and drink.'

'It is a tradition. Good food, drink and entertainment attract a healthy presence of buyers and sellers. These transactions help to maintain the wealth of the kingdom. The nobles would say it is reward for the people. Some of the people say the peasants are kept poor and given occasional relief. There are bards who say it has been this way for thirty or forty generations,' said Cormac.

'Every day at the farmstead I see bickering, drunkenness, and fighting, yet at the fayre with plentiful food and drink, and great merriment, I see none. Is there an explanation?'

'Patrick, when did you last eat cow meat or pig roast?'

'When I was in Britain.'

'Exactly,' Cormac replied. 'Communities here are too small to afford cows for food. Farming families live off the land. Daily food is always from the smaller stock, such as chicken, goose, fish, hen eggs, and the milk of cows, goats, and ewes. Even kings and nobles don't eat cow meat much between festivals.'

'I'm surprised that nobles don't. Is there a reason?' Patrick asked.

'It's costly, even for kings. They cannot eat their way through a cow, which means much meat would have to be given away or wasted. They cannot buy a part of a cow.'

'Cormac, that is amazing. I never realised how lucky we were in Britain to have coin, and weekly markets. But that doesn't explain the good behaviour, does it?' Patrick asked.

'It does when you know the reason. Make us a cup of warm milk, Patrick, while I'm explaining.' Patrick placed a pot on the fire and Cormac continued. 'Rowdy behaviour is against the law at a fayre or festival. There are important witnesses all around, with bards, guards, chieftains, brehons and other nobles from local and surrounding areas. Rowdy people will be seen by those who can hold them to account and no slave wants to lose the chance to become a freeman. No freeman wants to risk becoming a slave. All classes enjoy these occasions and respect them that they may continue.'

This barbarian land is full of surprises, Patrick thought as he served the hot milk.

'I find it hard to understand coins,' Cormac said. 'I know our kings will accept payment for livestock occasionally in Roman coins. They use them to purchase wine and jewellery and special fabrics from the Roman countries. Weekly markets though; the idea is beyond my imagination.'

Patrick thought about this comment. He concluded payment by exchange of goods was more difficult to comprehend.

'Let us put our heads down,' said Cormac as he finished his cup of milk.

'The Beltaine Fayre feels like a holiday to me; living in a warm and dry house, working at different tasks, enjoying an entertaining evening; so, thank you, Cormac, and goodnight.'

* * *

At the end of the week, Cormac, Patrick, Soldier, and the flock, returned to the hills. On reaching the top of the ravine, Cormac halted the procession, causing the sheep to bunch up and eventually, all were at a stop.

'This is a suitable place to leave you, Patrick. If you should need help, send Soldier. If that is not possible, light a fire beacon, and use your ingenuity to make it smoke as thickly as possible. Here, take my head-wrap,' Cormac said untying it. 'For sure your own will get drenched and they take time aplenty to dry out. I will return on the second full moon if you have not called me sooner.'

Patrick took a deep breath, delayed a little as he put the head-wrap in his bag and then asked, 'Under which circumstances should I call you?'

'If you are taken ill or break a leg perhaps. Even if you kill a wolf, call me. We'll use the pelt and meat. If thieves attack and steal sheep, call me. Good luck, Patrick.'

'Cormac, I've enjoyed your company these weeks.'

'And I yours,' Cormac turned and made for Voclut.

As the sheep grazed and wandered in the ravine, Soldier ran to his guarding duties. Patrick made his way to the enclosure and unpacked. Behind the wall he dug a hole and buried a pewter mug, the one the driver from Conn drank from and which Patrick offered to take to the returns table. The vessel was an unwitting gift, from King Miliucc. Patrick dropped the brooch into his miniature waterproof crypt and replaced the lid carefully. After backfilling with small stones, he covered his secret cache with soil and compressed it by hand.

Taking advantage of the solitude, he knelt and prayed to God. So far, he had not failed his vow to pray twice a day for a year, for forgiveness.

After prayers he enjoyed a prepared meal of bread and chicken, supplied by Cormac's friends at the farmstead. The day was dull and dry, as he set out to walk the sheep range. Patrick took Cormac's word when he said Soldier patrolled the unseen perimeter, warding off troubles that might visit the sheep and shepherd. He never spotted Soldier on patrol, but Soldier always arrived in time for guarding the count. Patrick walked south until he could see the farthest flung sheep. A sharp yelp in the distance worried him. He couldn't see Soldier which was not unusual, and the sheep were undisturbed. All he could do was stay alert.

An eerie wolf howl floated up the valley then stopped abruptly. Patrick's body hair stood to attention as he tried to make sense of the situation.

Has a wolf attacked Soldier? Has Soldier attacked a wolf?

Patrick dived into the gulley and ran towards the southern end of the ravine. Spotting a vantage point higher up the bank he took cover behind rocks and gorse, where he watched and listened. Far away some sheep were bleating, unhappily, but the sheep in sight were unperturbed. He scanned the valley carefully and spotted a stationary object at the end of the gorge.

Returning cautiously to the bottom of the gorge, and out of sight of the stationary object, he sprinted, leaping over logs, dodging around bushes and rocks. Glimpsing a two-wheeled cart he swapped his speedy, weaving and gliding for stealth; creeping cautiously closer. Standing guard at the cart was a fearsome looking naked warrior; strength oozing from his muscular torso and limbs. Wearing white face paint, his eyes outlined in red beneath a shock of stiff and spiky grey hair which fanned out like a reed broom; his face snarled as he cast his mean eyes around, alert to the slightest movement or sound. A grey, straggly, and unkempt moustache and beard, curling on itself a few inches below his chin, added unpleasantness to his ferocious facial appearance. His wrists were bandaged thickly with strips of swaddling cloth, as though he were an eagle trainer. Fiery red and purple flames were painted on his body and arms and he held, at the ready, an iron-tipped spear. A leather belt around his waist supported a dagger and sheath and superstitious looking items, including a rabbit's foot, a wolf's tooth, and a crow's skull. They dangled as though attempting to form a meagre skirt.

He could rip me apart with his bare hands.

Patrick turned his attention to the cart and spotted lambs' legs through the slits in the cribs. Sheep thieves at work, Patrick thought. He needed to fell the man, before the guard's fellow thieves returned. He took up his sling, confident he could hit the warrior with one shot, but certain he would need two to stop him.

He loaded his sling with a large round stone but the guard was too close to the cart for Patrick to get a clean shot. Flinging a small stone into the bushes, Patrick made the guard turn instinctively towards the noise and then he quickly looked the opposite way and all around. Seeing nothing, he moved towards the bushes for a closer look, dagger at the ready. Patrick now stood firmly. With the painted man looking the other way, he whipped his sling and released his shot. Painted-man saw nothing and dropped, like the stone that struck the back of his head. Patrick ran to the cart, released the gate, and pulled back the cover. Four lambs sprang out and scuttled off.

Just then Patrick saw Shifty running up the cart track towards him, wielding a long metal-tipped spear and fifty strides behind him, an accomplice followed carrying a lamb. As Shifty came nearer, he slowed, holding the spear level as he laughed at Patrick.

'First your blood and then your boots.'

Shifty knew exactly who he was looking at.

Patrick stood his ground calmly, in the posture of a shepherd, crook held upright standing on the ground, neither offensive nor defensive.

If he throws the spear, I'll deflect it. If he thrusts it, I'll deflect it and strike him.

An over-confident Shifty came close and thrust the spear to Patrick's belly. The shepherd, in one action, took a two-handed grasp of his staff and whacked the spear from Shifty's grip, deflecting the deadly weapon past his body. But the tip nicked Patrick's shoulder, slicing his flesh. Shifty was four feet away with a forward momentum and no spear. Patrick took one large stride towards his assailant and kicked his shin with a sturdy Roman boot. As Shifty hopped, he caught a right, left and right combination which Patrick had learned and practised in the Alauna boxing ring. Shifty was flat on his back, unconscious.

The third thief had seen enough. He dropped the lamb and ran. Patrick was short of time. He slung one shot and hit him hard on the shoulder. Third-thief flinched and continued running. Patrick rushed to his bag of life and grabbed a handful of swaddling bands.

He rolled Shifty over till he was face down, tied his hands behind his back and tethered his feet.

He then ran to the guard who was groggy but recovering. Dragging him by the ankles to a tree, Patrick wrapped the warrior's legs around the trunk and tightly tied his feet together, then pulled him into a sitting position, made possible by Painted-man's dazed and unwitting co-operation. Running out of ties, Patrick un-wound Painted-man's wristbands, noticing the cloth on one of the wrists was lacerated and mauled. He pulled Painted-man into a sitting position as though he was hugging the tree with hands and feet, then tied his wrists tightly, pulling his face into the trunk till his nose was squashed hard against the bark.

Having finished with the guard, he returned quickly to Shifty, who had rolled over and worked his way into a sitting position, knees up with hands behind his back. As Patrick bent down to pull Shifty by his feet to a tree, Shifty's kick sent him sprawling. Patrick had made the same mistake that the guard at the slave market made with Patrick. He assumed the ankles were tied.

Shifty sprang to his feet and gave Patrick a ferocious kick to his head before running to the same tree that Patrick had in mind for him. Patrick, though stunned, turned to see Shifty's hands were still tied behind his back, but they were clutching a knife. Patrick realised he'd failed to search Shifty before he left him. On arrival at the tree, Shifty turned and Patrick guessed he was trying to wedge the knife, to draw his bonds over the blade and slice himself free. Shifty succeeded and brought both hands to the front. But Patrick was upon him wielding the spear, and his adversary was without a weapon. As Patrick took aim, Shifty closed his eyes, not knowing that Patrick did not want to use his spear against an unarmed person. Neither did he see the spear passing high above his head, flighted like a javelin down the ravine, piercing the ground a hundred strides away; far from Shifty's immediate grasp.

Shifty opened his eyes to see Patrick in a boxing stance.

'I'll have you before the bard, Shifty. And once more I'll beat you with my bare hands.'

'Hah,' Shifty exclaimed, like a man who couldn't believe he was still alive. 'You've thrown your chance. This time your boots are mine,' Shifty smirked.

They exchanged punches. Shifty was faster but Patrick landed heavier blows. Equally matched, they drained each other's strength. Shifty caught Patrick with a left to the chin and followed with a stunning right. Knocked dizzy, Patrick went down on one knee. Shifty moved straight in to kick Patrick senseless. Patrick, fighting double-vision, took a deep breath. Gathering all his remaining strength behind one last punch he sprang up, the bended knee now straight and firm. His focus returned as he powered a perfectly timed punch to Shifty's chin, lifting him off his feet.

Staggering backwards Shifty slammed into the tree. He lingered upright and engaged Patrick's eye with a contemptuous smirk. Malevolence and malice contorted his menacing stare until his eyes bulged like peeled eggs; his head flopped on a neck gone limp. His upper body fell forward slowly as though restrained by an invisible harness. A red drip plopped onto the dusty earth, staining the dry mud as Shifty slumped and smacked, face down, into the ground. Patrick raised his eye to the source of the drip. Another blob formed on the pointed tip of a blood-smeared knife blade, projecting solidly from the tree trunk. A Latin expression came to Patrick's mind which he translated into Gaelic and said out loud to Shifty's corpse.

'By the sword you lived and by the sword you died.'

He took a swig of water from his pouch then crossed over to the tied-up guard and poured some onto the knots to make them swell. The guard had come round but for all his strength, sitting on his bottom hugging a tree was proving to be a difficult posture.

A shuffling noise in the cart caught Patrick's attention. He went over and removed the cover revealing a large grey bag, tied with a draw-cord. There was movement inside. He loosened the cord, half expecting rabbits to hop out. A muzzle poked through, followed by the whole of Soldier's head. He saw his master and whimpered, then wriggled out and leapt onto Patrick.

'Soldier,' said Patrick, hugging and comforting the hound. He untied the muzzle and noticed small strands of swaddling cloth between Soldier's teeth, which now made sense of Painted-man's wristbands. He was the dog catcher. Soldier ran round in circles celebrating his freedom, then lowered his head to the ground and with eyes fixed on Patrick, he snarled and bared his teeth, then yelped, then wolf howled.

'Good dog, Soldier. I heard your message.'

Soldier ran to Patrick's side, tail wagging. Patrick pulled out Cormac's head-wrap, he let Soldier sniff it and pointing down the valley said, 'Bring Cormac, Soldier, bring Cormac.'

Soldier ran off, out of sight in seconds.

* * *

Patrick was sitting on a rock trying to apply a dressing to his shoulder, when Soldier ran to him. As they fussed each other Patrick looked up to see Cormac on foot, followed by Eamonn on foot leading his horse, with a man tied belly down on the horse's back. Another man wearing a white flowing robe, mounted on a white horse, accompanied them. He had the appearance of a bard.

Patrick quickly pushed the bandages into his pouch and approached the visitors to greet them.

'Cormac, I'm pleased to see you. My lords, your presence is welcome,' he said bowing to Eamonn and the bard.

'How are you? We thought you might be seriously hurt,' Cormac said.

'I'm alright, but I wouldn't be if the thieves had their way,' Patrick answered as he walked up to Eamonn's horse and looked carefully at the captive.

'He's the one that ran away. How did you catch him?'

'Soldier did that. We are just giving him a ride,' said Cormac.

'You recognise him?' asked Eamonn.

'Surely,' said Patrick, which stirred Third-thief to shout aloud to the ground.

'I was never here. He's never seen me. He's mistaken.'

'I'm not mistaken,' Patrick responded. 'Let me tell you, I hit him with a slingshot at the back of his left shoulder, and I recovered the stone. Here it is.'

Eamonn took the slingshot, approached the captive, and pulled back his clothing, revealing a round and swelling bruise, almost the same shape as the shot.

The bard stepped close and took a careful look. 'Never been here, man-with-no-name? Then the shepherd has special powers.'

Patrick leant in to Cormac and, speaking in a whisper, said, 'It's a bad situation just around the corner. There is much to explain. Do we want this man to hear our discussion?' Cormac in turn spoke quietly to Eamonn and the bard.

'Can you chain him to a tree?' the bard asked Eamonn, pointing to the captive.

'I can, Bard Fichran.' Eamonn untied him from the horse and bound him to a tree.

'Lead the way, Patrick,' Eamonn said.

Patrick led them round a spur, to where a man lay dead, face down in front of a tree. The visitors stopped in their stride, to take in the scene.

The bard looked gravely at Eamonn and said, 'I think you should introduce me to the shepherd.'

Eamonn nodded. 'Patrick, let me introduce Bard Fichran. He is King Miliucc's legal bard and senior brehon. This situation is grave and your words will be your legal testimony.'

'M'lord,' Patrick replied, bowing his head to Bard Fichran.

The visitors walked around the scene. The day was dry and sunny, with no wind; perfect for keeping the site of the incident intact. A two-wheeled handcart contained a spear, a cover, and a bag. To the right a naked, battle-painted man was tied to a tree trunk. He was alive and unhappily scraping his nose and cheeks against the rustic bark in a largely vain attempt to view the visitors.

'I think you should give us your account of what happened,' the bard said to Patrick.

'Yes M'lord.'

Patrick retold the sequence of events. The bard listened carefully, then walked to the tree and felt the knife handle. It was wedged solid. Patrick followed the bard's eye as he estimated the height of the knife from the ground, and compared this with the distance of Shifty's back wound from his heels.

'Do you recognise this man?' the bard asked Patrick.

'I do. I saw him at a hostel in the east. At the time he brought himself to the attention of King Miliucc.'

'I was present, Bard Fichran,' said Eamonn. 'Bard Finian and King Miliucc will remember this man. His name will be known.'

The bard approached the tree caresser.

'I think I recognise this man. Patrick, wash the paint from his face.'

Patrick grabbed his water pouch and a swaddling cloth and found the face paint came away quite easily with a good rub of the damp cloth. First one side then the other, as the man's nose was hard against the trunk. With the paint removed Patrick saw Pig-cart-driver's face.

'You are Clan Fogha?' said the bard.

'I am,' he answered.

'Tell me your personal name?'

'Crimnan.'

Patrick looked at Pig-cart-driver. So, your name is Crimnan Fogha.

'Crimnan Fogha, what is your business here?' the bard asked. Fogha didn't answer.

'Let me help you to think,' said the bard. 'I am King Miliucc's brehon. This means your trial has already begun. What is your business here?'

'To guard the cart,' Fogha said.

'You mean to guard the cart and its contents, don't you?'

Fogha made a gulping sound as he swallowed hard and breathed deeply.

'That's what I mean, M'lord.'

'Who planned the raid?' asked the bard.

'The dead man,' he said.

'Of course it was the dead man. But who else?' asked the bard.

Fogha's face was fearful. He didn't answer.

'Fogha, if you were the guard, you will face a heavy fine. If you were an assistant to an attempted killing, or a planner of a violent raid, you may never recover.'

Fogha's hands trembled. He clasped them, only for both arms to shake.

'Is it the third man?'

'More.' said Fogha. Patrick glanced at Cormac. How many were involved in this raid?

'Was it someone higher up?'

Fogha nodded.

'A chieftain?'

Fogha nodded again. Patrick was surprised to hear that a chieftain was involved or even behind this raid.

'His name?'

'I don't know it,' Fogha answered.

'Is it the dead man's chieftain?' the bard asked.

Fogha nodded. Patrick looked again at Cormac. Shifty involved with a dishonest chieftain.

'Tell me the clan-name of the third man,' said the bard.

'I don't know it,' Fogha answered.

'Then how did you get involved?'

'I met him at a hostel when I drove for King Miliucc. We met again at the fayre, by chance. We drank ale together. He offered me fifteen chickens to do a guarding job. I agreed for twenty chickens.'

'Long-chain him round the waist, Eamonn,' said the bard and, grabbing the sack from the cart, he threw it at Crimnan Fogha saying, 'You'll scare the birds dressed like that. Cover yourself.'

Eamonn helped by cutting the bottom out of the sack to form a makeshift kilt. Bard Fichran moved over to the tree to study the wedged-in knife.

'Remove the knife from the tree for me, and clean it,' he called to Eamonn.

Eamonn nodded, and quickly discovered he needed to use a stone to knock the knife out.

The bard approached Patrick, who jumped to attention. 'Help Eamonn to load the cart.'

Patrick and Eamonn threw Shifty's body onto the cart. Man-with-no-name, too damaged to walk, was chained in the cart with Shifty's corpse.

'Eamonn, I'm sure you can make use of the cart cover,' Bard Fichran asked.

'I can. I have a request as we speak, from Cormac,' Eamonn answered.

Patrick looked across at Cormac, but his face was impassive.

'Very well, Cormac, it's yours now.'

'Man-with-no-name,' said the bard. 'Your day got worse. You will answer for organising a raid on King Miliucc's flock using violence, ending in an attempted killing. Today you refuse to say your name, but soon you may not have a name.'

Fogha pulled the cart while long-chained to the bard's horse. Eamonn guarded from the rear.

'I'll stay with Patrick tonight,' said Cormac.

The bard turned to Cormac and Patrick. 'Recently King Miliucc's farmsteads to the east have suffered raids. No one has been caught.' He looked at Patrick, 'today, young man, you served the king well.'

Eamonn gestured farewell. Patrick and Cormac returned the wave.

'Let me attend your wound,' said Cormac. He cleaned the deep cut and applied Patrick's ointment and bandage to his upper arm. As he made a sling with the remaining bands he said, 'Swaddling bands and ointment, Patrick. Your possessions are many and useful. How did you come by these?'

'Breege, the girl who dressed my blisters, gave them to me. She told me King Miliucc provided the ointment.'

'I'm pleased to hear this,' Cormac said, as he finished the dressing and sling. 'Keep your arm from working for a few days. Give healing a chance.'

'Shall we take these belongings to the pen? Then bring the sheep in?' Patrick asked.

'Just that,' said Cormac.

The count was good. The lambs, sheep and rams were all there, and so was Soldier. Cormac was relieved.

'I'll prepare supper, Patrick. You've done enough today.'

'Thank you, Cormac. Let me ask Bard Fichran's meaning when he said man-with-no-name might not have a name?'

Cormac thought about the question as he knelt to light a fire for cooking. 'He was referring to the law, Patrick. A serious crime, such as murder or armed raiding, will be punished with an Eric. It is a fine, and usually beyond the means of one person. If the guilty person cannot pay, then the clan must pay. If the clan cannot pay or will not pay, the offender will be made an outlaw, which means he will have no protection in law. He will be banished from living in the lands of his clan and will lose his right to the clan's name. The bard was saying that man-with-no-name may soon be an outlaw.'

'So, a slave in his owner's kingdom is higher than an outlaw.'

'He is,' Cormac answered as he began stirring a porridge.

Patrick reflected as they ate their meal, and then he confided in Cormac.

'Cormac, until recent times I felt I was nothing. A mere pampered person without skill or attribute and no substance of my own. Once I had position and power. I thought I was important but it was all given to me. Nothing did I earn and little did I learn. Now, as a shepherd I am useful, I am learning. In truth, I feel no shame as a slave. My shame is my previous life.'

'You learn quickly, Patrick, but the track is long. Keep going. It is in you to become a complete shepherd,' Cormac paused wistfully, then added, 'you have great principles, Patrick, and might achieve great things one day; better to live your principles, though, and not chase great things.'

'I believe you, Cormac. But now I'm ready for sleep, after I have given thanks for deliverance. I won't forget the sheep. I'll play "The Lord is my shepherd".'

'Oh. Your tune has words. "The Lord is my shepherd", did you say?'

Patrick nodded. 'I didn't remember the words very well to begin with, but now they are coming back to me.'

After prayers, he played the first line of the familiar tune, then put down the flute and softly sang the psalm. He was aware of Cormac watching him, an intense expression of concentration and curiosity on his face.

'Who are you, Patrick?' Cormac asked as Patrick finished singing.

'A happy shepherd,' Patrick replied, as he lay down to sleep.

CHAPTER NINE

Patrick knelt beside the dull embers, in the grey, predawn darkness, hands together offering his daily prayer for forgiveness. At length he finished, rekindled the fire, and boiled a pot of porridge, taking care to rest the muscles of his left shoulder. Cormac rose and sat with Patrick at the campfire eating the break-fast till the pot was empty. He didn't linger but gave Patrick some advice before leaving.

'Your shoulder cut is deep. Keep the sling on and let's hope for a few quiet days.'

Patrick nodded then said, 'Fogha, the only Miliucc man in the trio, probably knew I was about to work alone.'

'Maybe he did. Look after yourself, Patrick; I'll see you on the full moon.' Cormac set off for Voclut.

Patrick watched Cormac leaving and contemplated his responsibilities as a lone shepherd.

Patrick's daily life was busier than that of a hard-worked Banna Venta farmer. He grazed the rams in a separate, richer pasture, developing their health for the masculine task ahead. Watching the weight of the ewes, Patrick kept them as plump as possible, moving the flock to new pastures when needed. By mid-Autumn the rams and ewes were ready. He observed the rams servicing seventy-five ewes each and, at the end of the first cycle, with considerable awe, watched them completing a second round of duty. And so, the season passed.

Two bowls of porridge daily was not enough for Patrick and his stomach rumbled through the day and occasionally, when climbing the fells, his body trembled, and the strength of his legs felt weak. This day, though, he was hopeful of being able to catch fish. The last week had been wet and windy and the fast-flowing beck had run brown and deep. He couldn't catch fish in those conditions. No flies hovered above the river, but grubs abounded on the bed, frustrating Patrick's need for the trout to surface. However, yesterday had been dry and today was bright. He took up his spear and strode out in the sunshine to his river of life. Enjoying an interlude of lightness, his thoughts wandered playfully to the tups.

Three or four climaxes a day, every day for more than a month. Cormac does right to test the muscle strength of their testicles, he mused.

Approaching the beck, he dropped his smile as he concentrated on his next task. The grassy banks had been cropped short in the previous week by the grazing sheep. Poised in the shadow of a bush, spear at the ready, tip close to the surface of the river, Patrick watched and waited. The water was less than a foot deep at the bank. Midges were out and, upstream, the trout were rising. In Patrick's shadow, his prey silently arrived. Patrick was still as a tree and part of the scene.

I'll beat this fleet and nimble fish, he said to himself.

The trout waved its tail lazily in the current of the river, neither advancing nor retreating. After minutes of patient waiting, a colourful dragonfly came along, zigzagging erratically close to the water's surface, before stopping to hover. Nonchalantly, the fish rose, effortlessly accelerating towards the attractive morsel. With mouth opening for a deadly snap, a small splash pierced the water's surface. The trout's jaw remained open, fixed, with a surprised expression, as Patrick removed his speared target from the water.

By midday, hanging from a loop of twine on Patrick's belt were four fish, silent and slimy, dangling down like keys on a hoop. He made his way to the pen and gutted his catch.

Later that afternoon, while watching the flock, Cormac and a driver arrived with a fully-laden, ox-drawn hay wain. He hurried to greet them, and they continued together to the covered pen, where Patrick and the driver unloaded the fodder.

'What have we under the cover?' Patrick asked.

'Leave that for now. We'll take care of it later,' said Cormac, arousing Patrick's curiosity. 'Use this fodder for ewes that take sick,' said Cormac, nodding towards the hay. 'Move the healthy pregnant ewes on sooner. It's a strange thing, Patrick, but pregnant ewes lose their appetites. Better to graze them on the tips of the grass, where there is more goodness. See they eat well and shorten their day.'

'Thanks, Cormac, I'll do that,' Patrick acknowledged thoughtfully, then knelt to start a fire. 'I caught some fish earlier today. I can treat you to fresh trout.'

'Isn't nature's harvest wonderful? See here. I've brought you some bread, and for a change, a skin of ale.'

'It's a welcome gift, Cormac; I went hungry when the river was high.'

As the three enjoyed a cooked trout, the visiting slave sat on a stone further away from the fire.

'How many clean bottoms have we today?' Cormac asked. He was referring to the transfer of black staining powder to the ewes' private area from the ram's, which happened when the reproductive deed took place.

'Five,' Patrick answered without hesitation.

'The same number as last year. We'll take them with us and the tups too.'

'What will you do with the ewes?'

'If they don't come on heat, we use them for meat.' Cormac answered. Patrick took this in. A ewe has to pay its way, just like a slave.

'And the rams?' Patrick asked.

'We'll graze them on the lowlands. Miliucc owns a farm that lambs twice a year. The rams will be busy for another cycle before you see them again.'

Patrick's admiration for the rams rose higher still. Meanwhile the driver of the oxcart made no conversation. He was a slave and seemed uncomfortable eating with Patrick and Cormac. Patrick noticed the slave avert his eyes to avoid looking at Patrick.

I don't think he likes me.

'Let us finish unloading, Patrick. I have something to explain,' said Cormac.

'I'll do it,' said the driver, jumping at the opportunity. He lifted two wicker cages off the cart, each containing a hen.

'These are a gift from King Miliucc.' Cormac said.

Patrick beamed, 'A gift from the king?'

'Just that; your response to the raiders pleased him. The hens are layers, Patrick. You can eat them if you wish, but if you keep them, when spring comes, they'll provide you with five or six eggs a week through to winter.'

Patrick couldn't stop smiling. A wet and hungry week had made him fear the changeable weather.

'An egg a day! I'm delighted, Cormac,' he said laughing. 'How my life has changed in but three seasons. I indulged in extravagant dinners once a week at my parents' villa, and now I'm thrilled at the thought of an egg a day.'

Cormac nodded wistfully, and then cast his mind to the jobs. 'We'll set up the coops while you gather the flock, Patrick.'

They left the fire and set about their work.

Out on the range as Patrick played his flute to call the sheep, he heard the banging noises made by Cormac and the slave, building his hen hut. The same noise as Cormac made on the day of Patrick's arrival. In the same three seasons he'd gone from being devastated to feeling a sense of purpose in his life. On his return, as he counted in the flock, Patrick heard Cormac humming, in soothing tones, the tune to "The Lord's my shepherd, I'll not want". He's animated; I think he's humming the words, not the tune.

Patrick separated the unproductive ewes, securing them in the wain along with the rams. There were only four.

'We had an extra black bottom today, Cormac,' Patrick

announced, pleased that the ewe had saved her life for another season. The count was full, and Soldier arrived to guard the flock as Cormac showed the coops to Patrick.

'Here are the troughs for water and grits. Open the hatch in daylight and secure it at night,' he said.

'Will the hens stray?' asked Patrick.

'They'll wander and return, especially for fresh water. Here, Patrick, I brought you some pots and a bag of meal. It'll soon be weather for hot porridge and cooked eggs.'

'Thank you, Cormac,' said Patrick with a full-faced smile, eyeing the greying sky overhead. Patrick was about to speak further but Cormac continued.

'It's been a successful mating season. Better than last year. Let us hope for a mild winter and good lambing.' Cormac looked around at the cart, readying to leave.

'Let us drink some ale before you go, Cormac,' Patrick interjected quickly. 'I'd like to hear how it ended with the raiders.'

Patrick poured three mugs. The driver acknowledged, happy to be given a drink of beer, and then he sloped off, pretending to check the ox-reins and the load. Cormac and Patrick seated themselves on the log benches and Cormac began his tale.

'It isn't ended. Fogha was fined. He and the clan paid. Man-with-no-name confessed his name and to his crime as an accomplice. As expected, he insisted the dead man, Shifty as you say, was the organiser. Shifty served the same chieftain as Fogha, so trouble is fermenting for the chieftain. The Over-king's brehon has been called on to decide the matter.'

'Will this lead to a kingdom war?'

'That is a question for King Miliucc to answer.' Cormac paused to ponder the question himself and sip his ale. He shifted uncomfortably on his seat. 'The incident is small and alone will not cause war. The build-up of aggressions can.'

'Is Miliucc able to fight a war? Does he have warriors?' asked Patrick.

'He has trained warriors and also will take men from the land.

War is never far away, Patrick. If it does not come sooner, it will come later. Chieftain fights chieftain, and kingdoms fight kingdoms. You noticed yourself that Irishmen quarrel and drink heavily. They are poor in spirit, born of inescapable poverty over many generations. The Irishman's soul receives little nourishment. He drinks to dull his mind that sleep may come.' Cormac drained his horn of ale.

'Do they live in fear? Fear of dying?'

'It's worse, Patrick. They fear living. Theirs is a hopeless existence. They don't value their own lives. They enter war with courage, but reckless courage.'

Patrick set down his ale, the cup still half full. 'Which means a shepherd's life is a blessing.'

'I think so. It is a philosophy of good living. And you, a young foreigner, have arrived here with a tune and a song that captures the spirit.' Cormac cast an eye at the setting sun. 'I also think we should be going.' They busied themselves loading the rams and unlucky ewes on the cart and bade their farewells.

As soon as Cormac was gone from sight, Patrick checked his clucking gifts and felt like a boy on his birthday. Returning to the flock, with Soldier by his side, Patrick sang the sheep's lullaby and allowed warm tears of happiness to trickle down his cheeks.

CHAPTER TEN

For the first two moons of winter Patrick's bones were brittle. Wind gusts and harsh rain penetrated his clothes; he couldn't be colder or wetter naked. Mercy came at night. Changing into dry clothing and downing a bowl of hot porridge, Patrick would kneel for an hour of prayer beside an open fire. Nicely warmed, he would fall into a fleece-wrapped sleep. Dry nights were a relief. However, on wild and wet nights, keeping his fleece dry was difficult. It was essential though, for the shepherd to sleep in the open. The combination of the outside presence of Soldier, Patrick and the campfire was a deterrent to lone wolves or packs, from attacking.

Long before dawn he would waken and lose himself in prayer till sunrise. Patrick had analysed his flaws and developed a method and routine of prayer. His morning prayers would end like this:

Thank you, Lord, for your forgiveness. For forgiving me; a despicable sinner, an arrogant rent collector, a lazy youth, an ungrateful son, a neglectful employer, an uncaring person. Forgive me Lord for turning my back on your word; for refusing the message of the bishops. Praise be to you, Lord, for providing my food and drink, my occupation, my health. Praise be to you, Lord, for faithfully providing sunrise and sunset. Praise be to you, Lord, for my penance of slavery and shepherding. Praise be to you, O Lord, for giving me purpose, even in punishment.

At sunrise Patrick would blow on the dull embers, waking them to the new day, before piling on fresh kindling and branches. His spirits always lifted as he breathed the aroma of burning willow and listened to the crackling sticks cooking his kettle of porridge. However, the wet and windy days he found depressing; his body would shiver at the thought of worse weather to come.

One bitterly cold and damp day he decided he would discuss his thoughts with Cormac at their farmstead meeting, only a wax and a wane away, when he was to take the flock there for shearing.

Why shear the flock in late winter he thought? Why so soon before lambing?

He berated himself because he could have known. He'd collected rents long enough from Banna Venta sheep farmers. His lack of interest in the work of his tenants crossed his mind and the thought became another mental note for contrition, on his lengthening prayer list.

The moon came and went. Patrick led the flock and Soldier stirred the stragglers. Arriving at the farmstead in Voclut, Cormac, seeing them coming, opened the gates and the ewes ran eagerly into the playground of rich pasture.

'And how is the good shepherd?' asked Cormac.

'Cold,' answered Patrick. 'The shepherd's clothing is not a shepherd's friend.'

'Winter is a problem to you, Patrick?'

'It is Cormac. And the weather is not yet severe. I cannot keep warm in damp clothing.'

'Ah! You have a suggestion for some high-born comforts?' Cormac laughed.

'I do. Leg windings,' Patrick smiled. 'They'll stop water from getting into my boots. Could my clothing be made to repel water too?' he said, slightly tongue in cheek.

'Perhaps; maybe with tallow. I'll inquire for you.'

'Thanks, Cormac. I'm warm enough at night, but I struggle to keep my fleece dry. What about the cart cover? Could that be treated with tallow too?'

'Your needs are many, Patrick. Take care to remember your place.'

'I know my place. You know I've accepted my life as a shepherd. But can I not make use of that which I learned in Britain, both for myself and others? We used the wax of bees to make clothing resist rain.'

'I will help you, Patrick. I will always help with simple matters of food, clothing and shelter. Now, bring fifty sheep into the closed pen.'

Soon Cormac was demonstrating the way to shear sheep. By day's end he'd evenly sheared thirty-eight ewes. Patrick's twelve looked like he'd cropped them with his teeth.

'You'll get better each year,' laughed Cormac.

'In truth I will. But why do we shear them in the cold late winter when they are carrying young?'

'Cold or warm, it makes no difference,' said Cormac. 'Shorn sheep stay warm even in winter. Sheep use much energy feeding a big woolly coat. Shearing means more energy goes to the unborn lambs.'

'The opposite of what I thought,' said Patrick.

'Thoughts or no thoughts, I have some arrangements to advise of,' said Cormac. 'Pen the sheep then pay a visit to Eamonn at his workshop. Be sure to wear a clean tunic.'

'What is the purpose of my visit?' Patrick asked with a worried look.

'He didn't say.'

'Am I in trouble?'

'I've heard nothing, so you can't be.'

'I don't wish to be scruffy myself, Cormac, but I notice many slaves wearing grubby yellow tunics.'

'The grubby ones don't belong to the king. The next arrangement, Patrick, is that I'm leaving now. I have business some distance from here. See you much later.'

* * *

At sundown a smartly dressed Patrick knocked on the iron-studded workshop door.

'Come in,' a voice shouted.

Patrick entered and saw Eamonn putting the finishing touches to an oxcart repair.

'How is our young shepherd?'

'He's in good shape, master.'

'And the work; does it please you?'

'It does. It is a cold job, and lonely, but I find satisfaction in my work.'

'Good to hear. You'll get used to the cold. I called you here to talk about security. You and Soldier have gained a reputation. You've suffered no petty theft since the summer business. However, that might change when the lambs arrive so you must take steps to preserve the flock and yourself.' Patrick's brow creased. 'This week, Patrick, do not attend the festival of Imbolg. Your enemies will seek opportunity in the shadows. Back in the hills, when the lambs arrive, be extra watchful. Shorten the range and keep all in sight. Look and listen and stay alert. You know by stopping the raid in summer, you came to the king's attention. Only if the year ends well will this remain a good thing. Do you understand?'

'I do, master.'

'Then you may go,' said Eamonn, gesturing to the door.

Patrick returned to his lodgings at Cormac's small roundhouse next to the sheep pen. He thought how to act upon Eamonn's advice, and some ideas came to mind. Then he spent time on his knees. When they ached, he continued praying. Aching more, he prayed more and stopped only when he ran out of prayers.

* * *

Taking advantage of the extra resources Patrick was preparing a special hot drink when Cormac returned.

'Just in time,' said Patrick, while stirring vigorously. 'We're drinking our supper tonight.' He added back the yolks to the mixture of egg glare and cow's milk, and gently stirred them into a smooth, golden paste. 'Have you anything sweet, Cormac, honey perhaps?'

'That's not the request of a slave,' Cormac teased. 'I have mead. Will that do?"

'Perfect,' said Patrick, topping up the pot with cow's milk. Cormac reached to a wooden shelf for a crudely made amphora and added a few glugs into the pot as Patrick stirred, then poured the warm mixture into two mugs. Patrick thought of home on a cold winter's evening when he and his parents would take this hot drink. No garden herbs and fresh honey this time, he thought, passing a mug to Cormac as they sat on logs around the embers of the inside fire.

'You learned some kitchen skills,' said Cormac, slurping loudly.

'Mother showed me. Hen's milk she called it,' said a smiling Patrick, pleased with the compliment.

'Your meeting wasn't so bad then?' said Cormac.

'For now,' said Patrick with a little sigh. 'Eamonn instructed that I take extra care in protecting myself and the sheep, and, with intended menace, he advised that the highest has noticed the lowest.'

'Not a bad problem for a good shepherd,' said Cormac.

Silence added strength to the remark, as Patrick mulled over his shepherding ideas, prompted by Eamonn's warning.

'I will think of some practical steps to take,' Patrick added.

'I'm sure you will, by the way, I spoke to a cutter this evening,' Cormac placed his mug down on a flat stone slab next to the fire and continued, 'about leg windings. You may visit him after sundown tomorrow.'

'Thank you, Cormac.'

'Not a bother. Take the track north past the cattle farmstead to the craft village. Ask for Coren at the fourth workshop on the right. Show this token to identify yourself,' said Cormac, passing him a bright blue, ceramic-coated bronze disc.

Patrick looked at the disc curiously. The ceramic was a good quality, but he wasn't used to requiring this kind of identification.

'You're not coming then?' he asked.

'I can't get a guard for the sheep this time.'

'And if I find something suitable, how must I proceed?'

'Order them. Bring them with you if you can.'

'And the business of price and payment?'

'I've discussed the details. Payment is covered,' said Cormac.

Patrick hesitated and took a deep breath.

'Thank you, Cormac, but there is much for me to learn. Allow me to enquire; when King Miliucc issued clothing to his new slaves, he told us the first set was a gift and the second was to be paid for out of our allowance. Three seasons have been and gone and I have not been pursued for payment. Neither have I received any. I don't know what my allowance is. I don't know what I can afford.'

He hoped he hadn't stepped beyond acceptable boundaries, but he knew he could be more direct with Cormac than other masters would tolerate.

'Your allowance is paid, Patrick. But of course, you are a slave and the payments are small. Do you remember the king's bard on your journey from the slave market?'

'I do.' Patrick looked at Cormac in the dim light of the fire, interested to hear more.

'He's the king's counter. Each season he discusses your position with me. Your second set of clothes has already been paid for with your allowance. He records the pluses and minuses. You could not avoid a minus when you started, but now you've caught up you are not allowed a minus. To spend more than your allowance you need to trade personally, as you did with your sandals.'

'So, three seasons of shepherding is worth a set of clothing and some leg windings?'

'Just that,' Cormac replied.

'I drank at the alehouse during Beltaine. How was that paid?'

'You used my name to place yourself, Patrick. Your spending was charged to me and I charged it to your allowance when the bard came.'

Patrick stood to light a candle as the fire dimmed. This was a routine because the fire was subdued at night-time.

'Do the other slaves account to the bard?'

'They don't. They belong to their master. Remember, you are the property of a king.' Patrick suppressed a wince. 'This is to your favour. Craftsmen and suppliers will receive you willingly.' Patrick took the last comment thoughtfully.

As he learned more about the finer advantages of his lowly status, his thoughts switched to Banna Venta and his own treatment of the slaves he employed.

I've been cruel or kind, on a whim. Patrick resisted a negative headshake, but his head dropped and his eyes closed momentarily, as another shame from a shameful past, revisited this sorry shepherd. Deferring his thoughts, he addressed a question to Cormac. 'Did you have a reason for not telling me?'

'To everything its time,' Cormac replied.

'I don't understand,' Patrick replied, genuinely puzzled.

'When you arrived, how was your soul?'

Where is this going Patrick wondered? 'Dead,' he replied.

'Would I burden your thoughts with the working of wages when you had none?' Cormac paused briefly. 'How is your soul now?'

'Recovering,' answered Patrick.

'Now you understand.' Cormac knocked back his drink and turned to organise his bed.

But I asked the question, he thought to himself. Cormac didn't come to me.

However, Patrick knew the distinction would be irrelevant to Cormac. His message was that communication only works when the receiver is ready. If Cormac raised the matter when he thought I was ready; he would be judging me. Leaving the matter till I raised the subject meant that I thought it was time I knew. Cormac is right. Now I understand him. Then Patrick had a thought of his own.

The receiver must be ready, but is it possible to prompt readiness?

Cormac snored, prompting Patrick to prepare his own bed. He placed his fleece flat on the wicker mattress, like an under sheet. There was no need to wrap up, when he had the shelter of being indoors in a room heated by a central fire. Wearing his mantel, he knelt on the straw-covered, compacted earthen floor, said his prayers then settled to sleep.

* * *

Patrick's cloak, saturated and heavy, lashed and whipped his face. Leaning forward he pushed against the elements, left, right, left, right, squelch, squelch. Playing with the wind, Patrick leant forward at a low angle but couldn't fall on his face. He spread his arms and the gale forced him upright. Pulling in his arms again, he leant forward to stay on his feet and progressed, occasionally dodging airborne branches and boughs. Arriving at the craft village he loudly banged on the door of the fourth roundhouse, in the hope of being heard. There was the sound of a sliding bolt and the door opened enough for a young woman to peer out.

'I'm Patrick, here to meet Coren,' he said.

'Do you bring something?'

'I do.' He handed the token to her.

'Wait here.' She bolted the door. Shortly the door was opened again, this time by a smartly dressed man who looked, to Patrick, to be in his late thirties.

'You will be Patrick, the new shepherd?' he said.

'I am,' answered Patrick patiently as he caught bucket-loads of windswept water draining from the thatched roof.

'Well, you picked a good night. Here, this is yours,' said Coren, returning the bright blue disc. 'Come inside. Come up to the fire and take off your garment.'

'Thank you, master,' said Patrick removing his cloak and scarf.

'Bride, make this man at home would you,' he called.

A young woman came from behind a screen and passed a towel to Patrick.

'Thank you,' said Patrick, noticing she avoided his eye.

Enjoying the comfort of the warm dry towel he dried off his blond wavy hair, neck and ears then his face, mousey moustache, wispy beard and finally his hands. Without thinking he folded the towel and placed it neatly on a flat stone beside the fire. This genteel mannerism caused Bride's face to humour a little as she flashed a glance, with lifted brows, towards Coren.

'Take a seat by the fire,' she said, pointing to a well-crafted stool. 'Could you manage a hot drink?' she said to Patrick.

'In truth I could,' said Patrick, with a smile in his heart that his frozen face muscles could not transmit.

She brought him a large mug which he accepted eagerly. Cupping cold hands around the vessel he warmed his palms and purple fingers, lingering as he breathed in the welcome fatty smell of the chicken broth. Putting cup to lip the herbs and salty flavours were a delight to his palate. Small pieces of chicken and ham brought texture and taste to his excited senses, a reminder he'd not eaten the meat of a pig for more than three seasons.

'Cormac mentioned leg windings,' said Coren, 'but you tell me.'

Patrick placed his half empty mug on the slab next to the towel. 'I like my boots, but water gets in. My feet get very cold. May I show you?'

Coren nodded and Patrick removed a boot revealing a saturated woollen sock and an insole swimming in water.

Coren examined the boot. He poured out the water around the edge of the fire, where it evaporated quickly. 'This part is fairly dry,' he said pointing to the leather upper. 'Water clearly gets through the lacing, but look at yer socks, so high above the boots. Sure, yer feet are soaked, wrapped in these wonderful wicks.'

'I thought leg windings would help,' said Patrick.

'They could, but they are heavy. Hold a lot of water too. You should have a look at this.' Coren showed him a lighter fabric that stretched.

Patrick didn't like the look of it. Light weight. Not much of a barrier, he thought. Would it be warm?

'Does it repel water?' asked Patrick.

Coren shook his head, 'But it doesn't hold much water either. Not like your socks or leg windings. Dries out quick too. Try this one on.' Coren passed him a woollen tube.

Patrick pulled up the hose to just below his knee and then rolled up the bottom of the tube. He put on his boot and rolled the tube down over his laces, stood up and moved around a little.

'They're a good idea. A bit slack though,' said Patrick.

'Bride, measure him up. Both legs,' said Coren.

'Take yer boots off. And yer socks and dry yerself,' she said.

Patrick used the towel on his legs and feet, then dried the inside of his boots. When he'd finished Bride took his leg length and his girth at knee, calf and ankle. Clasping her smooth warm hands around his cold calf, Patrick enjoyed her touch. She moved his leg into position for measuring. Perhaps unnecessarily Patrick thought, or hoped, as he studied the top of her head of fiery red hair. Coren meanwhile had wandered off. He looked to be searching for something. He returned with a pair of short socks.

'Wear these for now. Bride will dry yer socks and shorten them. They're too thick to double up. We'll make you two pairs of tubes. Can you collect them same time tomorrow?'

'I can,' said Patrick, confidently, though he wasn't sure at all.

'Remember to bring my socks back,' said Coren.

'Thank you, I will,' said Patrick, then, turning to Bride, 'Thank you for the warm drink, and farewell till tomorrow.' Bride looked him in the eye briefly and handed Patrick his cloak and scarf.

The weather on Patrick's return was perfect for testing the wicking of short socks. The storm had calmed but it rained all the way. He arrived to find Cormac stirring a pot of hot porridge.

'And how is our soaking-wet shepherd?' greeted Cormac.

'Soaking wet,' said Patrick, sitting on a low stool and removing his boots. His feet and socks were damp but not swimming. 'I think we're getting somewhere. Coren wants me to pick up the goods same time tomorrow. I hope that's in order?'

'It is. I'm here.'

'There was a young woman there called Bride. She measured me up.'

'I'll bet she did,' Cormac smiled.

'Who is she?'

'She's Coren's daughter.'

'That explains,' said Patrick.

Mimicking Patrick's well used phrase Cormac said, 'I don't understand, Patrick.'

'She's bossy.'

Cormac laughed. 'You're getting there. But you're not there yet.'

Unsure of Cormac's meaning Patrick finished his porridge and prepared for prayer and bed.

The following evening, in dry and windless weather, he knocked lightly on the door. Bride answered.

'Come in, Patrick. Have you brought my father's socks?'

'I have them with me.' He pulled them out of his tunic bag and as he handed them over, he was drawn to her. Bride looked beautiful. Her reddish ginger hair was long and wavy and hung with a shine, over one shoulder, accentuating her fair complexion. Patrick resisted staring; unaware he was already mesmerised.

'Did they work?' she asked.

'I don't... er.'

'The short socks. Did you see a difference?' Bride asked, jolting him out of his daydream.

'Oh. I did. It rained all the way. But they soaked up less water.'

'Good. Now, come to the table,' she said.

Patrick approached the dark-stained oak table and saw the hose laid out. Leg ties were sewn into the fabric. His socks, clean and dry had been expertly shortened.

'Will Coren be joining us?' Patrick asked.

'Oh. I should have said. He's elsewhere tonight.' She picked up Patrick's socks and a pair of tubes. 'Here, put them on.'

He wanted to bow in exaggerated obeisance but Cormac's comment, you've accepted you're a slave but you don't think like one, came to him and he resisted. Patrick sat on a bench and removed his boots and long socks. Before he could pull the hose into place Bride was doing it for him, feeling the snug fit around his calves and lacing the ties.

'The bottom ties are slimmer for threading into the lace holes,' she said. 'It'll stop the tubes from riding up.'

Once again, he looked down, unobserved, on her hair. This time it was wavier and shiny. Patrick forced himself away from his staring to don the new leg wear, and took a few steps.

'Comfortable,' he said. 'But the true test will be in the hills.'

'And when do you return?'

'Tomorrow,' he said, stifling a sigh.

'So soon? Then we should discuss the other problems.'

Patrick looked puzzled. 'I think that's all,' he said gesturing to the hose.

'Cormac asked about treating a cover.'

'Oh, that. It was just a thought. It can wait.' Patrick reflected that he couldn't afford this and didn't want the embarrassment of enquiring, then having to back out.

'Share the thought with me,' she pressed.

Patrick chuckled, partly amused and partly in nervousness at being alone with her.

'Very well. I have a cart cover which I use at night to keep my fleece dry.' He took a breath to gather his words.

'But it leaks, and you'd like to treat it,' Bride interjected.

'I would,' Patrick answered, amused by her pushiness.

'Why can it wait?'

Patrick hesitated, searching the room for a reason other than the shaming truth. When he couldn't find one, he admitted, 'I have no means to pay.'

'That's a problem. I'll think about it. How did you come to possess a cart cover? You don't buy those with a couple of salmon.'

'There was a failed sheep raid. The thieves left it behind.'

'How did the sheep raid fail?' Bride asked, in a softer and curious tone.

'I stopped them,' Patrick answered, hoping she would push him for the story.

'Come on then. Tell me the tale.' Bride teased.

Her pushiness favoured Patrick this time as he fancied being in her company longer. They were sitting on the table bench facing each other side-saddle. Patrick could look at her closely while he was talking.

'It was my first day as a lone shepherd and the sheep were out on the gully. Soldier, our guard dog, howled from afar. I ran to investigate and found a raid in progress with an armed guard watching over a cart with three lambs already loaded. I took him down with my sling and tied him to a tree.' He watched her expression. It was cool, but she couldn't hide the sparkle in her eye. 'Another raider came, carrying a spear. He wanted to kill me. I deflected his spear thrust. We both lost our weapons and fought with our fists. I sent him flying and he landed awkwardly on his own knife, which killed him. A third assailant ran away and was caught by the dog, and Eamonn. The raiders lost their cart, cover and weapons and the brehon gave the cart cover to Cormac who gave it to me.'

Patrick had held her attention.

'So, you didn't just fight them off, you captured them; very impressive. You can walk me to the bottom then. I should be in safe hands,' Bride joked.

'The bottom?' he queried, delighted that she was opening up a little.

'I don't live here. I live with my father in the first house. This is our presentation house. I was escorted here by a guard and should call him now that our meeting is finished, but you can walk with me instead.'

Bride pulled on a cloak, showed Patrick the door, followed him out then closed the door and latched it.

'I believe you are King Miliucc's new hill shepherd?' she said as they walked down the track.

'That's right,' said Patrick, alert to their dark surroundings, lit only by a pale moon in a cloudy sky.

'When did you start?'

'Last summer,' he said, as he glimpsed a moving shadow in the moonlight. The village houses were set far back, obscured by dense bushes. Two men, one tall the other stocky, stepped out of the darkness and faced them.

'Take my arm,' said Patrick softly. She linked him.

'Clear off, lover boy,' said the tall one.

'It's you should go,' said Patrick, dropping the link.

The tall man pulled out a knife which he held menacingly in his right hand, away from his body, crouching low and counterbalancing with his left hand. The whites of his wide-open eyes, glistening in the moonlight, were intended to intimidate. Patrick tightened his grip on his slingshot.

The crack of breaking molars carried in the still night. Tallman grasped his mouth and spat out blood and teeth. On seeing the stone fall to the ground, the stocky accomplice ran off. Tallman quickly threw his knife like a reversed dart, piercing Patrick's forearm, then, falling out of the shallow wound it was quickly trodden underfoot by Patrick's boot. He eyed his adversary as he reloaded his sling. Tallman weighed his chances and he too ran off.

'You're bleeding, Patrick. Come to the house. We have bandages.'

'It's slight,' he said, but offered no further resistance. Patrick picked up the knife, recovered his bloodied stone and hurried back to her side.

The house was round with a high thatched roof. Inside was a centrally positioned log fire. The warmth of the large room was overwhelming to Patrick. He saw two straw beds with sheepskin covers against the perimeter wall, separated by wicker dividers offering a scant amount of privacy between father and daughter. A large table with benches stood in the open area. Patrick noticed an additional door, partially hidden behind a weaving frame, leading to a small cooking house. Coren was clearly a freeman doing well.

Bride brought a small basket to the table and sat on the bench sideways, patting the space next to her for Patrick to take a seat. He took his place. A dozen bee stings scalded his forearm as she dabbed a herbal salve on his open wound.

Fighting to maintain his myth of toughness, he gritted his teeth and calmly said, 'Your ointment has the kick of an ass.'

'For sure it has, but you'll be fine.' She smiled, bandaged his arm and put away the basket. 'Let me bring you a drink. I can offer you ewe's milk or fresh ale.'

'Thank you. Fresh ale. I… er… would like to ask, how should I address you?'

'Call me Bride.' She went from sight behind a divider and into the cooking house, returning with two horns of ale. 'You were quick with your slingshot: and accurate too. Where did you learn?'

'I am my own teacher. I practice speed and accuracy to protect the sheep and myself from wolves and people.'

'You didn't have much time. Did you see them behind the bushes?'

'Not clearly, but I saw a movement and prepared my sling. I was ready before they stood in the road.' He sipped his ale. 'Let me ask you, Bride', he hesitated, 'Ireland is a dangerous place for the unprotected. Did you walk alone to the presentation house?'

Her complexion pinked.

'I didn't. I was escorted. My guard was supposed to stay with me but I dismissed him.'

Patrick hid his smile. She planned to walk with me.

They chatted awhile, finished their drinks leisurely and said their goodbyes. She took him to the door.

'Will you be safe?' Bride asked.

'Not on the track; they'll outnumber me. But I'll be safe, and in bed before they are.'

'You'll hear a bell, Patrick. That'll be me reinstating the guards.'

He looked at her, restrained himself and said, 'I hope…'

As he hesitated, she put her finger over his lips and said,

'So do I,' and from her pocket she pulled out a cloth Celtic symbol. 'Here, take this. Keep it with you and it'll keep you safe.'

'What is it?' He asked, delighted to be receiving a small gift from her.

'It's a pishogue.'

'I don't know the word,' he said.

'Keep it with you. It'll keep you safe,' she repeated.

Patrick stepped out, headed straight for the dark shadows then for the hill to the west. He climbed the coarse and saturated terrain to the top and descended on the other side into the familiar territory of the ravine. As Patrick ran at a gentle pace he wondered if the villains were hiding aside the track to the south. It didn't matter. He was safely in Voclut now.

Cormac was in night dress when he entered the house.

'You took longer than I expected,' said Cormac, noticing the bandage. 'Had trouble then?'

'Two men ambushed us. Bride bandaged me and I came back the long way.'

Patrick was hoping Cormac didn't ask too many questions, for Bride's sake.

'Did they get what they wanted?'

'They didn't. I scared them off. I was in the way though. It was Bride they were after.'

Cormac looked surprised. 'Was Coren there?'

'He wasn't, but Bride was under guard,' said Patrick, protecting Bride from her indiscretion.

To Patrick's relief, Cormac, dismissing the incident, said,

'Let's look at your wares then.' Cormac inspected the socks and tubes. 'From the knees down, you'll be better dressed than a king. I hope they work well for you. How was Bossy?'

'She got her own way.'

'I'd say she did,' he chuckled. 'But sleep beckons. Good night most noble shepherd.'

'Good night, Cormac.' Patrick laughed.

Patrick's prayers took longer than usual, extended for additional thanksgiving. But this night his last thought was of Bride, as he fell into dreamy sleep.

CHAPTER ELEVEN

Back in the hills, Patrick kept the sheep in sight, as Eamonn suggested. He found a high vantage point from where, hidden in a hillside hollow, he could scan the sheep scene. Casting his eye wider, he systematically searched for signs of predators, intruders, and any hint of disturbance of the flock. On the near horizon he observed the behaviour of the sheep, looking for clues of difficulties or signs of lambing. All the while, Soldier guarded the perimeter of the range while skilfully remaining out of sight.

In response to Eamonn's call for extra vigilance, Patrick had been training Soldier to respond to his calls. The hound had learned and was reliable at close range.

This day the wind blew strong and Soldier could have been anywhere. The conditions were perfect for testing Soldier's training from a distance. Patrick, using a disguised voice command, launched a crow's call onto the stiff breeze. Would Soldier catch the call? Would he respond from a distance? The minutes passed by with no sign of Soldier. More minutes passed and Patrick began to doubt, then Soldier leapt with gusto onto Patrick's side and was rewarded with cuddles and strokes. Patrick was satisfied. The ability to call Soldier, surreptitiously, from a distance, would increase the safety of the sheep, his own and Soldier's. With a tail wagging and swishing, it seemed Soldier agreed too.

Later that evening, when the sheep were settled in their pen, Patrick sat around his campfire supping a hot drink. He thought over the words of Eamonn: your enemy is everywhere, ready to pounce on weakness. In looking after the sheep, he had listened and acted, but thought Eamonn had been exaggerating. He went through his experiences since setting foot in Ireland. On his first day a guard at the slave market had tried to take his boots; on his first night, Shifty, a fellow slave, tried to steal Patrick's boots and would knife another slave in order to succeed; in the hills he had witnessed raids whereby a king would steal from a neighbouring king. A slave would steal from a king. He thought finally of the failed attempt to ambush Bride at knife-point.

I'm living in a dangerous land, he thought. Eamonn is right. However, if there is a myth or reputation developing around me and Soldier, let's keep it alive. Today's progress at calling Soldier from a distance was an important step in safety.

Patrick was heart-warmed by Soldier's loyalty and his ability to understand and learn. He decided to think of some new tricks for Soldier, so they could confound their enemy.

Neither was Ireland all bad. He remembered many small acts of kindness he'd received. The guard at the slave market who understood Patrick's question and cut his ankle tethers; his own master, King Miliucc, treating a vagabond who had wronged him with fairness and justice; Breege, the sympathetic slave girl who bathed Patrick's blisters. Then he thought of his own traits. Without question, if one of Patrick's slaves crossed him, he would have treated them harshly. Patrick's intuition was that King Miliucc was wrong. Yet the situation of the slave girl, who didn't know Patrick, but showed him compassion when he needed it, seemed right. I prefer the compassionate view over the self-centred outlook that I have held myself, as a nobleman.

His mind returned to the sheep range and what the morrow would bring, hopefully the safe arrival of some newborn lambs.

The next morning, out amongst the flock, Patrick saw many signs of lambing. Pink sheep bottoms; ewes' tails arching, udders filling, teats swelling like four fat fingers, ewes pawing at the ground, preparing their bed for labour. Patrick stood back from one ewe and witnessed the flock's first arrival. The mother licked her baby's nose, cleaning her with love. Within the hour, the lamb found her mother's teat. Patrick felt relieved and then was joyous at witnessing the miraculous development of new life.

By day's end, three more ewes were tending their lambs. Patrick gathered the flock in the usual way, tallied the ewes and, with great pride, notched the new arrivals on the counting stick. Patrick had chosen the pen by the woods of Voclut, which gave shelter to the sheep from the prevailing winds. His own bed, however, was pitched aside a boulder and a bush. His roof was the doubled over cart cover and the stars. The sheep settled, but Patrick's mind raced like a river in the rains. Excitement from his first close experience of lambing mixed with the burden of his responsibility, brought on extra prayers for thanksgiving; for help in shouldering his responsibilities, and for the safe arrival of new lambs. Tiredness finally delivered his delayed sleep.

Patrick, as usual, was awake before sunrise and he found four new lambs had arrived during the night. Over the next seven nights he saw the flock increase by twenty-four. He'd helped struggling ewes to deliver; averted rejection of lambs by their mothers; reunited distressed ewes with their lost lambs; cleaned and tended their cuts and wounds, even saved a ewe from dying after a stillbirth. His eyes had welled at the loss of the lamb though. But through it all Patrick watched his flock with lifted spirits, his tired body shaking off fatigue.

* * *

In the sunshine of a fresh and brittle winter's day with the ewes and lambs scattered across the range, Patrick, seated on a large flat rock, wished his father could see him.

'You couldn't call me work-shy now...' He called out happily in Latin.

A few sheep turned to face him and then, with bored expressions continued their grazing.

The howl of a wolf brought Patrick to the present. He jumped quickly to his feet, thinking the howl might be Soldier's. From behind a hefty blow to his shoulder knocked him prone to the ground. He scuttled clumsily away, on hands and feet, putting distance between him and his unseen aggressor before jumping upright. On his feet, he turned quickly, to face his assailant.

A tall, grubby, mean-faced man wielding a long, sturdy stick, squared up to him, saying,

'I can break your bones shepherd boy, or you can lie face down and let me tie you. Either way we will take some lambs.'

Patrick quickly released the knot which tied his club to his belt and took hold of it. He shaped himself for combat but as he was about to attack, he was stricken painfully across the ribs from behind. He stumbled forward but kept his feet until a hefty push sent him to the ground. The two men overpowered him and rolled him onto his back. The tall man buried his massive fist into Patrick's nose, causing the shepherd's eyes to water involuntarily; for the second time that day.

Patrick let out two sharp crow calls and within seconds Soldier appeared, leaping at the tall man; clamping his jaws around the muscular forearm that wielded the stick. The man shrieked trying to shake off the hound, yelling at his companion to help him. The second attacker rushed towards Soldier, freeing Patrick to climb to his feet. He stepped back a few strides and, wincing in pain launched his slingshot, thankful that he'd shortened the action from three swings to two. A direct hit to the man's back dropped him to his knees. Soldier, shaken off the tall man's arm was now biting his heels as the raiders decided to run.

'Here Soldier,' Patrick called. Soldier ended his pursuit of the raiders and came to Patrick, who was on his feet but crouching in pain.

'You warned me. You're a clever dog.' He gave Soldier a hug but only briefly. 'Stay here, Soldier.'

Patrick lurched awkwardly to the hill top and scanned the middle distance. He spotted two heads bobbing hurriedly for the cover of the woods. Ignoring his pain, Patrick pursued them at a steady pace, keeping out of sight behind ridges and undulations. Reaching the woods and hearing voices, Patrick crouched low behind a cluster of bushes. Separating the branches carefully, he found the villains hiding a handcart under dense foliage. Certain now that his enemies would return, possibly in greater numbers, he tailed them to the edge of the woods and observed them taking a track to the south. He'd seen enough and headed back to Soldier and the flock.

As he ran in the midday sun, the temperature was pleasant, with fluffy clouds filtering the sun's rays. He studied the area around his rocky perch, trying to understand how his assailants came within striking distance, unseen. There were clusters of rocks interspersed with gorse and whin. Cover was possible but there was open ground between them and the assailants had managed to get close without being seen or disturbing the sheep. Patrick decided to be more selective when choosing his vantage points.

His thoughts switched to Soldier's late warning, and the conundrum of his proximity when called. *Am I expecting too much of the hound? The howl was supposed to let me know in advance about the presence of intruders. I would then be ready for them and could call on Soldier to help me catch them.*

Another thought crossed his mind. Soldier belonged to the king. He should have discussed ideas of training Soldier with Cormac. He should have sought permission. Patrick realised he was overstepping the line. Cormac was right when he said *I am accepting my slavery, but not thinking like a slave. I need to rein in my behaviour.*

He arrived back at the sheep scene. Soldier was out of sight but returned quickly to Patrick's call. Patrick counted the sheep where they were standing and, satisfied that no lambs or ewes had been stolen, he was ready to summon Cormac. He picked up a couple of sturdy twigs and tied them round Soldier's neck like a twine necklace and gave his instructions.

'Fetch Cormac,' Patrick said, pointing towards Voclut. Soldier ran off dutifully.

Uneasy about leaving the sheep scattered on the hillside when Soldier was not around, he pulled out his flute and called them in early. The Topp Mountain pen was surrounded by open land and Patrick could see the approach of predators more easily, but still he realised he'd made a mistake sending Soldier off before the sheep were penned.

He built up the fire and put a pot of porridge to warming, then soaked a woollen cloth in cold rainwater and held it in place over the ribs of his back to soothe his bruising. When Soldier returned, he sniffed for scents around the sheep pen area, before sitting on guard near to the fire. Later, Eamonn arrived on horseback with Cormac riding pillion.

'I see your boxing skills are slipping,' Eamonn greeted, looking at Patrick's colourful and closing eyes.

'You speak the truth. I never threw a punch. I wouldn't have got a slingshot off if Soldier hadn't come to my aid.'

The visitors joined Patrick and sat on stones round the fire.

'What happened?' Eamonn asked.

'I was attacked from front and back by two men. They tried to capture me. Soldier mauled them, I got a slingshot off and between us we frustrated their efforts and they ran away.'

'And the sheep?' Cormac enquired.

'They didn't get any but they'll be back. I trailed them to a handcart, which they've hidden in the woods,' Patrick stoked the fire. 'I can offer you a bowl of hot porridge.'

'We'll take the porridge then,' said Cormac, answering for both Eamonn and himself. He handed a packet to Patrick, containing a few pieces of bread and a flask of ale. Patrick handed back an empty flask.

'Have you seen their faces before?' Eamonn asked.

'I haven't. But the tall one had an accent. From the Lough Conn area I think.'

'How would you know this?' Eamonn asked.

'He told me what he'd do to me if I didn't lie down for him. His accent was distinct and the same as that of a man I spoke to at the fayre, who was from the Lough Conn area.'

'Do you think the man from the fayre and your assailant are connected?'

'I have no reason to think it,' Patrick replied. 'However, I would recognise the man again. His eyes were brown and his pupils a queer shape.'

Eamonn stood to leave. 'I'll find the cart and smash it,' he said.

Patrick looked across to Cormac, who had not moved.

'I'm staying till the end of lambing,' said Cormac, reading Patrick's face. He stood to bid farewell to Eamonn as he mounted, and they shook hands.

Eamonn turned his horse towards Patrick and asked, 'Where was Soldier when you were attacked?'

'I couldn't see Soldier, but he was nearby.'

'Then how did they get to you first?'

Patrick remained silent awhile, his face inscrutable. 'That's how it happened,' he replied.

'Something to ponder then,' Eamonn replied with a stern gaze.

Just then, Soldier lay down before Eamonn's horse, whimpering. He began to lick his side. Eamonn stopped and dismounted. He examined Soldier's fur where he was licking and found a mark in the flesh, surrounded by an area of blotching.

'Perhaps your answer is here. I would say your attackers used a poison tip to make Soldier unconscious. He's had a close escape. Look, they only nicked him,' said Eamonn, directing Cormac and Patrick's attention to the small wound. Patrick was doubly relieved. Firstly, that Soldier hadn't been knocked out by the poison and secondly, that Eamonn's suspicions about Soldier's behaviour had been allayed.

'You are the cleverest dog I know,' added Eamonn as he stroked and congratulated Soldier. He remounted and as he rode away called back, 'I'll be making some excellent firewood shortly. Keep well.'

Patrick and Cormac discussed the details of the attack, as Eamonn headed for the woods.

'The late warning, was it a howl?' Cormac asked.

'How did you guess?'

'I've heard Soldier howl when he's been injured. I think Eamonn is right about the close escape. Something is strange though. Your attackers have taken care not to kill the king's dog or the king's slave. Had they killed Soldier, you would have been overpowered or killed and they would have snatched up the newborn lambs.'

They heard a sudden crash from the ravine below the woods. Crows rose from the trees in a flurry and formed a black cloud, only to swoop back down to their starting point and quickly resettle.

'Our firewood,' said Patrick with a chuckle.

'I believe so. We'll investigate in the morning. Tonight, you need rest, Patrick, but before we settle, show me your back.'

Patrick pulled down his tunic and Cormac looked at the damage.

'Oh! Patrick. You're black and blue. And you've a mighty weal. The skin is broken but it's started to heal already. A cold night will do well for your swelling.'

Patrick could see the pain on Cormac's face.

'How can you take such a beating in your stride?' he asked, shaking his head in disbelief.

'It's better that I can't see it, Cormac. I'll sleep further from the fire tonight.'

* * *

Patrick and Cormac were sitting on stones around a generous campfire, listening to the cracking and snapping sounds as the flames devoured the sticks and splinters from the handcart, which Patrick had salvaged from the ravine the previous day.

'The flock will be doubled by Beltaine,' Cormac said.

'I'm looking forward to the fayre this year,' said Patrick, staring through the shimmering smoke at Cormac who appeared to be swirling and swaying like an escaping genie. As they spoke, Eamonn arrived on horseback accompanied by a man on foot. Patrick and Cormac rose to their feet in welcome, but their visitors were unable to raise a smile.

'Greetings, Cormac; Patrick, meet Donal, he's a valley shepherd for King Miliucc,' Eamonn said matter-of-factly.

Greetings were exchanged then Cormac gestured to two log seats, 'Please join us.'

They all sat round the fire. Patrick was apprehensive. Something serious was afoot and they were about to find out.

'That's a great fire you've got going,' Eamonn stated without any cheer.

'We have great firewood,' Patrick responded.

'That's the only good thing the handcart has brought us,' said Eamonn solemnly. 'I bring bad tidings. Let me say it straight, Cormac; Durmaid is dead. His burial is to be on the half-moon.'

Patrick and Cormac were gripped by silence. Patrick hadn't heard the name Durmaid but the grave faces of Eamonn and Cormac chilled the air. The news was somehow connected to the handcart, which worried Patrick.

After a long silence, Cormac asked, 'When and where did Durmaid die?'

'He was killed on the Lough Conn track, two nights ago.'

'In our kingdom or Conn's?' Cormac asked.

'Conn's,' Eamonn answered. Patrick saw Cormac close his eyes for a few seconds, as though bracing himself for disastrous repercussions.

'What were the circumstances?' Cormac asked.

'We were together,' Eamonn said, 'tracking the handcart.' Patrick winced. 'One of the wheels had been repaired with an iron clamp, which left an impression that stood out from the other wheel marks. It led us to the Carroncullin smithy.' Cormac nodded. 'We know Creann, the blacksmith there, and invited him to the Voclut Fayre to discuss pricing some large ironwork jobs for King Miliucc. He didn't hide the fact that they were desperately short of work

162

and were only surviving because of a small contract for King Conn's chieftain. He gladly accepted the invitation.'

Patrick saw Cormac's puzzled look and wondered where the story was leading.

'As we left and passed from the side track to the main track we were ambushed by farmers and ditch diggers. We charged the attackers. I was brought from my horse as the attackers pulled at the reins and led the horse into a field. Durmaid turned back to help me onto his horse. As I got on the back, Durmaid took a pike in the gut. I was the shake of a ram's tail from the same fate when the tallest of the attackers brought down his club on the back of Durmaid's attacker, "The horse, you idiot, not the man," he screamed and swore at the labourer. This action saved me. We made our escape. I looked back to see the tall man hoofing Durmaid's attacker on the ground, kicking his emphasis, "You kill the king's man, we lose everything." Durmaid died in my arms, on the horse, as we tried to put distance between us and the mob.'

'How is King Miliucc?'

'Sorely distressed. He's lost a trusted security guard and a loyal friend.'

'Has the king decided his response?' Cormac asked. Patrick held his breath as he waited for Eamonn's answer.

'He has. Patience and persuasion have failed. King Miliucc will take steps to recover his assets by force, while his kingdom is strong enough to win. Durmaid's burial will take place first. The war planning has begun and will be executed in the days after the burial. Which leads me to the arrangements affecting you,' said Eamonn, gesturing to Cormac, Patrick, and Donal. Patrick listened gravely. 'For now, Donal will stay with you, Patrick, to assist you with the sheep. Cormac, you will return with me tonight. The king wishes you to attend the meetings and discussions of his War Council, as an adviser. Afterwards, you will return here to release Patrick. You, Patrick, will join the warriors to fight in the battles.'

Patrick sat still, silent as stone, trying to take in the situation. He felt guilty that his skirmish with the sheep stealers had triggered a kingdom war. If he hadn't followed the raiders and found their cart, the guards wouldn't have followed the trail to King Conn's smithy. Durmaid would still be alive. Patrick stood up and turned to face the hills in contemplation. But killing the king's guard was the trigger, in an unprovoked attack. All the raids, all the thieving, the killing of guard dogs, the injury to guards: the entire situation was responsible. The next thought in Patrick's mind, seeping in slowly, pouring into every recess, overwhelming all other thoughts, and filling his mind with dread, was Eamonn's message:

'You, Patrick, will fight in the battles.'

Patrick felt fear and prayed internally, where he was standing, with eyes open.

Dear God, two seasons ago I didn't want to live. Now, thanks to you, Lord, I don't want to die. Help me to conquer my fear.

Having passed on the problem, he felt calmer, knowing he would be able to cope. Patrick's thoughts moved on to Durmaid and the king.

'Master, have I met King Miliucc's guard, Durmaid?' Patrick asked solemnly, having caught the eye of Eamonn. Patrick saw Donal's eyebrows lift in shock as he asked the question.

'He was the chief guard in the king's retinue when you journeyed from the slave market to Voclut,' Eamonn answered snappily.

Patrick remembered him. He gave the speech advising that no foreign slave ever escaped Ireland. Meanwhile, Cormac had packed his bag swiftly and was now ready. After brief farewells he left with Eamonn, Cormac riding pillion.

When they were out of sight, Donal asked Patrick, 'Where would you like me to lay my bed?'

Patrick was pleased to see that Donal, a man in his mid-thirties, was unperturbed to be assisting a younger man. As for sleeping, Patrick knew that inside the pen was sheltered from cold winds and breezes and he disliked the cold. However, if he slept outside the pen, he was nearer to the fire, close to Soldier and, in the event of intruders, he would be the front line and Patrick preferred to be the one doing the calling.

'Inside the pen wall,' said Patrick pointing to the general area. Donal nodded, unable to hide his delight.

They ended the evening with a hot drink, during which time Patrick told Donal the lay of the ranges and pens. Patrick didn't encourage conversation, but Donal slipped in an observation,

'I see you get on well with the king's men.'

'I do,' was Patrick's answer. 'Now let the day be ended.'

* * *

Five evenings later, Cormac arrived on foot while Patrick and Donal were penning the sheep. Patrick, seeing Cormac's serious face, stood respectfully but avoided greeting him, preferring to let Cormac speak first and set the tone.

'Carry on with your work. We'll speak when you are finished,' Cormac said to Patrick and Donal.

They continued penning and counting and, as they worked, Cormac stoked up the fire. Patrick was feeling grim. He already knew the news. Donal put on a show of apprehension, though fully aware that he was the lucky one. When the work was finished, they approached Cormac who was seated at the fire. The two shepherds stood like criminals waiting to hear their fate.

'Patrick, pack your bag immediately and go to Voclut. Tonight, you will sleep in my house. Report at sunrise to a commander in front of Eamonn's workshops, where you will join other warriors. Take your spear and dagger.' He turned to Donal. 'Donal, you stay here with me.'

As Patrick packed his bag, he felt afraid of battle. He placed his sling and two stones in one of the hidden pockets of his tunic and thought, as a shepherd I'm confident I can fight, to win or to survive, but I've never fought in a battle. I'm worried my life is in someone else's hands.

In another pocket he placed the pishogue from Bride. He had his own protection but he took the charm to hold when he was thinking of her. Patrick decided to wear his boots and socks but not the leg windings. His dagger and small knife were already secure on his belt. He took hold of the best quality spear in his collection. The one he acquired from Shifty, then turned to face Cormac and for want of better words said,

'How do I look?'

'There'll be prettier sights than you, Patrick. Good luck and try to stay out of trouble.' Cormac gave Patrick a hug.

Patrick bade farewell to Cormac and Donal and set off for Voclut.

CHAPTER TWELVE

The small roundhouse in Voclut felt eerie without Cormac and was dark as soot with the fire out. Patrick could have lit the candles but decided to settle straight into his night-time routine of prayers and sleep.

He rose before dawn and made his way to the workshop where he was pleased to see tables with bread and cheese and pots of rainwater for drinking. A few warriors had arrived, and more were drifting in. They were shabbily dressed; some wore sandals, others shoes, and many were barefoot. The well-equipped warriors carried pikes and wore daggers on their belts; some carried axes and knives. Many, from the farming community, carried work tools such as spades, wooden shafts; any implement that could be wielded. Those with no weapons were issued with a spear. Nothing Patrick saw gave him confidence that this "land brigade" was a fighting force.

Patrick grabbed a mug, which was tied with twine to the water tub, took a scoop and drank a good swig of cold water. As he helped himself to bread and cheese, more warriors arrived. The commander and his leaders gathered them into groups of ten to make a headcount practical. As this was happening a cart arrived containing shields. Satisfied there were sixty warriors present the commander directed ten at a time to take a shield and to follow their leader on the walk to the battleground. Patrick was careful to choose a shield with a leather body strap. He didn't see the point in carrying the shield in hand while on a march in friendly territory; something he learned from mixing with Roman legionnaires at the Alauna Fort.

He joined the second group of ten and walked briskly with pride, holding his spear upright in his right hand with the shield pushed round to cover his back, held with the leather shoulder strap. His left hand was free to swing his arm with the rhythm of the march; except there was no marching. The Roman technique of striding out firmly, in unison, exuding confidence, demonstrating control and capability, clearly hadn't reached this part of Ireland. He had to slow down as all the groups rambled along making sloppy, ill-disciplined progress.

Have these men been trained? I've never fought a battle, but I've received Roman army training. What kind of an army can this scruffy rabble make? Patrick felt confident he would be a capable warrior. I'm probably a better fighter than those around me.

Marshals maintained an element of order and pace by prodding and beating the stragglers with sticks. Day dawned cool and fresh but soon became cloudy and overcast. The rabble arrived at an area of common land; King Miliucc, his bards and chief druid were already there on horseback. Across the open space King Conn's preparations mirrored Miliucc's.

Patrick saw their overall commander ride up to a group of commanders, one of which was Eamonn. After discussions, the commander-in-chief bawled out his instructions:

'Line one, assemble.' Twenty Miliucc warriors formed the front line. 'Line two, assemble.' Another twenty warriors formed line two.

At last, some evidence of training, Patrick thought, although he was surprised to see the well-trained warriors in the front lines.

'Land Brigade, make six lines of twenty.'

Men jostled, looking at each other for clues. Most couldn't count but they didn't need to as commanders and leaders pointed out the lines with their arms and pushed the men into position. Patrick took a place in the fourth row at the edge. There was no warrior to his left. It was then that he noticed King Miliucc's bard, on his white mount, moving regally into position to the left of the first row. He was joined by Miliucc's chief druid, robed in black and scarlet, astride a shiny black stallion. Patrick had learned that bards were sacred in war. It was their duty to observe the battles and record the events in poetry.

Why the druid? Will he pray to the gods for deliverance, perhaps, or to put a curse on the enemy?

As King Miliucc's warriors chatted and murmured to each other nervously, Patrick cast his eye to the opposing side. Their warriors were similarly dishevelled, but they only had four rows of twenty. Patrick scanned the vicinity for clues of warriors in hiding. There was no cover and a surprise attack was unlikely; the nearest forest being on the Conn side, more than three hundred strides away.

The murmurs died down; stillness descended. No birds were visible. There were no animal noises. Not even a chicken or cow or sheep in sight. Patrick began breathing through his nose and, though his heart wasn't racing, he could count the strengthening beats. Patrick believed superior fighting won battles and received no comfort from their advantage in numbers. His brow was now baubled with sweat. Patrick had never fought in battle before. In fact, he'd never spared a thought before for those whose duty it was to fight. Battle was imminent and the reality that some of their number would soon be injured, others killed crept into his mind. It was time for a prayer.

'Praise be to God. Last summer I didn't want to live and now I don't want to die. Lord, you saved me then, please deliver us all.'

A piercing wail filled the air shocking Patrick out of his prayer. It was the opposing chief druid calling attention. Slowly his wailing transformed into a rhythmic chant. The druid proceeded to dance himself into a frenzy, and beseeched the God of Fire to consume the enemy. He then lay submissive on the ground, letting silence do his work.

Miliucc's druid pierced ears with his own call for attention, then prayed in a clear and projected voice to the spirits of East, South, West, and North:

'Let the trees run with blood before these men lose theirs.' Then he too lay prone on the ground before his chosen gods.

After a solitary silence, a farmer ran screaming from the woods. 'The trees are bleeding. The trees are bleeding.'

As both commanders hesitated, Conn's bard galloped his horse to the yew trees, saw for himself and galloped back.

'It's the sap. The sap runs red,' he roared, 'the trees aren't bleeding,' contradicting the farmer's account.

A murmur ran through both armies. Patrick knew that yews have red sap, but why did the farmer come running? Had he heard the druid's words from that distance? This occurrence would not be remarkable to a man living next to a yew forest.

The words of the bard, 'The sap runs red,' were heard by the warriors who passed it on; the message becoming progressively louder. The Conn bards faced their commander.

'The sap runs red; the trees aren't bleeding. Command your men to action,' he bellowed indignantly.

A Miliucc warrior called out what he thought he heard,

'The sap runs red; the trees are bleeding.'

The message spread like a headwind to the ears of every Miliucc warrior, compelling the Conn bard to yell at his commander,

'Send your men into action.'

But his instruction was drowned as the murmur on the Conn side became a unified chant, in both camps.

'The sap runs red; the trees are bleeding.'

Patrick couldn't hear the words clearly; the trees are bleeding or the trees aren't bleeding, but it didn't matter, the bard's contradiction, misheard by the warriors, had become an overwhelming confirmation of the Miliucc druid's request for the trees to run with blood before the men lose theirs.

Patrick strained to see and hear everything; then he saw the Conn warriors throw their weapons to the ground and lay face down. He couldn't believe what was happening. How could warriors disobey their commanders? How could they respond simultaneously without some form of coordination? Their commander, wild-eyed with fear, threw his own weapons down and joined his men on the ground. Patrick, relieved the fight wouldn't happen, laughed at the comedy he'd just witnessed. He glanced to Miliucc's commander, who began bellowing clear instructions,

'Guards, shackle the enemy. Land army, wait.'

The guards instructed warriors to pull hand carts filled with shackles from the side-lines to the arena. The front rows of trained warriors began chaining their docile enemy. Six oxcarts were signalled to be brought to the enemy front line. Once in position the commander called out,

'Land army; fill the carts with their weapons.'

Patrick looked around before joining the fray. He saw King Miliucc riding towards his bard but saw no sign of a trap. Baffled by the events, he followed instructions and began filling a cart with pikes and poles. Then he saw the Conn bard raising a green flag of surrender. Bards from both sides, with a group of guards, came together in discussion. Shortly, both kings and their retinues made their way out of the arena.

Patrick heard the chatter of the warriors around him.

'They're going for talks,' they were saying.

Meanwhile, Miliucc's commander directed the construction of a temporary camp and duties were doled out. Unexpectedly for Patrick, he was set to preparing fires, on which to boil pots of broth. Farmers hammered posts into the ground, joining them with twine to divide the field into sections. Shackled captives were brought before two legal and administrative bards, one from each kingdom. From where he stood tending the fires, Patrick could overhear the proceedings.

'Clan name?' King Miliucc's bard asked.

'Miurchu.'

Occupation?'

'Milk cow farmer.'

'Stand over there.'

Both bards scratched notes on their wax tablets and continued until hundreds of men had been segregated and grouped into clans and occupations. At the same time, pots of broth were bubbling for the servant classes and spits began turning as roasted pig and root vegetables were prepared for the enjoyment of the nobles. Patrick was instructed to work on the spits and serve. He heard hooves and looked up as the two kings and their retinues rode into the camp. All dismounted except the kings who took position in front of the warriors and servants. The crowd quietened eager to hear the pronouncements. King Miliucc spoke first.

'Today, Conn's Kingdom has repaid debts to my kingdom. I have accepted land as payment because Conn's Kingdom is poor in cattle. These lands include an outlaw settlement. Every male outlaw who fights for me will have his clan's name restored.' King Miliucc moved over, making way for King Conn who brought his horse forward a few steps and said:

'This day, I sold the lands from Cloonkala to Innisfall. King Miliucc now owns them. The clans affected are…' he nodded to his legal bard who called out six clan names. Patrick studied the faces of those concerned, who were conveniently grouped by clan. Patrick, oddly, he thought, witnessed most of the captives cheering, though a few dissenters shook fists and yelled insults at their king. King Conn, ignoring the insults of the clans who were unhappy to be sold, spoke again.

'The settlement of our debts to King Miliucc makes us smaller as a kingdom, but we are still poor in livestock, therefore I have sold two more territories to King Miliucc. We will receive cattle and swine in payment, ensuring our smaller kingdom enjoys better living.'

His legal bard once again read out the names of the clans affected. When the organisational arrangements were concluded Conn made an announcement to the people.

'King Miliucc and I have provided food and drink. Enjoy your meal and go as directed to your place of work.'

The kings dismounted and, as grooms led their horses away, the nobles made their way to the refreshments. Patrick was serving at the spits when King Miliucc approached him.

'How is my young shepherd?'

'Puzzled at today's events, M'lord,' Patrick replied, passing a serving of roots and roast to the king.

'You have a point, but take care of yourself, Patrick. Tomorrow the blood will be real,' King Miliucc said, before moving on.

So, King Miliucc too, thinks the events of the morning were not real.

Patrick and the other servants on the spits were lucky to enjoy the nobles' leftovers which were more substantial than the broth. Thereafter, King Miliucc's fighting force was assembled, now double in size, and they straggled five miles to the vicinity of the Eastern border.

Arriving at a defended hill fort, the warriors climbed a meandering track to a plateau surrounded by earthen mounds. The hill fort was a large farming community with many farmsteads and homesteads within the perimeter. The warriors were herded into sections of a field, some by clan, and others by trade. A guard directed Patrick and fifteen warriors into an enclosure, leaving them without any explanation of what would happen next. A slave standing near Patrick caught his eye.

'I'm Crimthan,' he said in a friendly manner.

'I'm Patrick.'

'You a cattleman?'

'I'm a shepherd.'

'Who ya work for?'

'I work for King Miliucc,' Patrick answered, wondering if he would receive a positive reaction.

'You know Bognan then? Hey Bognan. Meet Patrick. He's a shepherd for Miliucc.'

Bognan came over. He looked at Patrick quizzically, and asked, 'Where do you work?'

'In the Hills of Voclut. I've taken over from Cormac.' As they spoke, some leaders entered the enclosure. Patrick turned to see Eamonn and two guards arriving on foot. Eamonn spoke.

'Tomorrow, we intend to beat Moycullen in battle and take

livestock back into our kingdom. Everyone here will be called to bring the animals to Miliucc's hill fort. Defend well tomorrow and stay alive. In the cart over there you will find good quality shields. If you don't have a shield, take one. If you have a weak or damaged shield you must exchange.' Eamonn looked up the hill and pointed to a tall roundhouse. 'You will all sleep in this bed house. Leave your weapons by your bed and take further instructions from your house guard.' Eamonn strode out of the enclosure followed by his guards.

Patrick and most of the other Miliucc slaves followed the threadbare path directly to the bed house. Only a few headed to the cart for a new shield. A small spiral of smoke escaped from the pointed thatch, indicating there was a fire burning in their accommodation house.

A guard at the door called out to the group.

'Place your belongings on a bed, including all weapons, then go for food and ale over there.'

Patrick's eye followed the direction to hay barns made of wooden uprights, supporting a thatched roof. One was clearly in use as a kitchen and alehouse. He filed with the others into a dark, soot-lined sleeping accommodation. Fifteen straw mats filled the roundhouse perimeter, fan-like on the ground. A low central fire burned, dimly lighting the otherwise empty room. Patrick, Crimthan, Bognan and one other stayed together and claimed their space. Patrick placed his dagger and knife beside his mattress and covered them with his shield. He kept his sling and shot, which was hidden in an internal pocket, and made his way with the other three to the food and ale hostel. On the way they passed cattle enclosures filled with cows and the possessions of warriors, reminding Patrick of his own first night sleeping with cattle. At the time, his dignity had been offended, but he'd learned that once you had accustomed yourself to the stench, the place was dry and warm.

'Why is there a guard on our roundhouse?' Patrick asked aloud to anyone who would answer.

'We're the king's slaves. We get better treatment,' said Crimthan.

Patrick wasn't satisfied with the answer. 'What are we being guarded from?' he asked.

'Is this your first battle, Patrick?' Bognan asked half mocking.

'It is, if we actually fight.'

'We'll fight for sure. Miliucc wants his cattle back. King Moycullen has stolen too much from him over the last year or two. This battle is serious and when we've won, our job is to handle the livestock for him, so he doesn't want us caught up in drunken fights. Another reason is that he owns us. He paid for us, so he's looking after his property.'

'We're slaves, but special slaves then!' Patrick summarised.

'We are. Come, let's fill our bellies,' said Bognan.

Patrick followed his new friends, who seemed to know their way around. They entered an innocuous looking roundhouse rather than the large open-sided barn which was crowded with warriors, some already in high spirits. This building was an alehouse and less busy than the barns. There, slave girls ladled out bowls of mutton broth and served jugs of ale. The men, seated on scattered logs, ate and drank their fill. Patrick enjoyed the hot food and warm room. It was a welcome change from coldness that was his constant enemy in the hills. The conversation helped his Irish Gaelic speaking, too. Food and drink flowed and they all returned for more broth. As the men were exchanging stories, Memnon, the fourth man introduced himself to Patrick and was telling, at Patrick's request, how he came to be a slave.

'My father was a farmer under contract to King Miliucc. The king had issued him with a herd of milk cows and for a few years everything went well, until his herd caught a disease. He began failing payments then thieves stole some of his remaining cows. He couldn't pay his dues to the king so he sold me and my brother to Miliucc in settlement.'

The story upset Patrick. He struggled with the idea that a father could sell his sons into slavery to pay off a debt. It was the same tale as Cuchu told. Bognan was listening.

'Patrick, tell us your story. How did you become a Miliucc slave?' he asked.

'I'm from The Britains. One morning before sunrise, I was attacked from behind whilst working on my father's land. They blindfolded me and shackled me to other captives. We were bundled into a boat and brought to Ireland, where I was sold at a slave market to King Miliucc.'

'What was your work?' Bognan asked.

'I managed some of my father's business estate. He owned farms and craft businesses.'

'So, you've never really worked?' Bognan retorted.

Patrick squirmed a little. 'I worked. But I admit my position was given to me.'

'So, you can't fight either,' Bognan pressed.

'Not true. I can fight.'

'Born rich. Never worked. How can you fight?'

'I can box, stick-fight and throw a spear,' Patrick replied quickly, carefully using the word spear instead of javelin.

'How did you learn?'

'Our villa was next to a Roman Fort. I practised with Roman soldiers. They taught me to fight and I learned the tactics of fighting.'

'Was this in battle?'

'It was in sport.'

Bognan shook his head in disbelief. 'Tomorrow, if you want to live, stay at the back. Come on, let's go to the beds.'

Maybe I won't be as good as I think. I haven't fought in a life-or-death battle before.

They made their way to the hostel and bid their good nights to the guard. Some of the slaves were already sleeping, in sharp contrast to the revelry going on in the alehouses and barns. Patrick and the group quickly settled on their beds in the clothes they were wearing.

Patrick lay on his back in thought. His concentration was interrupted by a persistent nudge. He looked and saw Memnon offering him a tipple.

'Here. Get some strong stuff down ya. It'll help you to sleep.'

'Not for me, Memnon. I'll sleep anyway, because I'm tired,' Patrick answered.

'You not worried about tomorrow?' Memnon asked.

'I was, but I'm not now. I've given my worries to God. Sleep well yourself.'

Memnon, with a puzzled look, gave up trying with Patrick and took another good swig of spirit for himself. Patrick, not wishing to provoke Bognan anymore, prayed silently, not even mouthing his words. He finished off by internally humming "The Lord is my Shepherd", which comforted Patrick as it did the sheep. Aware of being free from guard duty and indeed being guarded himself, he fell into deep sleep.

* * *

Before sunrise the guard stirred the warriors and directed them outside. Patrick was first to a barrel of cold water which had been provided for the men to dip-wash their heads. Further along was a table of mugs and half a barrel of drinking water. Patrick dunked his head in the barrel and dried himself on the towel which was tied with twine to the to the table leg. He took a good swig of water and moved on to the trays of cheese chunks. By now all the men were outside, rinsing their heads in turn, scooping up mugs of water and standing around as they ate their cheese. Crimthan and Memnon joined him, but Bognan noticeably kept his distance.

'Finish your cheese, gather your weapons and stand over there.' The guard pointed to the top of the hillside track.

The men assembled slowly, still waking up on this damp and dingy morning. A young slave arrived pulling a handcart fully laden with spears.

The guard called out, 'Take a spear and make your way to the bottom of the hill, where you will turn left and keep walking.'

Motley groups of men merged uncertainly in the ground mists. 'Follow the king's men,' an anonymous voice commanded. Patrick and company turned left as instructed.

Most of these warriors wore dirty greyish-yellow tunics. King Miliucc's slaves, recognisable by their cleaner and smarter appearance, led the way to an area of open common land, busy with commanders and guards organising the arriving warriors into lines. Eventually ten lines of thirty men were formed, facing a similar arrangement of Moycullen warriors, only fifty strides away, across the open space. Patrick and his friends were in the eighth row, until Bognan glared at Patrick.

'Better you stay away from me,' he said.

Patrick was unperturbed. He had an idea for dealing with Bognan. He faced him, uncowed, their eyes locked. Bognan's stare was mean and aggressive, Patrick's, confident and inscrutable. They held the stare without blinking. Then Patrick halted the exchange and dropped back a line, taking position behind Memnon and Crimthan. Bognan fixed Patrick with a self-satisfied smile and glanced across at Crimthan and Memnon for recognition; Patrick had surrendered the staring-out victory to Bognan, tactically, and was satisfied. In row nine, he had in mind to use a Roman fighting technique.

By now Patrick was observing the relaying of messages to and from their chief commander. He saw druids in white, full-length robes, gathering at the sides, near to the front rows. Bards with coloured breast panels that indicated their specialities, arrived on horseback, taking position behind the druids. Their presence triggered a cackle of nervous chatter amongst the warriors on both sides.

On the Moycullen side a druid riding a shiny black stallion, came into view. He wore a cape of crimson and purple. Stopping his horse a few paces into the open ground, he remained mounted and began to chant quietly. The chilly morning mist thickened and drifted across the arena, creating mystique for Moycullen's chief druid. Chanting quietly at first then with rising volume and rhythm, words could be made out.

Mór Rio ghain. Mór Rio ghain…

The chant sped up gradually – until Patrick heard, 'Morrigan, Morrigan, Morrigan,' – becoming frantic, then desperate, and finally screeching until the druid fell from his horse in a trance.

His screaming pitch continued, rising higher and higher, his head rocking forwards, backwards; now violently forwards and violently backwards until his head was beating rhythmically into the ground, accompanied by the simultaneous slapping of both palms against the earth.

The scene scared everyone present. A solitary crow, circling overhead, wark-warked and, swooping down, landed a few strides from the head-banging druid. The crow, unconcerned by the priest's performance, had her eye on more interesting matters and began pecking at a handful of twitching, long-legged locusts on the ground. The druid, face down on the dry soil, opened an eye as he came out of his trance. The crow snapped up the last of the bugs. The druid opened his other eye and bowed before the bird. The crow faced the priest and still as a pond, looked at him with one eye. Her head twitched a notch and now she stared at him with the other eye, motionless; then took off to the high skies.

All the warriors gasped. But King Miliucc's warriors were shaking with fear.

Patrick heard the woeful wailing of warriors in front of him and behind him. 'We're doomed. She came to him.' Patrick listened, amazed at the strength of these men's belief in superstition.

'Morrigan gave a sign,' a warrior declared.

'I once saw Morrigan as a crow. She was on my side, the winning side.'

Patrick tapped Crimthan on the shoulder, 'Who is Morrigan?'

'She's the Goddess of warmongering.'

'Is she a crow?'

'Sometimes; she's a shape-shifter. They say being a crow is her favourite transformation.'

'Crimthan, are you scared?' Patrick asked.

'I am. Are you?'

'I'm not scared of Morrigan. I believe the crow was hungry and swooped down to eat some grubs and grasshoppers.'

As Moycullen's chief druid withdrew, Patrick saw their nobles congratulating him. But another druid grandly entered the arena dressed in red and pale blue robes, astride a white horse. Crimthan turned back to Patrick.

'He's Druid Eochaid, King Miliucc's chief druid.'

Fear-stricken Miliucc warriors waited on his words. Druid Eochaid took a more central position. He raised an arm and held a majestic pose. When total silence ruled, he spoke in prayerful voice, clear as spring water. His words carried like a breeze.

'Goddess Brighid, we love you. Goddess Brighid, your love of livestock is legend. We thank you. Goddess Brighid, you fill our fields with life. We thank you. Goddess Brighid, you fill our animals with life. We thank you. Goddess Brighid, you fill our people with life. We love you.'

As he prayed, the mist, obscuring the sunrise, thinned. Druid Eochaid saw his moment and didn't miss.

'Goddess Brighid let every man present witness your love.'

Patrick saw it too. As the golden orb rose above the horizon, the mist evaporated in its warmth and a new day dawned.

'Praise be to Brighid. Brighid. Imbolc.' Eochaid raised his arms, encouraging the warriors to repeat.

'Brighid. Imbolc,' the Miliucc warriors repeated. Patrick tugged at Memnon's clothing and, when he turned, he asked,

'What does Brighid Imbolc mean?'

'She's the Goddess of fertility,' Memnon answered.

'Brighid. Imbolc,' led druid Eochaid.

'Brighid. Imbolc,' the Miliucc warriors responded and a few Moycullen warriors joined in. Patrick saw the hold of the druids, on both sides, over the minds of the warriors; the Moycullen druid generating fear; the Miliucc druid presenting hope and love.

'Once more. Brighid. Imbolc,' Eochaid exhorted.

King Miliucc's men were rapturous by now and quite a few of King Moycullen's men were too.

'Brighid. Imbolc,' boomed around the arena and, with immaculate timing, druid Eochaid left the scene, as golden sunshine glowed, warming the bodies and the hearts of the men. The fertility of spring seemed assured to all present. Miliucc's warriors had forgotten their fear of Morrigan. Brighid would see them prosper. They were already chattering, fertility for crops, fertility for livestock and fertility for men and women.

Yesterday Patrick saw the druid rites as theatre. Today, he clearly saw the purpose and Druid Eochaid had done his job well. Patrick stretched to see his king's demeanour, spotting Miliucc expressing satisfaction to his chief druid.

Miliucc's commander rode to the front and bellowed out to his men, 'Morrigan won't fight Moycullen's battle, be sure of that.' He let the words reach ears and minds. 'But we'll fight ours. And Goddess Brighid will bless us.'

He moved to the side and called his men to action. 'Spears ready... Throw.'

'Spears ready... Throw,' came like an echo from the Moycullen side.

A hail of spears arched through the sky, passing each other and occasionally clashing. Within seconds the ears of the warriors were deafened by the frightening salvo of iron-tipped spears clattering against shields. The silent landings were the problem though, as shrieks of pain told the tale of tips penetrating flesh. Injured men fell to the ground, some to recover, others to die. The lines of warriors charged, axes swung, daggers plunged. Killing and maiming took over.

Patrick and company were now close to the middle of the fray. Patrick positioned himself behind Memnon and Crimthan, his dagger still in its sheath because he hadn't thrown it when instructed. Patrick was crouching in row nine, and along with his spear and tip, hidden by row eight. He watched the action and, when his fellow fighters were engaged in one-on-one battles, he intended to spear off the side attacks. Crimthan, fighting a dagger attack from his right, didn't see an axe-wielding warrior intent on chopping him in half, on his unguarded left side. Axeman was shielded but Patrick saw a small exposed area below the man's ribs. With a two-handed hold, Patrick buried his spear tip in the man's side. He felt resistance, like he was piercing tough leather and after a moment's standstill the spear continued easily. The man's face was a picture of pure shock as he opened his mouth wide. Crimthan was spared. As all power drained from Axeman's arm, he looked for the source of the mortal blow, but fell before seeing his attacker. Patrick, not fully realising that he'd killed a man, noticed how difficult it was to remove his spear. His victim's face, to Patrick's surprise, did not show agony and fear, but screwed up a little and frowned as though he had a headache. A flow of blood poured from the spear wound, forming a pool on the ground as Patrick's victim closed his eyes and lay lifeless.

Patrick reflected on his victim's fate. The man was shocked, caught by surprise and died before he knew what happened. His body didn't experience agony, his mind missed out on terror, and then a Moycullen warrior, who'd broken through the lines, attacked Patrick with a dagger. Patrick had recovered his spear, which was too long for close combat; and his attacker was on him. With his shield on his back, Patrick swivelled, just in time to protect his body from the plunging dagger. He pivoted round to face his attacker; taking his dagger from its sheath in the process, and with momentum, hacked into his assailant's dagger arm. Patrick's attacker dropped his weapon and clutched his arm as another warrior felled him from behind.

Patrick returned his own dagger to its sheath and noticed Bognan returning to battle having just glimpsed behind. Patrick tucked in behind Crimthan and Memnon again and in a slight lull in the action he began to realise he'd killed a man. It didn't seem real, but the fight was developing again. Haphazard fighting replaced the orderly rows of warriors, but Patrick stayed behind his friends who remained grouped together. Patrick moved over to the fighting on his right and positioned himself between Bognan and Crimthan. An enemy warrior brought down a fearsome looking axe heavily on a Miliucc fighter, splitting open his shield and bundling him to the ground. He was spared from the killing strike as Bognan struck the assailant with his dagger, badly wounding him and causing him to drop his axe. In an instant, Bognan snatched up the axe, but the half-second distraction was enough for his victim to make a final lunge at Bognan's gut with a small knife. Bognan, defeated, saw the knife stop short as the wielder faltered, having taken a spear thrust, deep into his side. Bognan turned to see Patrick with a white-knuckled grip of the spear shaft, pulling the buried tip from his victim's body. He nodded an acknowledgement to Patrick who returned the slightest of nods. The battle continued.

'Stay, stay!' Bognan shouted to Crimthan and Memnon. 'Don't be sucked in.'

They followed his advice and held back, fighting only when the fight came to them. The pace of activity slowed as men on both sides tired. The lull became an unannounced truce. Women entered the arena to care for the wounds of the injured warriors. Boys, not old enough to fight, were carrying away the dead and throwing their bodies into carts. The able took respite as women brought skins of water to the fighters. Bognan took a few glugs from a skin then passed it round to Patrick, Memnon and Crimthan. Patrick saw Bognan's eyes looking at him, thoughtfully.

'Patrick, did you throw your spear when the battle started?'

'I didn't. I kept hold of it and tucked in behind you three, watching out for the best opportunity to attack.'

'It worked. Where did the idea come from?' Bognan asked.

'Sport,' Patrick answered understatedly; satisfied that he had pulled off his plan for winning Bognan round.

'Let's swap places. I want to try for myself.' Just then their commander called attention for the warriors to line up. Patrick handed his bloodstained spear to Bognan and shifted his shield to the front before taking up his dagger. Bognan strapped his own shield to his shoulders, freeing both hands for the spear. Now both were ready for their new role.

Patrick estimated Moycullen's side had lost half of their warriors. King Miliucc's side were doing better. They had probably lost a third or less. Bognan was taking things in too, and cursing.

'Why hasn't Miliucc strengthened? He's got the men,' Bognan said to Patrick.

Something was happening. Patrick drew Bognan's attention

to the Moycullen side. An additional one hundred warriors were joining the lines.

'Strike me blind if I'm lying, we're outnumbered. What's going on?' Bognan uttered.

'I don't know. But Miliucc isn't stupid,' Patrick said, looking around for clues.

A hail of spears arrived in the sky, behind the heads of the Moycullen warriors. Patrick couldn't make it out. The Moycullen couldn't have thrown them; they'd been launched from further back. The spears rained down on the backs of the unsuspecting warriors. Iron spear tips pierced their soft, undefended targets, with deadly results. Moycullen commanders and warriors turned to see why their men were falling and were stricken with fear as they faced a second volley of spears from behind.

'Charge,' screamed Miliucc's chief commander.

Patrick, Bognan and all the Miliucc line-up ran to the battle. The front row of fighters picked off their bewildered enemy as a hundred screaming, hostile Miliucc warriors appeared at charging pace over a ridge, only fifty strides behind the Moycullen. The slaughter, inflicted by Miliucc's rear attack, intensified as the warriors stepped over speared corpses to battle at close quarters. At the front, Miliucc's warriors, like a hundred Setantas, tore through their opponents till the fighting slowed down.

'How have you found things with the dagger and shield?' Bognan asked Patrick.

'It's faster moving; and more to think about,' Patrick answered, 'And what about you, on the spear?'

'There's too much time to think. It's good for a group of men who know each other though.'

Warriors looked around as some called out excitedly. They began jumping up and down and cheering, pointing towards the good news. Patrick followed their gaze and saw a Moycullen bard riding forth with a green flag of surrender raised high. Moycullen's commanders were calling their men to cease battle. Patrick, jubilant that he'd survived, vowed to remain vigilant in the aftermath.

Patrick checked himself out for damage. His ribs at the back were sore and he felt a small flesh wound. He realised now, that he'd taken an injury when he'd spun round, and the dagger hit his shield. He investigated a large stain of blood on his tunic, above the hip and found his flesh beneath was untouched. It was someone else's blood. His hands were covered with sticky congealed blood. He spat on them and cleaned the excess on his dirty tunic. The little scrapes were not the cause; once again it was the blood of others, splashed around in battle.

'Let me look at your back, Patrick,' Bognan said. 'I saw you take the dagger hit.'

Patrick loosened his tunic and turned.

'It's just a nick. Your shield took the brunt. I thought you said this was your first battle. Your back is yellow and green with old bruises. You've been hammered.'

'Some sheep raiders did that to me. There were two of them. They didn't get any sheep though.' Patrick was glad that Bognan was seeing the real Patrick, and then their attention was called to other matters.

Miliucc's commanders were fast to take control. They called their warriors to stop fighting. Instructions were shouted out and soon oxcarts filled with chains were brought in from the sidelines. Teams of Miliucc's men were instructed to shackle the enemy warriors together. Patrick felt a sense of satisfaction that these captives had been beaten in battle, and he'd played his part. Empty ox-drawn carts and handcarts rumbled into the arena. The enemy, dead or alive, were stripped of their weapons, shields and any possessions of value. Miliucc soldiers, brimming with confidence and new energy, began filling the carts with the spoils of battle.

At the same time, a group of Miliucc's commanders, warriors and nobles could be seen disarming King Moycullen and his guards. Once King Moycullen and his nobles were surrounded by Miliucc's armed guards, the kings and noble retinues of both sides made their way, no doubt to a place where they could discuss the terms of peace. A Miliucc mounted commander worked his way through the warriors, picking out his master's slaves by their tunics. Fourteen were gathered and one had perished in battle.

'Join these men and their commanders,' he said pointing. Patrick, Bognan, Crimthan, Memnon and another ten Miliucc slaves were led through the battleground in an easterly direction. Patrick's practised eye scanned the lie of the land. He saw a slight depression along a gentle downhill slope, where warriors could assemble unseen by anyone from the battleground. The cover would have been within spear-throwing range of the enemy lines. Patrick was sure this was the spot from where the rear attack was launched. But where were the men hiding when Moycullen's reinforcements marched over this piece of land?

'Bognan,' Patrick called to his friend who was a few strides ahead of him. Bognan turned to see Patrick and joined him. 'Did you see the hidden ridge?'

'I did, and our commanders knew it was there,' Bognan answered.

'Moycullen's reinforcement didn't see our men. Where could they have hidden?' Patrick said, pointing to the open land.

'It's a mystery. Come on; let's catch up before the commander sees us lagging.'

The sun was high in the sky when they arrived at a large lake, stretching further than the eye could see. A massive island was situated in the centre, using the lake as a generous moat. Rich grazing lands, cattle houses, barns, workshops, and housing were visible on the island and access was by way of a wooden pier standing on posts a few feet above water level. Gated at both ends with a sturdy wooden lookout tower on the island, it was clearly built to keep out intruders.

'Whatever it is, it's a stronghold,' Patrick remarked.

'It's an island crannog,' Bognan answered.

'I've seen crannogs in Britain, but not so big and not in a lake,' Patrick said as more commanders and warriors arrived. All of King Miliucc's slaves were ordered, by their own commander, to join the new arrivals. They helped to build a day camp near the crannog entrance then sat around waiting.

'What are we doing here, Bognan?' Patrick asked.

'I guess Moycullen moved his cattle onto the crannog, he's probably housed a whole load of warriors here too.'

'So, the fighting hasn't finished?'

'It's finished. Moycullen's finished,' Bognan assured. 'We're waiting for the nobles to agree a settlement. King Miliucc has destroyed Moycullen. I thank our king that we are on the winning side. I've never seen such a decisive victory before.'

Patrick was finding a begrudging respect for Bognan. He was battle-wise with a grasp of the politics of kingdom rivalry. For a barbarian slave, Bognan was bright.

'Considering King Miliucc doesn't like war, he's good at it,' Patrick said.

The warriors stirred to their feet as a retinue of King Miliucc's nobles and warriors, led by Eamonn, arrived; they escorted Moycullen's disarmed commander and nobles. Patrick observed the commander instructing fifty warriors to support Eamonn's troop, as a Moycullen noble organised the opening of the gates. Moycullen, his men and Miliucc's brigade, crossed the planked bridge and entered the crannog as the second gate opened.

Patrick and the remaining warriors watched from the day camp and, after a long and restless waiting time, both gates opened. A single line of unarmed men, stripped to the waist, walked across the bridge. These forlorn fighters, heads dejectedly drooping, with only their hands held high, passed through the second gate, and were shackled by the Miliucc warriors.

The waiting resumed. Patrick, Bognan and Crimthan chatted in the sunshine, like it was the feast of spring. Patrick, aware that he had killed and maimed men earlier in the day, didn't show any signs of horror or regret in his demeanour. He knew, however, that his chatter was nervous, his humour, denial, and the fight wasn't over. They were still in enemy lands and more work, maybe dangerous work, had to be done. His first killing felt unreal and hadn't sunk in. He hardened his heart while he could, to see the job through and to not appear weak among his warrior friends. In truth he felt thrilled to have escaped death; a selfish emotion that worried him. Bognan broke his drift of thought.

'You were right, Patrick, you can fight.'

Patrick nodded modestly and responded with a gentle smile, 'Tactics were clearly in use today. I saw two good examples, would you agree?'

'I'd say three,' Bognan countered.

'Tell me them,' Patrick challenged.

Bognan obliged, 'When you speared from behind us, it was a good tactic. Secondly, our warriors launching a surprise attack from behind the enemy lines was a tactic so effective, it finished the battle.'

'Right,' Patrick agreed.

'You tell me the third example,' Bognan teased.

'It was you, Bognan, calling us to "stay, stay" when there was no value, but only risk, in advancing.'

'I agree,' said an obviously pleased Bognan. 'Now, let me ask you, how should Moycullen's commander have handled the ambush?'

'He could do nothing,' Patrick explained. 'It was too late, even before the battle started. A Roman commander would have formed his warriors into squares. Four facing forward, four backwards and two on each side, facing sideways, with four spearmen hidden in the centre.'

'How would they advance?'

'They would stand still and let the attackers come to them. But if they wanted to advance all the soldiers could run forwards, sideways and backwards, even at pace and keep their formation. They train and practice the movements. The commanders and warriors know what to do.'

'Why don't we think like that?' Bognan asked.

'I don't know, but I do know that blood in Ireland is spilled too willingly...'

Crimthan interrupted, 'Something's happening. A Miliucc guard has appeared,' he said looking at the inner gate.

'I think we're going in.' Patrick said.

CHAPTER THIRTEEN

Patrick looked up as a Miliucc guard rushed through the island gate and signalled to the waiting commander. He then called King Miliucc's slaves to enter the crannog. They quickly walked the planked pier where a guard met them at the gate. He led them into the crannog to a group of officials representing both kings.

'Gather round,' the Miliucc guard called. 'You each know your speciality, it is King Miliucc's wish that you identify good quality stock, free from disease, and bearing Miliucc or Moycullen markings. Livestock identified from neighbouring kingdoms are not valid as payment. Keep them separate. Your job is to count the stock which is Miliucc's due. When I call your name, you will step forward. Your bard will come to you, tell you your tasks and take you to your place of work.'

Patrick was third to be called.

'Patrick the shepherd.' He duly took a step forward. Two officials came to him, one from each king.

'We want three rams, twenty lambs and seventy ewes. Follow us,' his bard said, and signalled two slaves to follow them. Small gains, Patrick thought, when he considered how many lives were lost.

Patrick was led to a farm where several open pens, filled with sheep, were positioned adjacent to a barn containing equipment and tools. He worked out his approach then instructed his two helpers in their tasks. They settled into a rhythm, one of the helpers, with a strong and muscular physique was put to catching the sheep, Patrick to examining them, and the other, a weedy looking fellow, was to place them in the pens, as directed by Patrick. The helpers refused to assist Patrick in finding the best rams though. Grabbing rams by their testicles was not to their liking. Patrick enjoyed the tease and did the job himself. When all the one hundred and twenty-five sheep in the pens had been identified, tested, and segregated, Patrick called the officials, who then recorded the numbers and markings on scratch tablets.

Two thirds of the sheep and lambs carried Miliucc's markings; stolen in the first place. His helpers were from Conn's kingdom and recognised Conn's sheep markings. They pointed these out to Patrick, as a way of venting anger that the wealthy Moycullen would steal from starving Conn farmers.

Sadly, the men pointed out to Patrick a weakling sheep. The animal needed care and attention to have a chance of recovery. It was obvious to Patrick that the Moycullen farm would have other priorities. Patrick left the men working and approached the two officials.

'There is a sickly Moycullen sheep that needs a few days of nursing. Is there a shepherd at this location?'

The Moycullen official looked at the Miliucc official. 'We have but she's in the barn.' He was appealing with his look; a gesture Patrick didn't understand.

The Miliucc official directed two warriors to the barn, opened the door and the Moycullen official called. 'Moira, Moira come quickly.'

A woman, dressed as a shepherdess came to the door.

Patrick spoke, 'One of your sheep is ill. With a few days of help I think she'll survive. If I identify her with a twine round her neck, will you look out for her?'

'I will,' she answered, with a smile. 'Thank you,' and went back inside.

As the official closed the door, Patrick saw the barn was filled with women and children.

'What is going on in there?' Patrick asked his own official.

"You know Eamonn. Better to ask him,' came the answer. Patrick didn't have time for puzzles; he returned to his job, satisfied that his few minutes of attention may have given the sheep a chance of living.

Casting his mind back to his work, he thought, 'Any wonder that Ireland is poor?' He sighed, 'What now for Moycullen? A slave raid on Britain probably.' He imagined a raid where more young Britons like himself were stolen from the land and brought to Ireland as slaves.

Miliucc's bard came over to Patrick with new instructions.

'The next job is to place a new marker on the sheep we're taking. The powder will arrive on the next cart. While you are waiting, go to the roundhouse over there. You will find water for washing as well as food and drink.'

They followed the smell of roasting and came to the water barrels. Patrick stripped to the waist and washed his lean and muscly body, hands, and arms before dunking his dusty head and shoulder-length blond hair in the barrel. After squeezing the water out of his straightened mop, he made his way to the spits. Twenty cooked chickens were being removed and a further uncooked supply were being skewered. Servants were doling out chicken pieces and mugs of ale. There was a scramble for the bench tables, but soon the shepherds were sloshing down their food with gulps of ale.

As they finished eating Patrick called his helpers, 'Let's return to our place of work.'

The workers responded without delay. He could have been their commander and was shocked at how easily he slipped back into his former life's role of slave master. A scrawny carter arrived dragging a fully-laden handcart into their farm. King Miliucc's official immediately called him to account for his load. When the bard's list and the carter's load tallied, the official called Patrick over.

'Your powder and paddles are here,' he said, pointing to them in the cart.

Patrick's helpers took the supplies and were set to mixing a green paste. Soon all three were daubing the sheep with their new identities, applying the smear with wooden, spoon-shaped paddles.

The crannog farms were bustling with activity. A line of empty oxcarts had arrived, queueing to be loaded with sows and piglets. Commanders were shouting instructions to those at the near end of the bridge and more communications were being yelled from the far side.

Something is afoot, thought Patrick, looking round for clues. People had stopped working. Slaves were coming out of the fields and barns and forming lines at the track side, vying for position as if they were at a public event. The smell of cattle reached Patrick's nose, followed by mooing and snorting sounds. Cattlemen arrived, taking up positions on the track. The sound of hooves thumping the ground grew louder and louder and Patrick's excitement was already high.

The beasts came over the brow at a trotting pace, guided to the bridge by herders and slaves who stood shoulder to shoulder. Patrick, having never seen a cattle-run before, was astounded. No wonder people clamoured; this was an excitement not to miss. The procession of cattle, two or three abreast, passed before Patrick's nose. He spotted Bognan, running with the herd, waving a stick like a flail, hissing and hooing at the stragglers and strayers. The patter of hooves sharpened loudly as the animals entered the bridge and the bellowing bovines were drowned out by their own clatter as a thousand hooves beat out a rhythmic and ear-busting crescendo, crossing the wooden-planked pier in their hundreds.

Patrick's breathing pulsed to nature's drumbeat. Overwhelmed by the spectacle, he said aloud, 'There is the reason for the battle.'

The cattle noise died as the herd left the bridge and headed west. The people shifted back to work and, Patrick's official, striding through the crowd in search of him, commanded impatiently,

'Get the sheep ready to follow the carts.'

'Yes, master,' Patrick answered. 'Master, can we tie the rams to a cart?'

'You can. Be ready to move when the last cart is filled.'

Carters whipped their oxen into action and a dozen four-wheeled wagons, packed tight with swine, creaked heavily towards the bridge. Patrick opened the pen gate. His helpers secured the three rams to the cart and lay a track of broad leaves, a favourite food for the sheep, from the field to the track. The sheep took the bait slowly but Patrick was in a hurry and led the helpers in pulling and pushing and prodding the sheep until the entire flock was on the bridge, funnelled into following the procession of oxcarts. The sheep slipped and slithered on the greasy planks, made slimy with well-trodden, freshly dropped cow dung. The procession turned west, the way the warriors came and the sheep followed the rams and carts without thinking. The armed guards, some on foot, others mounted, served as herdsmen as well as protectors.

The procession came to the vicinity of the morning's battle and though making its own noise, the air became joyless, empty of birdsong, and the breeze died. A few corpses, stripped of weapons, some stripped of clothing, could be seen in ditches, missed by the burial boys. Even the pigs stopped squealing as the procession of warriors, livestock and wagons bumped and rolled over the field of the morning's battle. On they trudged, passing through deserted farmlands.

Patrick spotted the head of a boy, ducking out of sight behind a barrel; a woman scurrying with her head down, into a roundhouse.

'What next for them?' Patrick thought. In half a day, hundreds of women had lost their husbands and sons, and hundreds of children their fathers. There were farms without livestock, farms without farmers, and for the first time in Patrick's life, winning didn't feel good.

What next for us? We're victors but vulnerable; surrounded by unmendable grief, despair, hopelessness and, by consequence, vengeance. Patrick felt for the reassurance of his dagger, knowing well it was there. He checked his sling was in his tunic pocket and felt the two rounded stones. Redoubling his concentration, he cast his shepherd's vigilant eye on their surroundings, nervously looking ahead in the hope of seeing open ground. His wish was answered as they left the farmsteads and entered terrain that was safer from ambush.

They climbed a long and gentle slope then suddenly Eamonn called the train of wagons to a halt. Commanders passed the message rapidly up and down the line. Patrick was near to the problem. A pig cart was tilting dangerously where the track had crumbled away at the verge. Warriors were quick to put their shoulders to the cart, preventing it from rolling. Other warriors shored up the wheels with large stones and set to repairing the track; filling and digging and tamping down.

While at a standstill, the sheep wandered to the edges of the track on both sides and grazed idly on the succulent leaves and grasses growing out of the ditches. Patrick kept busy watching the sheep and scouring the vicinity, half expecting an attack while they were stopped. Nothing happened. Then the rhythm of a Celtic heaving song hit the air, as they pushed cart and contents back on track.

'Heave, heave all together, lift the wagon high,

Heave; heave, slave or servant, never shall we die.'

The procession moved on and Eamonn, one of the mounted commanders, resumed his trot down the line, looking out for trouble and communicating with leaders and warriors. He passed the sheep and Patrick without a sideways glance, and again on his return to the front.

He never sees me, thought Patrick, wanting to develop his own rapport with Eamonn. Then Patrick glimpsed the head of a crouching man, and was torn from his reverie. The man was moving with intent. The ground looked level between the track and the plain but Patrick saw the ridge line of a gully, and the gully was deep enough to hide the movements of an ill-intentioned man. Patrick's eye followed the ridge line forwards and saw that it converged to within a spear's throw of the track; he ran ahead then tucked in behind a wain and loaded his sling.

Should I call a warning to Eamonn? – but I might be wrong. Instead, he decided to focus his attention on the danger spot, the point where the gully and track were closest: the point where Eamonn was approaching. Immediately Eamonn passed the end of the gully – his back to the trouble – an attacker ran tall with spear drawn, aiming from close range at Eamonn's back. He launched his deadly missile clumsily, faltered on his feet and, with a muted yelp, clutched at his bloodied face. Patrick's slingshot had caught Eamonn's attacker on his cheek and mouth. The iron-tipped spear skidded along the ground, coming to rest by the side of Eamonn and his horse. Eamonn spun round in time to see the assailant's face, who turned and ran.

'Bring him to me,' Eamonn pointed. His warriors were already closing in on their quarry.

Patrick, with his sling held loosely, saw Eamonn glance down the line. His look was inscrutable. I'm still invisible to him, despite everything. He watched Eamonn walk his horse to the spot where the attacker had launched the spear. Eamonn dismounted and crouched to one knee, examining the ground. He picked up something small, studied it briefly then flicked it into the ditch. Patrick guessed it was a dislodged tooth from the attacker's mouth. Just then a scuffle caught Patrick's attention as Eamonn picked up another item. The two warriors were wrestling Spearman to the ground. Eamonn looked up, remounted and walked his horse down the line towards Patrick.

'This must be yours,' Eamonn said, tossing a rounded, blood-splashed stone to Patrick. 'Good shot.' He turned to face his attacker as the warriors brought him to his knees before the commander.

Patrick, pleased to receive the compliment, knew now that Eamonn hadn't been ignoring him. He chided himself as he recognised that he harboured a deeply ingrained need for recognition.

'Your name and clan?' Eamonn asked. The assailant wouldn't answer. 'Tie him spread-eagled in the pig cart.' The guards did so with relish, tying the attacker on his back, star-shaped and face up. The piglets sat on him, enjoying the warm cushion. A few minutes later Patrick saw the fully-grown sow crouch over Spearman and empty her bladder. The warriors laughed and jeered at their captive.

'You get a warm-water wash in the king's carriage,' one said.

'There's more to come,' another laughed.

The procession reached the top of the hill, bringing into view open lands to the south and dense forests to the north. The cattle train, visible by their dust-trail, were far ahead, approaching a river which glistened like a silver thread in the early evening sunlight. A cheer broke out among the warriors at the sight of the boundary to their own kingdom.

Passing the last small farmstead in Moycullen's land, six of Eamonn's guards drew their daggers and darted towards the roundhouses. Patrick saw a man running awkwardly towards the track, holding a hand on his hip, as though wounded. Another man, wielding a dagger, was intent on catching him. Eamonn held his arm up and called the procession to a stop. Within seconds the guards were dragging both men, like they were young boys, with feet hardly touching the ground. They were brought to Commander Eamonn. Patrick could see the man running with the injured gait was not hurt at all. He was holding up his trousers with one hand and clutching a knife in the other. Eamonn spoke to this man first.

'I know your face. I warn you to answer my questions truthfully. Tell me your given name and your clan.' A mounted Miliucc bard came close, listening intently, holding a wax tablet and stylus at the ready.

'Croghan of the Laithan clan,' he answered.

'What is your business in the farmstead?'

'Master, I put down my shield to help the wounded when someone ran off with it. I chased to get it back.'

'Lies,' the other man screamed.

The guard pressed the tip of his dagger into the screaming man's throat.

'Be quiet. Your turn to speak will come.'

Eamonn resumed questioning Croghan Laithan. 'Where is your shield now?'

'I didn't find it, master.'

Patrick moved closer, keen to watch Eamonn's handling of the situation.

'Where is your belt? Did this person steal your belt as well?'

'Master, I was behind a bush having a, you know, when I was disturbed.'

Patrick couldn't believe the man's words. Patricius would have ordered the man's beating at this point.

'Croghan Laithan, you are telling me someone stole your belt when your trousers were down?'

'I am, master.'

Patrick was surprised at Eamonn's patience.

'Liar,' shouted the other man.

Eamonn faced the shouter, silencing him with his look, before returning his attention to Croghan Laithan.

'You are a warrior. Why did you run from this man?'

'He had a dagger and I didn't,' Laithan defended.

'You lost your shield, your belt, and your dagger?' Laithan looked to the ground.

'Guards tie his hands,' Eamonn commanded as he turned to Laithan's pursuer.

'Your name and clan?'

'Dumnon of the Eochids.'

'Why were you chasing this man?'

'Because he's a filthy piece of turd,' he snarled. 'I disturbed him, about to rape my daughter.' He pointed to the house, 'She's still in there, tied up.'

Eamonn directed some warriors to check the houses. Patrick watched on and saw two warriors return with a young girl, a shield, and a belt.

This could have happened to Bride; Patrick shuddered.

More guards returned with an older woman from the second house. She was sobbing and shaking and wrapped in a woollen blanket. Eamonn addressed the young girl first.

'Do you accuse this man?' Eamonn pointed at Croghan Laithan.

'I do. He battered me till I was weak, then tied me to a table.' Patrick looked on, horrified.

'Then?' Eamonn asked.

'My father came in and saw what was happening. He picked up the dagger and ran at him.' She pointed to Croghan Laithan, and continued, 'He dodged and ran out. My father ran after him. You saw the rest.'

A warrior spoke, 'Master, she was tied with twine and this belt.'

This man had left a battle scene to pursue his evil bent; Patrick hoped dearly that Eamonn would severely punish Croghan Laithan. Eamonn checked the belt and the twine then switched his attention to the older woman.

Moving closer to her, he asked softly, 'Do you wish to accuse this man?'

She cried and trembled and as she tried to answer, her teeth chattered, overpowering her ability to speak.

'I can give you justice if you tell me what has happened.'

Her eyes bulging with shock and fear, darted about, giving a glimpse of her racing mind, overwhelmed with conflict and emotion.

'Let me help you. I'll ask the questions; you answer with a nod,' Eamonn suggested, speaking slowly. 'Have you seen this man before?' Eamonn pointed at Croghan.

She nodded to say, 'I have.'

'Has he hurt you?'

She nodded again.

'Try to tell me your name.'

She stuttered and faltered, then, like a bung popping from a barrel the word 'Brigid,' bawled out of her mouth.

Eamonn waited till she calmed a little.

'Brigid, can you tell me what happened?'

'We fought. I pulled this from his clothing.' She showed a ripped piece of cloth.

Eamonn took the cloth and approached Croghan Laithan and the guards restraining him. He matched the cloth to Croghan's shirt, then returned to the woman without making a comment.

'What did he do to you?'

She hesitated then opened her blanket to Eamonn. Patrick, from where he was standing saw remnants of ripped-off clothing, scantily hanging to her body. Eamonn looked carefully then told her to cover up. He leant into her and said quietly, 'I believe you. This man will be dealt with.' Eamonn turned to face Croghan.

'You left the battlefield without permission. For this you will spend two days and two nights tied to a tree.'

Brigid fell to her knees, bawling in frustration. She cried, thumping the ground with both hands.

'You don't understand. It's my blood on his body.' She sobbed as though defeated, empty of energy, then took a deep breath and screamed desperately, 'He didn't just leave the battle; he raped me.'

Eamonn paused as if taking in new information then strode towards the accused.

'Hold Croghan's legs and arms,' he instructed his guards. 'Pull forward his trouser.' The guard obeyed. Eamonn looked down at Croghan's private area and in an instant said, 'Do I see the blood of battle?' Eamonn fixed Croghan with his disgusted look. Croghan dared not answer. 'Tie him to a tree.'

Patrick was shocked at Eamonn's leniency. He looked around to see the response of the other commanders. No sense of surprise was visible. He glimpsed at the warriors and saw nods of approval, and then Croghan's shouting grabbed his attention.

'Please master, she lies.' He fell to his knees, his face distorted in terror. 'Please, please. It's as I said.'

Patrick was confused; Eamonn had almost let Croghan walk free, yet the despicable man was protesting like he'd been sentenced to death. Eamonn, having handled the situation well, was throwing away all the gains.

Brigid started again; convinced her attacker had been let off. 'Is that his punishment?' she shrieked, incredulously.

The young girl's father looked pleadingly at Eamonn and said, 'Master, can I help?'

Eamonn asked him in return, 'Do you understand?'

'I do, master.'

'Then go to her; explain.' Eamonn told the guards to release him.

He went to his neighbour, Brigid, and placed a hand gently on her shoulder. 'Brigid, Brigid, please be still. Let me explain something.' She calmed a little.

'The commander cannot move the sun back, but he's given you justice.'

'How is justice done? I don't understand,' she interrupted.

'Brigid, when a guilty man is tied to a tree through the night, the Gods send the wolves to him, and the wolves make sure the guilty man doesn't see the sun rise. This commander has the right to punish warriors in this way, for failing their duties. But if you press your claim of rape, the commander is not in control; brehons for both sides will be involved. It will take time, and if you succeed, the guilty man will be severely fined.'

Brigid sobbed and fixing a stare on Eamonn, slowly said, 'But how can I trust him?'

A murmur ran around the Miliucc men. Patrick too, winced at her questioning of the commander who was trying his best to help her. Eamonn, however, was unmoved.

The neighbour answered her softly. 'I came from the crannog myself, just now.' He glanced at Eamonn. 'All the women and children were locked in a barn. None of them were touched by a warrior.' The neighbour pointed at Eamonn, 'he gave that instruction.'

Brigid looked at Eamonn gravely, and half bowed her head.

'Go to your houses and stay there till we've moved on. Go now,' Eamonn announced to the girl, her father and Brigid.

As Eamonn watched Brigid go, Patrick read his expression. He was still thinking about her.

'Brigid,' Eamonn called.

She turned and faced Eamonn.

'Do you pray to Goddess Brighid?'

'Sometimes.'

'Pray to her now. I believe she will help you.'

Brigid bowed her head in acknowledgement.

Eamonn turned his horse and trotted to the front of the line. Brigid turned to home, to face her devastation. Patrick had seen a patient, sensitive side to Eamonn, but thought his parting comment, aimed at helping Brigid spiritually, was awesome.

Mulling things over as he stirred the sheep from their grazing Patrick thought of the solace that was available from belief in a kindly god, even though Goddess Brighid was a pagan deity.

One of the guards threw Croghan's dagger and shield on the equipment cart, and the procession began its long slow descent to the river.

Patrick now had to get the flock across the ford and keep them moving. He spoke to his helpers.

'Keep the sheep together. I'm going ahead to view the crossing.'

Patrick ran to the ford, pleased to see it was shallow as the official had vouched. The wheel ruts and stony riverbed were visible through the clear flowing water. The ditches by the track sides were open-ended where they met the river, allowing an escape route upstream and downstream for the sheep. Patrick ran back down the line to the first commander.

'Master, I'd like some help to get the sheep across the ford.'

'What help?'

'Two rows of men across the ford, starting here.' Patrick pointed with both arms. The commander nodded. As Patrick ran back to the sheep, he heard the commander shouting his orders. The sheep, however, were already out of control, running past the carts on both sides, now passing Patrick; some skidded into the ditches as they ran towards the river, their thirst whetted by the sound of running water. Patrick looked ahead to the ford and was relieved to see the warriors had formed the human walls. The sheep clamoured, in a noisy babble of bleating, eager to reach the water's edge. Those first to the ford stopped abruptly and drank greedily, standing their ground stubbornly against their mob. The new arrivals pushed with determination, forcing the first row of drinkers to step into the ford. More sheep arrived, springing onto the woolly backs to clamber their way over the top and into the river; others wriggled and writhed and squeezed down into the stream, between the bodies of drinking sheep.

The bleating stopped as a largesse of licking tongues attempted to drain the river. Patrick and all the king's men were powerless to move the sheep until they'd had their quench. Finally, with pushing, prodding, and channelling from the warriors, the flock emerged from the ford and settled into blindly following the line and the track. Patrick breathed easily once more and thought how, in the end, the sheep were easy to please. He went on to wish men could have more of this quality.

The guarded procession progressed deeper into Miliucc's kingdom and the land to the south changed from coarse and stony to boggy and marshy. A large and untidy looking settlement came into view. There was a striking absence of livestock. Haphazard attempts at cultivation were visible between thistle and gorse and saturated land. Smoke spirals were few from the poorly built roundhouses.

This place fits Eamonn's description of an outlaw settlement, Patrick muttered to himself.

The track elevated gradually, bordered still by woods on the northern side, as far as could be seen. As they reached the hilltop, the track turned to face north, revealing a breath-taking view. The red sun, low in the sky, painted the horizon and the patchy clouds crimson. In the foreground, farmsteads dotted the populous plain. Swirls of smoke rose into the sky from the thatched spires of roundhouses. Beyond the farmsteads, a belt of green and arable land surrounded a hill fort, itself visible in entirety from the higher vantage point, on which Patrick and the entourage were standing. The tiers of grass-covered perimeter mounds around the fort reminded Patrick of the ridges formed on a sandy beach by the receding tide. Patrick could see four parallel mounds, each taller than a roundhouse, artistically snaking around the contours of the hill. This, to Patrick, was an impressive level of defence. Two secure entrances were visible. One each on the northern and southern sides. The hill-fort top was a large plateau accommodating four distinct farmsteads, surrounded by open land. Patrick could make out at least twelve spaciously located buildings in each of the farmsteads. In one eyeful he could see an enterprise half the size of his own family's estate.

And now I'm beginning to feel safe again as I admire a large and tidy, working hill fort set against a shepherd's sunset. This time the crimson colour bodes well, at least for the weather in the morning.

The procession meandered down to the plain and, as they approached the gated and guarded entrance, guides came out to meet them. Commanders, warriors, cart drivers, special servants, were led to their destinations. Patrick, his helpers, and the sheep followed the carts into the hill-fort entrance and a guide wearing a green tunic approached him. His clothing indicated that he was a freeman and a farmer.

'When we reach the top, I'll show you to the sheep pens,' he said.

'Thank you,' Patrick acknowledged.

They followed the track which was walled-in by grassy mounds. The men and livestock followed the channel as it climbed gently, snaking forwards and backwards. The top mound was constructed as a rampart topped with a stone path for the soldiers to tread. A large presence of guards, armed with spears, daggers and shields, manned the defensive wall adjacent to the entrance. Further along, sentries stood on watch duties at observation posts, positioned at intervals along the perimeter wall. Patrick saw an example of defensive measures that could be instructive in Banna Venta – if he was ever able to return to share the information.

Their guide showed the way to the pens, a mere hundred strides from the entrance. They were open but sheltered from the prevailing winds by a dense cluster of trees on the south and west sides. Patrick led the sheep, and the helpers kept the flock in shape until a farm boy opened the pen gate. Even from distance the leading sheep knew the meaning of an open gate. They snapped out of their docility and ran to their new pasture, followed by the rest of the flock. Officials arrived to headcount the sheep and one with a wax tablet scratched the numbers thereon. Patrick thought about the rams, tied to a cart.

'Master, have you got the rams?'

'We have. They're in a separate place.' The official turned to the guide, 'Take these men to the hostel.'

'Master,' the guide answered, obediently. Turning to Patrick and his two helpers, he instructed, 'Follow me.'

They walked past shippons, breathing in the dirty cow-house smells until the whiffs merged with the more unpleasant stink of a pig farm. Two large boars, caked in dirt, oinked and grunted from the confines of their mud-meadow. On walked the trio, following their guide through open land. He took them to a cluster of buildings housing blacksmithing and carpentry workshops. Repaired wheels were stacked in open-sided barns, alongside newly made carts. The smell of ironworks had reached a large roundhouse, sectioned off behind a low wall, and now the mouth-watering aroma of roasting pig and cow meat wafted over from a row of spits located behind the houses.

The guide spoke to a guard at the entrance and announced, 'Three Miliucc shepherds.'

'Come inside,' the guard said.

They entered a typical roundhouse with a central fire burning. Twenty-four beds were placed around the perimeter most with personal belongings laid upon them. Patrick and his helpers copied with their identical possessions; spears, knives, headgear, sandals, and daggers, on the three remaining beds.

The guard took up a basket and doled out the contents, saying, 'Here, these are from King Miliucc.' He gave them each a new tunic and pair of sandals. 'There are tubs of water outside. Wash your bodies and wear the new clothing. Place your old tunic and sandals in the basket, over there. When you are washing, you will see the spits. Behind them is a long building. Go there for food and drink. Remember to leave your weapons here. Later, King Miliucc will speak to you in the hall. Do not leave until he has spoken to you.'

Patrick opened conversation. Until now he hadn't even asked his helpers their names.

'You're shepherds for Miliucc. Where do you work?'

'Doobehy Valley. We work together,' said the strong one.

'I haven't heard of it,' Patrick said.

'It's south-west of Voclut,' the strong one clarified.

'I'm Patrick. I'm Miliucc's shepherd in the hills of Voclut.' He extended his arm for a hand shake.

The strong one was caught off guard slightly but quickly recovered giving Patrick a hearty handshake, saying,

'I'm Dumnon.'

Patrick turned to the other helper, who put out his hand, half-heartedly. 'I'm Cuchulain but please call me Chulain.' He offered Patrick a limp handshake that was cold as a dead fish.

You're not the little finger of Cuchulain, Patrick thought to himself.

'Let's go to the tubs,' Patrick said and led the way. After washing themselves enthusiastically, Patrick was the first to the shared woollen towel, which was tied to a post. He found it saturated, bloodstained and reeking of sweat. A better idea occurred to him. He gathered up his clothes, returned to the roundhouse and dried his naked body in front of the fire. The soothing warmth relaxed his aching bones and Patrick wondered how he would adapt on his return to the hills. As he donned his undergarments Dumnon and Chulain returned, barefoot and partly dressed.

'There you are,' said Chulain.

'I'm here. Dressing in the warmth,' said Patrick.

'High standards for a hill shepherd,' Chulain teased.

'The life of a hill shepherd is a cold one, so I take every chance to be near a fire.' Patrick expected to be mocked by Chulain but the mocking didn't follow. Probably biting his tongue in case he has to work for me tomorrow, Patrick mused. They finished dressing and joined the others in the food hall.

The shepherds were the latecomers to a candle-lit hall crammed with chattering people, excited to be on the winning side of a battle. Patrick looked round the room for a suitable place to sit. A long table was filled with trays of meat pieces, jugs of ale and drinking mugs. Warriors jostled for position to get a plate of meat and a mug of ale, doled out by the slave girls. Many of those who'd eaten were standing in huddles, near to the ale jugs. The hall was filled with happy noise, as warriors, relieved of their worries, babbled out their tales to the appreciative guffaws and cackles of their listeners. Patrick spotted Bognan and Crimthan at the tables and pointed to the empty seats opposite. Bognan nodded.

'Let's sit with these friends,' said Patrick.

'You know Bognan?' Chulain remarked.

'I do. Seems you do too,' Patrick answered.

'We know him alright. But we don't call him friend. You join him. We'll sit over here,' Chulain said, moving off with Dumnon. Patrick set down his plate and mug opposite Bognan and Crimthan, and leant forward, arm extended offering his handshake. Both hesitated a moment then responded warmly. Patrick knew that the handshake was not customary amongst the Irish serving classes but they'd fought in battle together, looked out for each other and Patrick wanted to show his respect in accordance with his own custom.

'Good to see you both. Where is Memnon?'

'He's in the hill fort; in the trade's quarter,' said Bognan. 'Where are your little helpers? What did you say to them?'

'It seems they know you, Bognan, better than I do I suspect.'

Bognan laughed. 'They're not worth their tunic. I'll wager the king will sell them.'

Patrick listened without reply, before asking, 'What was your job in the crannog, Bognan?'

'Same as yours, only cattle,' Bognan replied.

'What markings did you find?'

'Half were stolen and half of those were King Miliucc's. The rest came from the south and east. None were from the north.'

Patrick thought about the news, then asked, 'Is the northern kingdom poor?'

'Just the opposite, their bogs are rich with iron ore. They have more ironworks than cattle farms.'

'Bognan, don't get onto politics again. Leave it to the nobles.

Look at that girl over there, the one in the middle. Good looking, eh?'

'Too good for you, Crimthan,' he said, trying lighter conversation.

'Do you think she's free?' Crimthan pursued.

'You can't afford her, Crimthan, she'll cost you a few milk cows.'

They refilled their mugs and chatted and laughed away. Crimthan got talking with another group at the ale refill table, giving Bognan his chance to discuss political affairs.

'Patrick, we talked about Roman soldiers forming squares, we were interrupted, you said they could advance in squares. How would they do it?'

'They practised running in unison. The sides could run sideways, the back row could run backwards, all in the same timing, keeping the formation.'

'Patrick, if Moycullen's warriors were trained and skilled like the Romans, after the surprise attack who would have won the battle?'

'Easy Bognan. Moycullen would have won, even with half the men.'

Patrick saw his certainty searing into Bognan's mind, like red hot iron dipped in water. Bognan's eyes glowed with new understanding.

'Phew,' said Bognan, blowing out a long hot breath.

'I've a question for you, Bognan. When Conn's druid prayed to Goddess Morrigan, why was the crow supposed to be a sign?'

'Ah! If you were Irish, you'd know Goddess Morrigan likes to shift her shape. She has many shapes, but the crow is her favourite.'

'It didn't work, Bognan.'

'That's because our druid called down powers with more conviction. He won the battle for the gods.'

'Do you believe Morrigan backed off in the Conn battle and Goddess Brigid fixed the outcome of the battle?'

Patrick watched Bognan's face, expecting to see pain or indignation.

'It happens sometimes. This time was different. Conn's kingdom is poor. People don't give their lives to protect their poverty.'

Patrick enjoyed Bognan's thirst for discussion and believed some of his opinions were wise.

Bognan continued, 'Miliucc's druid was clever when he appealed to Brighid, Goddess of Good Harvests. Horse sense told the Conn warriors not to fight. They would gain more by losing.'

Patrick was about to speak when the room noise reduced to murmurings. Commander Eamonn and his guards strode into the hall. Eamonn raised his arm and cast a firm stare around the room, sweeping all whispers aside.

With every ear attentive, Eamonn announced, 'Keep your silence. King Miliucc wishes to speak.'

The king entered the hall, dressed simply in gown and sandals, distinguished only by his purple cloak. He faced the room centrally with his back to the long wall, then pricked the silence.

'Our battles of yesterday and today were carefully planned and cleverly thought out. Our leaders and nobles served the kingdom well. You warriors,' he pointed slowly and deliberately to the men in the room, 'fought fiercely, fearlessly, and victoriously. We lost seventy-five of our own, while the enemy lost three hundred. Never has the kingdom fought with such success, taking four of them to one of us.'

Loud murmuring spread through the room. Heads nodded to the king and to each other. He allowed a moment of appreciation before raising his arm. Silence returned in an instant.

'You have seen the cattle, pigs, sheep, and other livestock that we have taken back. Most were ours, stolen from us. King Moycullen and his chieftains are in chains as I speak. When Moycullen provides his own daughter as hostage, I will release him. When his two chieftains provide a son each as hostage, then they will be released.' Patrick was surprised at this leniency.

'I don't want Moycullen's lands or any part of his kingdom. Do you want to live in a larger kingdom where half of the people hate you? My wish is for my kingdom, your kingdom, to prosper.' Patrick saw many nods of approval but Miliucc's audience remained silent, listening to every word he said.

'In the next few days new contracts will be issued for farmers and craftsmen. There will be an increase in work, to the benefit of all, but I want two things from you; first, your hard work, with hands and heart,' the king paused, 'second, an end to stealing. Do not steal, from your own, your neighbour or your neighbouring kingdom. Almost every battle happens because of stealing. I will protect the lands to my best. You, work the land to your best. This way your mothers might see you grow older, and you might live to see your grandchildren.'

Patrick was impressed. King Miliucc was giving his people values and hope. He couldn't imagine a Roman tribune saying this kind of thing to decurions and legionnaires.

'When the contracts are being delivered, everyone involved in these battles will receive a hen. Every fighting warrior two hens. Thank you all.'

King Miliucc turned to leave; the room erupted into rapturous cheering. The King smiled gracefully, wistfully, and continued smiling as the commanders parted the people, creating a path to the door. Patrick moved nearer to the door too. He wanted to be closer to the nobles to see their faces.

As King Miliucc and Eamonn neared the exit and the warriors moved towards the ale jugs, Patrick heard King Miliucc speak under his breath to Eamonn.

'Tonight, I have their bellies, Eamonn, but will their hearts be mine tomorrow?'

Patrick felt a tap on his shoulder. He turned, to see Bognan.

'Are you leaving?'

Patrick shook his head. 'I'm being nosey.'

Patrick, Bognan and Crimthan settled at a table with other warriors, chatting, drinking, and enjoying the special atmosphere.

Pondering Miliucc's question to Eamonn Patrick asked anyone of those at his table who would listen, 'Is Miliucc's way succeeding?'

'It is,' said Bognan, without hesitation. 'We haven't had a battle for three full years. Before it was almost every year.'

'Before?' asked Patrick.

'Before King Miliucc gave new rules to the clans. He stated no clan should steal from another clan, in the kingdom or out of it.

No clan should fight a clan from a neighbouring kingdom. Such a decision was for the king alone. It's why our losses are so high. We haven't been stealing back.'

Patrick thought for a while and then stood up saying, 'I have some prayers to pray. I'm going to my bed. I bid you goodnight.' He kicked himself for slipping into noble speech.

'Good night,' said Crimthan.

'Good night, mate,' said Bognan, grinning. To Patrick's relief, he didn't tease him for the lordly words.

Patrick entered the empty bed house. He was alone, the only one in the group who could resist free ale. He arranged his possessions in a neat pile; his boots and yellow tunic, checking his sling and shot were in their pouches, his dagger and knife, and finally the charm given to him by Bride, which he placed carefully, uppermost on top of the tunic. Then he knelt before his bed, placing his hands together palm to palm. After organising his prayers in his mind, he prayed them.

'Dear God, thank you for delivering me safely through the day, in answer to my prayer. Thanks for the gift of food and drink. Thank you for providing warm, dry and safe shelter. Thank you for giving me the gift of sleep. Thank you, Lord, for shortening the battle. Dear God, please bless the fallen and their families; the enemy chiefs, their guilty and their innocent people. Dear Lord, accept my prayer for the well-being of my parents; of Hermanus, of Cormac, Eamonn, the warriors, of my friends Bognan and Crimthan and Memnon. Dear Lord, please give me help and understanding, for today two kings and their warriors inflicted slaughter on their own country folk. I, too, wielded a spear and injured and killed many. I fought out of duty and to save my own life. Praise be to you, Lord, for the good things that came, even on such a day as this: men helping each other on the battlefield, Commander Eamonn treating a female enemy victim with decency. King Miliucc's magnanimity in victory, his leadership in setting values, his creation of hope for his people. For laughter and friendships, God, I pray for...'

Loud banging on the heavy wooden door broke Patrick's

concentration. It was the group of warriors returning; some were thick of tongue and loud of voice. He ignored the disturbance and continued to murmur his prayers.

Most of the warriors ignored Patrick though one exuberant man chose to listen closely and mimic him. Patrick lost his focus again and became aware that he was the cause of some mirth for one of those present.

'Thank you, Lord, this; praise the Lord, that,' came the mocking in high-pitched voice.

Patrick stood up and walked towards the teaser asking, 'Why clash like a cymbal in a room where men come to sleep?'

'Why clash like a simple...' the teaser mocked, but stopped abruptly when his friend, built like a tree, stood over him.

'The man talks sense,' said Tree-man, snapping his fingers against his thumb.

Clashing Cymbal cowered under Tree-man's gaze and closed his mouth. Tree-man ran his hand over his long, dark hair, as though he was working something out. He turned to Patrick. His overgrown moustache and beard revealed a wide mouth as he asked,

'What are you doing?'

Patrick, clean-shaven and slim, stood tall as he answered, 'I'm praying.'

'Who are you praying to?'

'To God.'

Tree-man looked baffled.

'Do you find this odd?' Patrick asked.

'Maybe.'

'Let me explain. Were you there when our druid prayed to the spirits of the North, South, East, and West, to spare our warriors' lives?'

'I was.' Tree-man nodded.

'Well, no one died, so a prayer of thanks would not be strange, would it?'

'I see your meaning. I'll interrupt you no more.' Tree-man turned to prepare his bed and Patrick returned to his prayers, mouthing them silently this time.

'Dear God, I miss Soldier. Thank you for providing me with such a loyal friend; let me be with the hound as soon as possible. Finally, Lord, I pray for Bride's welfare and share with you my hope that I shall see her again.'

As the sun rose, Patrick awoke to the noise of busy guards telling men their duties. Bognan and Memnon were given tasks distributing the reclaimed livestock. They wouldn't see their families for four or five more nights.

'Patrick, your work is almost finished. Today you will assist an oxcart driver taking supplies to a smelter. The ironworks is only a hill and dale away from the Woods of Voclut. Break your fast in the food hall. I will call you when we're ready,' the guard instructed.

Patrick tagged along with Bognan and Crimthan and entered the hall, which was only a quarter full. Warriors living locally had swigged the ewe's milk and left quickly, taking chunks of bread and cheese home with them. Although Patrick had left early the night before, he'd seen men drinking like they had second stomachs. He wasn't surprised that men lacked appetite this morning. Patrick put bread and cheese in his inside tunic pocket, for later. He ate a small amount, standing, the way he would have done at home in Banna Venta. As he drank down a cup of ewe's milk the guard entered and beckoned Patrick.

Turning to his two friends Patrick said, 'I hope our paths cross again.'

'If we stay alive, they will,' said Bognan. Patrick shook their hands and his friends complied politely. Bognan followed up with a bear hug.

'Coming,' said Patrick, narrowly beating the guard to a comment.

Stepping outside, Patrick was surprised to see an oxcart, driver and six armed guards on horseback. What are we carrying? He thought. Gold coins?

'Sit with the driver. If the cart gets stuck, your job is to get it going. There are tools to help.' The guard pointed into the cart.

Patrick saw spades, some long and narrow, others broad. All

had long shafts. There was a heavy tamper, made from a tree trunk, placed on a pile of coarse woollen cloths. The load, spread across the bottom of the cart, consisted of a mixture of crudely shaped, brown shale pieces and tan coloured, irregular-shaped pellets, about the size of Patrick's thumb. He'd never seen the like before and scooped up a handful, the weight of which caught him by surprise. Patrick jumped on board and took his seat as the guard called the driver to start.

CHAPTER FOURTEEN

A harsh crack of the whip on the ox's backside stirred the beast to pulling. The wooden joints of the sturdily built wagon creaked as they slowly moved off.

'I'm Patrick,' he said to the driver.

The driver turned to face Patrick with bleary and bloodshot eyes, set in a sour-looking face. 'Eochaid,' he grunted.

Patrick recognised last night's clashing cymbal.

Feigning indifference, he asked, 'Eochaid, what are we carrying?'

'Pig turd,' snarled the driver.

'More of a dog's, I'd say,' Patrick quipped.

The driver whistled, shaking his head from left to right. 'You really don't know, do you?' The driver let his disbelief sink in, then continued, 'It's turd because it looks like turd. It's pig turd because it's pig iron, straight from the bog.'

The day will be long, Patrick thought to himself, and for the next ten miles they didn't speak a word. Passing some common land, Patrick noticed a shepherd looking after a mixture of goats and sheep. He spotted a dozen different markings but as he pondered on this he was rocked and shaken from his thoughts. The cart listed from side to side; the ruts were rougher and deeper and a high ridge with a green mossy stripe had formed in the centre of the track. Looking further along, Patrick saw two ragged men approaching, hauling a handcart.

Miliucc's guard trotted his horse up to them to sort out priorities.

'We travel for the king,' said the guard, 'Move your cart into the ditch that we might pass.'

'And if our cart gets stuck?' asked one of the carters.

'It's a handcart. You will get it out,' the guard replied curtly.

The carter muttered and moved over. Cribs held their half load of turf intact as they tilted their cart into the deep ditch. The king's men and their heavy load passed slowly and stopped, to be sure the handcart returned to the track. But the carters struggled as the wheels locked under the dead weight.

'Help them,' the guard rapped out to Patrick.

'Master,' Patrick acknowledged, jumping down from his perch. He stood over the carters and boomed out his instructions, 'Push the cart back into the ditch.' They followed his command. 'Swivel the cart at an angle,' he ordered, indicating the position with his arms in parallel. They obeyed. 'Pull, till one wheel is over, then hold.' The men pulled and this time the wheels turned. 'Pull again till the second wheel is over.' The wheel rolled and the men pulled till the cart was back on the track. Patrick had unintentionally slipped back into the role of the master giving out the orders.

Everyone cheered the carters except the hung-over driver.

Using an old Celtic phrase, the leading guard said, 'Brain beats brawn.'

Patrick saw the scowl on Eochaid's face and worried that he was becoming his earnest enemy. He hoped the friction wasn't leading anywhere and that it was the result of the driver's poor night's sleep.

During a long downhill stretch the ox sped up and the cart began bouncing and shaking. As the wagon gained momentum, Patrick could see the ox was running faster to avoid being pushed by the cart, yet the driver made no attempt to curtail the beast.

'Rein in,' called the guard. Eochaid made a feeble attempt.

'Rein in or I will,' the guard commanded, readying himself to mount the cart and take the reins.

Eochaid reined in the ox. The cart lurched and swayed as the wooden yoke rode up the ox's back and neck. The ox displayed huge strength resisting the increasing momentum of the load. The yoke rode above the ox's shoulders as if in a battle of wills. Uncomfortably but dutifully, the ox persevered until the yoke settled on his shoulders and stability returned. The guard faced the driver.

'You never let the ox take control. You should know this.'

'Sorry, master,' muttered Eochaid, head down looking sheepish.

Patrick didn't believe the apology. He was suspicious and watched Eochaid like he was a prowling wolf. A couple of sharp pulls on the reins caught Patrick's attention. Eochaid had tweaked the ox's right nostril first, then the left immediately afterwards, so snappily that the movement of the reins passed unnoticed to the guards. But everyone saw the momentary stumble of the ox, unaware the beast had been wrong-footed by his driver. They reached the bottom of the hill without mishap but the level track brought more potential hazards as the ruts deepened. The undercarriages of previous carts had gouged and occasionally dislodged the stones making up the central ridge.

'How are you going to get through that?' Patrick asked.

'Slowly,' said Eochaid, with a distinct lack of conviction.

A guard shouted out and called the procession to a halt.

'You,' he pointed at Patrick. 'Fill the ruts.'

'Master,' Patrick replied, jumping off the cart.

He took up a scoop-shaped spade and crowbar. Levering at the ridge stones till they were loose, he rolled them into the ruts. Patrick was strong and worked fast. He finished by scooping up small stones, throwing them into the crevices and, grabbing the heavy tamper, he compressed and flattened his rut fillings.

Patrick had time to think about Eochaid while he was working. He believed the driver was harbouring a much deeper grudge, possibly a hatred. Whatever it might be, it was nothing to do with last night's exchange. Patrick finished the job, put the tools in the cart and returned to his place next to the recalcitrant driver.

'You're right, Eochaid, slowly should do it,' Patrick said, carrying on from where they left off.

Eochaid looked sourly at his companion as the ox and cart passed safely over the repaired track. They journeyed on, through wooded areas and into open countryside. Patrick was watchful and once more spotted Eochaid making a double twitch of the reins, wrong-footing the ox yet again. The guards looked with concern at Eochaid who shrugged his shoulders as though blaming the beast. The guards had only seen the animal stumble but Patrick had seen enough to suspect that Eochaid was planning an accident. As the track narrowed beside a sheer drop on the left-hand side, Patrick saw places ahead where the track was crumbling. It made sense to steer to the right. Instead, the duplicitous driver reined the ox gradually to the left. Disaster was one twitch of the reins away.

Patrick slid along the bench till he was close to Eochaid. Underneath his clothing he drew out his dagger, thankful that he'd sharpened the tip and blade the previous day. Holding the dagger horizontally, he jabbed the tip into Eochaid's ribs. As the driver winced, Patrick leant into him, saying softly,

'If this cart has an accident, you will have an accident too.'

Eochaid thought for a second, then responded with a smirk. 'You haven't got the courage. The guards would work you out.'

Patrick was losing the battle of wills. His next move would have to be convincing. Eochaid edged the cart nearer to danger. The crumbling track was looming; the driver's moment only seconds away. If Eochaid was ready to die, he wouldn't need to blame the ox, Patrick reasoned. He sunk the dagger suddenly into Eochaid's ribs. The driver yelped as a bloodstained patch appeared on his tunic.

'Move to the right,' Patrick instructed, holding the pressure. There was no response. Patrick twisted the blade, and could immediately hear the pain in Eochaid's groan.

'Take the blade away,' he snarled through clenched teeth.

'Tell me a reason,' said Patrick, twisting the dagger more.

'No accidents,' Eochaid gasped.

Patrick twisted the blade further, saying, 'Convince me.'

'No accidents,' Eochaid repeated, then reined the ox to the right.

Patrick withdrew his dagger, relieved his bluff had worked. The driver pressed his left arm firmly against his ribs to stem the bleeding and they travelled on without incident during the rest of the morning.

After noon the guards directed the company into a side track through the woods. The cow path, well maintained and sheltered from bad weather, gave a smoother ride. A smell of ironworks polluted the air, but Patrick could only see trees. Finally, the woods gave way to open land and a cluster of roundhouses came into view, accommodating a forge, workshops, and stores. Spearheads, dagger blades, gate frames and other ironmongery were stacked under the cover of open-sided barns. Further back there were houses and small farmsteads. Eochaid was instructed to stop the cart next to the pig-iron bunkers beside the forge.

A grey-bearded man wearing a leather blacksmith's apron came out to greet the guards. He snapped his fingers and the servant following him jumped to unshackle the ox before leading the beast to a cattle house. The blacksmith hugged the lead guard in welcome and invited all the guards inside for refreshment. He interrupted for a second to give out an instruction and, grabbing a spade he threw it vertically towards the driver.

'Catch.' Eochaid caught it. 'Unload the pig iron into the bunker.'

So, this is Eochaid's place of work.

Just then Patrick's lead guard said, 'Give a spade to our man. He can help.'

'Catch.' Patrick caught the spade, and the two began scooping the pig-iron pieces into the bunker. Patrick worked at a faster pace than Eochaid but saw that Eochaid quickly caught up.

'You work better under the master's nose,' Patrick commented.

Eochaid scowled and continued. Patrick noticed the smelter came to the door occasionally, keeping his eye on the slaves. By now the servant who unshackled the ox was busy giving water to the guard's horses. Another servant came with half a mug of ewe's milk each for Patrick and Eochaid. She placed them on top of a barrel along with two pieces of dried and curled bread.

The two slaves made quick work of unloading the pig iron and were soon drinking their ewe's milk. Patrick took out his cheese and bread which he'd pocketed earlier at King Miliucc's hill fort, and left the stale bread. As he was eating, the lead guard came out and addressed Patrick.

'Your work is finished now; return to Cormac and take up your duties at sunrise.' He turned to Eochaid, 'Tell Patrick how to get to the Woods of Voclut.' The guard returned inside to the hospitality of the blacksmith.

Patrick took Eochaid's instructions, but they didn't fit with his own sense of direction. He swigged back his milk and set off heading west as told. At twenty paces he turned; his sling and stone at the ready. Eochaid was eating the second piece of bread and wasn't watching. Patrick released his shot and sent Eochaid's mug clattering off the barrel to the ground. Surprised, Eochaid looked up and saw a smiling Patrick calling out.

'I've decided to go north.'

Patrick's sense of direction was sound and by sundown he was closing in on the pinfold at the top of the ravine. He thought of Eochaid's instructions which would have led him to the wrong side of the mountain. He wouldn't have made it to Cormac by dawn the next day. Even taking the direct route, his legs became weary.

Eventually the familiar Voclut landscape gave his spirits a lift. He recognised Cormac's white hair and beard from a distance and was pleased the sheep were penned at the nearest location. With thirty strides to go, Soldier bounded down the track, tail swishing with excitement. Patrick braced himself as Soldier leapt onto him in welcome.

'Me too, Soldier, I've missed you too.' After hugs and strokes Patrick was able to look to Cormac.

'How's that for homecoming?' Cormac commented.

'Mighty. It's how I feel too. And you, Cormac, how are things with you?'

'I'm well, enjoying a few days in the hills. The flock is sound too; almost doubled.'

'A few days, that's all it's been, but so much has happened, it feels like an age,' Patrick said.

Cormac handed him a skin of ale.

'Have a drink while the porridge is warming and tell me news of the battles.'

Patrick put down his shield and dagger and bag of life and sat on a log next to the fire. He took a long swig of ale and began his tale.

'The southern battle with Conn never happened. Every one of his warriors threw down their weapons before them and lay face down on the ground. Maybe our druid put them under a spell. King Miliucc's men took all the enemy weapons and shackled their warriors. At this time, the nobles from both sides moved to a large roundhouse to discuss a settlement.'

'Did you hear the terms?' Cormac asked.

'We all did. Both kings made a public announcement. King Miliucc took his dues in land and men, including outlaws. He purchased additional lands from Conn, paying with livestock, then hired additional fighters.'

'A wise course of action,' said Cormac. 'It is well that they pulled it off,' he added, trying to take in the achievement.

'I agree,' said Patrick. 'In Britain we are told the Irish pay little attention to strategy but rush to fight. It seems we are wrong.'

'You are not wrong in general, Patrick, but King Miliucc is cut from a better cloth.'

Patrick digested Cormac's comments. He felt lucky that King Miliucc was his master. He could have been a master like the smelter he saw earlier. Patrick snapped out of his thoughts and retold the story of the Moycullen Battle, remarking on the surprise spear attack which shortened the fight.

'I selected and led seventy-five sheep to King Miliucc's hill fort and witnessed a cattle-run that was spectacular. Unfortunately, it showed the extent of Moycullen's thieving. This morning I was placed with a cart driver for the purpose of delivering a load of pig iron to a smelter in Glenedagh. After unloading I was told to return to my place in the hills for sunrise.'

Cormac had listened carefully. 'Do you know what has happened to Moycullen?' he asked.

'I do. He's been taken captive. When hostages have been delivered, he will be freed to return to his kingdom,' Patrick replied.

'Do you know how Eamonn is?'

'He's well and in control, organising things for the king.'

Cormac passed a bowl of hot porridge to Patrick, saying, 'I suppose you've been eating meat recently.'

'Thank you, Cormac. Indeed, I have. King Miliucc clearly believes full bellies fight better battles.'

Cormac laughed.

As Patrick sipped the porridge he asked Cormac, 'Did you know I was returning?'

'I did. A messenger arrived calling Donal back to his farm. I was told to expect you by sunrise tomorrow. I guess you are tired.'

'I am, but glad to be back,' Patrick answered.

'Shall we close the day?' Cormac asked.

Patrick nodded. 'I'll prepare my bed. But first I'll look at the sheep.' Patrick rose to his feet and looked over the ewes and rams resting peacefully in the pen, and he felt at home.

It'll soon be Beltaine. He pulled out the woven, Celtic wheel from his pocket and eyed the charm with pleasure. He didn't believe the superstition, but Bride had made it for him and he treasured the simple gift.

Patrick completed his bed time routine and lay his head to rest, thinking, and saying quietly to himself, I hope I meet Bride at the craft stalls.

CHAPTER FIFTEEN

Beltaine came. Patrick and Cormac led their largest and healthiest flock in years to Voclut. For Patrick, the market work was a repeat of his first season, but this time Patrick chose which rams to buy. The lamb sales were Cormac's responsibility and they were fetching good prices, which pleased Cormac.

Patrick cast his eye around the trade stalls at every opportunity but two days and two nights passed with no sign of Bride or her father. On the third evening Cormac offered Patrick an opportunity.

'You go to the fayre this evening; I'll watch the sheep. Enjoy some meat and ale.'

'Thank you, Cormac that would be a pleasure.' He felt a flush of excitement at the thought that he might see Bride.

Patrick donned a clean tunic and made for the stalls. He wasn't buying but he thought of the brooch he'd acquired last year for his mother, kept safe among his meagre possessions, and wondered if he would ever get the chance to give it to her.

This time he passed through the jewellery and craft stalls with a greater understanding of the Celtic symbols; the wheel, the cycle of seasons, the cycle of life, death, and renewal. He thought longer about renewal; a kind of life after death but in a different form. The lucky ones might become bulls; and wretches, perhaps a rat or a snake. He thought of the mythical gods, their powers over seasons, their powers of shape-shifting, of Morrigan becoming a crow. Worse still, he'd learned of the fearful belief of the Irish people in the reality of myth. He pondered this as he joined a queue to get a cut of cow meat and root vegetables, musing that their clinging to superstitions meant that the Irish people allowed fear into their own hearts too easily. They were powerless to change their material poverty but had more control over their spiritual well-being. And yet their spiritual beliefs were filled with misery, fear, and too little hope.

Nearing the front of the queue, Patrick was pleased to see the rump was hardly touched. He was humoured by the quirk of snobbery whereby the nobles commandeered the topside cuts for themselves, leaving the lower and rear for the servant classes. Patrick, on his turn to be served, pointed to the rump, and was given a couple of chunks and some turnips. Someone tapped his arm. Patrick turned.

'We met last year,' the man said.

Patrick recognised the man from Lough Conn.

'You on your own?' the man asked. Patrick nodded. He continued, 'Go to the table there. I'll bring some ale.' Patrick sat by the table on a log bench and his pal arrived, a jug of ale and two mugs in one hand, carried with large fingers and thumbs threaded through the three handles, and his plate of pig meat in the other.

'Much happened in a year, what about you?' he asked Patrick.

'The same. Most of it this week,' Patrick answered, between slurps of ale.

'You been in the battles then?'

Patrick nodded, 'And you?'

'I was, and I live in the Miliucc Kingdom now.' He smiled, as though pleased with the new arrangement.

'How does that feel?' Patrick asked.

'Good. We won't starve under Miliucc.'

'Is that just you talking?'

'The clans think the same.'

Patrick pierced a chunk of meat with his spike and ate from it. He sloshed the food down with a good swig of ale, happy with his imitation of the slave's style of eating.

'We haven't swapped names. I'm Patrick.'

'I'm Cuchu. You still shepherding?'

'I am. It's why I'm here. Cuchu let me ask you about the battle that didn't happen. Did you lie down?' Patrick immediately regretted his directness. Luckily Cuchu didn't seem to take offence.

'I did.'

Patrick softened his approach. 'Cuchu, was the crow really Goddess Morrigan, and did she make the trees bleed?' he asked, trying to make his enquiry sound innocent.

'I see why you doubt, not being from Ireland and that. We were brought up with these stories. It's all we know so we believe without thinking.'

'Do you ever wonder about how true…?' Patrick caught himself asking what he felt might be another impertinent question.

Cuchu smiled slightly. 'Some of us ask questions inside our own heads, but we'd never tell.'

'Thanks, Cuchu. I won't ask any more.'

'No harm. You're from foreign lands; you have some catching on to do. Don't be asking too many questions though. You never know who you're talking to. If a druid gets the wind of it, he'll put the devil in your heart.'

These words stunned Patrick. I've already been loose-lipped, he thought. It wasn't the devil in the heart threat, but he didn't want his words to get passed on to one of King Miliucc's druids. He had a better life than many slaves and being reined in by Cormac or Eamonn on King Miliucc's instructions was something he'd prefer to avoid.

'I can see I've scared you. Don't be scared by me, Patrick. But take my advice, be scared of black druids and don't let them know your mind.' Cuchu shrugged and swigged his ale then changed topic. 'Anyway, our clans are happy and so are the people in Conn's Kingdom. Mind you, some of the nobles aren't. Most people would say you are lucky to work for King Miliucc.'

'I'd say that myself,' Patrick answered. 'I'm unlucky to be a slave, but I'm lucky to slave for a decent master.' Moving the conversation to safer ground, Patrick asked, 'Did you come through the Moycullen battle unharmed?'

'Hardly bruised. The outlaws took the brunt of it. Forty out of a hundred perished. They fought like hungry wolves, desperate to get their names back. King Miliucc kept his word. They're slaves now, back with their clans. You look alright yourself. Did you fight?' Cuchu asked.

'I did. We were near the back but we still had to fight. Four of us stuck together and looked out for each other.'

'Good that it worked. I just looked after me. What did you think of the spear attack from behind?'

'It took us by surprise,' Patrick said.

'And Miliucc's commanders too,' said Cuchu, continuing, 'I heard tell that Miliucc's informers saw the movement of cattle to the Crannog. They thought it was preparation to pay for extra warriors from the south. Miliucc's commander hid warriors until the fighting started, and then they moved to go south to fight off any arrival of reinforcements. But their leader saw the lie of the land and realised they could get close to the back of Moycullen's men, without being seen. So, he changed direction and gave Moycullen a stuffing.'

'He did that for sure; and saved a lot of lives on Miliucc's side. Terrible slaughter of the Moycullen warriors though,' Patrick added.

'The bastard deserved it. Conn's Kingdom was poor and Moycullen's rich, but he still stole our cattle. He didn't take our surplus; he took our need. Miliucc should have cut his balls off.' Cuchu's vicious response made Patrick wonder whether Moycullen fully understood the consequences of his thieving, or did he just not care.

'Grievous,' Patrick remarked. 'I heard it said that Conn's Kingdom stole out of necessity and Moycullen's out of greed.'

There was a moment of silence which they both filled with chewing. Cuchu picked up the ale jug and filled up their mugs. He leant forward and spoke slowly. 'Got any plans for going home?'

'None. I've stopped thinking about it. I'm making the best of what I've got.'

'You're getting the hang of it, Patrick,' Cuchu smiled and gave him a wink. 'Even so, let me tell you: if you ever see the boats on the west coast, don't get any ideas. They're all coast hoppers. They don't cross the seas. You need the east side, but where you came into Ireland is too busy. If you don't get caught on the journey you'll be caught at the harbour.'

Patrick cut in, embarrassed at the conversation. 'Where are you from, Cuchu?'

'The south-east.'

'And now you're in the north-west. Is there a story there?' Patrick watched Cuchu's face closely.

'There is. My father's farm was having a bad time. He sold me to Conn to pay off his debts.' Cuchu spoke without emotion.

'How did you travel here?'

'I walked, tied to one of Conn's carts.'

Patrick though of his first days in Ireland, chained to the last cart in King Miliucc's train.

'Did that upset you?'

'Not really. I got some blisters.'

Patrick smiled; he knew about blisters. But if my father sold me, I'd be upset...

'Do you miss your family?'

'I never knew my mother. I miss my father but I'm a slave. We get sold; we get moved on; sometimes for better, sometimes for worse. That's our life and our home is where we make it.' Cuchu stood up and made ready to leave.

'I think I know what you mean,' said Patrick, 'Anyway, good chatting to you. I hope we meet again. And may King Miliucc stay good for you.' He raised his cup of ale to Cuchu.

'Oh, he will. He keeps his word. I got my hens. Did you get yours?'

'I did, and they've started laying eggs,' Patrick said proudly.

Cuchu gave Patrick a bear hug and was off. Patrick sat a while, taking in the richness of the conversation. He was jolted from his thoughts when someone called his name.

'Patrick, I saw you earlier, but you were talking.' Patrick looked up to see Bride's father, Coren. Patrick stood but Coren said, 'Don't be rising for me,' so Patrick extended his arm and his handshake was received. 'Bride asked me to look out for you; she's away for a few days but sends a message. She's had an idea to waterproof your canvass. You'll need a large boiling pot,' Coren said, indicating the size with his hands. 'It's something you can do yourself once she's shown you. When is a good time?'

'Early evening. When the sun is half down,' said Patrick. 'I return in two days. She'll find me at the hill-pen,' said Patrick with forced calmness, thrilled to learn that Bride had been thinking of him. 'By the way, master, the leg-wraps and socks are working well. At last, I'm keeping my feet dry in wet weather.'

'Glad to hear it. Call at the workshop if there is anything else.'

'Master, do you have a stall here?'

'Not this time. We have more work than we could wish for.' He turned to leave.

'Good day, master, give Bride my thanks for the message.'

'I will indeed. Pass on my regards to Cormac. Goodbye.'

Patrick sat down again, to savour the conversation, but first, he kicked himself. I keep forgetting to speak like I'm a slave. Thankfully he spoke to me as an equal. Upper classes don't usually ask slaves to pass on their regards.

Then Patrick let his feelings fill his face. He smiled from ear to ear, delighted that Bride was thinking about him. And now he knew exactly where to go: back to the craft stalls to look for a boiling pot.

He found a selection of cooking pots exhibited by a trader. The business was based in Voclut, so Patrick proceeded to discuss the price.

'Can I pay you with eggs?'

'You can. Five dozen eggs will do it,' said the trader.

This seemed a very high price to Patrick, but for now he was just gaining information.

'I can deliver one dozen each week. How will payment work?' Patrick asked.

'You bring me the eggs each week and on the fifth week you take the pot.'

'Let me think about it,' Patrick said.

'It's my best price. I'll not be lowering if that's what you're thinking.'

'It's the waiting,' Patrick countered, which was partly true, but it was getting the pot after he'd parted with the eggs that concerned him the most.

'Bring the hen. If it's a young layer, I'll exchange the pot for the hen.'

'A good idea. Thank you. I'll sleep on the thought.' Patrick turned quickly and left, before the trader could apply more persuasion.

He returned to Cormac's little roundhouse, knocked at the solid wooden door with his knuckles, and entered.

'Ah, you're early,' said Cormac, glancing up from trimming his beard with what looked like a miniature pair of sheep shears. He was sitting on a bench next to the fire, leaning forward to view his reflection in a small, irregular-shaped piece of polished tin, which was pinned to a post.

'No worry, I've enjoyed the roasted rump of a cow, ale and two conversations,' Patrick said as he took a log seat by the fire.

'Who did you meet?'

'The man I met last year from the Lough Conn area. He's called Cuchu and he's one of us now.'

'What do you mean one of us?'

'He's from the Conn Kingdom's borderland, which King Miliucc gained in the settlement of debts. So now they're in our kingdom. He fought for King Miliucc in the battle against Moycullen.'

'Was he a willing fighter?'

'He says he fought with all his heart.'

Cormac nodded sagely as he took in the information.

'I met Bride's father too. Bride is away for a few days but she sent me a message.'

'The lady has missed you then,' Cormac interjected.

Patrick felt a blush rising in his face and rushed to explain the down to earth nature of the message.

'She's going to help me to waterproof my cart cover but I need a boiling pot. I found one on the stalls which I can pay for with five dozen eggs. I can deliver a dozen each week, but how can I be sure he'll hand over the pot on the fifth week?'

'You can't be sure but there are middle-men who are trustworthy.' Cormac dried his face on a cloth. 'They'll hold the pot for the trader, and take your payments, handing over the goods when you've paid. They'll want a fee too, probably a dozen eggs. Don't rush Patrick; I'll see if I can help you.'

'Thanks, Cormac.'

'I spoke to Eamonn briefly while you were out. I'm going to the fayre with him for meat and drink, then back to his place for a chat. He says he wants to speak to you before you go back. I don't know any more, but he seems pleased with you.'

Patrick's face lit up. 'There's something I haven't told you. After the Moycullen battle, when we were transferring livestock to the hill fort, a Moycullen warrior, hidden from view, crept up on Eamonn from behind and was about to spear him. None of the guards saw him, but I did. I gave the attacker my best sling shot, which made him miss his target. The guards caught him after that.'

'It seems your star is shining, Patrick, and it may yet become brighter when Miliucc sees the flock figures. We've had the best year ever for lambs, and we're getting good prices too. One way or another, you'll get your cover waterproofed.'

'Thanks. When should I go?'

'Tomorrow, before you start work. I'll tell him to expect you at the workshop.'

'Thanks, Cormac.

'Now, boil a pot of water. We'll have a hot drink before I meet Eamonn.'

Patrick placed the partly warmed kettle of water over the embers. When it boiled, he mixed the water with white wine and added a small spoon of honey. Cormac was treated well by King Miliucc, who supplied him with the occasional bottle of mead or pot of honey. Cormac didn't mind sharing this luxury with Patrick.

Patrick new that other shepherds and slaves were not treated this way, nor were they comfortable holding conversations with their superiors. Patrick believed his background was responsible for this.

If I remain humble and modest, maybe I can keep this favourable treatment going.

The luxury made him think of home in Banna Venta and he missed his parents. He supped the mulled wine, and watched Cormac heading for the door.

'You're the smartest sage in the kingdom,' Patrick complimented.

Cormac, enjoying the playfulness, responded, 'I probably am, if not the best dressed.' They both laughed. 'I'll be late. Don't stay up for me,' and off Cormac went.

Next morning the workshop door was open and Eamonn saw him coming.

'Walk right in,' Eamonn called.

Patrick stepped into the crowded room. The benches and shelves of this usually tidy workshop were filled with clutter, quite clearly from the lesser spoils of war.

'How do you feel about your first battle?' Eamonn asked, filling a shelf with daggers as he spoke.

Patrick hesitated. His true thoughts might be too direct for a slave to express to his king's commander. He expressed the view anyway, but in sorrow.

'In truth master, sickened. Glad to be alive but shocked at the slaughter.'

'Stay that way. There is nothing good about war.' Eamonn walked over to a shelf and pointed, 'I want to give you a little reward. Choose any one thing from this shelf.'

Patrick looked over the items, a leather belt with a fine metal buckle, a small dagger, a vertical weaving frame, a paring knife, and a smartly crafted skinning knife.

'Thank you, master, but what have I done to deserve this?' He asked, as his eye lingered on the skinning knife.

'You selected the sheep well, protected my back, and kept the pig-iron cart on the track,' Eamonn said, moving over to the shelf of items that Patrick was studying.

'Do you mean that I filled the ruts for the pig-iron cart?' Patrick asked with a slight frown on his brow.

'Not exactly. I'm told you kept the cart on the track without touching the reins.'

Patrick's face coloured, 'The guard saw me persuading the driver?' he asked, shocked his actions had been observed.

'Of course,' Eamonn said. Patrick's blushing subsided as he realised that he was not being reprimanded.

'Can I trade my reward, or would that be disrespectful?'

'It's yours. Do with it what you will.'

'Then I'd like the skinning knife, thank you.' Patrick took it up and examined it with pride; he was becoming a wealthy slave, possessing a lamp, a cart cover, a brooch for his mother, leg wraps, four laying hens, and now a skinning knife; a considerable accumulation in just four seasons.

'Cormac says you need the use of a boiling pot.' He picked one up from behind some ironmongery. 'Take this, and return it to me when the job is finished.'

Patrick's smile beamed again. 'Thanks, master. That means I don't need to trade the knife. I'll be able to skin some rabbits in the summer.'

Eamonn briefly returned Patrick's smile of enthusiasm then returned to business.

'Before you go, have you worked out why the last raiders didn't kill you or Soldier?'

'I think I have, master. They were from Conn's Kingdom, desperate to feed their families. Beyond that, they didn't wish to harm king Miliucc or his Kingdom.'

'That's what I think. But stay alert Patrick. The southern border is further away now and less of a risk, but we will have made some new enemies, powerful ones, who now live in our kingdom.'

Patrick had only arrived at this conclusion yesterday, after listening to Cuchu. He believed Eamonn's advice to be sound and the kingdom lucky that Eamonn hadn't fallen in the ambush. Patrick left Eamonn's workshop feeling privileged, and so light-headed that his last two days in Voclut passed in a blur.

The trading of livestock ended and Patrick led a refreshed flock of one hundred and thirty ewes to their range in the hills. Over the year, Patrick's faith in God had strengthened. He'd been shown a new way of life, gaining satisfaction from shepherding; even occasional recognition in his work. His life of penance was working. Patrick was seeing rewards and felt at last, forgiven.

CHAPTER SIXTEEN

One pleasant sunny evening, on the quarter moon, as Patrick was playing his calling tune for the sheep, a figure, wearing a long, flared skirt, strode along the rugged hillside; catching his eye. He stopped playing the flute; as she came nearer, her hair, tied in a back bun, showed-off her fair complexion. Patrick's eyes drank her beauty. She wore a short-sleeved cloak, clipped at the front with a brooch and carried an unflattering shoulder bag. Patrick's heart raced. He greeted her excitedly, with a peck on the cheek and a quick hug. Their meeting, over a cart cover, was far from his mind.

'Let me carry your bag,' he said taking it on to his own shoulder.

'What a welcome, Patrick,' she smiled, 'is this what going to battle does for you?'

Having counted the minutes to seeing her, thought of all he wanted to say, Patrick was suddenly unable to express himself.

'Good to see you,' he mumbled.

'Thanks,' Bride said. 'Don't let me stop you working. Get back to your flute. I'll walk with you, to the pens.'

Patrick took Bride's invitation seriously, and observed the sheep carefully as they responded to his call. He'd lost his concentration a few days ago, thinking about Bride's forthcoming visit, and had to turn out again in search of a missing sheep. The last thing he wanted was a repeat this evening. His wish was fulfilled; he counted a full flock into the pen, whilst Bride stoked up the camp fire. Patrick closed the pen, checked the hens, brought two fresh eggs and some oats with him and joined Bride by the fire.

'Let me make refreshment for you. I can offer you porridge and a cooked egg?'

'Don't go short yourself,' said Bride.

'It's not a problem. I have four hens now,' Patrick mentioned with pride as he placed a small pan of water on the fire and put two eggs down to boil.

'I'll do this,' Bride said and began preparing a pan of porridge. 'How did you come by the hens?'

'King Miliucc gave me them; two for preventing a raid on his sheep and, after the battle, he gave two to every warrior who fought for him.'

She raised her eyebrows, seemingly impressed.

'I heard King Miliucc's warriors fought well,' Bride said.

'We lost seventy-five men; Moycullen three hundred,' Patrick responded.

'How did you gain such advantage?'

Patrick recounted the story of the battle and the surprise spear attack.

'Moycullen raided King Miliucc's cattle too often. He must have felt unbeatable,' Bride commented.

'If Conn's men had fought us, I don't think we could have beaten Moycullen; instead, we lost no lives against Conn but gained more warriors, which tipped things in our favour.

'We were lucky then,' Bride stated.

'I wouldn't say lucky. King Miliucc planned to get a peaceful agreement with Conn, he tried and it worked. There's something else, Bride. King Miliucc is a decent man; he respects his people and does not send them into battle easily. When he does, they fight for him.'

Her eyebrows arched. 'You've only been here a year, and you see all this.'

Patrick shrugged his shoulders and prodded the fire. As they ate porridge and eggs and drank fresh water from the river, he enquired. 'You have something to show me?'

'I'm going to teach you how to make your own wax sticks. When you have made enough, I'll show you how to waterproof your cart cover with them.'

They finished eating and cleared the cooking pans.

'Did you get a large boiling pot?' she asked.

'I did,' he said and fetched it from the covered pen. Bride opened her bag, which was filled with special leaves.

'Quarter-fill the pan with water,' she commanded.

Patrick brought his half-full leather water bucket and poured some into the pot. Bride stirred in the leaves and boiled the contents until greasy oil came to the surface of the water.

'It smells terrible. Like goose fat,' said Patrick, holding his nose.

'You'll not know when it's cold.' Bride took out three copper moulds, the shape of tall candles and using a flat stick skimmed off the oil from the pan into one of them. 'Keep on boiling, pressing, and skimming off into the moulds,' she said.

'How many sticks will it take?' Patrick asked.

'Nine or ten will do it.' She watched Patrick skimming off the fat for a short time. 'I think you've got the idea. Now just keep working at it.' She hesitated, 'It's time for me to go.' Bride stood to leave.

Patrick quickly rose to his feet and from his tunic pocket, produced the Celtic wheel that Bride had given him.

'I thought of you every day,' he said, wanting to say more. As he tried, his face struggled awkwardly and tied his tongue.

Bride took over. 'It seems my woollen trinket worked.' She pecked him on his cheek. 'See you on the full moon,' she said, kindly, then turned and made for the hill, beyond which was her home.

Patrick looked on, mesmerised by her movement, amazed at her aura. Bride finally went from view behind a ridge. She didn't look back. He spotted Bride's guard catching up with her. The guard's presence, he could see, was not a secret to Bride. She, or perhaps her father, had organised the security. But if she'd told the guard to keep out of sight, then he'd made a bad job of it.

* * *

Over the following weeks Patrick tended his sheep, his wax making and his prayer life. Bride was always in his thoughts, and he looked forward to her next visit. One evening, as he called the sheep to their pen, he heard the nearby howl of a wolf. He stopped and listened carefully. Hearing a distressed bleating from further up the ravine, he investigated and found one of his lambs caught up in a bush. Returning her to the flock, he resumed his calling of the sheep and led a full count into the pen. Casting his mind back, Patrick realised that he hadn't looked around when he first called the flock. Bride had been on his mind; he was so much looking forward to seeing her. The wolf howl came at the right time; making him listen carefully. He'd had a lapse of concentration and a lucky coincidence had come to his assistance. Patrick resolved to pay more attention.

Keeping up the wax making, he completed his candles before Bride's next visit was due.

'Warm a section of the sheet like this,' Bride said, holding the cover over the fire, then flat on the ground, with the warmed part uppermost, 'rub the candles into the sheet, like this.'

Patrick saw the wax soaking into the fabric. Bride demonstrated until a third of the candle was used. Patrick watched her movements, mesmerised.

'You do it now, Patrick.'

He followed but the wax didn't soak in.

'Get the fabric warmer,' she told him.

Patrick had been watching Bride closely, but not her technique. Now he paid more attention.

'Press hard and rub faster,' she said, holding his hand with the candle in it, to indicate the pressure and speed.

Patrick copied Bride's instruction and this time he succeeded.

'You're on your way, Patrick. By the next moon you'll have a cover fit for a king. Let's change the subject. Do you like mead?'

'I do,' he answered, smiling as Bride pulled a skin out of her bag.

'Tidy up the work place and I'll warm the mead,' she said.

Patrick did as he was told with pleasure and came up with two mugs. Bride poured the hot drink and sat beside Patrick on the log.

'Slainte,' she toasted.

'Slainte,' he replied.

They chatted for a while, sipping their mead. Patrick could feel its warmth in his chest and the warmth of Bride's body as she sat close beside him.

'Last time I was here you said you thought about me while you were away. I'm glad you did. I thought about you too.' She leant in and kissed Patrick on his lips. Speaking softly, she said, 'Did you spot my guard last time?'

Patrick nodded a yes.

'Did you spot him tonight?'

Patrick nodded a no.

'That's because I didn't bring him,' she said in a seductive tone. 'I thought I'd stay the night, if that's alright with you?' Bride didn't wait for an answer as she embraced Patrick and ran her fingers through his blond locks.

Patrick returned her kiss in earnest, but the log wasn't made for passion and they found themselves holding onto each other for balance as much as romance. Patrick didn't know what to do about it. Not wishing to break out of Bride's embrace lest he ruined the moment, he clung on precariously. Bride solved the dilemma. Carefully she untwined herself from his arms.

'Where do you sleep?' she asked, looking through her wavy red locks at him.

Patrick pointed to the covered pen. She nodded and stood to take a woollen blanket from her bag.

'Patrick, you do your duties and I'll arrange the blanket and sheepskins.' Patrick quickly checked the sheep, the hens and spoke to Soldier, before rejoining Bride.

His night was the warmest, cosiest, and loveliest in over a year. It was obvious to Patrick that Bride, although a well-off, freewoman, enjoyed the night too. They both woke up at sunrise. Bride kissed Patrick and quickly prepared to leave.

'See you next moon, Patrick.'

He nodded, split between happiness and sadness as he savoured her kiss and watched her depart.

Over hot porridge by the campfire, he thought of his misery a year ago, how his spirit had been broken. Now he'd found satisfaction in hard, but useful work. He spoke out loud:

'I found God through prayer. I found forgiveness through God. And now, I've found the warmth of Bride's caresses and my feet can't feel the ground.'

He allowed himself to reflect on keeping his new, simple, and contented life in Ireland, in preference to his old life of comfort, status and elements of discontent in Britain. After all the reflection, Patrick pondered a little longer this morning on his decision, last night, to omit his evening prayers.

The moon counted his days and, square at a time, Patrick waterproofed the cover.

Bride arrived at the hill-pen after the sheep had been gathered, once again carrying her shoulder bag. Patrick was sitting next to the fire, partly sheltered by a tree and large boulder, with Soldier by his side. The weather was windy and dry but large black clouds loomed, promising a downpour. Patrick stood to greet Bride, checking his urge to run to her.

'How are you, Patrick?' she enquired. Putting her bag by the log seat, she walked up to him and planted a kiss on his lips.

At her touch his resolve to greet her modestly, crumbled; Patrick hugged her, then lifted her off her feet, spun round in a full circle, and returned her feet to the ground.

'I've counted the days,' he said.

'How's the work on the cover?' Bride asked, cooling Patrick's excitement.

'It's done. I needed a tenth stick but the job is done. I know it works too; we've had a couple of wet nights to test it.'

'Show me then.'

'Over here.' Patrick took her to the tree and boulder. The cover was fixed to a bough of the tree and sloped down to the ground, disappearing below the surface.

Bride studied the detail, 'What have you done there?' She asked, pointing to the ground.

'I've buried the edge of the cover. If I put rocks on the edges to weight it down, the wind can get a hold of it. Laying the edges in a trench and backfilling the soil stops the wind getting under it.'

'Clever. You sleep outside on this pasture?'

'I sleep outside on all of them. Last time we slept in the covered pen to favour the visitor.' He blushed at the memory of their night together and, hoping he wasn't being too presumptuous, asked,

'Are you staying tonight?'

'I like the thought. And if you can sleep outside, I can.'

He smiled, partly at her competitive comment but mostly because she was staying.

She dived into her bag. 'I've brought you some food,' Bride said, putting down a large skin of ale and a cloth-wrapped pack of bread and chicken pieces.

Patrick beamed at the thought of having a change from porridge and eggs for a day, and could see Bride was charmed with his enthusiastic reaction.

They sat down on rocks around the small campfire, to eat their meal. Patrick wanted to devour the food hungrily but he controlled himself to avoid behaving like a slave. He laughed internally at the thought that there could be any dignity in drinking beer from a skin and eating chunks of bread and cheese with his fingers, whilst sitting outside in coarse terrain with rain threatening. They chatted away about the weather and the sheep and how trade was for her father then ran out of conversation.

Bride broke the silence, asking, 'Did you have a girlfriend, at your home place?'

'I didn't. I met a girl and took her for a ride on my horse. Alas, I was snatched away before our second meeting.' Patrick put the memory aside. 'And you, Bride?'

'I never owned a horse,' she teased. 'But I was married once. My husband left me after three years. That was two and a half years ago. I've been single since then.'

'I can't imagine anyone leaving you,' Patrick said. He was describing his own feelings: he meant it.

The rain began splashing so they moved under the cover and sat on the ground, satisfied with their food and drink and the company of each other. The shower became a downpour which pummelled harder and harder until they could barely hear their own voices. Nature was giving the waterproof cover a searching test.

'Don't ask me to silence your cover,' Bride joked, enjoying watching the deluge of pear-shaped water bombs exploding as they hit the ground.

Patrick and Bride huddled together as the torrential rain tried to pound their shelter into the ground. Lightning flashed, thunder rumbled and a ferocious wind arrived, whipping at their cover. The fun became fear. Patrick called Soldier, who emerged soaked, from under a bush. The hound shook the rain off his straggly brown fur, sharing the splashes generously with Bride and Patrick. Bride pulled a handcloth from her bag and dried down Soldier's coat. The wind, cruel and bitterly cold, froze their noses, ears, and fingertips. Wrapping themselves tightly in their sheepskin bed covers, with Soldier squashed between them, Patrick and Bride could only watch on and wait for the storm to die. The cover held out and the storm calmed, the rain reducing to a drizzle. Soldier, without prompting, returned to the shelter of his bush. What a smart dog, thought Patrick. The storm is over and he's left us to our privacy.

Patrick and Bride made their bed and soon were enjoying frivolous fun touching each other's warm bodies with cold noses and fingers. Bride stroked Patrick's lithe body, firm muscles, and toned skin. Patrick couldn't believe his luck. Bride was beautiful, her complexion smooth as Egyptian silk, her long hair tickling against his skin as he held her in his arms. Even in sleep he clung to her.

'I love your sleeping embrace.'

The softly spoken words woke Patrick and, as he felt a gentle kiss on his cheek, he realised where he was and didn't want the day to break. Waking up fully, he looked over to Bride. She was kneeling in front of her bag, taking out some clothing for the day.

'What a night, Bride. Did you get any sleep?'

'I did, eventually, and you?'

'I had sweet dreams,' Patrick said leaning over and giving her a quick kiss. 'Hey, Bride, the fleeces are dry, except for a few damp edges,' he announced excitedly.

'Now I understand your need for waterproofing. This will happen again, won't it?' she stated.

'It will, many times a year.' Patrick rose from his bed. 'Let me check the sheep, then I'll start a fire.'

The sheep were standing around the sides of the pen where they had sheltered from the strong winds. Solider was on duty, touring the perimeter of the grazing land watching out for predators. Patrick returned and took the lamp from his bag of life. Bride was already dressed in boots and a woollen outfit. The boots were farmer's garb but, combined with her dress and wavy red hair, she was shapely and attractive. Bride looked like she owned a goldmine. Taking his flint and tinder he created a spark at the first attempt and lit the candle. Patrick's discipline of keeping dry sticks in a wooden-topped wicker basket at each fold proved its worth. He soon had a crackling fire and a pot of porridge on the simmer. As they ate, Bride began the conversation.

'Patrick, I'd like to see you more often. How do you feel about that?'

'After last night's storm I expect you to never visit me again,' he joked.

'You're right, the accommodation was terrible,' she laughed, 'but the company was good.'

He saw Bride watching his face. 'I'd like that,' he said without hesitation. 'What do you have in mind?'

'One night every quarter moon,' Bride said.

Patrick could hardly speak for happiness, but he didn't need words. They finished their break of fast and hugged their farewells.

'See you in a quarter,' Patrick said, filled with joy.

As Bride left for home, he watched her all the way to the hill, Bride's Hill he called it; then she disappeared. Bride never looked back.

Cormac called unexpectedly the following evening, just as Patrick was penning the sheep.

'Pay no heed to me while you're counting. I'll make myself useful.' Cormac stoked up the fire and examined Patrick's cover.

Patrick finished his work and came to the fire.

'Good to see you, Cormac; is everything well? This is a surprise visit.'

'All is well. I came because of last night's storm; to see if you had weathered it well. Your camp looks in good shape to me, and you're looking well yourself.'

'Thanks. The waterproof cover stood up to the storm and kept my fleece dry.'

Patrick felt tempted to mention Bride's visit, but resisted. He wanted to ask Cormac about marriage customs in Ireland; especially about a slave marrying above his station. But he couldn't ask this question unless he'd already told Cormac about his feelings for Bride and he feared repercussions with the king, if he did this.

'How did Soldier manage in the storm?' Cormac asked.

'He joined me under the canvas, after shaking himself dry on me.'

Cormac laughed. 'I thought Soldier would have joined you. I've brought you a chunk of bread,' he said taking a small pack out of his pouch. 'By the way, if you've finished with Eamonn's pot, I'll take it back for you.'

'I've finished with it, but don't burden yourself with the carrying.'

'It isn't a burden. If it's at the covered pen, I'll collect it on my way back?'

'It's there. Pass on my gratitude to Eamonn please.'

'I will. He'll be pleased to know the exercise was fruitful. You'll see me as usual on the full moon. Goodbye Patrick.'

'Goodbye Cormac.'

A quarter-moon was seven nights and the more Patrick longed for Bride; the slower time crawled. He caught a couple of trout on the day of her visit, to serve as a treat, cooked over the camp fire. Bride brought bread and ale which they ate and drank with the fish. As night closed in and bedtime beckoned, Patrick wanted to tell Bride about his prayer life.

'Bride, the last time we met I mentioned I had a horse.' He stopped as a memory of Shadow filled his mind. 'He was a black horse and I named him Shadow.'

Bride smiled warmly to Patrick.

'My family in Britain are noble. I managed my father's grain farming business, and from this land I was snatched by raiders and brought to Ireland. I was broken in spirit at the time and wanted to die.'

Patrick saw compassion in Bride's eyes; she was listening, perhaps imagining his horror.

'I received kindness from a few people, which kept my spirits alive. Working and living in these hills, in the beauty and harshness of nature, raised my awareness of the marvel of creation. I began praying to God, the creator, and he's helped me.' Patrick smiled at Bride to lighten a little. 'I've just shared with you why I pray and the reason for my belief.'

'Thank you, Patrick,' Bride answered through raised eyebrows.

Was she impressed or mildly surprised?

'Do your checks, Patrick. I'll prepare the bed, and listen to your prayer.'

Patrick checked the sheep, the hens, gave a hug to Soldier and then prayed an abridged version, in Bride's presence, as she waited in the bed for him.

'So, I'm on your list. Did God send me to you?'

'Absolutely not; you certainly came of your own accord. And I'm thrilled you did,' he said as he joined her.

Entwined in each other's arms and legs, she asked, 'How thrilled?'

'Remember that cup of broth you gave me, on the night of the gale?'

She nodded yes.

'It was the best taste since I left Britain. Almost that thrilled,' he teased.

'Almost? I was beaten by a broth, then,' she giggled.

Patrick enjoyed their intimacy but held back and was relieved that Bride hadn't pushed him further than he wanted to go. The first night he'd been reluctant because he'd never had the experience before, but now it was more serious. He didn't want to become a father, while he was a slave.

* * *

It was only the second, quarter moon stop-over and Patrick knew he'd fallen completely in love with Bride. He couldn't stop thinking about her. But he realised that his love for Bride would make Ireland his permanent home and he wasn't sure how he felt about that. He had to raise the subject soon; this was Bride's fifth sleepover, or Bride would do just that. But once again he prevaricated.

In the morning, in his arms before sunrise, Bride said coyly, 'Patrick, I'm falling in love with you.'

It wasn't the way he expected the subject to be aired, but Patrick was relieved that the matter was about to come out in the open. 'I feel the same way about you,' he answered.

Bride smiled, but put her forefinger gently over his lips, to stop him from talking. 'I must tell you something important, before you, before we, get too serious.'

Patrick lost his smile. What was coming next?

Bride paused, then looked into his eyes as she said, 'I'm barren, Patrick. I can't give you a child.'

'You are?' Patrick asked, momentarily floored. He'd held back with Bride to avoid making her pregnant. Now he didn't need to worry.

He immediately despised his selfishness. Dear God, what is the point of purging my soul for past misdemeanours if I am wrong-hearted in the present?

'How do you know this?' he asked.

'It's the reason my husband left me. He's married again and they have two children now.'

'Oh, Bride, I'm sorry.' He hugged her face against his chest. They held each other for minutes in silence. He considered his selfish thought, and felt ashamed.

'How are you coping with this?' Patrick asked.

'It's a great sorrow, but I have no choice. I'm not worrying though, so don't you worry for me.'

'Let me confess to you, Bride. I love you, but I've been holding back. If our love develops, then Ireland becomes my permanent home. If we have children, my paternal responsibilities do the same. I have accepted that I will not escape from Ireland and I no longer think about it. However, falling in love with you has made me think about the future more seriously. I have discovered that I'm not completely reconciled to making Ireland my permanent home. It makes me a bad choice for you.'

Patrick was on his back with Bride by his side.

'And I'm a bad choice for you too,' Bride said. She rolled on top of him playfully.

Patrick's response was cool.

'What is it, Patrick?' she asked softly.

'It isn't respectful. I've held back because of me. Now it's alright, it would feel selfish to let go.'

Bride smiled. 'Thank you, Patrick.' She slapped his face playfully, 'Now don't you dare give me any more respect.' She rolled back, this time taking Patrick with her.

The sheep were pastured late that morning. Patrick and Bride, still drunk on love, rushed breaking their fast.

'Have you the time to walk with me this morning, as I lead the sheep? Once they're grazing, we'll be able to talk.'

'I have time. I'm not working today.'

They sat on smooth flat boulders high up the hillside overlooking the grazing sheep.

'Bride, I am deeply in love with you. Ever since the night of the storm I have had thoughts I would never have believed possible. I move forward in my feelings for you every time we meet. I think it is possible my soul will find peace with the idea of settling permanently in Ireland. I feel to be getting closer to this every day, which means I shall have to pay attention to becoming a freeman. I know little of what is involved. Let me not rush ahead though; what are your thoughts about our future?'

Bride took a deep breath, 'Whoever I fall in love with, there is a risk he won't stay with me once he knows I can't have children. In your case, Patrick, the risk is twofold. You have been ripped from your homeland as well. Should an opportunity arise to return, your heart will be torn.'

Although Bride spoke the truth, Patrick was disturbed by her reasoning and responded directly. 'So why are you here, with me?' he asked, fearing his openness may have put her off.

'Because I have fallen in love with you; with you, I see some hope for our future.'

This better-than-expected answer returned a guarded smile to his face.

'I'm intrigued. I haven't yet associated hope with my prospects. Please tell me more.'

'You don't have a clan, Patrick. To become a freeman and stay free, without the support of a clan, is more difficult than for someone with. I can help you to develop your wealth and your social belonging. I don't have this value to other men. It will take years of working together, but therein lies the hope.'

Patrick was lifted with Bride's response. He needed more knowledge about the process and costs of gaining freeman status, but he was pleased that Bride had thought ahead and was thinking about him, in the long run. He was sure of his love for Bride and now felt sure of her love for him. We both come with problems, he thought, which strangely, might be a benefit, though there was much to consider.

'Where do we go from here?' Patrick asked.

'Maybe we could continue as we are for a couple of quarters. Think things over and talk again?'

Patrick nodded his agreement as he cast his eye across the sheep range, without really seeing the sheep, then asked, 'Bride, does your father know you visit me?'

'I've told him. It's alright as things are, but if we become more serious there are some customs we should respect.'

Patrick wondered what these customs might be, but he thought they had said enough for now. He decided to leave the question for another day.

'Have you said anything to Cormac?' Bride asked.

'I haven't said much. He can see I'm taken with you but he doesn't know you've stayed overnight.' He thought for a moment, 'Unless your father has mentioned it?'

'You can be sure he has said nothing to Cormac. My father is a supplier to the king. He would not pass on stories about one of the king's slaves to an employee of the king.'

Bride's response was emphatic, but she hadn't taken offence. Nevertheless, Patrick regretted his thoughtless enquiry.

'Cormac is visiting me in a few nights. I intend to let him know our situation. Would it be safe for me to discuss the freeman question with him? And if it is, would it be alright with you?'

He watched her face as she answered. She was spontaneous and earnest.

'You will be safe discussing with Cormac.'

Patrick nodded in agreement.

'If you reported directly to the king your enquiry could be rebuffed because you haven't been with him very long,' she added.

How long is reasonable to the king? Patrick thought, then remembered Pig-cart-driver saying it could take ten to fifteen years to work your way out of slavery. This meant the king needed ten to fifteen years to get the value from his investment, in which case, questions within two years would indeed be premature.

'From my point of view, I would be happy with you talking to

Cormac. Secrecy over a dalliance is acceptable, but beyond that it would cause offence.' Bride stood up and swung her bag over her shoulder.'I need to go now and you need to be watching those sheep.'

Patrick got to his feet, gave Bride a long hug and they parted with a kiss; both with rosy cheeks.

'I'm already wishing away the days, Bride. See you in a quarter.'

'I am too. I hope your chat with Cormac goes well.' She turned and strode off.

He watched her all the way to Bride's Hill where she went from sight, as always, without turning back. Patrick fell to his knees in prayer, delighted Bride had been thinking of a future with him.

* * *

Cormac arrived on foot and saw Patrick taking a lamb from his shoulders, returning her to the fold.

He's caught me out, Patrick thought.

'Our shepherd is working late, I see,' Cormac greeted.

Soldier interrupted and ran to Cormac, tail swishing and, after some fussing, returned to his guard-dog duties.

'I was one short. The lamb had strayed beyond the river and couldn't find the ford.'

Thankfully for Patrick, Cormac didn't make any more of it.

'I've brought you bread and a skin of gruel,' he said.

'Thanks Cormac. Hot gruel is perfect, now the nights are getting nippy. Can I serve you porridge?'

Cormac shook his head, 'Thanks for the offer, but I'm not staying long.' He handed over another small package. 'Here are some ointments and cloths for treating the sheep. I passed your pot back to Eamonn. He was pleased to hear your waterproofing plan worked.'

'Thanks Cormac, I'll put these away. Please take a seat,' Patrick pointed to the logs. 'I hope you'll stay long enough to drink a mug of ale. There is something I want to discuss.'

'I will,' Cormac answered agreeably.

Patrick took the packet to the covered pen and returned with two mugs and a half-full skin of ale, which he poured and set down on a flat stone before Cormac. The evening was dry and cold and the light was fading. The fire lit their faces, giving the two men a healthy hue.

'I'm surprised you have ale at this time in the month,' Cormac commented.

'That is a perfect lead in to my conversation. Bride and I are, well, er, things have moved on from waterproofing a cart cover. Now she visits me, to see me.'

Patrick waited for Cormac's response.

'How serious are things between you?' Cormac asked.

'She's visited me a handful of times, and that explains why I have some ale, because Bride brought me a skin when she visited a few days ago. Our relationship is young, but we are both fervent, which prompts me to enquire about the customs here in Ireland. Am I treading dangerously because of my status as a slave and Bride's as a freewoman?'

'It is allowed to have a relationship out of one's class. For a freeperson to marry a slave often brings social disapproval to the freeperson, but it's their choice.'

Patrick was relieved with Cormac's response. 'How would King Miliucc view the situation?' he asked.

'If your relationship becomes serious, he would expect you to conform to custom.' Patrick turned towards Cormac, listening intently. 'In your case that would mean entering a third-degree marriage whereby people who live in separate homes bind themselves for a year, to each other. This establishes respect and correctness.'

Patrick thought of a pagan British tradition of hand-fasting where a couple are tied to each other by the wrist, symbolising faithfulness to each other in a lead up to marriage.

Cormac continued. 'Thereafter the marriage dissolves or is replaced with a full marriage which will need the king's consent in respect of your finances.'

Patrick was impressed with Cormac. He spoke with the succinctness and certainty of a brehon.

'You will be bound to pay a dowry to Bride's father and the king will need to see you can pay without reducing your worth to him.'

Patrick paused to digest this information. 'In practice, that must mean I will need freeman status? I cannot pay a dowry from a slave's allowance.'

'That's right, Patrick. The financial process would be a lifelong commitment of around twenty-one years.'

Patrick could feel his face muscles tightening at the thought of twenty-one years of debt. He saw Cormac reading his face.

'Don't be daunted; the people around you will help, and I believe you and Bride have the ability to prosper in time.'

'Thank you, Cormac. Bride herself said the roads to freeman status, and to keeping it, were long,' he laughed, 'she implied there was hope for me.'

Cormac smiled and then turned a little serious. 'Have you discussed Bride's situation?'

Patrick understood the question. Cormac wasn't just a customer of her father, Coren, he was a friend too. He would know Bride's personal circumstances and would not wish to speak out of turn.

'She's told me of her previous marriage, and, why it ended.'

'It is a sad situation. Bride has it tough. Do you know, Patrick, that there are twice as many young women in Ireland as there are young men.'

'I'm not surprised, with all the unnecessary battles and reckless fighting,' Patrick interjected.

'It's difficult for many young women to find a husband. She succeeded once, but could struggle to do it twice. If there is love between the two of you, I believe she will climb mountains to help you.'

Patrick poked the logs and arranged them, as he thought sympathetically of Bride's plight.

'Thanks for your advice, Cormac, I didn't want to upset the king's cart, and I was reluctant to burden you.'

'I'm glad you did,' Cormac interrupted, with a smile. 'How are you conducting your affairs?' he said, supping the last of his ale from the mug.

'Bride is visiting me every seventh night. We will discuss matters and decide a course. Bride told me herself there is custom to be mindful of.' Patrick stood up and Cormac followed.

'I wish you well, Patrick, and if that is all,' he pointed to the darkening sky, 'I would like to be home before the weather breaks.'

Relieved that Bride's visits hadn't raised any eyebrows, Patrick watched Cormac begin his journey to Voclut then turned to make a later than usual meal that evening, his mind already digesting Cormac's words.

CHAPTER SEVENTEEN

'You're working late I see,' Bride called out.

Patrick stood up from rekindling the fire and ran to her. He swept her up, hugging her tight enough to merge body and soul and, as he returned Bride's feet to the ground said,

'Could six nights be any longer? I've thought of you every minute.'

It was true, and this evening, as his mind was occupied with Bride, he had failed to spot a straying sheep and the search had lengthened his day.

'I have too, but we're together now.' She dived into her bag and pulled out a pack of bread and a skin.

'You've brought me some bread and ale?'

'Bread yes, but not ale,' she interrupted. 'Take a taste.'

He took out the stopper and breathed in the aroma of the most welcome broth he'd ever tasted: the one she had served him when he was a soaked wretch in search of leg wraps.

Tears welled in his eyes as he relived his feelings on the evening when Bride gave him a generous mug-full of a first-class broth; when the flavours took him home to Banna Venta, when Bride's beauty took his breath, and when she studiously avoided looking at him or smiling. He hugged her again.

'What a thoughtful thing to do. Let's eat the treat tonight. Take a seat Bride and put some sticks on the fire; I'll fetch a warming pot and some mugs.'

The evening was cold and dry with a gentle breeze as they sat in front of the fire eating a supper of chunky, dark-brown bread and hot broth.

'How did your chat with Cormac go?' Bride asked.

'It was helpful. He speaks highly of you...'

'Oh. I see. You asked about my character then,' she commented mischievously.

'He wouldn't have given me one, had I begged.' Patrick laughed. 'Our conversation, not surprisingly, was technical. He said there was such a thing as a third-degree marriage, valid for a year. A procedure, he advised, that would keep me on correct terms with King Miliucc. Is that the custom you had in mind?'

'It is. It's a custom I'd like to keep and it protects the reputation of the couple. There are ways to proceed on which I have an opinion but we're not there yet; we have earlier bridges to cross,' she said, fixing Patrick with a polite but firm look.

'Bride, my love for you grows every day and for the first time I am beginning to think about settling in Ireland as a choice, in order to be with you.' Patrick knew he had to be sure and sincere on this point. 'If I was in Britain, I would be thinking of a romantic setting for asking you to marry me.'

Bride's eyes sparkled.

Patrick continued, 'I would be planning which gifts to shower you with. Instead, because I'm stolen from a foreign land; have no clan in Ireland and am not free to choose my occupation, I am forced to discuss the knots and twine with you first.'

'Patrick, are you saying that you are trying to marry me?'

After a moment's hesitation he said, 'I am.' He watched Bride's reaction. She was studious. She looked gorgeous too. Her milk-white complexion, pinked by the conversation and enhanced by the warming glow of the fire, was accentuated by the plain background of the grey night. 'Cormac encouraged me not to be daunted. Bride, when I know what is involved in buying my freedom from the king, paying the dowry to your father, and earning our living – when I know I can see a way – I will ask you to marry me.' Patrick spoke in earnest and saw this reflected in Bride's slow and understanding nod.

'Patrick, you've just satisfied my wishes. I believe a third-degree marriage should be a declaration of intention, not a trial, and the idea of the year's duration should be for planning and preparation.'

A look of relief crossed his face. Patrick liked the idea of a committed third degree and this arrangement would be valuable for his freeman preparations.

'I will marry you as a slave,' Bride said. Patrick breathed in deeply, his chest swelling with pride in this amazing woman, 'and I'll share the burden you will face to gain freeman status. And while you sort your way through these things, let us enjoy our love without rush or fuss.'

His eyes welled with joy and he gave her a long clinging hug, thinking how lucky he was to have Bride's love and selfless support.

She plunged into her bag and brought out a small skin. 'Two good portions of mead,' she announced, with a twinkle in her eyes.

'I'll wash the mugs out,' Patrick responded, rising to his feet.

He returned, shaking the mugs dry and over mead they small-talked about favourite colours, music and childhood memories.

'Let's drink up and have an early night,' Bride suggested.

'Good idea. We'll use the visitors' bedroom again,' he said, smiling happily.

'I'll prepare the bed while you say goodnight to the animals.'

Bride was under the blanket when Patrick returned and he quickly joined her, feeling like the luckiest man in the world.

'What about your prayers?' she asked.

'I forgot,' he sucked in breath and put his hand to his mouth. 'Thanks, Bride.' He jumped out of bed and dropped to his knees.

'Forgive me Lord for I am the least of the most contemptible. You favour me with blessings and I forget you in an instant. I beg your forgiveness...' and then he prayed as usual, finishing with thanks for the love between Bride and himself. He returned with enthusiasm to Bride's embrace, but in the back of his mind he knew the luckiest man was spilling his substance and needed to mend the leak.

Next morning Patrick was up long before dawn saying his prayers outside, kneeling on a flat stone a few feet from the fire. There was a cold and damp mist swirling in the predawn light and the weather was dry. Patrick loved the freshness of the chill and the gradual coming to life of the world around him, as birds called and sang, then the sun peeped and the birds chattered in excitement. Patrick had built up the fire and prepared a pan of porridge before Bride rose. As he was drinking his cup of porridge, standing up by the pen and looking out over the valley, he heard the sluicing of water behind him and guessed Bride was washing herself in the outside tub. Resting his mug on the wall, he felt two hands and arms wrap around his waist from behind; and Bride's warmth radiated into his body as she hugged herself to him. He savoured the moment then turned to see Bride, dressed for her ramble home, her cheeks pink and pretty from the cold-water rinsing.

'Did you sleep enough, Patrick?' she asked.

'I got some sleep. Some is enough when I'm with you,' he laughed.

'It's the same with me, but come this evening I'll be ready for an early night.'

Patrick thought so too but kept it to himself.

'Can I pour you some porridge?'

'Not today, Patrick. I'll be on my way. Thanks for everything; I'll see you on the seventh night.' She gave him a parting hug and a kiss, then made for the hill.

Patrick refilled his cup with Bride's portion of porridge and watched her all the way to the foothills.

My slave status is a chasm between us. He thought of how he could change his life to be with Bride. He needed to become a freeman, which meant developing his wealth. Bride was already trading his surplus eggs for more hens and looking after them for him at the craft village. How many hens would I need to trade them for a lamb? How much livestock would I need to become a freeman? Less than five cows said the slave-raid captain. I need good and accurate advice. Would Cormac and King Miliucc discuss this detail with me or would they frown upon it?

* * *

As thoughts of his situation continually filled his mind, the shepherd's concentration slipped and he found himself spending hours looking for lost sheep. He tried harder to keep his mind on the work at critical times, which worked for a while until he lapsed again.

Patrick pined for Bride and the more he thought about her, the more his attention drifted away from the sheep. He needed to be with her, to live with her, to marry her.

During one of Bride's visits, they discussed the Irish ceremony of marriage.

'What is an Irish wedding like?' Patrick asked.

'It's a ritual where we promise ourselves to each other in the witness of our communities and in front of our chosen gods, who are then called down to bless our coupling,' Bride explained.

'Who conducts the ceremony and where will it take place?' Patrick asked. He saw Bride looked a little nervous as she answered.

'The ceremony takes place in the woods in the evening and is led by a druid.'

'Will a druid take objection to a Christian?' Patrick asked.

'No objection at all. They believe in many gods. I have an uncle who married a Christian woman. She witnessed before Jesus Christ and the druid called on Christ's blessing. What about you, Patrick, have you any objection with a druid marrying us?'

'If I am free to worship as I wish, that is enough for me,' Patrick answered. He thought how his father and grandfather would view this situation. They would be intolerant of a Christian marrying in a pagan ceremony.

* * *

A quarter of a year had passed since their first kiss and now Patrick was learning more about how to become a freeman in his own circumstances. Cormac advised Patrick that Bride's father, Coren, would only be able to ask a quarter of the dowry that he'd asked for on Bride's first marriage. The payment was traditionally made with a tenth of a person's wages paid every moon until the agreed sum was settled.

Patrick learned that his freedom price to the king reduced as his service lengthened and that it may be possible for the king to employ him in different work, allowing him to live with Bride. Patrick was beginning to see his path for gaining freeman status and becoming hopeful about his future with Bride.

* * *

One morning as Patrick rose to pray, it occurred to him that he'd forgotten to pray the night before. He was dismayed.

'Please God, when I think of the sheep, I think of you. Yet the more I think of Bride the more I forget you and the sheep; help me in my weakness.'

Later that afternoon, he found himself picturing Bride's face, imagining the feel of her skin against his. He lingered in his thoughts of Bride. Before he'd fallen in love with her, God had filled his thoughts, day and night. He enjoyed thinking of Bride and the love they'd found. But he was forgetting God, and the sheep, too often. He knelt immediately, praying for forgiveness and help, and soon, his burden eased and he worked away with a happier heart.

Patrick redoubled his effort to maintain his prayers; to concentrate on the shepherding. It only worked for a short time.

'I'm one short again,' he said despairingly to Soldier. 'Guard the pen, I'll see you later.' Patrick hadn't watched the sheep carefully enough to have any clues where to start looking, so he headed for the furthest point on the range.

Halfway back as he was checking some gorse, a wolf appeared from the bushes. Patrick stopped, instantly. His pulse always raced when he was confronted by a wolf, but this time the predator was more menacing. Blood dripped from the wolf's teeth and jaws as he stood in Patrick's path snarling defiantly. Patrick slowly pulled out his sling. The wolf growled and walked slowly towards him, head down, eyes looking up with a fixed, attentive stare at Patrick.

Usually, a lone wolf would retreat from a human but Patrick had a sinking feeling that the blood was from a ewe and that he'd disturbed the wolf while eating. The wolf looked mature but starving and might defend his catch like it was a newborn cub. Patrick made noise and waved to scare the predator away. The wolf hesitated briefly then continued his menacing walk towards Patrick; eyeing him, revealing his blood-soaked jaws.

Is the wolf telling me to back off? He certainly isn't rushing to attack.

If the wolf had already achieved hunting success on Patrick's range; if he scared off the shepherd as well, he'd come back for more. Patrick swung his sling and released his shot, on target for the wolf's face until he dodged at the last second and took the hit on the shoulder. The wolf yelped and ran with a bloody snarl straight at Patrick, who released his second shot, smashing the teeth of the wolf. But the wolf kept coming; bit Patrick's leg viciously, then howled in agony, probably pained by the broken teeth and the power of his own bite. Patrick clubbed the wolf in the ribs with the full force of his bulbous rod, knocking him to the ground and the second blow rendered the wolf unconscious.

Searching the bushes, he found their missing ewe, still entangled but dead and half eaten. The ripped open flesh of the sheep was excessively bloody, explaining the dripping red face and jaws of the wolf. Turning to head for home, Patrick noticed one of his stones on the ground and picked it up, kicking himself for almost forgetting to recover his slingshot. He found the second shot and pocketed it with his sling and began his journey to the pen, limping lightly. Filled with remorse for failing to safeguard the sheep and riddled with guilt over his inability to keep his mind on his job; Patrick felt tortured.

He stopped on the way, at his river of life, to wash his wounded leg, which revealed that much of the blood on his leg had transferred from the wolf's mouth. As his leg washed clean it became clear that his own wounds only bled slightly. He thought his calf wound would have been much worse if the wolf had all his teeth, but still, the remaining fangs had penetrated his flesh. He wrapped a sheep's bandage around his leg and continued home; thinking how to solve his concentration problem. If he lived with Bride the pining would cease. It was the living apart that was the problem.

He arrived at the pen and despatched Soldier to call Cormac.

Soldier returned and shortly after was followed by Eamonn on horseback with Cormac riding pillion. His visitors dismounted as Patrick greeted them.

Good evening, master; good evening, Cormac.'

'How are you, Patrick, I see your leg is bandaged?' Cormac remarked.

'I'm alright, but the news is bad. We've lost a sheep.' Cormac gestured with his hand palm up, for Patrick to continue. 'I was one short when penning.' He saw Cormac raise an eyebrow. 'Soldier stayed here. I found trouble at the gorse bushes north of the river, when a wolf stood in my path. His mouth was dripping with blood and he wouldn't scare off. He tried to make me back off and when I didn't, he ran at me. I hit him twice with slingshot, injuring him but he kept on coming and bit my leg. I beat him unconscious with the rod and then found our ewe, tangled in the bushes, dead and half eaten. I'm very sorry; if I'd noticed his absence before I led the sheep in, this probably wouldn't have happened.'

Patrick was clearly distressed by the event but his reaction was exacerbated by the turmoil and conflict he was suffering in balancing his relationship with God and Bride.

'Show me your wound, Patrick,' Cormac asked.

Patrick removed the bandage. Eamonn, still holding the reins, and Cormac looked closely.

'I think that's going to turn bad,' Eamonn said, have you some ointments for the sheep?

'I have; shall I bring them to you?'

Eamonn nodded.

Patrick returned with a pot of brown and a pot of green ointment.

'The green paste will protect you from infection,' Eamonn said, 'Cormac, would you apply it?'

Cormac took a cloth from his pocket.

'Take a deep breath, Patrick,' and he smeared the teeth marks where they'd pierced the flesh. Patrick sucked in as the ointment stung his skin and continued stinging and burning. After the initial shock, he stifled his extreme discomfort, and noticed Eamonn chuckling. 'If it hurts it's working,' he said.

As Cormac bandaged him up, Eamonn said, 'I'd like you to stay here Cormac while Patrick shows me the place.'

Cormac nodded, and Eamonn mounted. Patrick began walking.

'Jump on the back if you think you can stay on. We'll be trotting.'

Without reply, Patrick jumped on the back, landing softly in place. He glanced at Cormac as if to say, did you see that. Cormac nodded in approval.

Patrick loved the feel of the horse and his technique for bareback riding came straight back to him. His left calf ached as he gripped the horse with his legs, but not enough to spoil his enjoyment of riding with Eamonn who was noble, a guard to the king, and a man Patrick admired.

They dismounted at the scene. Eamonn examined the sheep and pointed out teeth marks around the sheep's neck to Patrick.

'A lone wolf is unlikely to kill a sheep in the open but if a sheep is ensnared the wolf will get at the sheep's neck. It must be strangulation because there is very little bleeding. Once they are eating the flesh, they get a blood lust and human beings no longer frighten them. I think if you had backed off, he would have left you alone and returned to the feast.'

Eamonn examined the dead wolf. 'You knocked half his teeth out,' he said.

'He bit me with other half, though,' Patrick quipped, 'but I didn't think I'd killed him.'

'Patrick, regarding your word earlier; you feel guilty for not spotting the missing sheep. It's good that you never want to lose a sheep, or never want to make a mistake, but don't whip yourself. You haven't lost a sheep or a lamb in three years.' Patrick's chest filled out. 'We know Soldier is very clever, but he can't guard the range when he's at the pen. It is a weakness of the system. This wolf happened to come along when Soldier was out of range at the pen. It's happened before, but if you could train Soldier to make a closer perimeter check for strays and caught-ups before you lead the flock in, you could plug this weakness. Soldier responds to you; I think you could do it.'

These words made Patrick feel better and he liked the idea of training Soldier to make a tighter perimeter check at the end of the day, knowing he could already call him from a distance. It could be a solution to his lapses with the sheep too and the idea could be implemented quickly.

They returned to the pens and on this occasion, there was no opportunity for a private chat with Cormac. Eamonn and Cormac departed immediately after returning Patrick to the camp.

Bride's visits continued happily and the sheep counting improved as Soldier learned very quickly to operate the additional check. However, as Patrick learned the finer details of his route to freeman status, he was informed by Cormac that the king was open to discussing with Patrick once his third-degree marriage to Bride had taken its course, through to full marriage. However, Patrick's longing to live with Bride was intensifying. Could he ask King Miliucc to make him a valley shepherd, immediately, especially so soon after the king had expressed willingness to flexibilities once he was married?

Patrick now, was forgetting about God entirely during the daytime and occasions of missing night prayers were still happening. Continuing as they were for another year and a half weighed heavily on Patrick's mind. The wolf and dead sheep had come back to worry him. Eamonn had lifted his spirits but on reflection Patrick new his performance over three years was not the issue. The horror of the event would not leave him and he blamed it on his inner turmoil. He blamed himself.

This week, after five full moons of romance, Bride had left after break of fast and Patrick's mind was filled with exciting thoughts of Bride and their future together; and torn with anguish as usual, he was churning through the possibilities. Soldier had completed his close perimeter check and Patrick called the sheep, but they didn't respond. He called again but they continued grazing. Then Soldier ran up to Patrick, muzzled into his tunic pouch and came out with the flute in his mouth. Only then did Patrick realise that he'd been voice-calling the sheep. Patrick laughed aloud, and fussed Soldier, but the nature of his distraction dismayed him and he cried on the inside as he played Psalm 23 on his flute. The sheep gathered and followed as usual to their calling tune.

After much thought and prayer that week, Patrick finally saw the solution to his problem and now it stared at him. He had no further mishaps that week. Patrick knew he would need courage and determination to see the challenge through and he prayed for the necessary resolve.

* * *

Bride arrived, bringing with her a treat of bread and ale. As they ate and drank a mug of ale, Patrick started the big conversation.

'Bride, I have something serious to say to you. It's a message that I deliver with pain in my heart.'

Bride's look became sombre. She nodded gravely, as though she knew what Patrick was about to say.

'I must stop seeing you. I love you Bride and...' Patrick struggled with his emotions. He couldn't speak for a while.

'I'm sorry too, Patrick. I love what we have, but this day was always coming. I'm just sorry that it's here.'

'You can't possibly have known the day was coming. I didn't know myself till now.' His voice was raised and filled with anguish. 'I haven't told you why yet.'

'Patrick, you love me and you love your God, but you want to give all your love to God.'

Patrick jerked his head back, shocked. He felt robbed of his thoughts. Glistening little rivers trickled down his ruddy cheeks. 'Your words, Bride, they are better than my words. How do you know?' Patrick had braced himself for this moment, expecting Bride to be taken by surprise, to have no answer for his reason, only to find she was ahead of him by weeks.

'I know you, Patrick.'

Patrick was exasperated. He rubbed away his tears on his sleeve. 'You know my inner thoughts; my new thoughts?'

'You're honest, Patrick. And we are close, it's not surprising,' Bride said.

Patrick took a deep breath. 'Bride, I apologise to you. When I think of the sheep, my thoughts take me to God. When I think of you, I forget about God and the sheep. I've made my choice, Bride, and you don't deserve this.'

Bride, about to speak, stopped 'There's no point talking,' she said, resignedly and picked up her bag.

Patrick saw Bride fighting her feelings. She gathered a measure of composure and gave Patrick a hug.

'It was good while it lasted, Patrick. I lived in hope.' Her face saddened as she continued, 'I've lost two good men in my life, because all I had to offer wasn't enough.'

'No Bride. There is nothing lacking on your part. You offered more than could be expected. Your words say it. I want to give all my love to God.'

'I was hoping you would love both of us. People have faith in God and still love their husbands and wives. Can't you?'

Patrick didn't answer. He wanted Bride to turn and go.

'Can't you?' Bride asked again, softly, pleadingly.

Patrick was weakening. He was desolate. Please go, I cannot bear the pain much longer; he silently willed her to leave, but she stood there, waiting for his answer.

'It's my weakness. But I can't,' Patrick said, hoping his answer would close the matter. He looked at Bride's expression. Oh no! She's reading my face, which means my heart and soul; my frailty.

'Oh! Patrick. I can see the deep distress in your face. And I see the determination in your already dry eyes, too. Both tell the truth, but your eyes speak the bigger truth.'

Patrick couldn't take any more. If she would go now, he could keep his resolve. He was close to turning his back on her.

'Forgive me, Bride.'

'I forgave you on the night you forgot to pray.'

'You saw this coming on the night I forgot to pray? How?'

'When you dropped in an instant to your knees, I saw your obedience to God. You called yourself the least of the most contemptible. I remember a line of your prayer, "You favour me with blessings and I forget you in an instant, I beg your forgiveness."'

Patrick's eyes opened wide, as Bride continued, 'I saw your fear of god. But once you'd asked, you felt forgiven so completely, I could see your belief; and by the time you'd given thanks, your love of God was plain to see. It was then that I understood the strength of your relationship with God; out of the ordinary, truly exceptional.'

She really knows me; and understands. What a remarkable woman. She's known for weeks and has waited for me; accepting me for who I am. And, I will use Brides words, she is out of the ordinary; truly exceptional. Patrick's eyes filled with water and his head drooped, but relief was already entering his look.

She turned and strode for the hill.

Patrick wanted to run after her; to change his mind. He was denying the strength of his feelings for her and his resolve was failing. But he knew where to go for help. Kneeling with his back to Bride's Hill, he asked God for courage to see this through. While praying at length he heard a voice inside his head. 'Harden your heart no more; wave to her.'

He stood up and turned towards Bride's Hill, looking to where she passes from sight. Bride was there, looking back. She made a big sweeping wave. Patrick returned the wave with both arms and kept it going. Bride stopped waving and stood upright with both arms outstretched in the shape of the Christian cross. Patrick imitated the posture and Bride lingered for a second and was gone.

She really has forgiven me. We are both free.

CHAPTER EIGHTEEN
Look Your Ship is Ready

Patrick prayed for Bride on each festival day, and thought of her often through the year after their parting. She was written in his heart and soul and, as time passed, he found he could think of her fondly, without pain or anguish. Patrick thanked Bride in his prayers, for her forgiveness, which had set him free.

The shepherd settled deeply and comfortably into work and prayer and, in the certainty that his youthful sins were forgiven, his purged soul found the love of God. He walked every day with the Lord and, when asleep, God entered his dreams. Patrick stopped thinking about wealth and possessions. The little he had was sufficient. Even the quality foods of his former life were gone from his mind. Neither was his physique skinny. Patrick was tall and slim, muscular and fit. His daily diet of oats and ewe's milk and an occasional trout, had been supplemented with eggs and occasionally chicken, satisfying his appetite. His previous level of hunger had abated.

One day, in most months, Cormac brought a treat of bread or a skin of ale. Patrick had all he needed, except warmth. The inhospitable weather in the hills was, at times, cruel. Patrick's efforts to improve his clothing and shelter helped, but when the elements were harsh, most efforts were futile. He resorted to prayer and was toughened. The harsh weather taught Patrick to change what he could and to accept what he couldn't. When misery tried to afflict him, he turned his energy or his mind to positive things. Even his thoughts of home changed from homesickness to fondness and happy memories. And so, the wheel of life turned and turned.

Three years passed without a Kingdom battle, until Patrick, now twenty, was called again to fight, this time on the southern border of Conn's Kingdom. King Miliucc sent his warriors, as allies, to repel an attack by a starving kingdom to the south. The battle was cut short as the attackers retreated when their commanders saw the combined strength of the Conn warriors and King Miliucc's force. Some of Conn's warriors were injured and killed, but the skirmish was over before Miliucc's forces – lined up and battle-ready – were called into action.

In the retreat camp, Patrick renewed his contact with Bognan, but after a quick snatch of conversation, Bognan was called away. Patrick was marshalled into a separate enclosure and was pleasantly surprised to come across Joshua, his fellow captive from Banna Venta and son of the leather man. He learned from Joshua that he'd prospered as a craftsman for King Miliucc and was now a freeman with wife and child.

'How are you progressing?' Joshua enquired. 'I'm not. But I don't push for it. I'm a better Christian as a slave and shepherd.'

Joshua's breath was taken, and he didn't disguise it.

'You've travelled a long road, Patricius,' Joshua declared, humorously emphasizing Patrick's Roman name, and shedding his own subservient term, master. 'I'm glad you've found happiness.'

Patrick was delighted with Joshua's goodwill towards him. Indeed, it was goodwill for Patricius. The conversation, however, was short-lived as the commanders gathered their warriors, sending Patrick and Joshua separate ways.

* * *

The seasons passed and six years on from Patrick's first Beltaine, Cormac was walking with a stoop, and Patrick had grown from a wiry boy to a tall and slim, strong young man. Patrick led the business now, at the Festival of Beltaine and Cormac, in practice, was his assistant and adviser, though still his official senior. One evening, early in Patrick's seventh Beltaine, he returned to Cormac's house having completed a purchase of two rams.

'Patrick, Eamonn wishes to speak to you.'

'Oh good,' Patrick responded. He admired Eamonn and enjoyed meeting him. In recent years the audiences, though few, had always been positive.

Patrick presented himself to Eamonn that night.

'I have something to show you,' said Eamonn. 'I think you will know what it is.'

He handed him a highly polished, dark-brown leather case about two feet long, a foot wide and four inches deep. The lid was held closed with two leather thongs tied neatly in a bow. Patrick, immediately recognising the item, received it carefully, with both hands. He looked for a generous space to set it down and fixed his gaze on a clean portion of a bench top. Eamonn, seeing Patrick's train of thought, cleared away a few tools. He put up his hand, motioning Patrick to wait a moment and found a length of clean cloth with which he covered the bench. Patrick held the case and examined the leather; he sniffed the surface, checked the corners and joints, examined the stitching, held it high and looked at the bottom of the case then placed it centrally on Eamonn's cloth.

The smell of the leather and sight of the pouches transported Patrick to Banna Venta on his twelfth birthday, when his grandfather, Potitus had gifted him a similar precious box: a writing set, only slightly more modest than the one he now held. Patrick noticed Eamonn was appreciative of his reverence for the box. He opened the hinged lid till it lay flat, revealing pouches, small and large, housing ink and tools. He opened the next leather layer to the left and finally the same again to the right. Patrick and Eamonn were now beholding a typical British noble's writing desk-top. Patrick glanced at Eamonn and saw he was enraptured.

'Eamonn, this is beautiful.' Patrick realised that he, the slave, had called the commander by his given name, but neither of them responded to the accidental slip.

Inside, Patrick found the larger pouch contained six sheets of unused vellum. Smaller pockets held glass pots of India ink, a selection of quills and a small knife. Patrick's feelings of enthusiasm flattened to stony as his mind flashed back to his last evening in Britain, penning the security report for his father.

'What is it, Patrick?' Eamonn asked, his concerned tone revealing he'd detected a change.

Patrick came back to the present and his smile returned. He chose to answer the question as though it was about the case, not the thoughts it had triggered, which surely had shown on his face.

'It's a writing set, master.' By now Patrick was inspecting the vellum sheets. 'High quality; probably from the Mediterranean,' he said.

'You are right. It was a gift to King Niall from his Roman wine merchant. Niall gifted it to King Miliucc, who doesn't know what to do with it. Could you do something useful with it? I mean, for the king.'

Patrick mused. King Niall didn't know what to do with it either. He thought about charity gift competitions in Banna Venta. If you won a gift you didn't like, you offered it as a charity gift in a different society. He laughed. It's the same over here. But now he took Eamonn's request seriously. Ireland didn't have a written language. He thought for a while and looked across at Eamonn, whose face was serious and silent as he gave Patrick thinking time.

'I could teach Cormac to write and read.'

'How would you do that?' Eamonn asked.

Patrick searched in one of the leather pockets and found some vellum trimmings.

'Shall I demonstrate to you on these coarse pieces?'

'If you wish,' said Eamonn, looking puzzled.

Selecting a quill Patrick took up the small knife and, with a flourish, sliced off the end at an angle, making a perfect nib. He removed the ink-pot lid and dipped his quill into the India Black.

Holding the parchment strip, he practised a few strokes and then wrote the letters A m o n, on the vellum scraps.

'Each of these shapes is a letter, and letters have a sound. You learn the sounds.' He pointed, 'This is an 'ay' sound. This is 'emm', this is 'oh' and this is an 'enn' sound. Together from left to right you merge the sounds, and say them fluently, Ay-emm-oh-enn: Eamonn.'

Eamonn gaped.

'That is how to write and read your name,' Patrick explained. 'With this beautiful set I would write down all the letters and teach their sounds to Cormac.'

Eamonn, with practised understatement said, 'Interesting; are you sure Cormac is not too old?'

'His mind is still sharp. He would learn quickly. Then he could use what I have written down, to teach others,' Patrick responded.

Eamonn considered a while. 'This is good use. Take it and I will speak to Cormac. You are about to become a teacher as well as a shepherd. Remember, the writing set belongs to the king. You should return it when you have finished. Take care and you can expect the king will ask to see your work.'

Back at Cormac's home, by candlelight, Patrick wrote the Latin alphabet and some word examples, neatly on a sheet of vellum, to be used for teaching Cormac, who slept, unaware he was about to become Patrick's student. Patrick also wrote Psalm 23 carefully spaced to fit on one sheet, for Cormac to practise reading. Whilst doing this, he had the idea to spend some time in the hills writing an extra psalm carefully with flourishes on the first letter of every verse. This ornate version would be for King Miliucc.

* * *

By the end of Patrick's seventh Beltaine, Cormac could read and write his own name and some short sentences, in Irish Gaelic, using Latin letters. Cormac treasured the script that Patrick wrote for him.

On Patrick's last evening, after the markets, Cormac spoke movingly to his charge.

'Patrick, you have taught me something very special. To see letters, in a special order, describing the sounds of words in my mother tongue, is a joy. However, to know that a king called David wrote the words of Psalm 23, seventy generations ago in a foreign land, is thrilling. After all that time, his thoughts become my thoughts. It stretches my mind beyond imagination.'

'Cormac, you've taught me so much about life. I'm happy that I could show you something of value, but right now I must prepare for my social appointment.'

Patrick changed into a clean yellow tunic and left to join Cuchu for food and ale at the festival. They met up and chatted easily about all manner of things.

Before parting, Cuchu whispered, 'Any thoughts of escape?'

'None at all,' Patrick answered, sincerely.

'You've learned well,' said Cuchu, disbelieving Patrick's words. 'Let me tell you. Don't think of looking on the west coast. The boats are land hoppers. You'll get caught. Don't think of the north coast either. It's too nearby. The dogs will catch you. Let me tell you; the best plan is the maddest. You know the southern part of Conn's Kingdom, where we fought?'

'I do,' Patrick nodded, going along with him.

'Go there, follow the river. Get far south as fast as you can. Eventually this river meets a bigger one. This is your sign to go east. Keep the tall mountains on your right till they end. Follow the next river in the south-east direction for a few nights. It'll take you to the south-east coast of Ireland. The harbours are busy down there. You will find merchant boats from over the seas.'

'Thanks, Cuchu, but like I said, I've no plans for escaping.'

'We know that. But save your food. You'll need twenty days or more.'

'Thanks, Cuchu. Always good to meet you, but it's time to go.' Patrick gave him a hug. 'I hope we meet again next Beltaine.'

Cuchu hugged Patrick long and firmly and said, 'In a way, I hope we don't. But you've learned well, now fare well.'

Patrick was puzzled by the fuss. For some reason Cuchu never seems to accept that I'm not going anywhere. This time it was Cuchu that extended his arm in the noble manner, giving Patrick a hearty handshake. Patrick watched him walk away, losing sight of Cuchu too quickly, and yet the fayre wasn't crowded.

* * *

One night, towards the end of summer, when the people of Ireland were looking forward to the Festival of Lughnasa and the celebration of harvests, Patrick was sleeping as usual by the embers, outside the covered pen. The sheep were settled in the open fold and Soldier was asleep next to the pasture.

Patrick heard a voice in his dreams.

'You do well to fast since you are about to go to your own country.'

Patrick turned restlessly in his sleep.

'You do well to fast since you are about to go to your own country.'

The voice woke him this time; it was a man's voice. He sat up in bed and listened. Disturbed, he rose from his bed, his heart in a flutter. His breathing shortened and his pulse rattled in his throat, like a woodpecker tapping at a tree. He went down on one knee for a while to settle himself, then, in the middle of the night he dressed and called Soldier, simply to check the hound was there. Soldier came faithfully appearing undisturbed.

Patrick scouted the area with Soldier and knew from the hound's calm reaction, there was no one there. He stoked the embers into life and sat on his log, looking into the fire, and thinking. Soldier returned to his bed. Patrick slowly realised the voice was God's and he was devastated. He prayed where he was sitting.

'Dear God, I'm happy with my life; the sheep and prayer; it is all I want for, I'm already yours.'

But the voice returned; he heard it plainly and this time he was wide awake:

'Your hungers are rewarded. Look, your ship is ready.'

His time to escape had arrived and he knew it was God's wish.

He thought of Cuchu's conversation and now realised he was God's angel, and had been for all those years. This means that God has forgiven my youthful sins. I felt he had, but now he's told me directly.

Soldier, uncalled, came to Patrick silently and settled snugly, leaning against Patrick's leg.

'And you know something too, don't you Soldier?'

Patrick stroked Soldier lovingly as the realisation of leaving began to sink in.

My capture; my six years of slavery; this was my penance, and I've served it. I am about to return to my own country. God is sending me home. He will guide me home. Was my punishment equal size to my sin? No. It was only punishment when my heart treasured material wealth and status. As I learned humility, the same treatment educated me, developed me, and purged my soul.

The fire needed more sticks and Patrick broke out of his train of thought to stoke it. He sat on the log to prod the fire and Soldier snuggled up to him again.

'I'm going to miss you, Soldier, and how empty life will be without you and Cormac. And dear Bride, God bless you, we didn't know at the time what the future would bring. King Miliucc, I'm about to leave you. My slavery could have been much worse with a different master.'

Patrick felt empty. There was no elation at the thought of escape. No excitement over God's direct words. The purpose in my life has been removed. I don't know what is ahead.

Over the next three days Patrick planned his exit. He cooked a chicken and pulled the meat; cooked some eggs, filled a skin with ewe's milk. He emptied a shelf in the covered pen and set out the items for packing. He only partly filled his second skin with fresh river water, reasoning that he could replenish water easily on his way. He decided to take his small knife and dagger to protect himself from predators.

His rod and staff he would leave behind, along with his bag of life and the shepherd's head scarves. These items now reminded Patrick of his first day as a shepherd, in Eamonn's workshop, filling his bag, discovering that the sky was about to become his roof. He thought of his devastation, and how he had adapted. Now, the same scene was his home. A home he didn't want to leave.

Snapping out of his reverie, he decided to take the sheepskin and leave the bulky and heavy cart cover. After a second thought, Patrick cut a strip off the cart cover, sufficient to wrap around the fleece, to protect it from rain when he would be walking. In a medium size bag, which Bride had given him, he packed one change of clothing and sandals, in case his feet blistered in the boots. Finally, he hung his candle lamp – which Bride had kindly replenished for him – on the outside of the bag.

On the evening before his departure Patrick secured the sheep then took the writing set and penned a couple of messages, by the fireside, with Soldier moping at his feet.

'My dear friend, Cormac, I thank you for your kindness and friendship and for sharing with me some of your plentiful wisdom.

May God bless you, Patrick.'

'My Lord, King Miliucc, please forgive me, you did nothing to deserve this. I leave for you the words of "The Lord is My Shepherd". If you ask a harpist and singer to perform this for you, I believe it will bring you pleasure. I have given to Cormac the tune and the words.

May God bless you, Patrick.'

Patrick lit a candle and placed the message to Cormac on the hidden shelf in the low-roofed pen, alongside the writing set. Inside the writing set he placed the letter to King Miliucc with the handwritten psalm.

His final preparation was to recover the brooch he'd bought for his mother at his first Beltaine Festival. The ground in the corner of the pen looked undisturbed. Using his dagger as a spade he began to unearth his buried treasure; surprised that he had to dig deeper than he thought. Expecting to find a mug he was shocked when he came to a box. He removed the wicker container with both hands, opened the lid and there, to Patrick's relief, sat the mug. His earlier and thorough preparations had paid off, as he lifted out the bone-dry vessel. Removing the cover of the tankard the brooch sparkled as it bounced back the light from the candle. Picking up the mug he tipped the brooch into his palm; examining it with pride. He didn't mind that the stones were glass; he'd bought the brooch as a slave, trading a new pair of sandals for it. Patrick ran his fingers over the jewels and the rim of the brooch, savouring the moment, before placing the gift in his pocket.

The appearance of the box was still a mystery. Looking carefully at the empty container he recognised the bottom was lined with parchment, which he picked up curiously. Suddenly his breathing quickened and his neck hair stiffened as he found a written message on the underside.

'Patrick, it was only a matter of time. I wish you well and may your Christian God bless you.' It was signed in normal writing, 'Cormac.'

Patrick's mind raced. The note had to have been placed there in recent months; since Cormac's writing lessons began. Once again, those close to him had read his thoughts, and again before he'd had the thoughts himself. He rolled the parchment note and taking some twine from the shelf, tied the bow, then stepped outside to the fire and placed the scroll into his bag.

Cormac guessed my intentions yet never raised the subject. He didn't question me but allowed events to take their course. That was Cormac. The note is a treasure, a specimen of Cormac's newly learned writing skill and in between the lines is Cormac's wonder and appreciation of the written word.

Patrick returned to tidy the soil back into the hole and placed the mug and the box on the shelf next to his letters and the writing set. He finished his packing and went to sit by the fire.

Soldier walked around listless; moping. 'Come here, Soldier,' Patrick said as he sat on the log by the fire.

Soldier sat on Patrick's feet resting against his shins. 'It's time to go, Soldier,' said Patrick, staring into the fire. 'But I don't want to. I'm happy here. I regret the nature of my leaving. I'm walking out on you, Soldier, on Cormac and King Miliucc. Yet I must go. My time here has run its path. God is my guide and yet I feel nervous. I don't know what lies ahead. I wish you were coming with me, Soldier.'

Patrick looked up from the fire and watched the lifeless, pale sun disappearing behind the horizon. He didn't see the closing of a day; Patrick saw the closing of a six-year chapter in his life.

CHAPTER NINETEEN

It was dusk and Patrick was ready. He'd placed his farewell messages carefully for Cormac to find and now the time was right to steal the last hour of twilight.

'Let's get moving,' he said aloud to himself.

Soldier was watching him, head on his paws, sad eyes raised to Patrick.

'Soldier, it's time for me to go. I'll miss you. Take care.' The dog's downhearted face was saying 'don't go', to Patrick, then Soldier, all-knowing, leapt onto Patrick licking his face, whimpering all the while. Patrick hugged and stroked the hound in return, steeling himself as he did so, against the wrenching of his heart.

'Soldier, when the sun rises, go to Cormac.'

The dog barked his understanding.

Patrick strapped his rolled-up fleece to his back, as Soldier stood and watched, whining loudly. Slinging his bag over his shoulder, Patrick cast his eye over the sheep pen and the ranges. He looked around and marvelled at how this rugged, often inhospitable landscape had become his home. He'd found God here and now that God was firmly in his heart, he was free and could move on. God's directing words rang in his ears.

'Your hungers are rewarded. Go, your ship is ready.'

Patrick turned and took his first hopeful step to freedom. The weather was dry and breezy as he strode briskly across the valley and up the fell. The landscape looked and felt different. He wasn't looking through the eyes of a shepherd now. He was a Briton making his way home. Then he shivered as he remembered the words, "No foreign slave ever escaped Ireland". He was a runaway slave on a perilous path. If the saying was true, he was about to become the first foreign slave to break the record.

Patrick headed south for the cover of the trees, where his earlier attackers had hidden their handcart. His eyes adjusted to the darkness of the woods and, with the firm, dry ground underfoot, he increased his pace. By the time he'd emerged from the trees, the crescent-shaped moon was low in the sky, the breeze had dropped and the night was still. No wind rustle. No animal noises, except the occasional hoot of an owl. Then Patrick heard the distant, lonely, howl of a wolf. He stopped and listened carefully. The doleful cry came from high in the hills, where the sheep ranges lie.

'Are the sheep in danger?' he wondered. No other wolves responded. It's a lone wolf, he thought, briefly reassured, and Soldier can handle that. Then another possibility struck Patrick. Was the howl Soldier's? Patrick launched his harsh, wark-wark sound into the night air. A few seconds passed before two short, sharp howls soared in the sky, imitating the timing of Patrick's crow-call.

'Clever Soldier; you have stayed in the hills with the sheep, and you've let me know,' he said quietly to himself. Patrick knew now that the night was his. He needed to travel far and fast, not only tonight but every night, in order to be at his destination before the Harvest Moon was lighting the nights, filling the fields with farmworkers, and providing a lantern for lovers.

As Patrick searched far across the vale, he spotted a thread of moonlight tracing the course of a river. This was his guide to the northern bank of Lough Conn. He lost sight of the river as he descended the hillside, and found it again just before entering the plain. Patrick knew, from his time at the Lough Conn crannog, that the river meandered through farmsteads, so he progressed stealthily, occasionally crouching low, to check his surroundings against the night sky. Spotting the light-grey silhouette of roundhouses, he stopped to work out his next course. Deciding there were too many houses between himself and the lough, he back-tracked and made a lengthy detour.

His progress was halted at times when the cloudy sky plunged him into blackness but he eventually made it to the lakeside. He didn't find a bank, though, just an indistinct reed marsh. Moving to firmer ground, he made progress, veering occasionally too close to the settlements, setting dogs barking. Correcting his path, he stepped accidentally into marsh. The terrain was slowing his progress and Patrick hoped the marshy edges would give way to solid ground soon.

Hearing a splash in the lough he stopped abruptly and stood still, vulnerable in open ground, darkness his only cover. Listening carefully, he heard voices whispering. If they have a dog, I'm in trouble, Patrick thought. A light flickered in the lough and he caught a glimpse of a boat beyond a clump of bushes near the lakeside. He crept to the cover of the foliage from where he could hear the voices more clearly. Two figures emerged. One lowered a lamp near the water's surface; the other appeared to be holding a pole in the water.

'Now,' cried the one holding the lamp, in a high whisper.

The stick wielder pivoted the handle with both hands, quickly raising a wide-rimmed net from below the surface of the lough. There was a great splashing around of fish wriggling and writhing, flicking tails and leaping, as they sensed their coming separation from the water. A few flipped free of the net and gravity delivered them quickly home. Patrick was impressed. The lough seemed to be teeming and these fishermen filled their net in one go. Close to the activity and with eyes accustomed to the dark, Patrick could see a tall man holding a large bag. The other figure, much shorter, was shaking their catch into it.

'Enough, let's go,' said the lamp-man, holding his light high. 'This way,' he said pointing at the bushes exactly where Patrick was hiding.

Patrick missed a heartbeat as he feared the fishermen would see him. He looked around for better cover and saw a cluster of denser bushes, just before lamp-man quenched the light. He'd seen enough to know his way, though, and was soon crouched behind his new hiding place, in the cover of bushes and darkness. No longer able to see the fishermen, he heard the hurried sloshing of their wading coming nearer. A gap came in the clouds illuminating the shore and Patrick, peering through the foliage, saw a man and a boy holding a circular boat above their heads, threading their way through waist-high stalks. He dared not retreat lest he alerted them to his presence, instead he watched nervously, willing the men not to come too close. To Patrick's relief, under the hanging branches of two twisted and intertwined trees growing out of the partially submerged bushes, they slipped their lightweight boat through the fronds until it was perfectly hidden. Patrick could hardly believe his luck.

Waiting till the men were gone, he crept around the bushes and waded in the shallow marsh towards the hidden boat. Suddenly he heard rapid steps approaching and saw the dark outline of the boy against the grey, cloud-covered moonlight, darting towards the boat. Patrick, standing shin deep in water, needed to move fast and silently, but he couldn't do both. He was in between the boy and the boat, covered by shadow. Taking two slow and silent strides in the shallows he concealed himself behind the gnarled trunks, then held his breath and hoped the cloud cover would remain. The boy, now less than a stride from Patrick, grabbed something quickly from the boat and ran off, as the clouds parted and lit his path.

Patrick again waited patiently for the shadows of the clouds to return. When his moment came, he moved quickly to the hidden boat. Like Shifty in the darkened cow-shed, he was intent on stealing. Inspecting the boat by sight and touch, he was pleased with his find. It was a lightweight coracle; an over-sized circular basket, clad in animal hides; a tiny version of the currach used in his capture. Pushing the boat before him, he waded into the shallows and tested it for leaks. There were none. He jammed his boat against a clump of reeds, threw his bag and fleece to the opposite side and clambered in, tipping the boat, and narrowly avoiding sinking. He found two oars wedged under the seat and taking up one of them, paddled to the centre of the lake where he stopped, listened, and observed. There was no flow of water so he began paddling due south, down the centre of the lake, too far from the shore to be heard or seen. He found the shallow, flat-bottomed boat awkward to propel but managed to create a gentle, steady pace.

Patrick was happy with his new situation, and reckoned he was moving slightly faster than walking pace. The additional advantage of travelling on the level and in a straight line, added to the speed of his escape. Passing an isolated cluster of houses on the shore, crammed tightly, with no space between them for cart-tracks, he reasoned they couldn't be workshops. But there were no smoke spirals, leaving Patrick to guess the occupants were too poor to maintain a continuous fire. This was probably an outlaw settlement and perhaps the homestead of the man and boy trying to feed their families by fishing the king's waters, illegally, in the dark of night.

Patrick paddled rhythmically and automatically; his thoughts focused on the morality of starving people stealing to live. There was enough food on earth to feed everyone, but if the affairs of man were organised such that some went without, were they committing an offence by taking their need? Patrick also believed mankind should obey the laws of the land in which they lived, other than in extreme circumstances. In fighting off starvation, Patrick believed their actions were justified. They were taking God's provision.

He paused to drink water from his skin and to eat his chunks of chicken and boiled eggs. With arms rested and feeling refreshed he returned to his task of paddling. He thought of Cuchu and their many discussions over the years. Cuchu's unsought advice was proving to be a guiding light. He'd learned from his friend about the length of Lough Conn and that it extended to the southern border of Conn's kingdom.

By dawn, I will have travelled half the night on water, leaving not a trace of scent or a single footprint. But the daylight hours are longer than the night. Will King Miliucc's men catch up with me while I am sleeping? Will they find my route? Cuchu proudly called it madness and now the least obvious direction was a comfort to

Patrick. He wondered if Soldier was still with the sheep; if Cormac, Eamonn and King Miliucc were still sleeping. The predawn sky, a barely perceptible light-grey glimmer, brought him to the present.

Where can I hide in daytime, safely? So safe that I dare fall asleep soundly without fear of a wolf or a dog, or an adult or a child, finding me? I need a refuge where a turn or a snore can't be heard. Can I find this place in poor light before the sun comes up?

To his right, a range of mountains edged near to the lakeside, encouraging Patrick to steer his boat close to the shore, looking for a place to land. He came across a small inlet, into which he directed his coracle. Spotting a gently sloping bank he paddled towards it as fast as he could, which was slower than he'd have liked as the purpose of the oars was for gentle movements and direction changes. Patrick managed, however, to gain enough momentum to skid a few feet up a grassed-over, sandy beach, before grinding quickly to a halt. He jumped out carrying his fleece and bag and placed them on a flat dry stone then searched for some heavy loose rocks. He found a couple of large specimens which he carried one at a time and placed them in the boat. Taking off his boots and tucking his loose clothing into his belt, he pulled the boat into the lake, wading till the submerged bank steepened and the water level was above his knees. Grabbing the dagger from his belt sheath, he began stabbing into the hide and slashing the waterproof hull till the boat leaked. He pushed the coracle further away and watched the scuttled vessel sinking deep, before wading back to dry land. Grabbing a small piece of swaddling cloth from his bag, he dried his legs and feet and put on his boots.

The foreground which he faced was coarse, like the sheep ranges he'd left behind. The lake, reflecting dim light on the mountain face, assisted Patrick's search, but increased his risk of being seen. He ran quickly across the open space and found a place to scale the rock face. He climbed to a ledge about twelve feet above him, with his fleece and bag on his back. Footholds and hand grips were plentiful and Patrick made it as easily as climbing steps.

Searching along the rocky platform, he came to a small elongated fault in the rock, which opened into a shallow cave. He didn't like it. Access was far too easy, but he was encouraged by the nature of the crag and scanned higher up the rock face for further opportunity. Several surface slits were visible about forty feet higher up. The climbing looked more difficult, though Patrick was happy with this complication. He unpacked a coil of twine and tied one end around his fleece and bag. Counting out forty-five feet loosely onto the ledge, he placed the remainder of the coil diagonally across his shoulder and began his climb, slowly making it to his chosen gap in the rock face.

The tall and thin recess was only a few feet deep. Although out of sight and secure, the location was exposed to the weather and Patrick was fussy about the importance of keeping dry when living under the stars. He decided to climb horizontally to the next recess. This time the narrow, vertical aperture was tight. Sliding his shoulder blades along the rock wall, his chest almost touching the opposite face, he passed through the narrow gap, which opened into a broader, low-ceilinged cave. He followed the tunnel, and turned a corner into a cavernous space. Patrick had found his lodgement.

He rushed back to the entrance where he hauled up his trappings. Thereafter he coiled the twine, packed it in the bag, and took out his lamp. He entered the tunnel, rounded the corner, and put down his fleece and bag. Kneeling, he sparked up the lamp, opened the shutter to give a generous light and investigated the cave. The place was dry, with a stale and dusty smell. There were no signs of footprints or animal traces. He came across a nook in the cave wall, above head-height. With an outstretched arm he placed the lamp on the shelf and scrambled up to the secluded recess.

I'll lay my bed here, he said quietly to himself. His find was like a small hidden room within the cave. He passed his fleece and groundsheet into his new-found bedroom before returning to the cave entrance with his bag in hand. Dawn was approaching and a small amount of light filtered through the slit, illuminating a patch of floor space, enough for Patrick to see some loose rocks inside. He dragged one to the entrance and used it as a seat.

Out of sight of prying eyes, Patrick enjoyed a breakfast of water and chicken chunks as he watched the sun rise and the ground mists evaporate. From his vantage point he could see the whole green vale, the position of the farmsteads, the dense woods to the south and he even caught a reflection of sunlight on a far-off river.

You, my friend, are tonight's target.

The farmsteads and the industrial enclosures were divided by a main track which led into the distance, towards the river. On each side of the track were open crop fields and occasional farm buildings, probably hay and threshing barns. The houses were grouped in enclosures surrounded by mounds and were situated next to the fields. Cow paths connected the houses and farmsteads to the main track, itself a good distance from the houses. Patrick decided this was his route to the river.

By dawn tomorrow I want there to be three kingdoms between me and the Woods of Voclut. But now I need sleep.

Patrick returned to his elevated bedroom and placed all his possessions out of sight in the recess. He prayed at length and, assisted by darkness, fatigue, and faith, fell into a deep sleep.

He woke up in a black hole, briefly unaware of where he was. He looked around and saw partial light, then remembered he was on a shelf in a cave and outside should be daylight. Patrick took off his mantel, donned his sandals and tunic and lowered himself to the cave floor. Turning the corner, towards the entrance he saw a narrow shaft of sunlight beaming through the aperture, showing off particles of dust like a starry night in reverse.

Patrick peeped out of his cave over fields crawling with labourers cutting crops and filling oxcarts. His heart gladdened to see such bustling activity as he recalled how close the Conn Kingdom had been to war with their neighbours; just two seasons ago, here in the south and four years ago against King Miliucc in the north. On both occasions, Miliucc, their neighbouring king, had been a good influence for these people. Looking more steeply down, he saw the coarse ground between the crag and the lough was scattered with scrawny brown goats. He was shocked to see a goatherd sitting on the ledge below; on the very spot he'd placed his bags this morning and begun his climb. The boy stretched out and began humming a tune, clearly enjoying the warmth of the sun as he watched over his trip of goats.

Patrick stepped back into the safety of the shadows and continued to study the scene. A moored boat caught his eye on the far side of the lake. A line of strong men, three on the boat and three on the pier, threw logs to each other, rapidly unloading the cargo from the boat into an oxcart.

A fishing boat, returning from the centre of the lake to the shore, was passing over the spot where Patrick had scuttled his coracle. He watched nervously and was relieved to see no reaction from the fishermen. Although Patrick was satisfied that he'd chosen to sink the boat rather than hide it, he was sharply reminded of his constant need for caution. This thriving area had looked isolated in the dark hours before dawn. His judgement to seek hidden shelter here had been flawed. He decided to wait long beyond the afterglow of sunset before resuming his journey in this bustling locality.

Fetching his bag, he took out a cooked egg, a few chunks of chicken and his skin of water. Sitting in the small shaft of sunlight he warmed the bones of his body and ate his afternoon break-fast, as he studied the main track of his intended route. Bounded by ditches and occasional bushes, this direct route would serve him well, Patrick thought.

After eating, with nothing else to do but wait, Patrick returned to the darkness of his lair, where he prayed and rested.

Dark rain clouds filled the sky, blackening the dusk. Patrick's waiting time was over. Moving swiftly down the crag face and across the open land by the southern shore of Lough Conn, Patrick found the main track. Stepping forth briskly in his leg wraps and leather boots along the dark and desolate track, a fine rain descended, wetting Patrick thoroughly. My scent is being washed away and by dawn I'll be three kingdoms distant from Voclut. Grateful for the waterproof cover over his fleece, he thought of Bride, fondly, and felt her warm hand on his as she guided his candle waxing technique. The rain persisted but was no deterrent to Patrick. Who else would travel in this weather, in the dark? Patrick strode out and never met a soul.

He came to a river, but it wasn't the one Cuchu spoke of. This was smaller and meandered northbound; no use to Patrick. He continued, and as the rain stopped, the track reduced to a small cow path leading into an enclosed farmstead. The fields ahead were probably part of it, Patrick guessed, as they were surrounded by a deer-leap ditch, intended to keep unwanted people and animals out. Patrick kept out, and headed across the open land towards a wooded hillside, continuing his journey south-east under the cover of trees. His clothes dried out a little but his body was cold. The woods were small with well-trodden paths, and likely to be busy with scavengers in the daytime. For this reason, he emerged from the trees and descended the hillside in search of safe daytime shelter. He came across a lough reflecting pale moonlight from a gap in the clouds, and made for the bank where he scouted for opportunity. Hoping to find a derelict building perhaps or a disused souterrain, he crouched low to scan his surroundings and felt a blow to the back of his head before losing consciousness.

* * *

Patrick opened his eyes to find a scruffy face staring at him.

'He's coming round,' the scruff said, sharing his breath and spittle with Patrick. By now, Patrick was aware that his hands were tied behind his back, his feet tethered and his dagger removed from his belt. Another man, tall with a dirty beard, moustache, and shoulder-length hair, held a dry and bloodstained spear tip to Patrick's throat.

He scrutinised his spear tip, cautiously feeling the point in mock appreciation of its sharpness, whilst asking, 'What is your name?'

'Who is asking?' Patrick responded, as he took in the situation.

'The one with the spear is asking.'

Just then a small fishing boat beached nearby and two men stepped out. One gestured to the other to upend the boat, and walked towards Scruff, Spearman, and Patrick. 'What have we here?'

Patrick suspected these men were outlaws, in which case the reward for turning in a runaway slave would be handsome.

'We caught this git watching you,' said the scruff.

The leader looked Patrick in the eye and asked, 'What is your clan name?'

'I don't have a clan name,' Patrick answered evenly.

'I think you do,' the leader said. 'See if he bleeds.'

Spearman pressed the tip under Patrick's chin, piercing his skin till blood dripped.

'I used to have a clan name,' Patrick said with indignation.

'So, you are worth nothing,' the leader stated.

This exchange could go badly wrong, Patrick thought. 'Probably,' he confirmed.

'That's what a runaway slave would say,' the leader declared, taking a step closer to Patrick. 'Tell me your given name.'

'Fichran,' Patrick answered.

'And your clan name at birth?'

'Fogha.'

'Why are you not in Conn's Kingdom on this miserable night?' the boss said, worrying Patrick with his knowledge of the clans.

'I am travelling to the place of my childhood, where I hope a trusted friend might adopt me.'

The boss turned to his men. 'Noose him. He's coming with us.'

At this point, Scruff slung the fleece and bag over Patrick's shoulders and snarled, 'Carry your own bags.'

The leader's accomplice from the boat stepped forward and placed a slip knot around Patrick's neck, and, holding the lead he said, 'Follow them,' pointing to Spearman and Scruff who were carrying the boat.

About thirty paces later, in a normal conversational voice the leader said, 'Fichran.'

Patrick looked round immediately, as though it was natural. The boss said nothing more, but with a false smile held Patrick in his gaze. Patrick was expecting the trick and knew his reaction had passed one of the leader's tests.

As the outlaws talked among themselves, Patrick learned their fishing catch was poor, again. They came to a shabby looking copse with all the trees stripped of their low-lying branches; probably taken to fuel a fire. Through the trees they came to a clearing, with a large, ugly looking stink-pond, surrounded by algae and plant-life, emitting a stronger smell of fish than the fisherman's catch-net. Near to the pond was a small henhouse, and on the opposite side of the clearance was a dirty-walled roundhouse with poor, moss infected thatch.

This looked like a patch of no man's land and enough to convince Patrick that his captives were outlaws.

Patrick was taken to the henhouse where he was stretched out by Spearman and Scruff, face down on chicken muck. With arms extended, his wrists were bound and tied firmly to a post. His feet and outstretched legs were bound and tethered in a similar way, to the opposite post. There Patrick was left, without a word spoken.

He looked around to no avail. The interior was black as soot. He wriggled and writhed to test his bonds but there was no slack to work with. He found he could twist onto his side and then bouncing and twisting he made it onto his back. There was still no play from fingertip to toe, but it was better than breathing in dust from the henhouse floor. Resting on his back he thought through his situation. He disliked praying for himself. The more he thought about it, the more it seemed like an implied lack of faith in God. He believed if he needed help, God would come to him. For mundane problems he was happy to help himself.

Dawn wasn't far away. In daylight, the leader will check my story. If someone in the community knows Fichran Fogha I'll be exposed. They'll hand me back to King Miliucc within days. My captors will be rewarded and a brehon will strip me of my status as a slave. I'll be at the bottom of the social order, an outlaw.

On the other hand, if the leader's contacts don't know Fichran Fogha directly, my facts will stand up to scrutiny. Either way I'm going to live through this, but will my plans to escape, survive? I'll offer up my problems to God.

Patrick finished his prayers and was calm of mind. Even the gurgling and clucking of the hens and the discomfort of his posture did not stop him from sleeping.

* * *

The door flung open suddenly, banging noisily against a wooden feeding trough. Patrick opened his eyes and blinked at the bright light. Two men entered and quickly cut his ties.

'Stand up,' said the leader.

Patrick obeyed and learned that his hands and feet were still tied. Only the tethers to the posts had been removed. The second man, Scruff, placed a slip knot, once again, over Patrick's head, and cut his feet free.

'Follow me,' the leader said, and they stepped out into daylight. The sun, high in the sky, announced midday. The leader walked over to a space with three logs positioned in a U-shape. A clean-shaved man in a green tunic was standing with one foot perched on the central log. His eyes drilled Patrick as he approached.

'Sit here, my friend will ask you some questions,' said the leader, pointing to the ground. Patrick sat lithely, with legs crossed and faced his examiner, calmly and uncowed. He bowed his head respectfully to the freeman, who pretended not to have noticed the politeness. The leader sat to Patrick's left, Scruff to the right, and the freeman directly in front. Patrick understood the set-up, whereby his face could always be observed unseen, by one of the scrutineers. Patrick determined his expression would remain inscrutable unless he deliberately wanted to plant an impression.

'You once belonged to clan Fogha?' the freeman asked.

'I did,' Patrick replied.

'What is your given name?'

'Fichran.'

Patrick noticed the freeman unconsciously tilt his head, to listen intently, probably to Patrick's pronunciation. But Patrick's grandmother was Irish and as a boy he'd learned her Gaelic twang.

'Tell me the name of the bard who stripped you of your clan name.'

'Bard Crimnan.'

'Are you sure of this?'

Patrick knew Bard Crimnan was not the usual legal bard and he could be incriminated if the freeman didn't know the case.

'I'm sure, master, it wasn't Bard Culleen, as you might expect.'

'I expect only the truth.'

'Yes master.'

'So why didn't Bard Crimnan deal with your case?'

'Some evidence incriminated King Moycullen, so his own bard couldn't be used.'

'What was your crime?'

'Stealing sheep.'

'Stripped of your clan name for stealing sheep?'

'Master, I could not pay the fine. My clan would not pay because I'd dishonoured them. I'm an outlaw for not paying the fine.'

Freeman nodded as though he knew the story.

'Why are you not in your own kingdom?'

'I'm returning to the place of my childhood. I have a good friend there who might adopt me.'

'That is all for now. Face the other way.'

Patrick turned his back as the freeman, the leader and Scruff retreated a few paces and spoke in whispers. Ridiculously, Patrick could hear most of their deliberations. Freeman said his facts were right and his accent right. I think he's telling the truth, but I don't know Fichran Fogha's clan. If I find someone who knows him this will cost. If he confirms your captive is Fogha, how will you pay when there is no reward?

'I don't have the means,' the leader said. Patrick allowed himself a smile, while no one could see his face.

'Fichran Fogha, turn round.'

Patrick turned to face the boss. Freeman had gone. The leader and Scruff remained seated on the logs.

'You really are worth nothing, so what shall I do with you?' the leader said, as though thinking out loud.

'I can be of value to you,' Patrick announced and stood up without invitation.

The leader rose and walked towards him, 'Spit it out then.'

'I'll feed you for a lifetime, but I want your boat in return.'

'Food for a lifetime; how exactly?'

'I'll show you how to fill your nets with fish.'

'Huh. Your price is too high. I have a better idea. Help me to steal some piglets and the boat is yours.'

Patrick didn't expect this answer, but he was interested in learning more.

'Where are these piglets?'

'On the opposite side of the lake, we've been watching the farm.'

'Why do you need my help?' Patrick asked.

The leader called to Spearman.

'Fetch drinking water.' He pointed to himself and Patrick. Looking at Scruff he rapped, 'Start mending the boat.'

When no one was within earshot, the boss began to explain.

'It's a secure farm, but we've worked out a method to steal some piglets, only I'm a man short.'

Patrick was suspicious. Maybe he wanted someone to sacrifice. Spearman returned with a coarse pitcher, followed by a pubescent girl dressed in rags. Her shoulder-length mousey-coloured hair was unkempt and matted. She smiled at the leader and avoided looking at Patrick as she passed a mug to each of them. As Patrick took his mug in tied hands, she returned to the roundhouse, leaving behind an odour which Patrick detected, even though he'd spent the morning on a dirty henhouse floor.

Spearman handed the pitcher to the leader, who said, 'Thanks. Now help Duggan with the boat repairs.' He poured a mug of water, which Patrick picked up with both hands and drank greedily.

'Fichran, I have a wife and daughter, who you just met, and a son of nine years. I don't want to die, so we need to succeed or not start. Neither must we get caught afterwards. They always search the outlaw settlements after a raid.'

'What's your plan?' Patrick asked.

'I need two lookouts, my son and one man to go over the fence, and me on this side of the fence.'

'So, you have all you need,' Patrick stated.

'Let me tell you, the man with the spear is trustworthy to defend us – he saw you before you saw him – but he has no brains. We can't trust him over the fence. Duggan is too short for the job. The one who held your noose at the lough-side isn't from here. He's from another settlement. He helps here and there, for a fish, but he can't be trusted. He'd tell all to a freeman for a couple of hens. You, Fichran, are young and strong which right now would be very useful to me. And I have a boat, which can take you far on the river. Are you ready to strike a deal with me?'

'You could go over the top, with your son. You must have a reason for not doing so, which worries me.'

'Let me show you something.' The leader turned round and pulled up his clothing. Patrick stared at a huge gash across the leader's spine. He covered quickly and explained, 'I took an axe blow, in battle, and luckily it didn't kill me. You cannot see my problem when I walk, but my back has no strength. This plan could feed my family for a month or two, but I haven't got the agility to go over the fence.'

Patrick's mind flashed back to the axe attack he witnessed in the Moycullen battle. He believed the leader's sincerity, and his determination, which included making use of Patrick. Neither would the leader return Patrick's food, fleece, and dagger until he'd got the piglets. But Patrick believed he'd get his plans back on track if the leader was genuine. It was a risk he decided to take.

'What's your given name?' Patrick asked.

'Guigan,' he replied.

'Guigan, for the boat and the return of my possessions I will help you to raid the piglets.'

'We have a deal,' Guigan said.

Patrick stood up and held his tied hands forwards. Guigan came towards him and cut Patrick's bonds. Patrick remembered not to offer a handshake; he was, after all, an outlaw called Fichran. However, Guigan extended his arm to Patrick, which momentarily caught him by surprise. Patrick recovered and returned a firm handshake.

'Sorry,' Guigan responded to Patrick's surprised look. 'A few years ago, I fell from a higher status. Some of my old habits remain.'

Patrick completely understood but only nodded in mild acknowledgement.

'There's a tub over there. You're welcome to have a wash. I'll tell the men you're in.'

Patrick wasted no time. He plunged his head in the water, washed away the chicken muck, and dried his hair and face as much as was possible on the damp grey towel tied to the tub. He watched to see how the men took Guigan's news; they waited till his back was turned then shook their heads, clearly not pleased.

As Guigan returned to Patrick, a barefooted boy emerged from the trees carrying a bundle of sticks.

'That's my son,' Guigan said.

The boy looked at Patrick curiously then ran into the house.

'My wife is cooking the night's catch. We don't have much but you can join us. You must be hungry.'

'Thank you. I don't want to eat your food; you need it yourselves. I've got my own in the bag. I'll get it from the henhouse,' Patrick said, testing Guigan.

'It's not there, Fichran. We've put it somewhere safe.' He turned to Spearman, 'Bring Fichran's bag.'

Spearman vanished from sight, giving no clues about the location of the bag.

'Let's go in,' Guigan said beckoning Patrick to the house.

They entered through a dilapidated door and the first thing Patrick saw was the fire being tended by the boy. A hanging pot, directly over the fire, was already boiling. A plump and smiling lady dressed in dark colours, was preparing a meal. Patrick saw half of the circular room was in use as a cooking and living area. The rest was set out for sleeping.

'Roisin, meet Fichran.' Guigan introduced.

'Pleased to meet you,' said Patrick, nodding politely.

'Please, sit down. I'm making a fish stew; it will be ready soon.' She gestured towards three logs positioned in an L-shape.

The stump of a broad tree acted as a low table. Patrick sat alongside Guigan and took in the other half of the house. Six beds, with heads to the wall and feet to the fire, lined the perimeter. A double and a single were separated by a willow-wicker divider. Mother, father and daughter, Patrick thought. Next was a single bed, a large space and two more singles. The son and two workers, separated from the family by a larger gap. Spearman arrived and handed Patrick's bag to Guigan.

'Here, Fichran, take out what you will,' Guigan said. Patrick took out his own ration twice and went to Guigan's wife.

'May I call you, Rosheen?' he asked, pronouncing her name carefully.

'You may,' she said, embarrassed by Patrick's courtesy. Patrick handed over two cooked eggs and four chicken pieces.

'You shouldn't have,' Roisin said, taking the offering gladly.

'Roisin, Fichran is going to help us to come by a few piglets,' Guigan said.

'For sure we could use some meat in the house,' she answered agreeably.

Patrick watched Roisin drain the cooking pot into another, leaving behind the fish heads and skeletons. Taking roots from a steaming, warming pot, she chopped the vegetables into pieces and stirred them into the fish liquamen. Next, she cut the boiled fish and Patrick's chicken into small chunks and dropped them into the stew.

While the pot was bubbling, Scruff and their daughter arrived. He took a seat and the girl began handing wooden spikes to all present. Her mother peeled and quartered both eggs, added them to the pot, and rubbed her hands as if to say the meal was ready to serve. Her daughter placed a ladle and a stack of wooden porringers on the tree trunk.

Patrick enjoyed seeing the children contributing to the running of the household. This was something he couldn't remember ever doing in Banna Venta himself.

Roisin carried the blackened pot and placed it with pride, like a centrepiece, on the log table and dished a scoop into each bowl, passing the first one to her husband. When all had received their stew, including Roisin, who sat beside her husband, Guigan held up his pauper's bowl like it was silver.

'Slainte mhaith,' he greeted.

'Slahn cha va,' responded Patrick and everyone, in unison. Patrick's eyes moistened as he witnessed the togetherness of this family and friends. *The appreciation and celebration of a stew, which, without the chicken would have barely been soup, yet celebrated nonetheless; where the head of the family expresses gratitude for health, before everyone eats. And this poor family, eating only one meal a day, shared their food with me.*

'That's a mighty stew,' Guigan declared.

'Helped along with Fichran's egg and chicken,' Roisin answered.

'Thank you, Roisin. You're spoiling me with such a tasty meal,' said Patrick. He looked across to the daughter. 'May I ask your name?'

'Aoife,' she answered.

'I like your name, Eefa.'

'What's to like about it?' she fired back. Her father put up his hand, palm forward signalling his daughter to stop the moodiness.

'I like its history. It's the name of an Irish princess,' Patrick said warmly.

'I don't feel like a princess,' she replied, curtly.

Patrick thought of Guigan's comment about falling from a higher status a few years ago. *Aoife has been uprooted from her friends. She's isolated now and is suffering.*

'Do you know her story?' Patrick asked.

'I do,' she nodded.

'Then you know she was a fighter.'

'And she was beaten,' Aoife responded.

'Not true. She was mortal and beaten by no person, except a God. You are like her. You're a fighter. You are fighting now. Don't feel defeated, Aoife, triumph will come to you.'

A slap of hands on the table came from the boy. 'I think An tUasal is right, Aoife. Anyway, you are my princess already,' the boy said.

'Hurrah for the princess,' Guigan said, and everyone in the room applauded. Even Aoife managed a smile.

Patrick asked the boy, 'What's your name?'

'Cashel,' he answered.

'What do you like doing, Cashel?'

'I like helping Ma to get wood and Da to get food.'

Patrick saw the pride written across Guigan's and Roisin's faces.

'What are you good at, Cashel?'

'Throwing stones,' the boy answered. 'I'm good at hitting targets with a sling.'

'You can use a sling?' Patrick asked.

'I can. Here it is.' Cashel pulled out his sling from a hidden pocket and passed it to Patrick, who examined the boy's treasure. The sling was like Patrick's, except the shot pouch was smaller; made for a pebble, indeed made for a boy.

'Daddy, can I show An tUasal my target practice?'

'You can, when we've finished, Cashel, but quickly, because Fichran and I have things to do.'

When mealtime was over, Patrick was led outside by Cashel, to a place behind the henhouse. Here stood five circular posts, driven deep into the ground, topped by woven willow mats, secured to a wooden dowel. Cashel unhooked them and stood them up in a V-shape. These were his targets. He ran enthusiastically to a tub and pulled out a handful of stones.

'Watch me, mister, I can hit three out of five most times.'

Cashel produced his usual best.

'Can you sling, mister?'

'I can.'

'How do you know how to sling?'

'I'm a hill shepherd, I have to know.'

'Would you like a go?' Cashel offered his sling to Patrick.

Patrick wasn't sure he'd be any good with the smaller sling and pebbles, but he tried. He missed the first target and then hit the rest. The boy's mouth was wide open with surprise.

'Oh, An tUasal, how did you do that? I hope you can show me.'

'You're nearly there, Cashel. You missed two because your sling was too long. Do like this, hold further forward.' The boy copied. 'Now, on your final swing let your wrist work more than your arm. Try it without shot.' Cashel took in the advice and practised the action.

'That's good. Now, try it with shot.'

Cashel hit four out of five. Bouncing with delight he couldn't stop smiling.

'How did you learn mister?'

'First I learned from someone who was good.' Patrick made up this bit, in order to give Cashel a good principle. 'I concentrated to try my best then I practised every day till I was good. When I was good, I practised every day to stay good.' The boy was listening, and looked like he was learning. 'Cashel, I want to chat with you about something else, before your father comes.' Patrick could see Cashel had enjoyed being involved with the grown-ups. He didn't disguise his enthusiasm for having a chat with An tUasal. Patrick had finished imparting his advice when the boy ran to his father.

'Daddy, I hit four out of five, and mister showed me some tricks.'

'Well done, son.' He patted Cashel on his back. 'Practise your tricks and show me when we return.'

'Thank you, Daddy. Oh! Will Mummy let me dig up the roots later?'

'She will, Cashel. There's enough daylight left for both.'

Off ran Cashel, skipping on his way.

'So, you're good with a sling, Fichran?'

'I am. It's part of a hill-shepherd's life. Though I'm not as good as I used to be,' Patrick added as an afterthought, to cover his momentary lapse.

'Fichran, I want to show you the boat in daylight. I expect our mission to succeed and don't want any disagreements when it comes to payment.' He led Patrick across the clearing to a thatched, open shelter, a short distance from the house. His men stopped their work on the upturned boat as Guigan and Patrick arrived. He examined the repairs. Patrick looked closely too and thought the patches were rabbit hides, stitched with gut.

'Can I feel the weight?' Patrick asked. The two men lifted the boat off the bench. Sideways, Patrick took a grip and the men let go. He could shift it around without help, but the shape was awkward and the weight too much for one to carry far.

'Let it down on the ground, Fichran, and see what you're getting into,' Guigan said. Patrick wasn't too fussy. It was a boat and would transform his chances. He sat on the currach and imagined how he would manage on the river. The boat was too wide to paddle on both sides from one sitting position. But it would be his boat. Stealing a boat would leave clues and create enemies therefore this opportunity suited Patrick well.

'Have you seen enough?' Guigan asked.

'I have, but I have some questions.'

'Come with me then,' Guigan led the way into the woods and down a lightly trodden path to the river.

'My men will carry the boat to here, then it's yours,' said Guigan, anticipating Patrick's most important question.

'Will we use the boat in the raid?' Patrick asked, as he took in the detail of the river.

'We will.'

'Are we raiding tonight?'

'We are, but don't worry. We're planning to succeed.'

Me too, thought Patrick.

'When do you expect me to leave, if the raid succeeds?' Patrick asked.

'In the middle of the night, I expect. You don't want to be here when the guards come, do you?'

'That's my thought too. Guigan, do you know the river?'

'I know it well.'

Patrick was heartened by Guigan's confident answer.

'Good. What direction does it take and how far will it take me?'

'The river travels south. Your journey will end when it flows into a much larger river. It'll take you two full nights to get to this place.'

Guigan's answer was welcome news to Patrick, aware he was still within the reach of Miliucc's men and dogs. Two nights of travel by boat would put that worry behind me.

'I will need to hide and sleep tomorrow morning. Can you suggest a place to look?'

Guigan nodded 'Half a night from here you will pass densely wooded mountains, on your right. There are places in there where no one ever goes. For your second day, walk east after you meet the big river. On the south, large mountains from west to east will guide you. There are caves aplenty in those hills.'

'Thank you, Guigan.'

'Come. Let's go to Cashel, he's got work to do before day's end.'

Cashel saw his audience arriving and moved quickly to set up the targets.

'Watch me,' he called out.

His first shot clipped the target narrowly. His second attempt missed. Visibly concentrating, he hit three more in a row.

'Dad, that's the fourth time I've hit four!'

'You're a good shot, Cashel, well done. Now, get digging those roots before the daylight fails.'

Cashel ran to his duties happily, giving Patrick a chance to tackle Guigan further.

'Guigan, when do you intend to return my bag and its contents, my fleece, and my dagger?'

'Don't worry, Fichran, all your possessions will be given back to you, when you have kept your promise.'

Patrick knew his risks. He couldn't expect to have his dagger and possessions returned before the raid. That would be too risky for Guigan; however, if Guigan wanted to go back on his word after I have handed over the piglets, he would be taking an unnecessary risk. How would he stop me from informing? Would it be realistic for Guigan to kill me, just to avoid handing over the boat? One piglet would feed the family for two moons. A second piglet could be traded with an outlaw settlement for a coracle or a good number of laying hens. Patrick reasoned that if the raid produced two piglets, his own position would be at the mercy of Guigan's honesty. Three piglets, however, would provide food for the immediate future and plenty of trading power for hens and a replacement boat. Guigan would be unlikely to take chances with me in these circumstances. A successful raid is my security, Patrick concluded.

Guigan had gone into the house; Cashel was out of sight digging; the two workers had finished on the boat and were cutting straw to make thatch bundles. Patrick was unoccupied until darkness and, to keep busy; he offered his help to the workers.

'Can you give me some work?' Patrick asked.

Spearman answered, 'You can make some spars. Do you know how to do it?'

'I don't, but show me.'

Spearman breathed heavily as though his patience was being tried then he demonstrated reluctantly, in poor spirit. Patrick picked up the task and produced spars until the willow was used up. He now had a better idea for filling time. Patrick sat down against the wall, in sight of Spearman, who was under the leader's instruction to keep Fichran in his sights; then fell into a long nap, which lasted till darkness. He woke to Guigan's voice, calling his team together. Patrick rose to his feet and paid attention.

'I'll go through the plan now, because once we've crossed the lake we don't speak unless necessary, and then it has to be in a quiet whisper.'

Patrick concealed a smile. Guigan and Spearman were loud whisperers.

'The farmstead on the opposite side of the lake is ringfenced and mounded. There are no night patrols. It is a pig farm and the pigsties are near to the houses. Dogs will bark and men will stir before anyone gets near them. One building, remote from the farm, is surrounded by a ten-foot-high fence, and is situated inside the perimeter mound of the farmstead. The building often stands empty but is occasionally used for sows and sucklings when extra space is needed. For the last five nights it has been full of piglets and sows.'

Patrick had listened carefully. With each passing day the piglets would gain in strength, ready to be placed in the pigsties near the housing. It was down to chance that they would be there tonight. Patrick needed this luck or things could become complicated.

Guigan pointed to Spearman and Scruff, 'You and you guard the north and south banks, to warn us of intruders. Fichran and Cashel, you will go over the fence. I will stay at this side.'

Trusting me with his son, Patrick thought. It's a good sign that Guigan is genuine.

'Cashel is small enough to get through the hen hatch. So too are the piglets. Here are three hoods.' He passed them to Patrick. 'Cover the piglets' heads quickly and they'll stop squealing. A small amount of noise won't be heard, but an all-out squealing tantrum means we abandon, in this case the lookouts return on foot, the rest of us by boat. If we get in and out undetected, the maximum number of piglets we can take is three, and we all come back in the boat. Cashel, you sit on the fence coming out and Fichran passes the piglets to you. Then Cashel, you hand them down to me, butt first. By now you lookouts come to me and take a piglet each to the boat. Fichran brings the last piglet. Are there any questions?'

'Have you got a good length of twine that I can carry? It might be useful,' Patrick asked.

'We have.' The leader looked at Scruff. 'It's in the henhouse.'

Scruff made off quickly and returned with a coil, which Patrick placed diagonally across his shoulder.

'Let's go,' said Guigan.

Scruff and Spearman carried the boat. As they walked Patrick noticed they both wore a dagger on their belts. At the lakeside, Scruff and Spearman held the currach steady as Guigan, Fichran and Cashel climbed aboard.

Guigan, pointing to the front seat said, 'Fichran, sit here between me and Cashel.'

Scruff and Spearman sat behind and pushed off, using the paddles as a pole. Patrick noticed how low the boat was in the water. Three piglets as extra passengers would probably take the boat to its limit, and the oarsmen didn't row in unison. One plunged deep and pulled strong, the other shallow and weak, causing the boat to rock, but with no harm done. Patrick thought it would be an issue on the return journey.

At the other side, Spearman moored to a landing and secured the boat, with a plaited twine, to a sturdy wooden stump. On a windless night and a still lake, the crossing had been quick and easy. The night was dark, with not a star, nor the moon, to be seen. Even the umbrella of cloud was invisible. Everyone alighted, Spearman and Scruff immediately walked in opposite directions to take their positions.

Guigan led Patrick and Cashel over the mounds to their carefully selected part of the formidable looking fence. Without hesitation, Patrick sat on his haunches in front of the fence and pointed to Cashel to stand on his shoulders. Cashel was there like a shot, grabbing Patrick's vertically outstretched arms, to steady himself. Patrick stood up, raising the boy halfway up the fence on his shoulders. He tapped the boy's ankles. Cashel looked down, stood on Patrick's waiting palms, and was pushed higher. Nimble as a squirrel, Cashel was up and over. Guigan, expecting to give Patrick a hand up, was too late. With one high spring and impressive arm strength Patrick scaled the fence and joined Cashel on the other side. Patrick beckoned the boy to follow him. A few strides along the outer fence he examined a large, disused door, before signalling the boy to go to the hatch. He watched Cashel wriggle through a generous little door made for hens. The boy returned quickly, popping his head through the hole, nodding left to right.

'Empty room,' he whispered.

Patrick saw there was a second room with a separate door.

'Can you get into this room from inside?' Patrick asked pointing.

Cashel vanished. He reappeared, opening the second door inwards and beckoned Patrick in, whispering, 'There's something in here.'

They looked around the darkened room and came across two stalls, each housing a calf.

'We can't pass these over the fence. Come with me,' Patrick whispered, and led the way outside to the barn door in the perimeter fence. He tried to slide the bolt, but it wouldn't shift. Looking closely Patrick found a dowel had jammed the slider.

'If only I had my dagger,' he said under his breath. Cashel produced a small knife and handed it to Patrick. It did the job, allowing Patrick to slide the bolt. He stopped just short of the open position. With his thumb he directed the boy to come to the shed.

Inside Patrick put his finger to his lips then whispered, 'Don't tell your father you lent me your knife, he will not be pleased that you trusted a stranger. Now, look around for water and food and bring it to me.'

Patrick used the coil of twine and tied a lead around a calf's neck. Cashel arrived with a bowl of water. Just in time. Patrick held a length of twine in both hands and Cashel cut it.

'You found water?'

'I did, there's a tub of grain, a trough of water and another bowl.'

Patrick took a piglet's hood from his pocket.

'Fill this with grain, and bring another bowl of water.' Patrick tied a second lead to the remaining calf, and again Cashel returned and cut the twine to length. Patrick placed the water under the calf's nose and it drank immediately. He slid the bowl away from the calf. The calf stood up, took a few steps, and found the water.

'Try that with your calf.' Cashel's effort had the same success so, by moving the bowls of water they led the docile calves through the door. The calves by now had emptied the bowls.

'Take the bowls to where you found them and leave the grain bag here.'

Patrick tried the calves on a handful of grain. They ate readily.

'They're weaned,' Patrick smiled. 'That's good news for Guigan.'

Cashel returned to Patrick who was studying the door. The outside face was plain with no handle or lock.

'Can you work out how to close the door?' Patrick asked. Cashel looked for a few seconds.

'I need some twine please, An tUasal.' Patrick held the coil, Cashel cut a piece, and wrapped it around the locking bar, holding it in a raised position. Pushing a dowel back with his knife, he pulled the door gently closed, removed the knife, and lowered the bar, removing the twine afterwards.

'Good enough?'

'Five out of five,' Patrick whispered, inducing a broad smile to Cashel's face.

They led the calves to the barn door. Patrick slid the bolt and the door was open. Guigan and the rest of the team were there, waiting.

'No piglets, Guigan, just a big problem.'

He led the calves through. 'Two heifers.'

Cashel, of his own accord, stayed inside, closed the sliding bolt and was over the fence to his father in seconds.

'It means we can't all go back on the boat,' Patrick whispered.

Guigan allowed himself a shake of the head in disbelief and then thought through his problem.

'Duggan, Cashel, go now. Meet us at the landing on the other side.' He turned to Spearman and Patrick. 'Get these in the boat,' he said, pointing at the heifers.

Guigan held the currach steady as Patrick and Spearman coaxed the calves onto the vessel, with the help of the grain bag. Applying gentle pressure on their backs, Patrick encouraged the calves to sit down. Guigan boarded, and Spearman pushed them away from the moorings, but as the dim-witted assistant clumsily jumped on board, the overloaded boat tilted, taking on water momentarily. Luckily, the boat rocked once and stabilised.

Guigan gave a paddle each to Patrick and Spearman. Spearman, as though in a competition to show his speed and strength, once again demonstrated his lack of wit by immediately digging his paddle deep into the water and pulling hard. His exertions tilted the boat to his side and the currach shipped a huge amount of water. Patrick was on his feet immediately scooping out water with the only tub available. The heifers now sat in a tidal pond as water sluiced to the other side of the currach. The boat tilted again, taking a further scoop of water from the lake. Patrick continued scooping with urgency to keep his own hopes afloat and Guigan, with perfect timing, counterweighted by standing on the opposite side to the water. Patrick glanced at Spearman who looked on, hapless. The third tilt didn't take on water as a result of Patrick's bailing having reduced the weight in the boat. Guigan helped to stabilise the rocking and finally calm was restored.

'I have an idea, Guigan; look how calm the lake is. We just made our own waves. Let's have one rower. Let me row from the front.'

Spearman was about to protest when Guigan nodded his approval.

Patrick snatched up Spearman's paddle and glared at him, 'You don't need this.'

Patrick saw Spearman choking as he subdued his resentment of the intruder. He also could see that the leader's word was final to him.

Using his earlier experience on Lough Conn, Patrick stroked his oar gently from left to right, pulling the boat through the water. Traction came from twisting the angle of the blade. The currach responded slowly and moved forward. Calmly they made progress towards the opposite bank.

All the while, Patrick's back was to Spearman, armed with a spear and a dagger, and Guigan by his side armed with a dagger. They both could have killed me when I was bailing water and dumped me in the middle of the lough. This meant, so far, the balance of risk was steady. And now that Guigan was worth two heifers, the price of a boat was trivial. Spearman being a liability in the boat, and Patrick an asset, tipped the balance of risk in Patrick's favour.

'It's not fast but we'll get there. How are you going to manage your wealth, Guigan?'

'It's a nice problem. I'll keep one and think about the other, assuming we don't sink.'

'We'll get there, though Cashel and your man might beat us to the landing.'

Cashel and Scruff were waiting.

'Why so long?' Scruff teased.

They disembarked. Patrick and Cashel led the heifers and Spearman and Scruff carried the boat.

Arriving at the homestead Guigan told the men to put the boat down, and said, 'Take the heifers to the hideout then come back and clean the boat.' He turned to Patrick and Cashel, 'Come with me to the henhouse.'

They entered the building, which last night was Patrick's prison cell. A dull light shivered in the room as the flame from a low candle bobbed left and right, trying to dodge the draughts. Patrick wondered where things were leading.

'Cashel,' Guigan said. 'Please wait outside with the door closed.' Cashel stepped outside dutifully and pulled the ill-fitting door noisily into its frame.

'Fichran, I want to give you a choice of boats. Don't get me wrong, the boat outside is yours if you want it, but look at this, it might serve you better.' Guigan took down a small boat, one of a pair hanging on the wall. 'It's a single person fishing currach.'

Patrick was looking at a boat just wider than his hips. On end, it reached to his shoulders. A broad leather strap was attached to both ends of the sitting plank. The hull, as with larger currachs, was clad with animal hide, and was surprisingly deep, allowing the sitting plank to be set lower in the boat. Patrick liked this feature.

Safer and steadier, especially in faster currents, he thought.

Guigan placed the currach on the floor.

'Sit in it. See what you think.'

Patrick did so. He could paddle left and right from the same sitting position.

'Can I see the paddle?' Patrick asked.

Guigan took it down from the wall. 'There is a holder in the boat, under your seat. Get out and I'll show you what the strap is for.' Guigan stood the boat upright, lifted it onto a half barrel, put his arms through two looped straps and as he stood up, the boat settled securely on his back and shoulders. 'You can walk for miles like this,' Guigan said.

'This is an interesting idea,' Patrick said.

'Try for yourself,' Guigan added.

'Usually, I carry my fleece on my back,' Patrick stated.

'If you wedge your fleece under the seat, you can carry the boat in the same way.'

As Patrick mounted the boat on his back, he was reminded of a shield, shifted round to the shoulder blades when the soldier needed both hands free. He walked a few steps with the boat on his back, extending above his head, amazed at the light weight. He wouldn't need to abandon the boat when his river journey ended.

'You will come to dangerous rapids on your journey. With this boat you can get off the river, walk past the danger, and re-join downstream.' Patrick didn't need any more convincing.

'I'll take the small boat,' he answered.

'I thought you would. However, I don't want you to take either of the boats. I have another suggestion. Why don't you join our family, stay with us? You can make a life here. My family like you. I think you could make it work.'

'Guigan, that's very generous. I like your family too. But I can't. I'm on a bigger mission.' Patrick paused a short while. 'Thank you, I'm honoured, but I must move on.'

'I follow you, Fichran, but I wanted to try.'

Patrick nodded appreciatively. 'Guigan, you have much to do before sunup, let's conclude our business.' Patrick, with the boat on his back continued, 'If I can have my bag and my fleece, I'll make my own way to the river.'

'Cashel and I will come to the river with you. Let me organise your things.' Guigan walked to the door and opened it.

'Cashel, bring Fichran's things to the front of the house.' Cashel ran off quickly.

Guigan, and Patrick, with the small boat on his back, made their way to the house. Cashel appeared, with his mother carrying the bag, followed by his sister with the fleece.

'We want to thank you,' Roisin said. 'We tied you up in the henhouse, and in return you helped to bring us riches.'

Patrick nodded and smiled as he thought of the peculiar turn of events.

'You're special, Fichran,' Aoife said, jumping in. 'I hope we meet again, when I'm a princess.' She placed the fleece at his feet.

'I hope so too, Aoife.' She's already started, Patrick thought.

'I'll take the fleece,' Guigan said. 'You carry Fichran's bag, Cashel.'

'Roisin, meeting you was a pleasure and I'll miss your fish stew. Aoife, good luck with your preparations, I think you will be what you want to be.' He waved farewell as they walked to the river.

'So, you're hiding the boat?'

'I am, Fichran. Did you notice the boat you've taken is one of a pair?'

'I did.'

'Well, you can't put calves in it.'

Patrick smiled, 'Good luck to you. You have great faith in your hideout and your workers.'

'Thank you. My biggest risk will be choosing who to trade with, but no more of this. I would like to have learned how to fill my nets, but tonight is not the time for a fishing trip.'

'I've already shown you,' Patrick answered.

Guigan looked puzzled. Cashel searched Patrick's face and received the nod he looked for.

'Daddy, I can show you. I know how to do it. An tUasal explained to me.'

Guigan raised his eyebrows.

'And when did this teaching take place?'

'After sling practice,' Cashel said.

'Very well, my son, we'll have to go fishing soon.' Guigan looked at Patrick, 'You did this before the raid. I thank you for that.'

Patrick shrugged off the comment, picked up his fleece and packed it in the boat.

As he reached for his bag, Guigan said, 'You'll find your dagger in there.'

Patrick opened his bag, took out his dagger, which was uppermost, and fixed it to his belt. The dagger had covered a small package wrapped in swaddling cloth. He opened it and found a few boiled root vegetables and a small skin. Taking out the bung he caught the smell of fish stew and immediately took a swig.

'Delicious; this was prepared before the raid too.' He looked at Guigan, who looked back, and they both laughed heartily, easily. It was the laughter that comes with pleasant surprise, as two minds meet.

'Before you go, Fichran, if you need to pose as a fisherman, let me tell you that the boat is one of a pair for river fishing. The boats position at opposite sides of the river with a net spanning below the surface. When the nets are full, the fishermen pull in their haul from each end simultaneously until the boats meet in the middle. With the catch shared they walk home, boats on their backs and their catch-bags in hand.'

'Thank you, Guigan.'

The two came together and shook hands, each wishing good luck to the other. Patrick was keeping calm, but internally was bouncing with delight and utter amazement. His brief captivity had seen him safely through another day, and once he was on the river, he'd make up the few hours of night he'd lost. To have gained a small boat; one that he could carry, would shorten his journey time. And he'd helped a needy family on the way.

'Good luck to you, Cashel, I enjoyed meeting you.'

Cashel ran to Patrick. 'Can I shake your hand?'

'You can.' Patrick shook Cashel's hand, warmly.

'Farewell,' he waved, then sat in his boat and pushed off.

CHAPTER TWENTY

Patrick paddled gently for a short time, learning the feel of the one-person fishing boat and the mind of the river. The breeze, cold on his back, gave him and his floating basket, a welcome push. The slapping of water against stony banks was the only sound this lazy river produced.

Now Patrick was ready and, impatient for progress, he pulled rhythmically on the paddle, twice on the left and twice on the right, zigzagging down the river at double his previous speed. He was hungry for food, but hungrier still to put distance between him and the pig farm. Ten Roman miles, then I'll stop. It occurred to Patrick that he hadn't thought of distances, or time, in Roman terms for over six years. Yet on only the third night of his escape, the early beginning of a long journey, his mind was already anticipating a return to Roman life.

Body warmth from Patrick's exertions protected him from chilling as the breeze grew into a strong tailwind. Conditions were favourable for making fast progress, and once again Patrick dismissed the thought of food. He stopped paddling for a moment and took a few greedy glugs from his water skin then continued till the glow of predawn arrived, by which time the wind had calmed. Spotting a backwater, he paddled into the stillness of the side stream where he stood in the boat to stretch his legs. Reaching into his bag for Roisin's stew, he noticed another package and opened it quickly, discovering a porringer and a wooden spoon.

'Thank you, Roisin,' he said aloud as he poured the stew into his bowl. He ate his meal with the wooden spoon and recalled the earlier sense of ceremony he'd felt, eating at the Guigan household. After washing the bowl and spoon in the river, he shook them dry and returned the utensils to his bag. He manoeuvred his boat into the gentle flow of the river, determined to travel another half hour before sunrise. Again, his mind had brought forth words and thoughts from his motherland; "hour, half hour". Ireland hadn't divided the day into twenty-four equal parts. As his mind was about to linger on thoughts of home, a pervasive sound came to his attention. It wasn't wind in the trees; the wind had died. It sounded like a continuous version of someone blowing on embers. A clue came as the river began flowing faster.

The current was grabbing hold of the boat. Patrick paddled aggressively for the bank and heard rapids; but his efforts were like rowing in the air, except now the white clouds were below him, roaring, hissing and spraying. A wall of moving water angrily whacked the bottom of Patrick's boat, launching him into the air. He landed spread-eagled on his back, feeling lucky to be reunited with the boat. His eyes peered through a fog of spume at a dimly lit sky. Bouncing around and fearful of being flung from the currach, Patrick rolled onto his stomach. Now he was facing backwards and looking upstream. He clung desperately to the frame. Fearsome buffeting forced the fishing boat to twist and bend and all Patrick could do was hold tight. Now spinning, next tossing and tilting; left and right had no meaning. He barely knew which way was up till the raging river reminded him.

And then it all stopped. Patrick felt like he'd sailed down a mountain in a rainstorm. Looking back, on a short stretch of foaming rapids, with not a rock in sight, he laughed in self-mockery.

'You're a mouse, Patrick,' he said aloud, and did what he thought to do earlier.

He paddled to the bank and came off the river. Standing the currach upright, he poured out the water and checked the boat for damage. There was none. For the second time Patrick had experienced the amazing resilience of these leather-hulled, basket-framed boats. His bag, sodden, and fleece wet at the edges, had at least remained with the boat.

Standing on the bank, Patrick scanned his surroundings. The mountains and trees that had accompanied Patrick for miles were indeed isolated as Guigan had told. Patrick strapped his boat and possessions to his shoulders and plunged into the woods, heading for the high ground. The trees were tall, with few low-lying boughs, but the horizontal light beams could not follow Patrick as he weaved his way around the trees. Soon he could only see a few paces ahead, just enough to stride over logs and avoid fallen tree trunks. The earthy smell of the undergrowth filled his nostrils as the riverside fresh air was left behind. Underfoot he felt gnarled and knobbly tree roots crossing his path. As he climbed higher up the mountain, the trees too, stretched higher in the sky. Patrick heard birds cheeping and before long he was surrounded and serenaded by birdsong. The sun had risen. Angular shafts of light penetrated the gaps between the foliage and tree trunks. The ground he was treading became a soft blanket of nature's detritus, formed from the decayed and decomposed sheddings of the tall trees. He saw squirrels scurrying, lizards, and mice darting, but he had yet to see a place to lay his head.

The thickets and bushes grew denser. His boat snagged on overhead vines and Patrick, from time to time, had to hack a clear path with his dagger. Spider strings tickled his face and arms. His legs left samples of skin and blood on the prickly tips of gorse and briar. Beams of sunshine revealed the shape of the mountain and Patrick was encouraged when he saw that the line of the trees followed the contour of a steep-sided gully. He chopped his way to the feature and found a small ravine, flat-bottomed, dry, and covered with a dense blanket of undergrowth. Descending to the base, he noticed the short gully widened to the shape of the mountain, ensuring the location was impossible to see from a distance. Indeed, Patrick only saw the gully himself because he came across it.

Beneath him wasn't the ground, the mountain, the earth. Underfoot was pure, dense undergrowth. Patrick placed his boat on the vegetation and hacked a shallow pit around it. Spreading his possessions and clothing on the ground, to dry in the sun, he found himself yawning. But he had more to do. He turned the boat down side up on the ground sheet and fleece, with the wet edge exposed to the sunlight, and placed his food under the boat in the shade. Gathering up the choppings of undergrowth, he scattered them over the hull and then walked a complete circle around his hideout, scrutinising its visibility from a distance. Satisfied it was well hidden, he returned to camp, wriggled under the boat, and though surprised at the warmth of his accommodation, Patrick slept soundly.

He woke up in darkness but remembered where he was; that it was daytime. He peeped out cautiously before rolling from under the boat, then, crouching behind it he scanned all around. Satisfied that he was safe, he stood up and came out into the open. A few wispy clouds, floating in a blue sky, offered no obstruction to the rays beaming down on Patrick's camp. The pads of his fingers felt the hot dry fabric of his previously drenched clothing and bag. He felt his fleece; it too was bone dry.

Patrick sunk to his knees and with palms together thanked the Lord for providing the sunshine that dried his clothing and all of this while he slept. Now he checked his food. One of his wraps was black and seething with the to-ing and fro-ing of creeping things. Under his nose, a line of ants marched along a vine, away from the chicken chunks, before descending a stalk deep into the undergrowth. Patrick leant in to examine closer; each creature was carrying a small white crumb, half its own body size. Using the tip of his dagger he opened the wrapper and to his shock the parcel was almost empty. The chicken meat had gone, carried away by a disciplined and determined army.

'Fussy eaters,' Patrick thought when he saw the root vegetables were untouched. Putting aside the stew and water skins, he packed his bag and fleece placing them under the boat. Climbing up the side of the gully he sat between two bushes in a shaft of sunlight, and whilst overlooking his camp he took a drink of water and finished off the stew. The warmth of sunshine on his body lifted his spirits.

He knew he was only living for the moment, but the moment upon him was good. The sun was lowering in the sky. Plenty of daylight time to make a net before dusk. With only root vegetables in his bag, it was time he caught a fish.

Surrounded by materials, Patrick chopped down lengths of willow, slim green vines, a long and sturdy bough and set to work, using his upturned boat as a bench. He made a hoop from plaited willow, stitched, and tied with the tough sinews of the green vine. While making a net from the vines the light began to fade and the sun set as he fixed his hoop and net to the handle. Gathering up some tinder, he sparked a light and successfully lit his candle lamp. Satisfied that he could create a flame, he quenched the candle. Next, he gathered a mugful of larvae and various creeping insects and covered the top with a tightly tied piece of cloth. Ready now to finish packing, he tied his bag under the seat of his boat, secured all loose possessions to the frame, mounted the boat on his shoulders and began the descent of the mountain. The musty smell of decaying forestation gradually gave way to the sweeter smells of birch and grass, and then fresh air wafted into the woods and soon Patrick was on the river.

He enjoyed a long stretch of east flowing water as mountains of rock on both sides channelled the river into a deep and narrow gorge. Eventually the river widened as it entered flatter lands. Patrick became nervous as the larger river flowed slowly, passing banks and fields that were close enough for vagabonds to mount an attack. The value of the boat alone made Patrick a target. However, he passed a few tributaries and his river swelled into a major waterway, making attacks less likely. Now Patrick felt like he and his little boat were a floating acorn on a calm ocean. Remembering Guigan's advice that this river joined a larger river, he visualised a confluence too turbulent to take on. But that was a problem for closer to dawn. Right now, it was the middle of the night and a matter of importance needed his attention.

He paddled to the shallows and watched out for a fishing opportunity, which appeared as a bend in the river, partially isolated by erosion, had created a backwater. Paddling out of the main current he found a spot as still as a pond, lit his lamp and set the shutters to deflect the light downwards. At that moment Patrick's mind brought forth his last night in Banna Venta, holding a lamp as he walked in the dark to the threshing barn. The girl in the barn entered his thoughts. He'd never considered who would have found her body, and when. He began to think this episode hadn't finished. His return to Banna Venta would probably lead to questions.

Returning to the present he removed the cover from his mug of grubs and threw half of them over the side. Lowering his large hooped net into the river he waited for a short time, then with his other hand held the lamp over the water, close to the surface. He saw a few fish below, snapping up the bait, but when the light caught their attention, curiosity attracted fish large and small to the surface, swimming over and under each other in irregular circles. When Patrick couldn't see his net for fish, he put down the lamp and raised his net as fast as he could, but the fish were quicker. Thinking they'd all escaped, he was delighted to see a perch and two large trout in the bottom of his net. With a sharp knock on the back of their heads Patrick delivered a bloodless death blow to his catch. He gutted the fish and washed them in the river before wrapping them in large green leaves, grabbed from some of the riverside plants. Satisfied he had caught enough fish to feed himself for a week, he paddled his boat to the faster flowing water, refilled his water skin and resumed his journey. The fishing technique, gleaned from the outlaws on Lough Conn, had served him well. He hoped Cashel too would enjoy similar success.

The night darkened as the moon faded from sight and, as dawn drew nearer, he took the caution of travelling closer to the bank. After a lengthy time, he noticed the pace of the river was gaining and a background sound, like a wind rustle, rose and receded. Recognising the signs this time, without hesitation he came off the river and walked. In half a mile, Patrick was standing on the south bank of the largest river he'd ever seen. This magnificent flow of water made the Eden into the Solway, look small. He studied the junction of his river with the big river. The scene wasn't turbulent at all. The confluence looked serene. The master river could take in all the water of Patrick's river, seemingly without a splash. Perhaps the size of the rivers created an illusion where waves looked like ripples and splashes were unseen. But Patrick was happy not to be afloat in a basket putting his theory of illusion to the test.

The predawn light was strengthening and Patrick was regretting his hunger for speed and distance as the locality, which was flat and arable, would be teeming with people by sunrise. Deciding to follow the river, due south, he launched his miniature craft on the mighty flowing river and paddled steadily toward the centre, hoping to find a suitable place to land on the far bank. Instead, he discovered he could not pass the imaginary centre line of the river. Trying harder seemed to strengthen the flow which opposed him.

Patrick shook his head in disbelief. He needed to reach the far bank of this huge river quickly, to have any hope of finding safe and secret refuge before daylight. As a stranger to these parts in the daytime he would find himself having to prove his clan; risking being exposed as a runaway slave.

His efforts were futile, the current his master. Looking downstream, the river ahead entered a long bend to the south-west, which was the wrong direction for him. He needed to travel to the south-east. Then, without any paddling, the current took him gently over the centre line. Patrick tried paddling towards the far bank and immediately his efforts were rewarded.

Patrick breathed a heavy sigh, exhaling his worries. He realised the current was pushing in that direction because of the forthcoming bend, and he was reaping the benefit. Keeping close to the bank he went with the flow of the river, passing farmsteads and cattle ranches. Looking further south he spotted hills and his hope began to seem well founded. Studying the landscape, a yellow expanse of furze and whin came into sight, leading to the hills, as rich farming lands gave way to a coarse and rugged landscape. He came off the river at a small inlet and headed for the hills. Patrick's hopes lifted again when he spotted a gully in the barren land, leading up to the hills. He strode out urgently. If the area was grazed, he could expect within the hour that sheep, a shepherd, and guard dog would enter the land.

As Patrick maintained a brisk pace, he saw no signs of sheep droppings, old or new. Coming to a cluster of bushes he stopped and, under their cover, scanned the area all around. Although the place looked desolate, before moving on he tied creepers and vines around his boat and tucked leaves and furze under the ligaments, attempting to hide himself in the landscape, in case he was still searching at dawn.

He came across an elevated valley with no river, where two hills met. Enclosed naturally on three sides it was a place where a sheep pen would be sited. He speeded up his stride and came across a run-down, rectangular building made of wattle and daub. The entrance, robbed of its door and posts, was wide open to the world. The roof was stripped. Only a few corner rafters remained with some rotten bundles of thatch that weren't worth stealing. The derelict building appeared too badly run-down to offer refuge, but Patrick ran to the building all the same. Inside was empty, except for a broken bench with two steps leading up to it. He guessed sheep would climb up the steps and stand to be milked, making the building a disused milking station. He couldn't take the risk of sleeping here, but before leaving he checked the walls for hidden spaces. There were none. He looked up, fearfully at the dim but growing light of the sky, and saw a third of the loft remained boarded. There were no steps, but some evidence of where they once had been. He leant his boat against the wall and used it as a ladder from which he sprang onto the beams and boards. They were strong enough to bear his weight, especially in the corner, which was dark and completely out of sight. Patrick smiled. Unexpectedly, he'd found his lodgings.

Before settling down for the day he had an important detail to take care of. He strapped his boat to his shoulders and climbed to the summit of the hill, where he stood in the shelter of a group of rocky peaks. The sun was risen, low in the sky, shining above the clinging ground mists, illuminating the mountains that peaked through in the distant east.

'The mountains will guide you to the east,' Guigan had said. Patrick checked the foreground, looking for a route. The lands were rich, the farmsteads large. These were wealthy cattle ranches and the king didn't need to graze the scrublands. Patrick could probably walk the low-lying hill slopes without meeting shepherds. He had learned enough for now. Returning to the derelict farm building hungry and tired, he couldn't risk starting a fire to cook the fish, so he organised his hideaway. Safely out of sight, he ate the last of his boiled roots and drank them down with fresh water, before falling asleep during payers.

Voices woke him. They were close, relaxed, and laughing voices. Listening carefully, Patrick made out two men chatting light-heartedly. Peeping from under the canvas he couldn't see down to the source of the chatter. Quietly he moved the cover aside and, crouched in the boat, he stretched his neck until he could see two men sitting around a fire in front of the doorway. Each had pierced a fish onto a stick, which they were holding over hot embers.

'I didn't believe the night nets would work. I mean, how can a trout get tangled and caught, when he's got all night to escape?' said one.

'I told you it worked,' the other teased.

Patrick lay back in his boat and listened. The men commented on every bite of their fish as they giggled and knocked back their ale. Eventually they were ready to move on.

'I'll piss the fire out,' one said.

'Don't be stupid. We'll use the sticks again. Leave it. Stamp on it, if it bothers you.'

Patrick thought about the comment. The reveller didn't expect people to pass by this place. The sticks would still be there for next time.

The man relieved himself noisily against an inside wall.

'Ah, you're not so stupid. You thought to kill two birds with one strike,' his friend laughed.

Patrick heard their chattering fade into the distance and came down from the loft. He sneaked a look outside. It was mid-afternoon on a cloudy day. He'd had a long sleep, but better than being awake with nothing to do, he thought. Encouraged by the visitors, Patrick took advantage of the hot embers, cooked all three of his fish and enjoyed a tasty meal of perch at the same time. Happy that his gamble had paid off he packed away his cooked meals, including the perch carcass, and hid in the loft again till darkness came.

The rain poured. The weight of the boat was no problem, it was the chafing. Using his spare tunic as padding between the straps and his body, he solved the problem of carrying his boat in wet weather. His route along the foothills had proven to be successful, assisted by a few hours of rainfall. The boat on his back completely sheltered his bag and fleece and was a welcome advantage to Patrick.

During the night, a man, who was probably a thief, crossed Patrick's path without seeing him. From the shadows Patrick had watched this man behaving furtively. He seemed to be making off with a piglet tied up in a shoulder bag. Patrick wondered if the man was stealing to alleviate poverty or just trying to make an easy living. He couldn't himself avoid stealing in his quest to escape from Ireland.

By dawn, Patrick had reached the mountains and found a suitable cave for shelter. He built a small fire inside and, with his pot, he boiled the perch skeleton and fish head to make a hot gruel, then he kept the fire burning to dry out his clothes.

While drinking his hot fish stew, he contemplated his faith in God, which he thought was total. After five nights of fleeing and five perilous days of hiding, here he was with a roof above him, fire beside him, food in his belly and two full fish in his bag. He didn't know exactly where he was going, other than to a busy harbour on the south-east coast. But God was guiding his way, of that, he was sure.

Sleeping soundly, a tickling sensation on his face woke him up. He opened his eyes and met another pair of eyes at the end of a short brownish snout. He couldn't see if his visitor was a kitten, fox cub or puppy dog. All he could see was a small, furry, whiskered, non-aggressive animal that had woken him by licking his cheek. Patrick moved slowly away, sparked up his lamp and saw a young fox cub watching him with a tilted head and pleading gaze. As Patrick moved, the cub shuffled painfully towards its object of torment, Patrick's bag, and tilted its head again. Patrick saw the wounded animal had one front leg hanging limp and the other bleeding from an open wound. The poor thing was probably starving, but hadn't the strength to rip open Patrick's bag to claim a fish supper. Neither could the cub drag the bag away, as it was tied to the boat.

Patrick picked up the cloth in which the perch had been wrapped and, using his dagger, cut it into strips. Speaking gently to the cub he felt the broken leg to estimate the damage. The fox lay down; sensing help was on its way. Patrick used a stick from his firewood and all the care and learning he'd gained from years of tending sheep, and applied a splint to the cub's leg. Patrick felt in his bag and brought out a small vessel of ointment that King Miliucc had issued to Patrick for treating sheep's wounds. He washed the sore on the cub's other leg, gently with a damp piece of cloth, applied the ointment and wrapped the wound with a small bandage.

The cub stood tentatively on three legs; limped around a little, then he was moving quickly on three legs. Patrick thought the animal's chances of surviving were poor, but still he reached into his bag and pulled out one of the remaining trout. As he removed the leaf wrapping, the cub snapped up the fish with the head hanging out of one side of his mouth and the tail, the other. He three-legged it quickly to the cave entrance, turned back, fish in mouth, looked at Patrick and off he went. Patrick stared at the space the cub had just vacated and lingered in thought. Was there a purpose in all things? One thing was sure; Patrick was short of food again.

The mountains, Patrick's guide and host for three nights, came to an end, replaced by fertile plains and a fast-flowing river heading east. Dawn was far away but Patrick decided against continuing his journey. He tracked back into the mountains, found a suitable cave, and changed out of his boots into his sandals. Unfettered by his boat and possessions he headed for the plains in search of a small farmstead. Passing the larger enterprises, he came across a cow path leading to a small cluster of buildings. Moving close and hiding behind bushes, Patrick accustomed his eyes to the darkness and distance until he could see details. He identified two family houses and some smaller animal houses. The entire farmstead was surrounded by two parallel earthen mounds, a means of security to prevent the running of cattle, or large-scale theft of smaller livestock carried off in carts. But against the intentions of an opportunist thief after a chicken and a clutch of eggs, the mounds were of no use.

Patrick thought of the heifer raid, to help a family in need and to acquire a boat and freedom for himself. Now he was stealing to feed himself for a few days. He looked forward to getting home and leaving the cusp of moral and immoral living behind him.

Patrick crept over the mounds and hid behind a water barrel, where he studied the buildings. Creeping to the henhouse, which was furthest from the family homes, he stood motionless and listened. Sensing his presence, the hens made gargling noises. The shoulder-high door was closed and bolted with a sturdy slide bar, which he pulled to the open position. Making sure no one was watching, he quickly stepped into the henhouse, and closed the door behind him.

Patrick squatted and peered around the dark room, kicking an egg as he crouched. He felt for the egg and found it, then placed it with a handful of straw in his tunic pouch. By now he could see the floor was scattered with resting hens. He felt around and pocketed a few more eggs before turning his concentration to the main task.

The unlucky bird failed to raise a fuss. The only extra sound she made, unnoticed by the other chickens, was the snap of her neck. Then, the futile fluttering of an already dead bird triggered a chorus of clucking among her feathered friends. Patrick stepped outside, his left hand firmly holding the hen by its neck. He slid the bolt into place with his right hand and crept quickly to the cover of the water barrel from where he watched the doors of the family houses.

One of them opened and a tall, bearded man wearing a nightshirt came out. By now the henhouse choir had calmed itself and Patrick hoped for the best. His wish seemed to be granted when the man relieved himself against the pigsty wall and headed back to his house. But the aggrieved bird's body was not listening to its lifeless head. With gut instinct she launched a frenzied flurry of wing-flapping, alerting the man, who immediately summoned help and grabbed a spear from inside his door. He was joined by two more gown-wearing spear carriers.

'I heard a noise,' he said, and pointed instructions to the other two.

Patrick belatedly pulled out a bag – one of Guigan's piglet head covers – from his tunic and stuffed the hen into it, hoping to restrain any additional bursts of life, then, as though oblivious to his surroundings, he knelt and, placing his palms together, he prayed in a most extraordinary manner.

Patrick had thought often and deeply about his attitude and approach to prayer. He prayed generously for others. He prayed to give thanks, to ask for forgiveness, to ask for strength, but was uncomfortable with praying for his own situation. His belief was strengthening that prayer for self was an implied lack of faith. Passive faith, in the way of not asking for help, showed trust in God, who would send help if necessary. He thought about having the courage to show faith in difficult or even dangerous circumstances, when consequences would be immediate. This moment presented an opportunity for Patrick to test his own faith in God and more; to show God the strength of his own faith, if only he had the courage.

The armed farmers fanned out. One headed for the track, one for the perimeter behind the hen houses and the bearded one strode across the yard to check the area from the water barrel to the perimeter mound. Patrick was surrounded. He was about to be caught red-handed.

He'd worked hard on a prayer of faith since his experience at Guigan's farm and it was written in his mind. He chose this moment to offer it to God, aloud, in full voice.

'Dear God, I arise today, through a mighty strength, the invocation of The Trinity; through the belief in the Threeness; through the confession of the Oneness of the Creator of creation.'

The farmer, spear poised, ten feet away from Patrick in plain sight, looked Patrick's way – through him and beyond him.

Patrick continued, 'Christ be with me, be within me, be behind me, be before me.'

Patrick heard the farmer call to his man on the track. 'What do you see?' he said looking straight through Patrick once again.

Patrick crossed himself and said out loud, 'Praise be to God.'

'I see nothing,' the farmer on the track answered.

He called to the other farmer, 'What do you see?'

'Nothing.'

'I too, see nothing, but I hear the cry of deer. Let us return to our beds.'

Patrick saw two of the men enter the house as he crept over the mounds and down to the track, where he hid behind a bush and watched. Thinking the retreat of the farmers might be a ploy, he waited, intending to witness the third farmer going home, before making a move. After a long wait Patrick was considering leaving, when, directly across the track he heard a noise, like the plucking of leaves. He ducked his head down lower, worried that the solitary bush would be insufficient cover. Suddenly, and only twelve strides away, the third farmer stood up from down in the ditch, tidied his clothing and looked around; then picked up his spear and strode out for home.

Patrick, stifling a laugh, felt he could do no wrong. He continued his journey to his own home, a cave residence in the mountains. Unable to feel the earth under his feet, tears of joy ran down his cheeks and, as the enormity of the exchange sunk in, he cried without restraint. Suddenly, a flash of fear struck his heart as the experience of proximity to God hit him. He was burdened by the unburdening. The fear of God troubled his heart awhile, until new joy so filled his soul that he was becalmed.

Coming down to earth, in his cave, Patrick drained the chicken, plucked it and cooked it. Feeling this moment like his existence was a prayer; he lay down his head and slept with the angels.

* * *

During the next four nights, Patrick skilfully avoided rapids and waterfalls and as the river grew wider and deeper, it flowed slower. The farmers were arching their backs into the late evening as the waxing harvest moon illuminated their fields. Patrick floated by, a harmless, unchallenged dot in the middle of the river. The banks widened and moored boats gave the impression that Patrick was near the sea. The riverside became ever more distant and the flow of the river almost stopped. He paddled to maintain progress and yet an hour later he still hadn't arrived at the sea. Boats of all sizes were visible, pulled up the sloping banks, occasionally moored against wooden structures. Patrick wanted a harbour as close to the sea as possible and now he was faced with a choice. Directly ahead of him was land. The river became T-shaped; leading left looked like an estuary, but so too did the river to the right. Which way should he turn? There was no wind so Patrick tried an idea. He paddled his boat to the centre of the T and brought it to a standstill. Lifting his oar from the water he let the boat drift. He reasoned there would be a flow, however gentle, to the sea, only possible to detect in the absence of wind. For a while he seemed not to move, as though settled in the centre of an invisible vortex; but slowly, he drifted to the east and as the flow became unambiguous, he took to the oar again.

The predawn light crept in. Ahead he spotted a silty beach and just beyond that a pronounced promontory on which several boats were moored. He came off the water and took careful note of the boats. One larger boat stood out, fitted with enclosures for goods or livestock. The hull was wooden and three pairs of oars were mounted on iron spigots. There was a central mast which was lowered. This looked like a trading vessel and the design was not typically Irish. This vessel could be from the Britains or beyond. The other boats looked Irish-owned, being lightweight and leather-hulled. They were probably coast hoppers, meaning their destination was simply another location in Ireland. Asking one of these captains for passage would be the same as handing himself in.

Patrick felt nervous. Risk was upon him. However carefully he approached a captain, as soon as he made a request for passage, his identity as a runaway would become obvious. Worse still he would have embroiled the captain, who was forbidden by law to turn a blind eye to a suspected runaway slave. Patrick was intending to ask a foreign captain for a job on board, exactly as he was putting to sea, to minimise the risk for the captain and himself.

A sandy, dune-riddled hillside overlooked the moorings. Patrick wedged his boat upside down between two dunes. Tilted like the top half of an open clam, he disguised the hull with sand and, from the cover of his boat, thirty strides from the moorings, he watched the still though scary scene, and waited.

The weather was dry and windy as the sun promised to rise. Boats were already leaving the estuary, including the ones on either side of Patrick's target. He heard the Irish twang of their crews, which confirmed his decision not to approach them.

Patrick's heartbeat suddenly raced as men appeared on board the merchant vessel, moving with urgency, gathering tools and materials. A ramp was lowered and six men came to the harbour side, four carrying stakes and heavy wooden mallets. The fifth man gave instructions to the workers in a Gaelic language, but their accent wasn't Irish or British. The workers immediately marked out the ground and began hammering a row of fat, circular spears into the earth. The sixth man was overseeing two fearsome looking bulls as they were led from their on-board enclosure, down the ramp to the quayside. Each was tied to the newly installed stakes. Six men, carrying shields and armed with spears and daggers, ran down the ramp and took up position guarding the bulls.

It was obvious to Patrick that the foreigners were ready to trade. Step by step he was closing in on his goal, but the minutes dragged like hours.

Along the track came a company of guards on horseback. They

were protecting an ox-drawn cart and a leader on a white steed. Perhaps a chieftain or a king, Patrick thought, although the leader was plainly dressed. A driver and bard were seated at the front of the cart which was filled with excitedly yapping young pups. As the company halted alongside the bulls, the overseer approached the customer.

'King Eoghan. Pleased to see you. How was your journey?' he greeted.

Patrick thought this overseer might be a merchant or trader as he knew the king by sight and name.

'My journey was noisy. The young guard dogs are excited, but they may soon be yours. Shall we inspect the bulls?' the king asked.

These words were welcome to Patrick's ears.

'Of course,' he gestured towards the animals.

The king and one of his guards examined the beasts in detail. Finally, he nodded to his chief guard to fetch the dogs. They were let down from the cart, collared in five groups of eight and secured to the remaining five posts. The overseer and a crew member examined the pups, slowly and carefully, stretching Patrick's nerve as the day began and people were coming and going. He preferred not to have witnesses when the time came to reveal his intentions. At last, the buyer and seller seemed to agree their terms of trade as tablets were scratched and notes exchanged. The bulls were hitched to the king's cart and the company moved on.

The merchant guards became busy loading the dogs, the water tubs and food; Patrick's big moment, for escape or capture, had arrived.

CHAPTER TWENTY-ONE

Carrying his bag and fleece, Patrick made his way briskly to the merchant's boat, catching the attention of a crew member lugging tools up the ramp.

'I'd like to speak to your captain,' Patrick said to the crew member; a wiry man with long brown hair and an unkempt beard and moustache.

He stopped, looked down his nose at Patrick then shouted, 'Hey captain, a young blond slave would like to speak to you.' He sneered Patrick's way.

Patrick winced; his cautious approach ruined. A short, dark-haired man, wearing no identifying garb, looked across to him.

'What do you want, young man?'

'I'm Roman-British and I want to return home. I have my own food and I would like to work my passage…' Before he could say 'please' the captain's face froze, then contorted in suppressed rage.

'Stranger, I wish you hadn't asked me.' He hesitated and then in anger said, 'Go, just go,' and turned away.

Patrick glanced around fearfully but was relieved to see no one was in close proximity. He hoped he'd get a second chance on a different vessel. Making his way quickly to his upturned fishing boat, praying as he walked, he arrived at the dunes and heard an urgent voice behind him calling.

'Hey, stranger.'

Patrick turned to see the wiry crewman who'd relayed his message to the captain with the diplomatic skills of the bulls they'd just delivered.

'The captain has had a change of heart, come quickly. We are ready to leave.'

Why the rethink? What has changed? Is it my prayer being answered? He looked across at the boat and saw the captain waving them urgently to return. Patrick was fifty strides from freedom with God on his side, so he took the chance.

He pointed to his boat, 'I'll grab my food. Can I give my fishing boat and equipment to the captain...?'

'Leave it,' the sailor interjected. 'Come quickly.'

Patrick turned, with just his bag and fleece.

As they rushed, the sailor said, 'The captain will take you on trust – and I will let you suck my nipples.'

Patrick stopped abruptly. He didn't like the sound of the sailor's suggestion.

'If that is the price of my journey, I decline. Tell your captain thanks.'

The crew member quickly backed off. 'Have it your way. I was only being friendly.' His arms rose helplessly.

Patrick couldn't see the friendliness. 'I feed myself and work for the captain. Nothing else, is that clear?'

'It's clear,' said the baffled crewman.

Patrick and Friendly boarded the vessel and the crew immediately pulled up the ramp. Six oarsmen were in position as a crewman pushed them away from the mooring using a long sturdy pole.

It's happening, thought Patrick. He looked back across the dunes at his fishing boat. The unlikely looking vessel had halved his journey time and helped him avoid capture along the way. Now he was mid-river on a large, rigid, wooden-hulled boat, being rowed down the widening estuary, with the open sea in sight. His heart raced as every pull on the oars propelled him to freedom. He looked around; there were no boats in pursuit. He really was leaving the shores of Ireland.

The captain came to him. 'What is your name?' he asked, showing no sign of his earlier annoyance.

'Patrick.'

'I believe, Patrick, that you will not accept the bond of nipple-sucking, in which case, choose an oath that is serious, and to your liking. I want you to accept my rules and commands on board this boat provided they are lawful.'

Patrick now understood Friendly's offer. It was like rubbing sweaty foreheads together, or slitting wrists and mixing blood: a symbolic swearing of trust.

'I believe in God,' Patrick said, watching the captain's face for reaction.

'Your oath before God is acceptable,' the captain replied.

Patrick was relieved and responded without delay.

'I swear by God Almighty that I accept your rules and commands so far as they are lawful, while I travel on board your vessel.'

The captain nodded to Patrick in satisfaction.

'I'll take that from you,' the captain said, pointing at Patrick's dagger. 'You'll get it back when our journey ends.'

As Patrick handed over his dagger the captain beckoned him to the enclosure; opened the door and said, 'Find a bed space and put your things there.'

Patrick found a gap and marked it with his bag. On the right were forty dogs, chained, but free to yap, bark and defecate. Cows had a better odour Patrick thought.

'Captain, where are we heading for?' Patrick asked.

'Gaul.'

'We pass Britain on the way to Gaul. Will you leave me in Britain please?'

The captain's eyes flamed. 'I helped you too much already,' he turned and in raised voice commanded, 'there are tubs on board, feed the dogs.'

Patrick filled buckets with water and dished out bones and meat for the pups. When he finished the captain thrust a blanket Patrick's way. 'Put your head down. You'll be rowing in a couple of hours.'

Opening the enclosure door, Patrick saw two men sleeping. And there was Friendly, rooting around in Patrick's bag. Undisturbed by Patrick's entry, Friendly put the bag down and showed the brooch to Patrick, mocking him. 'Isn't this nice?' He ran his finger over the jewel. 'Our runaway has a girlfriend.'

Patrick was working out how to take back the gift for his mother.

'Don't worry; I'll sell it back to you in Gaul,' Friendly said.

Friendly's dagger was in its scabbard and tied to his waist belt; this would give Patrick the few seconds he needed. His opponent's casual arrogance was careless; he was wide open for a punch. Friendly taunted Patrick as he held his pouch open, clasping the brooch between finger and thumb he released his grip, dropping the brooch cockily into his tunic pouch. With both of Friendly's hands occupied briefly, Patrick delivered two fast and hard blows to his adversary's stomach. Friendly bent forward in pain, winded so deeply he couldn't even groan. Patrick removed Friendly's dagger and recovered his mother's brooch. Friendly fell on to both knees, weak with pain, as Patrick made for the door.

'What are you doing with my dagger?' he gulped.

'Putting it somewhere safe,' Patrick answered.

He tucked it under his belt at his side and left the enclosure. The only prying eyes were those of the rowers. Keeping the dagger on their blind side Patrick moved to the edge of the boat and took in the sea air. Easing his belt away from his body he let the dagger drop silently into the ocean, and returned to the enclosure.

Friendly was back on to one knee.

'What have you done with it?' he snapped at Patrick, clearly having recovered his breath.

'It's at the bottom of the sea. Give me any more trouble and you will follow it.'

Friendly snarled defiantly. Still bent forward, he left the enclosure, just as someone very large came through the door.

The giant took Patrick's fleece and was about to lay on it, when Patrick, tiring of conflict, took a deep breath and, bracing himself for a reaction, said, 'Excuse me, that's my fleece.'

'But I don't have a blanket,' the man replied nodding towards the dogs. Somehow the pups had made his blanket theirs.

'Take mine,' Patrick held out his blanket. The man took it with a nod and passed the fleece to Patrick. Relieved that the situation hadn't escalated, Patrick rested his head. He briefly wondered why there was so much friction in his life at the moment, then said a few silent prayers and slept.

Shaken out of deep sleep, Patrick turned to see his big neighbour leaning over him. 'We'll be rowing soon. Get some food down ya. You'll need the energy.'

'Thanks,' Patrick said as he looked around.

He delved into his bag and took out his water skin and chicken pieces. 'Let's smell the sea air,' Patrick said aloud, leaving the enclosure to eat his breakfast in a fresher place.

Sitting against the enclosure wall Patrick watched the two leaders talking, preparing for the crew change.

Were they both captains? Patrick wondered. One was for sure. The other looked like a trader, having recognised the king and used his name. They both seem to lead at times. Is one more senior? He drank his water, ate a few chicken pieces, and finally was called to duty as the rowers changed shift.

All the oars were singles and Patrick was seated beside his bedtime neighbour. A few rows ahead on the opposite side, was Friendly. Patrick was glad they were on the same shift as it reduced Friendly's opportunity to make mischief.

And so, for two nights and three days they alternated every four hours, rowing, feeding the dogs, sleeping, and eating. With no tailwind to speak of, the sail was never hoisted. Patrick thought of the storm on the night of his capture, when he believed he was going to die. He was happy to be rowing this time and delighted the sea was calm. He heard the second captain detailing crew members to clean the dogs and the enclosure. Sounds like we'll be landing soon, he thought. He searched the coastline as well as he could manage, looking over his shoulders, but couldn't see signs of a harbour.

Shortly, under the captain's instruction, the boat was manoeuvred into a small bay on a remote part of the coastline, where a similar sized boat was already moored. Why are we landing here and not in an established trading port? Patrick wondered. The trading captain left the boat to meet someone from the other boat, on the quayside. As the oarsmen stood to stretch their legs, Patrick saw three men disembark from the waiting boat; their leader greeted the trader. The trader shook his hand and invited him and his two assistants on board.

By now Patrick believed that the bulls he saw traded for dogs, in Ireland, were stolen. The seller was probably the thief and the trader knowingly handling stolen goods. Why else would the parties meet in such a remote place?

They entered the enclosure through the wide-open double doors, and carefully checked every dog, arguing hotly over the health of some of them. Patrick and the crew watched on as the haggling continued. At times it seemed that there would be no deal. Finally, it appeared they'd agreed a sale, as Patrick watched the trader-captain counting Roman coins into a leather purse. Thereafter he allowed their customer's crew on board to lead the dogs to their own vessel.

Patrick's trader-captain now appeared to be the main leader as he paid the boat captain, who in turn called the crew around him and doled out the wages. As he did so, the trader-captain called Patrick and Friendly to gather their things and get off the boat. Patrick, on his way to the enclosure, took his chance to speak to the boat captain. He was out of earshot of the merchant, who had the puppies on a lead.

'Captain, where are we?'

'You're on the west coast of Gaul.'

'Does the place have a name?' Patrick asked watching the captain's face carefully.

'I don't know this area. You are probably two days from the

nearest village and perhaps five from a town.' Patrick was dismayed, but thought the captain was speaking straight.

'Where are you going to next?'

'Oh no. You can't come with me. I'm going home and I'm not taking strangers to my home place. I'll give you some advice, though. Don't use the coastal route north, it's dangerous. Go east with the merchant and get onto the main Roman road. Head for Parisium and Bononia. That's your way home. Now, please go. I'm in a hurry.'

'My dagger, please,' Patrick asked.

'The merchant has it. Good luck, young man,' he smiled with a hint of sarcasm.

Patrick grabbed his things and disembarked. He watched both boats pull away; the sight induced a huge pang of loneliness and a twinge of fear.

I'm a freeman now with little food, no coin, and no possessions of worth. I expected to land in a busy harbour but I find myself in a remote place, five days from the nearest town, at a time when I need work and earnings, fast.

The paymaster came to Patrick, 'Young man, you are in Gaul. The Britains are ten days that way,' he pointed northeast. 'The way is hostile, so you must take care,' he said.

'Who is fighting?' Patrick asked.

'Barbarians are fighting Romans. You haven't heard this?'

'I have heard nothing for years,' Patrick answered, worried now about the situation in Gaul.

'Do you know the news about Britanniae?'

'I have heard no news.' Patrick shook his head, looking concerned.

'The Romans pulled out of Britanniae last year.'

Patrick stopped; motionless, disbelieving. Slowly he began to wonder what that meant for his parents, for Banna Venta and indeed the administration of the country. The merchant seemed taken aback by Patrick's response. He waited; let the news sink in for a while.

'You really didn't know,' the merchant stated.

Patrick nodded a no.

'Home will be a different place. We are from Condate, which is three days east,' he pointed over the hills. 'It's a fortified Roman town. The roads from there to the north are good. It's a supply route with some large towns, including Parisium. Your journey will be safer but four or five days longer. Travel with us to Condate if you wish. You have a choice to make.'

Patrick reasoned that his chances of earning money would be better nearer to towns and cities, and his Roman citizenship would probably be more useful in these places too. And as this echoed the boat captain's advice, he thought it was the best option.

'I'll travel with you,' Patrick said and held out his hand, 'my dagger please.'

The merchant answered coolly, without missing a breath.

'I believe you threw one of my daggers into the sea, but it's not a problem. I will accept yours in its place. There it is.' He pointed to Friendly who was wearing it on his belt.

Friendly smiled with a raised nose to Patrick.

Why couldn't Friendly have been one of the captain's crew? Patrick was regretting having thrown the dagger overboard before considering the consequences.

'Let's get moving. We're sleeping in those woods tonight,' the merchant said, pointing to a densely forested hillside. The three men and two puppies walked a few hours before nightfall and slept in a disused lumber cabin. Patrick kept the brooch on his person in case Friendly had further ideas, but nothing happened.

The next day they came across a burned-out village with no residents left. This posed a problem as the merchant was expecting to buy food there. By evening Patrick was disturbed by the situation. No one could walk in Britain for days and not see anyone. Where are we? We're going hungry and need to find a village or a town.

'Get that God of yours to provide us with food,' the merchant mocked.

'He's your God too. Have you asked him?' Patrick retorted.

Eventually Patrick persuaded his sceptical companions to join him in prayer, to relieve their hunger. Nothing happened and an hour later the merchant was berating Patrick.

'Your God isn't true. It's all a lie,' but before he finished his words, a herd of boar charged out of the woods.

Friendly, quick on his feet, tackled the smallest boar to the ground, thereby providing several days of sustenance for the group. They all enjoyed a campfire roast that evening, including the puppies and Patrick's standing was raised. Conversations became more amicable after the show of faith produced results.

* * *

Two evenings later they slept in the hills in sight of their destination. The weather since leaving Ireland had been dry and warm. Patrick could not remember experiencing seven consecutive days without rain during his time in Ireland. He fell asleep with a more contented mind, imagining how things would be tomorrow, in a Roman town called Condate.

Somehow his dream darkened and he felt the weight of a bull on his chest, restricting his breathing. The devil, in his dream, danced on his muscles. Trapped and slowly dying, his mind mixed up dreams and prayers. Christ came and went in stirring, swirling vapours, from which Elijah stepped. Patrick saw himself crying out, 'Elijah, Elijah'. The mists vanished in sunlight and Christ appeared and, as the light brightened, he could be seen no more. The sunlight warmed Patrick's bones and flesh; his muscles gained strength and the paralysis was lifted. Patrick thought the light of Christ had saved him from the devil and, waking from his dreams, he called out, 'Let it be thus on my day of tribulation.'

Patrick opened his eyes to darkness, and realised he was blindfolded, arms tied behind his back and feet tethered. His mind flashed back to his capture in Banna Venta. It's happening again.

It was deserved retribution then, but this time; after years of steadfast faith?

He hardly noticed he was being pushed to walk. God, how can it be? I don't understand. The dream: was it a message to strengthen me, in time for this bad turn of events? His blindfold was removed and he was prodded brutally with the butt of a spear.

'Keep moving,' snapped the merchant.

'Where are you taking me?'

Friendly slapped him across the face, 'I offered you a bond of friendship and you turned me down. So now, shut your mouth.'

Is he telling me he wouldn't have tried to take my possessions if I'd bonded with him? Patrick wasn't sure there was any lesson to learn here.

In silence the three men and two puppies descended the mountain and made for the grey and rocky hillside opposite. A large and active stone quarry was visible from this side of the valley and they seemed to be heading towards it. It was lost from sight as they crossed the valley and climbed the other side. The track they walked led to a Roman road which they followed until they arrived at a forbidding, stone-built entrance, set in a perimeter fence twice the height of the one at the pig farm. The place looked like a prison.

The merchant rapped the knocker on the pedestrian door situated at the side of the hardwood, double leaf gates. A guard opened the dark-oak door, the black hinges creaking, and recognised his friend.

'Step inside,' the guard greeted, cheerily closing the door behind him.

Patrick weighed up his chances of escaping; now it was one against one. His ankles were chained with enough slack to walk, but he couldn't stride or run. His arms were tied behind his back. He needed to get close enough to Friendly to head butt him, grab the dagger and slice his hands free. Then he would need to incapacitate Friendly, and walk away and hide, in order to work on freeing the chains. He turned to face Friendly and felt the spear tip pressed against his throat.

The door opened. This time the merchant's expression was serious.

'You,' he said, pointing at Patrick, 'come inside.' He turned to Friendly. 'Wait and watch the baggage and the dogs.'

Friendly almost fell over trying to get in front of Patrick, in order to give him his best smirk. Patrick ignored him and stepped through the door into a small courtyard where two armed soldiers guarded an internal doorway. *This is more than slavery, it's a prison.*

Meanwhile, the merchant was speaking to a man wearing a high-quality, plain coloured toga. To Patrick's eye, he was dressed as his own father would be. This senior looking figure stepped across to Patrick and looked him up and down.

'Show me your hands,' he said, gesturing a guard to cut Patrick's bonds. A sharp dagger sliced his hands free, allowing Patrick to extend his arms before him.

'You two, what are you doing?' Patrick asked, fixing the supervisor with his stare.

The supervisor, temporarily taken aback by this unexpected insubordination, recovered, and smiled into Patrick's face, 'I am the quarry manager and we are preparing you for work in the quarry.'

'But I'm a Roman citizen. My father is a Roman decurion and that man,' Patrick pointed at the merchant, 'does not own me. I am not his to sell.'

'Roman citizen, eh? Rome is on the other side of the gate. On this side, only my rules count.' He beckoned the armed guard. 'Take out your cosh and stand ready. If this man speaks, bruise him till he learns not to speak.' The guard nodded and stood with cosh drawn.

The merchant watched on; his face inscrutable.

The manager, facing Patrick said, 'Follow my instructions. Hands out with palms up.'

Patrick obeyed and the man in charge studied them at length.

'Turn over.'

Patrick faced his palms down. The backs of his hands were weather-beaten, scratched and grazed.

His scrutineer said, 'Come this way,' and led Patrick to a row of three chiselled grey stones, increasing in size from left to right.

'Place the small stone on the middle stone,' Patrick did so, wondering what the point was. 'Now put it back and place the middle stone on the large stone.' Patrick obeyed. He was at the limit of his strength lifting the middle stone, which gave him a clue about the weight of the big stone. 'Put the middle stone back and place the large stone on the middle stone,' he instructed. Patrick stood the large stone on end, lowered it onto the middle stone and shifted it into position. The manager asked Patrick to return the stones to their original position. Patrick reversed his moves, completing the task without lifting the deadweight of the large stone.

'Bring the ankle chains,' the manager commanded the guard.

The merchant didn't disguise his smile. Patrick had just fetched him a good price. Coins were pressed into the merchant's palm.

Patrick took advantage of the guard's absence. He looked the merchant in the eye and said, 'Is this why you changed your mind in Ireland?'

'I didn't change my mind,' he leered, 'I changed the captain's mind.'

The merchant counted his coins and shook hands with the quarry manager. 'We have a fleece and a bag of clothing.'

The manager interrupted, 'He doesn't need possessions.'

Patrick's spirit was crushed by this offhand decision. Cormac's written scroll – lost forever – the bag, the fleece, and the waterproof cover too; his mantle. He'd been robbed of all his ties to Ireland.

The guard reappeared, shackled Patrick's ankles and unclamped the merchant's chains. Smiling, the man in charge handed over the shackles to the merchant.

'It's not too late. Take back your money and put me outside the gate.' Patrick called out. The guard smashed his fist in to Patrick's face. Patrick shook his head and turned to the trader, 'Merchant man,' said Patrick earnestly through bloodied lips, 'you will pay for this misdeed, as sure as the sun comes up tomorrow.'

The guard was ready to punch Patrick again but the quarry manager waved his hand.

'It's enough,' he said.

The merchant, however, had lost his smile. Indeed, his face was drained.

'Are you alright? You're shaking,' the quarry manager said.

Patrick answered for the merchant. 'He's taken a step too far and has just realised it. A herd of boar came to haunt him.'

The quarry manager shook his head in puzzlement as he escorted his shaking, ashen-faced friend to the door.

Patrick felt devastated. He'd been reduced to slavery, for the second time in his life, possessing only the clothes he stood in.

CHAPTER TWENTY-TWO

Two guards pushed Patrick roughly through a courtyard door into a sunny, open space and marched him for a mile in sweltering heat, across stony terrain, to a slate quarry. Chain gangs laboured at a rock face under the watchful eye of whip-cracking supervisors. Patrick felt sick at the sight of this rock-breaking prison. Worse than slavery, this was tyranny.

The guard checked Patrick into a hut where an old man fitted a clasp to his ankle.

'Carry this,' said the old man, and, with two hands, passed over the coil of chain leading from his ankle clasp. Patrick's guards turned and left.

As he carried his chains he thought, why is this happening to me? I'm a Roman citizen on Roman soil.

'Follow me,' a supervisor said and led him to the foot of the rock face. 'Watch how these men break the rock.'

Patrick looked on. The men swung a mallet made of granite, strapped to a long, tough, wooden shaft. Most men used brute force.

'I want a flat face like this, and thickness like this,' his supervisor said, pointing to a specimen broken down by one of the gangs. 'Twenty-five pieces a day buys you a hot meal. Thirty gets you a large mug of ale as well. Come this way.'

Hard labour, whilst chained, earns you a meal; this is barbarism.

He led Patrick to the end of the gang where the old man was waiting; implement in hand.

'Put down the coil,' the old man instructed.

Patrick dropped the chain to the ground, noisily.

The old man knelt and linked Patrick's chain to the last man's ankle clamp, then took from his cart a huge mallet, which he stood on the ground; and a small one, plus a couple of iron wedges, he handed to Patrick.

The line supervisor spoke to Patrick a second time, 'Today your target is one piece, for which you will receive hot food and ale. Any more pieces today will count towards your target tomorrow. Learn fast and make good use of this advantage.' He turned and went to the head of the line.

Patrick observed the workers high up the rock face. When their efforts succeeded and boulders tumbled, the lives of the workers below were in danger. Stepping forward to the nearest boulder, Patrick searched his rock specimen for flaws to break open, but found none. Perhaps the use of brute force was best. Keeping an eye on the rock-breakers above should boulders fall, he raised the mallet then let it crash down, guiding the breaker to its target. In two hours, he'd made his first piece, but his strong hands became blistered, unused to the repetitive swinging of a heavy handle.

His thoughts turned to God. Why am I here? Every swing of the mallet chipped away at his faith. He'd been happy in Ireland once he'd adapted and reconciled. He hadn't wanted to leave. God inspired me to leave, and look at me now.

Seeing the workers wearing identical kirtles suggested to Patrick that he might be parted from his tunic. It was time to hide his brooch somewhere safer.

By sundown Patrick had made six pieces, and as the light faded the gang's labour was called to an end. They walked a mile to a row of hostels behind the main building. In a secured place their chains were removed. Here, Patrick was given a numbered wooden disc and directed to his accommodation.

Patrick's hostel consisted of a large room with a table and six chairs placed centrally. Along a wall was a bench with a water tub and towels for washing. Further along, two guards were dishing out food in exchange for a numbered disc. Along with the other men, Patrick washed and collected a bowl of broth, generously filled with meat pieces and root vegetables. A sign maybe that the owners were interested in output more than punishment. Patrick put down his bowl and took his seat. A mean looking man, the size of a mountain, was sitting opposite. He slid Patrick's broth to his own side of the table.

Patrick tapped the back of the man's hand, gently, and said, 'Excuse me, that's my meal. Slide it back please.'

Man-mountain looked at him and laughed, then ignored his request.

Patrick spoke again, 'If you want my meal, ask me and I'll give it to you.'

Man-mountain hesitated then smirked, 'I've already got it.'

The rest of the men were silent, watching every move.

'Ask!' Patrick asserted, preparing to take the fight to the bully.

Man-mountain made as if to slide the meal back, then suddenly threw the bowl and contents over Patrick. The guards moved quickly and pulled the bully out of his seat backwards.

'It's the bucket shift for you, big man,' a guard said as they removed him, kicking and writhing, from the room.

At the table, an orderly came to Patrick and passed him a cloth, which he used to clean himself up.

'That one is yours,' he said to Patrick, pointing to the broth in front of the empty seat.

Eating resumed as the atmosphere relaxed.

'He eats two bowls every night,' explained the man to Patrick's right. 'Then everyone else gives a portion of their broth to the one he robbed. You are the first person to challenge him.'

'Yes, and he'll make you pay,' said another.

'More turbulence tomorrow then,' Patrick said.

'No, you'll have five or six days before you see him again. They mix us up every night. We take turns at getting farters and fighters.'

'Or a crier or a boyfriend,' another one interjected.

'You get two in one with the big man,' someone else chipped in.

And so, the banter flowed as they supped their ale. Two men rose from the table. Patrick watched their movements as they went through separate doors. The two remaining workers lingered over their ale and one pointed out to Patrick:

'That's the bedroom, and that there is the bucket room. Big man will be the bucket cleaner for eight hostels tonight.'

Just then an orderly came to Patrick. 'Here is a blanket and a tunic; every Friday a clean one will be placed on your bed. You change after meal time and put the dirties in a basket over there.' He pointed.

When he'd gone one of the men said, 'He's decent, that orderly. They usually issue tunics in the mornings. He's saved you from sleeping on soup.'

Patrick managed a rueful smile. 'I jumped in too quickly,' he said.

'You weren't to know. I'm glad you challenged him, but you'll need more than words next time.'

'Sup up,' said the other one. 'It'll soon be locking up time.'

Patrick entered the dormitory. It was a prison cell with three bunks on the right and three on the left. A four-inch-high horizontal slit, where the outside wall met the ceiling, served as a window and a ventilator. The bed frames were wooden structures, and the pallets had no padding. There were two empty spaces for Patrick to choose from.

'Which bed would Man-mountain use?' Patrick asked to anyone who would answer.

'The bottom one,' a voice replied.

Patrick chose the other and said, 'I stepped on his toes already so I'll not sleep in his bed.' He paid a quick visit to the bucket room. A batten on the floor divided the room; two buckets for peeing on the left and two for solids on the right. Patrick turned left and wasted no time as one of the buckets on the right was in use. Patrick thought of the basic fresh-air toilets of the Irish hills with heightened appreciation.

Back at his bunk he changed tunics and transferred his brooch, grateful he'd managed to hold on to this one small possession.

His prayers were shorter, sincere, but tinged with sadness and a sore heart. Faith, self-defence, turning the other cheek, all swirled around in his thoughts, like fog, choking off the sunshine. He prayed for strength and guidance and for the first time in years fell asleep with a confused mind.

At dawn the door bolt opened noisily and the banging of dishes and pans followed. The workers were given a large bowl of porridge and a chunk of cheese. Patrick saw the men pocketing the cheese.

One saw him watching and said, 'It's a long day if you eat all, now. Better to save the cheese till midday.' Patrick nodded and took the advice.

At the rock face the men were chained in the same positions. Patrick's neighbour, a strong, fit man, took the time to give him some tips to help his speed. Patrick produced twenty pieces, and with five from the previous day he'd earned a hot meal. Over the next few days Patrick worked his way into the routine of the hard labour, earning hot food and ale on most days.

One blistering, hot day at the end of Patrick's second week, he noticed his neighbour was struggling with the work.

'Are you alright?'

'I'm not. I'm in a fever, my strength is sapped.'

'What's your count so far?'

'Twenty-three,' his neighbour replied.

The supervisor, suspecting they were slacking, was already on his way. Patrick pre-empted the situation.

'Master,' he called, 'I'd like to help this man.'

'In what way?'

'I'd like to make some slabs for him that he may rest.'

The supervisor came closer; he could see the man's baubled brow and trembling body.

'What's your tally?' he asked him.

'Twenty-three.'

'And yours?' he said to Patrick.

'Twenty-six.'

'You'll probably miss your ale,' he said to Patrick, 'but go ahead.' Looking at the feverish man he added, 'Rest against the cart if you wish.'

'Thank you, master.'

Patrick's neighbour slept deeply to the end of the shift. He woke to find twenty-five pieces in his cart. Patrick finished on thirty.

'How are you?' Patrick asked his neighbour as they traipsed back to their lodgings.

'Grateful to be having hot broth, I can tell you. I owe you a good turn.'

'It's nothing. You need plenty of liquid. Here; take my ale token.'

The man shook his head in refusal.

'You need it and I don't.' Patrick insisted, handing over his token. 'I'm Patrick, and you?'

'Thanks. I'm Saul, but we don't use names here.'

* * *

Having completed three weeks of labour, Patrick's date with the devil arrived when he was placed in the same hostel as the big man. Saul was one of the other four. The prisoners took their seats at the table; bowls of broth before them. Patrick sat opposite the big man, who seemed much larger this time.

He's so big he's frightening, Patrick said to himself. This time Man-mountain made no move for anyone's bowl. All ate in silence, sure there was trouble to come.

Finishing his broth, Man-mountain pointed his spoon at Patrick, saying, 'Pretty boy, I'll have you whenever I want you.'

Patrick wanted the confrontation here and now, one-on-one. He felt his neighbour's foot, under the table, pressing on his. He thought for a moment. Patrick wanted the initiative and couldn't see any alternative, but he'd misjudged his previous encounter and decided to ignore Man-mountain's comment. Man-mountain stood up, smiled sarcastically at Patrick and made for the bucket room. Two stooges from the table followed him.

Patrick's neighbour lingered till there was just the two of them.

'If it breaks tonight, fight furiously, hands and feet. I'll help you. We'll bring him down.'

Hands and feet? Patrick wondered.

Lock-up came and the room darkened. A small peek of night light bounced through the slit, painting the room grey. Everyone was in bed except Patrick, who was on his knees, on the floor, praying silently.

'Prayers won't help, pretty boy,' Man-mountain taunted.

'I'm praying for you,' Patrick retorted, though his heart was thumping.

The man in the bunk above him was already snoring so there could be little help from that quarter, and the waiting and wondering wasn't Patrick's way; it increased his nervous urge to act. But he avoided acting rashly and climbed into bed, knowing he wouldn't be able to sleep.

The expected came and still the speed caught Patrick by surprise. He was seized suddenly by two men; taken by his arms and legs, jerked out of bed and slammed face down onto the floor. Lashing out with his fists and kicking like a madman, he nevertheless found his right arm extended and lashed to the bed-frame opposite. His neighbour dropped from the top bunk onto Patrick's assailant, knocking him unconscious before the knot was tied. Patrick's kicking enabled him to get to his feet and face his opponent at the other end, but the man was quick and punched Patrick on the jaw. Patrick instinctively moved his head and dodged what would have been a telling follow-up punch. Stamping his heel on the man's bare instep, Patrick had him hopping, and he followed with a three-punch boxing combination knocking his adversary senseless.

Saul was swapping and dodging punches with Man-mountain and once again Patrick, with a mean adversary, was able to pick his spot. He delivered, for the second time in his life, a fast and hard kidney punch. His fist sunk into flesh that closed softly round his knuckled fist. To Patrick it didn't feel to land. He withdrew his fist and recovered his position but no return punch came. Man-mountain instead, went down on all fours, growling like an angry bear about to clear the room of nuisance.

But Patrick knew better. He felt guilty and prayed it was his last kidney punch. Man-mountain's pain intensified, he groaned deeply and rolled over onto his side, feeling his soft spot. Saul called the guards. They arrived in seconds, one holding a spear, the other a candle light. As the cell was illuminated, everyone saw that Man-mountain was entirely naked. He looked like a baby white elephant rolling around in dust.

The stooges were coming round and snorer, now wide awake, stared studiously at the wall. The guards searched everyone wearing clothing. Patrick, Saul and wall-starer had no possessions. Man-mountain's assistants both were found with tethers and bands in their pouches.

Four guards were present by now. Two escorted the stooges at spear point. The other two carried the big man out on a pole bed.

'Reaping as you sow, big man,' laughed one of the guards, before closing and bolting the cell door.

'What will happen to them?' Patrick asked his roommates.

'They'll go back to hard labour and bucket emptying,' said wall-starer who'd found his courage now the trouble had gone.

'And the big man?'

'He's in trouble. He's not fit enough for hard labour; they might sell him. Fool. He could have been a freeman in a few years.'

Patrick held out his hand to his chain gang neighbour, which he received willingly.

'Thanks.'

'You deserved it. But let's get some sleep.'

The three bade each other goodnight and returned to their beds. Patrick prayed silently. He thanked God for deliverance. He confessed his lack of courage to turn the other cheek to someone like Man-mountain. Did you want me to let it happen? Did you send my neighbour to help? By the end of his prayers Patrick asked, 'Lord, why have you led me from slavery to slavery?'

Sleep came to him, and in his dreams, Patrick was grumbling about his second term of slavery to a friend, who dismissed his moaning with the question.

'Are you not a Roman in a Roman land? Leave here in the sixth week.'

'How can I leave when I'm shackled and guarded?' Patrick responded to his friend.

Morning came and after break-fast Patrick and his neighbour were called by a guard.

'Your duties are changed. Come with me,' he led them to a different part of the quarry, with buildings and forecourts, workshops, and warehouses. Craftsmen were busy with hand tools, chiselling and dressing slate slabs. Joiners were making boxes and packages for finished products. He and Saul were chained to a stone pillar and set to work on opposite sides of the same bench.

As Patrick chiselled away at excrescences and shaped the slate pieces, his mind thought over last night's dream. Was it a reworking of his inner thoughts or a message from God? I've been here four weeks. How can I leave here in the sixth week? There's no time. How can I escape; I'm chained, supervised, the perimeter fence is twenty-five feet high, the ground up to it is wide open, and the gates are guarded with armed men?

At noon Patrick and his friend sat together to drink their water and eat cheese.

'The big man and his helpers worked here, so the trouble turned out well for us,' Saul said.

'In what way?' Patrick asked.

'This job is a stepping stone to freedom. We've got their jobs. They lost them as a punishment. We could become freemen, perhaps in two or three years.' As they were talking, higher up the hill a pony and cart and two women were leaving a store house. Their supervisor left the chained men and walked up to the departing visitors, chatted briefly, and put something in his pocket.

'What's happening there?' Patrick nodded towards the pony and cart.

'I believe they deliver vegetables,' Saul answered.

'And a bit more,' Patrick observed.

'There's a rumour they supply mead,' Saul said.

Patrick was thinking of possibilities. 'That makes sense. How often do they deliver?' he asked.

'Every week. They never miss, nor does the guard.'

Patrick attempted to disguise his thoughts and picked up on the mead in his conversation.

'I used to drink mead, in better times,' he said.

'You weren't always a slave then?'

'I wasn't, but I didn't mean that. I drank mead as a slave once a year at Beltaine. My supervisor would share his portion with me.'

'I've noticed you're a lucky man.'

'I don't feel lucky, what do you mean?' Patrick asked.

'You came here and they put you on slabs. You missed two or three years on the rock face. Now you're on the tools after five weeks. It's taken me five years to get here.'

Patrick wondered if the stone-lifting interview had anything to do with it. 'I've no idea why,' he said.

'We could both be freemen in two or three years,' Saul added. 'With your luck you'll probably beat me to it.'

'Why would they free a person who makes money for them?' Patrick asked.

'They set up the brightest in business selling stone. The freed man owns the business himself and sells on the open market, but has a purchasing contract for supplies with the quarry. That's what I'm told.'

Patrick nodded and returned to his work, keen now to keep a mask on his true thoughts. He turned his face away from Saul and kept an eye on the cart as it progressed down a gentle, sloping bank, before the track U-turned on its way to a well-guarded gatehouse.

He started work on a wedge-shaped piece of granite, immediately after the visits of the supervisor on his circular tour of inspection, hiding his craft work under the table top by wedging it in a recess. He surreptitiously tested the wedge for size in a chain link as he worked it. After daily honing, his accessory was ready; a week early. Perfect. He had other things to study in the next six days, and the seventh day was execution day. He frowned at the pun in his own thoughts.

It was Friday and the delivery cart came again. As Patrick sat with Saul, he watched the cart and counted the seconds of its journey from the gate to the store house; the seconds to the reappearance of the cart. He timed the guard's walk up the hill to the cart, the time of the transaction and the chat and his return to the line. He timed the cart's downhill journey to the U-bend and the prison gate. He observed the shadows cast by the guard, the cart, the store building, and the workshop.

Saturday was day one of his last seven. He rehearsed his thoughts and timings. His plan was simple, everything was in place. He was confident, provided nothing unexpected would occur, like a simple change of work place, which would dash everything. Patrick was ready too soon. There was only so much checking and rechecking he could do. The days felt longer and his apprehension grew.

It was night five and Patrick's prayers were repentant. He was aware of his miserable lack of faith. Every time he doubted God he resolved not to doubt again. Then events occurred and the doubts returned. Patrick, once again, saw that God was with him. Saul had saved him from brutalisation. The issue with Man-mountain was necessary for Patrick to be transferred to a job on the tools. These same tools would help him to loosen his shackles. The new location was close to the gates and Patrick could now see how to beat the guards.

Day six and Patrick was confident his plan would work; it was simple and quick. He visualised once again the outlook from the line-guard's perspective, when he was purchasing his mead from the ladies on the cart. Patrick calculated that his shepherd's running pace down a ravine would work here in the quarry landscape.

However, Patrick wasn't sure how to stay free, even though he was a legitimate citizen. Moving from no job and no money to having a job and an income wasn't going to be easy in a foreign land where he knew no one. It was too easy to fall foul of the scurrilous. Another chance to show faith, perhaps, but even now Patrick couldn't understand why he had to be enslaved in the quarry in the first place. *My faith, solid as a rock in Ireland, shakes like a trembling hand.*

He checked his timings, went through the sight lines, hoped for a dry day tomorrow. He thought of the instruction in his dream, "leave here in the sixth week". His mind had been blank at that time. He couldn't see any hope of escape, yet it all changed by the following noon.

Day seven – execution day – was dry and sunny. Soon he would sit with Saul and eat his cheese, for the last time. The pony and cart clip-clopped its way up the circuitous track and Patrick's stomach muscles tightened. He took a deep breath. Calmness, timing, and confidence would do the trick, he told himself, and took his signal to collect a slab from the slate cart.

Out of the line-guard's sight he pressed a carefully honed slate wedge into the weakest eye of his clamp chain. Lifting a slab, like an upright paving stone, he guided and dropped the full weight onto the small wedge. The iron eye splayed open and burst. Patrick's chain was freed. But the stone slab bounced off its target, gashing Patrick's leg above the ankle. Denying his pain, he calmly leant the slab against the cart then bent over and hooked up the open link loosely. The pain in his ankle was registering and as he took a deep breath, he saw that blood was already pouring from the gash. Patrick couldn't afford to leave a trail, and time was not plentiful. Quickly ripping out the lining of his tunic pouch, he tied it tightly round his ankle like a bandage. Returning to his work place he sat nonchalantly with his back to the workshop wall and began to eat his lunch. Saul joined him, quietly as usual. Patrick watched the line guard making his way to the top for his brief meeting with the women. Their pony and cart appeared from the stock yard.

'I'm just going for a pee,' Patrick said to Saul.

'I'll bet you are, Patrick. Good luck to you.'

He used my name. He's saying goodbye.

Patrick smiled, 'The same to you, Saul.'

Behind the gable Patrick unhooked his chain, and with the speed and agility of a leopard, ran down the dry, uneven bank in a diagonal line, heading for the U-bend in the cart track. He was in the cover of the craft workshop provided he made it to the bottom before the pony and cart set off. Two hundred strides later, Patrick was behind the bushes watching the line guard pay for his mead.

The bonneted women were on their way. With head down, he let the pony and cart pass him. The cart swivelled round the U-bend, almost stationary but rocking left to right; grinding the grit noisily under the wheels, turning the women's backs to Patrick. He leapt on the cart and crawled under the folded tarpaulin, in the twitch of a ram's tail. A minute later the wheels stopped. Patrick risked a quick peep and saw a guard leave the gatehouse, striding towards the cart. Just then Patrick saw a pool of blood from his ankle wound, trickling under the cover onto the open cart. He stopped the flow with the side and palm of his hand and edged the canvas over the spill. Had the guard seen anything? Patrick held his breath and hoped. Through a tiny hole in the cover, Patrick saw the guard look over the empty cart. He said goodbye to the women and called the armed guards to open the gate. The cart passed through without stopping and Patrick heard the welcome creaking of the gate hinges as they closed. He was further relieved when the pony reached trotting speed.

Patrick wanted to be far from the prison gate before he jumped off the cart.

CHAPTER TWENTY-THREE
AD 405 – Cassian School, Gaul

'You can show your face now,' a woman's voice called. She pulled back the cover.

Patrick, bewildered, thought of running off, but hesitated. She knew I was on the cart yet didn't report me to the prison guards.

'You do want to escape, don't you?' the woman asked.

Patrick saw two well-dressed women, one holding rein, the other doing the talking. Before he'd worked out how to react, he was asked, 'What are your plans now?'

'I don't have a plan,' he answered.

'Then we'll help you. Get back under the cover. We'll be at the lodge in five minutes.'

Patrick covered himself but left a large tuck, out of which he could see some of his surroundings. Trees with generous, even spacing between them, lined the track. They were heading downhill towards rich farmlands. The stone-paved track looked public and was well maintained. The trees and verges were cultured as though they were in a wealthy municipality. Patrick was reminded that he hadn't seen a public road for six years, and he'd almost forgotten the word municipality.

But who are these women? Is their offer of help genuine? Why would they help me?

The five minutes passed and they stopped. The talking woman opened some gates and closed them after the cart had entered.

'You can sit up now.'

Patrick took in his surroundings entirely. They clip-clopped along on the path of a country residence set among well-tended gardens and arrived at a grand entrance to the reception door of the house; a groom placed wooden steps to assist the ladies as they alighted. Patrick jumped off the cart at the far side and stood a distance from the women, feeling self-conscious in his prison clothes. The groom, he noticed, eyed him from top to bottom, lingering a second when he saw the ankle clamp.

'Please clean the cart and the cover,' said the talking woman to the overweight groom, as he wiped perspiration from his forehead, on the back of his hand.

'Follow me,' she said to Patrick and led him into a vestibule.

'Mary, please bring the skeletons to the library, and something to dress that wound,' she said, pointing at Patrick's bandage.

As Mary took off down the corridor, Talking-woman opened a door into a private library. 'Take a seat,' she said directing Patrick to a long chair, of the style in his parents' home. 'I'm Angelina, and your name?'

'Patricius,' Patrick felt strange calling himself Patricius, but it was his Roman name and eventually he'd make it back to his parents and would use the name they gave him.

'Well, that's not a slave name.'

'You're right, but it's a long story.'

Mary arrived with a tray carrying a jug and bowl, cloths and a hoop of skeleton keys. Angelina quickly tried the keys on Patrick's ankle-clasp opening it successfully with the third key.

'Mary, please put away the keys and hide the clasp then return quickly.'

Angelina removed the temporary bandage, bathed the gash and applied a clean bandage, by which time Mary had returned.

'Let me introduce you: Mary, meet Patricius,' Angelina said hurriedly.

Patrick nodded, 'Pleased to meet you, Mary.'

Mary took up the tray, jug and bowl, plus the used and clean bandages and headed for the door.

'I'm taking Patricius to the private room.' Angelina said to Mary. 'If visitors arrive, I'll be in the chapel. Follow me, Patricius.'

Angelina took him through a studded door into a small dark room. Proceeding quickly down the aisle and behind the altar, she opened a hidden entrance disguised as wall panelling.

'I'm afraid it's prison once more, Patricius, but you escaped at the same time as we left the grounds of the quarry, so of course they will visit us. I'll be back. Don't be tempted to light the candles. Darkness will serve you better.' She closed the door and he heard a bolt locating in a slot.

'Faith, Patrick, faith,' he said in a low voice and tried the comfort of the accommodation. Stretched out full-length on the chair, he rested and closed his eyes. 'Is this a lucky break, or another sinister turn of the wheel?' He gave faith a try and, with the help of darkness, fell asleep.

A light shaking on his shoulder woke him up. The door was open and Angelina was speaking in a gentle voice.

'The guards have been and gone. They checked the cart and cover and found nothing suspicious.' She called Patrick into the chapel and carefully closed the secret door. 'Follow me,' she said, and led Patrick into a dressing room where he saw a washing stand equipped with cloths and towels, a washing bowl and a jug giving off the shimmering vapours of hot water. 'Everything is here for you to wash. Do please change out of your quarry tunic; there are clean clothes and sandals on the chair. When you are ready, come to the library and we'll talk.'

This was a dream to Patrick. In the space of ten minutes, he'd left a world of imprisoned slavery and now was surrounded by the comforts of home. Patrick cloth-washed thoroughly and last of all washed his shoulder-length, wavy hair. He thought about his brief experience of Roman slavery. Till now he'd considered slavery was decent. His own slaves, his father's slaves, weren't chained and imprisoned. He was shocked to have seen, and experienced, brutal slavery in Gaul; he thought of his own attitude towards slaves at Banna Venta and how he bullied the girl in the barn. The reflection made him realise how far he'd come from his earlier way of thinking. Yet Ireland was considered barbaric, uncivilised, simply because it was a land outside of the Roman ecumene. Patrick hadn't seen the Irish chain their slaves.

He dried himself down and enjoyed donning the linen loin cloth and woollen tunic. He loved his boots but they were ragged. Changing into new sandals was a treat. Transferring the brooch once more, Patrick clipped the jewel to the lining of his tunic, out of sight.

He found the library and wondered what would happen next as he knocked on the partly open door.

'Come in,' Angelina called.

He entered, hesitantly.

'Ah, Patricius, how do you feel?' Angelina asked.

'Clean. Very clean,' Patrick replied.

'How is your ankle?'

'Comfortable. Thank you for your kindness.'

She shrugged off the thanks with a wave of her hand. 'Would you like a drink, Patricius? We can offer you honey mead, summer fruits, or ale.'

The room and the drinks on offer could have been home in Banna Venta.

'Summer fruits would be welcome.'

Mary poured him a generous filling in a porcelain mug. Placing the drink carefully on a low table in front of a formal chair, Mary gestured Patrick to take a seat. He sat, stiffly on the edge and briefly remembered his discomfort at his last business meeting with his father. Angelina brought him to the present.

'Patricius, we'd like to know who you are and how you came to be working at the slate quarry.'

'My name is Patricius Succat from Banna Venta in Britannia Prima. My father is Calpurnius, a decurion and a deacon. My mother's name is Conchessa.'

'Thank you, Patricius. And where is Banna Venta?'

'It's in north-west Britain near Luguvalium.'

'Please continue,' Angelina prompted.

'I was captured by slave raiders, shortly before my sixteenth birthday. Along with many hundreds more, I was taken across the sea to a foreign land called Ireland, and sold at a slave market. A king from the west of Ireland bought me, and employed me as a hill shepherd. After six years I found a way to escape, and gained passage on a merchant boat travelling to Gaul. The merchant promised to take me to Condate, he said it was a main route to the north, but one night he and his assistant attacked me while I was sleeping. They bound my hands and feet and sold me to the quarry. In truth, I don't know exactly where I am.'

'You're in Gaul. You're near Condate, but you are not on a main route to anywhere,' Angelina confirmed.

'Why did you accept a boat travelling to Gaul?' Mary asked.

'It is an offence in Ireland for a captain to give passage to a runaway slave. It is an offence for the slave to ask. To run from Ireland onto any Roman soil was good enough for me. I was confident as a Roman citizen that I could work my way through Gaul or any Roman country to Britain. With God as my guide, I felt safe.'

'You are safe now. Let me tell you who we are. Mary and I are sisters. We are sisters in Christ but also real sisters. Our surname is Cassian. Our brother, John is a Roman Catholic monk and the founder of two abbeys in the Massala region. One of these abbeys, St. Sauver in Place De Lenche, is for women. Mary and I run a preparation school to supply novitiates for a monastery that is based there. We teach in this house and, as our pupils live here during their course, upstairs is a dormitory. We have farming land here, and grow crops and vegetables for our own use and for monasteries without the ability to grow their own. We run the farm as a business to generate income. We supply to local customers; the quarries are an example. So that is who we are,' Angelina concluded.

Mary added, 'It isn't our intention to provide an escape route for dissatisfied quarry slaves.'

356

'I can see that, but you knew I was on the cart before we passed through the gate, and you did not tell the guards. I am happy that you didn't, but you must have a reason.'

'We have a reason.' Angelina stared. 'But first, you said you don't have a plan. If we can help you, what sort of help would you like from us?'

'Let me express my thanks that you didn't hand me back to the quarry. But I'm very glad you didn't. Do you think you could help me to contact any Roman administrators who deal with Britain? I believe Turonum is an important Roman centre?' Patrick asked.

'Do you know Rome has withdrawn from the Britains?' Angelina asked.

'I heard it from the merchant,' Patrick said, shaking his head.

'The Roman administration may not be your best option. I think the brothers in the monasteries would be a better help to you. This course would take time, but your chances of success would be high.' Angelina paused and searched Patrick's face as he concentrated. 'Would you like me to put out some enquiries?'

'I would, but what do I do in the meantime?'

'What a perfect question. We are short of labour on the farm and there are no spare workers round these parts. When we knew you had hidden on the cart, Mary and I looked at each other. If we took you through the gates, at worst you would run away. At best you might work for us. It only took a whisper.'

'You could work on the farm to earn your keep. We have spare accommodation for workers,' Mary added.

'Will I be safe here? So close to the quarry?'

'Of course; the quarry is a business and a customer. They are not the law or the administration.'

Patrick wasn't so sure and being close to the quarry worried him.

'You mentioned Roman administrative presence,' Angelina said. 'Turonum is a large Roman centre, three days south-east of here. It's the wrong direction for you. North-east of here is a large town called Autricum, situated on a great Roman road connecting to Parisium and Bononia This is your best route to Britain.'

'Thank you. I don't know the map of Gaul but my mother's cousin lived in Turonum.'

'Does your cousin still live in Turonum? Angelina asked.

'I'm afraid not. He was a prominent clergyman in the Catholic church when he died.'

Angelina and Mary looked at each other.

'Tell us more,' Mary prompted, filling all three drinks, as though she was settling into an interesting story.

'Mother never met him. Her aunt married a Roman tribune and moved to Pannonia with him. Their son pursued a military career. His mother wrote to our family at special times; when he joined the army, when he was baptised in his teenage years, and when he left the army.' Angelina stared, wide-eyed at Mary as though the teenage baptism meant something. 'He penned his own letter to Mother on his consecration as a bishop. That news was the source of great excitement and pride to my mother. It was also the last of the letters until someone wrote informing us of his death. I was twelve at the time.'

'Such a coincidence,' Angelina said. 'What was his Christian name?'

'Our family knew him as Martin.'

'Not alone a coincidence; it's a thrill,' Mary added.

'May the Lord save us, Patricius; you're a random prisoner from the quarry, who climbed on our cart to escape. Yet it turns out you're a relative of Martin of Tours,' Angelina marvelled.

'Tours. The last letter said Tours. All the others referred to Turonum,' Patrick remarked.

'Some like to use the traditional name, others the Roman name. The place is the same,' Angelina said.

Mary picked up the conversation, 'Patricius; let me explain our excitement. Martin and our brother John Cassian were friends. Martin gave much encouragement to John when the two Abbeys were in their project stage.'

What an amazing coincidence, Patrick thought as Angelina asked, 'What is your relationship to the church, Patricius?'

Patrick hesitated. 'I sadly did not take the message of the bishops seriously in my youth. My fall from a position of great privilege to slavery broke my spirit. Through fear of the Lord: prayer for forgiveness, through praise of the Lord, through the purging of my soul, and through relinquishing the desire for material wealth, I have truly found God. He lives in my heart. But I don't have any relationship with a church.'

'How interesting; I don't want to leave this conversation but unfortunately, Patricius, Mary and I have some preparations to discuss. Can we leave you for a short while?'

'I'm quite familiar with solitude, but if you don't mind me using your chapel, I could spend some time in prayer.'

'That would be perfect. I'll take you there.'

Angelina led Patrick down the hall; turning a black, ring-handle on the dark-oak door, she opened it, and led him into the chapel. The light of a single candle illuminated the room dimly. On the right-hand wall hung a sketch in coloured inks on vellum, depicting a mounted Roman soldier handing half of his bright red stola to an almost naked beggar. Angelina pointed out this picture to Patrick.

'That is Martin, serving in the Roman cavalry, being charitable to a beggar. Such action did not sit well with his position, but that is a conversation for later. We'll meet you in the library in fifteen minutes.'

'Thank you, ma'am.'

'Call me Angelina.'

'Thank you, Angelina,' he answered.

She smiled, then turned and left the chapel.

Patrick studied the picture of Martin. He was a young man in cavalry uniform, riding a white horse. Patrick couldn't resist comparing their lives. Eighty years later, he, Patrick, Martin's second cousin in Britain, was riding a black horse, supervising grain farms in Banna Venta.

Patrick turned to two short rows of kneeler-stands, each with a tilted shelf for elbows or scriptures. He knelt in contemplation then prayed aloud in soft tones: 'Lord, you delivered me from Ireland, for that I thank you.

Enslaved at the quarry, my faith in you failed, please forgive me.

You showed me, in dream, how to strengthen my faith during adversity; tested, I spilled your message in minutes.

Escape in the sixth week, you said. Forgive my unbelief.

Lord, let my faith be as strong as I think it is, but it never is.

I offer this prayer through Jesus Christ.'

Patrick knelt in contemplation for a while. He finished and quietly made his way to the library, where Angelina and Mary were chatting leisurely.

'How was the chapel, Patricius?' Angelina asked.

'Spiritual. I'm used to finding God anywhere. I've prayed outside in all weathers, but the chapel adds something, especially to the giving of glory.'

'I'm pleased. Now, Patricius let us explain our thoughts on helping you back to Britain. Our brother is patron of several small monasteries throughout Gaul. Autricum and Parisorium are major towns, both with Cassian monasteries. These locations are on the main road to Bononia in Belgica. From there you can cross easily into Dubrae.'

The mention of Dubrae raised Patrick's hopes as the name often entered conversation in his family's household.

'Please God that day will come,' Patrick said.

'It's coming. Fortune is favouring you, Patricius. This house will be lively on Sunday and Monday with pupils arriving for our new semestris. A group will arrive from Autricum, which means we can send a message to our brothers in Autricum with the returning driver. We can expect an answer to our request for hospitality, when an Autricum monk visits us next month,' Angelina explained.

'Your help is much appreciated. Thank you.'

'You're welcome. If he brings news that the abbot can accommodate you then you can travel to Autricum with the monk on his return journey, which means you will only have to pay the cost of your lodgings on the way, and your employment on the farm will cover that.'

'Thank you, Angelina. I can't believe my luck. How can I receive such help from people who don't know me?'

'Patricius, I showed you the picture of St. Martin of Tours giving of his Roman army clothing to a beggar. Martin and my brother, John Cassian, set the guiding principles of the monasteries I have mentioned. They will help a person in need. It is part of their credo.'

Patrick was taken aback. Angelina paused then continued. 'Mary and I have discussed your accommodation. We invite you to stay in the house in a ground floor bedroom at the back. You are also welcome to eat with Mary and myself for breakfast at 7am and dinner at 7pm. We dine privately, keeping the refectory for pupils and teachers.'

'Thank you for your generosity. I feel like I am an imposition on you. It would be no inconvenience if I were to dine alone in my room,' Patrick offered.

'Lord save us! A relative of Martin does not dine alone under our roof. You may use the wash room as before, and we ask you to wash your hands and feet prior to dining. Come, Patricius, I'll introduce you to Domitius. Perhaps when you are working you will feel less of a burden.'

Patrick couldn't count his fortune. A successful escape from the quarry; two ladies prepared to help him and give him employment. They knew my second cousin, Martin of Tours, whom I never met myself, and the connection is opening doors.

Angelina led the way.

'I'll prepare your room while you're out,' Mary said, flitting down the corridor, as Angelina led the way to the outside explaining things to Patrick on the way.

'Domitius was the groom you saw when we arrived from the quarry. He's our farm manager and will be your supervisor while you are working here.'

Outside the day was dry and sunny. As Angelina descended the front steps of the house Patrick observed her clothing. Her dark blue stola was like the type his mother would wear, except for the long sleeves. A simple dark blue rope, knotted at the hip, gathered her otherwise shapeless clothing at her waist. She wore black socks and black leather shoes, clearly visible below her ankle-length dress. She's put a bit of thought into looking plain, but hasn't quite succeeded. Patrick thought of Bride and how good she looked in plain clothing. Angelina walked with elegant deportment; a feature undiminished by her austerity.

Patrick saw workers in the fields, filling hand carts with the fruits of their harvesting. The track led to a collection of farm buildings. The farmhouse itself was stone built with a stucco wall finish that needed repair and painting. The roof, clad with terracotta tiles, was green with moss and lichen as a result of its proximity to the surrounding trees. Located opposite the farmhouse stood a wooden barn, next to stables and a workshop. The cart, which had carried Patrick to freedom, was standing in an open-fronted store.

A hugely-built, bald man over six feet tall appeared at the workshop door. He walked towards them, feet wide apart, dressed in sloppy trousers and a tunic. His face, unsmiling and carrying no plumpness, told a lie about the rest of his body, which looked firm and fat; he carried a formidable air.

'Domitius meet Patricius.' The men nodded to each other. 'Patricius is staying with us for some time and will lodge at the house. I'd like you to give him useful work for that period. Perhaps you can catch up on the fence? It's an overdue project.'

Domitius raised an eyebrow.

'Staying at the house, ma'am?' he asked.

'Yes. He's a friend and we have much to discuss.'

'I see, ma'am,' he answered, giving a reverential nod to Patrick.

'Domitius, how did you clean the cart so convincingly? When the quarry guards came, they were looking for blood,' Angelina enquired.

'Come this way,' he said, smiling with satisfaction. 'The cart was easy. I cleaned it dry. The blood came off with the caked-on mud. There was blood aplenty on the cover though.' Walking past the cover, neatly folded on the cart, he opened a large cupboard door, revealing the bloodstained canvass. 'These things don't dry quickly. When I saw the quarrymen coming, I swapped them.'

'Good work, Domitius. Now, I'd like you to show Patricius the work you have for him. Let him return to the house in time for dinner at 7pm.'

'Yes, ma'am.'

'We'll see you later,' Angelina said to Patricius, then turned and walked back to the house.

Domitius looked at Patrick. 'Staying at the house, eh? It never 'appened that one of my workers stayed at the house.'

Patrick felt embarrassed to be receiving favour of this kind while labouring manually.

Domitius started again, 'What work 'ave you done?'

'I've been a shepherd and a farmer,' Patrick answered.

'Come this way.' He led Patrick to the back of the workshop and pointed.

Patrick saw wooden planks and circular posts, stacked high against the wall, for the full length of the store and workshop.

'You want me to build a fence?' he stated.

Domitius nodded. 'Round the whole perimeter. Come with me. We'll walk the job.'

Patrick passed workers harvesting vegetables, some fields lay fallow and others were being planted. He witnessed a thriving farming business. Angelina and Mary were running an enterprise much larger than required to feed a school and a few monasteries.

On the way, Domitius rapped out instructions to workers and occasionally questioned the supervisors in the fields. Patrick saw fear in their eyes. These workers jumped to Domitius's tune. He'll expect me to do the same. The perimeter was partly fenced; there was evidence of dilapidated, and in places rotted, fencing. Other parts were completely open to neighbouring lands separated by large ditches. Behind the school and near to the track, Patrick saw the ground was stony, perhaps explaining the presence of hedgerows.

Arriving at the farmhouse having completed the circuit, Domitius asked, 'Reckon you can do it in six weeks?' He spoke in a challenging manner.

'Not alone. It's a two-man job,' Patrick said, not sure how Domitius would respond.

'There'll two of you,' he fired back.

'I need to pickaxe the stony ground, to see if the posts will set. What do you want me to do with the old fencing,' Patrick asked?'

'Gather the rubbish into the fallow field. We'll burn it. Can you do it in six weeks?' Domitius asked impatiently.

'Give me two days and I'll tell you.'

'Oh, yes? And in two days I'll tell your lady friend if I want you. Best you get off to the house. I believe you have your hands and feet to wash.' He chuckled sarcastically. 'Report to me, nice and clean after your break-fast tomorrow.'

Patrick returned to the house in no doubt that Domitius did not like workers to be foisted upon him. He summarised the situation: I can build the fence. He'll put up with me and I'll put up with him. I wonder what is important about six weeks.

With clean hands and feet, Patricius entered the library. The women were already waiting.

'Good timing, Patricius. Are you ready for dinner?' Angelina enquired.

'I am; my hands and feet are washed,' Patrick answered.

'I meant are you hungry?' she laughed.

'I could eat a horse.'

'Well, you'll have to be satisfied with a portion of chicken and some roots. The food is ready, shall we repair?'

They crossed the corridor to a spacious but sparsely furnished dining room. The walls, panelled in light oak, stood out from the darkly-stained floor planks. A table and four upright chairs proudly occupied the centre of the room. Three places were set with crockery and cutlery; dishes of cooked foods were placed centrally. The upright chairs made the room look strange to Patrick's eye. More like a school room for children. Angelina and Mary stood behind their chairs and gestured Patrick to his place. He saw, now that he was close up, that the chairs were designed for adults and wondered if the Roman traditions for long chairs and low dining tables had somehow not replaced the Celtic traditions in Gaul.

'Mary, please lead us in blessings.'

'We give thee thanks, Our Father, for the resurrection. And, as the bread on this table is made one, with contents from near and far, so may thy church be united from the ends of the earth. Amen.'

Mary finished and pulled out her chair to sit down. Angelina and Patrick voiced their 'Amens' and joined her. Patrick, delighted to be in the presence of like-minded company, prayed a message of thanks internally for the gift of his situation.

As they ate a bowl of hot wheat porridge with chicken pieces and a side plate of varied root vegetables, the sisters probed Patricius's background. These cheerful and charming women were hungry for anecdotes on the swirl of his family life in Britain. As they finished their meal, Mary poured three glasses of mead.

Angelina raised her glass and said, 'We offer this meal and drink to you, Our Lord, and pray your blessings on Patricius and his journey home.' Mary joined Angelina and drank to the blessing. Patrick raised his glass, tipped it to his hosts and bowed his head in thanks; conversation resumed.

'How did you get on with Domitius today?' Angelina asked.

'He wants me to build a perimeter fence.'

'Oh, jolly good, we might get our fence, before all the wood is stolen,' Mary interjected.

'Is theft a problem?' Patrick asked.

'Not in general,' Angelina answered, 'but since we took delivery of the fence materials, we've experienced pilfering. They have been sitting there too long because Domitius has been slow to get the fence built.'

Patrick was surprised to hear the sisters speak so openly in front of him. He thought, perhaps, they were treating him as family, or management, because of the connection to Martin. The fifteen-minute break, immediately after he'd told them of the connection with Martin, was probably to allow the sisters to discuss accommodating him at the school. If true, that was a welcome strike.

'I hope my work will be of help to you,' Patrick said.

'I'm sure it will. We only recently set Domitius a deadline of six weeks. Providing him with your labour unexpectedly will be a great help to him,' Angelina explained.

'Is there a reason for the six-week deadline?' Patrick asked.

'None whatsoever; it is an arbitrary number aimed only at getting the job done. While we are on the subject of work, we eat twice a day, Patricius, but if you would like to take a lunch with you, we'll happily provide you with cheese and dates,' Angelina offered.

'Thank you, Angelina. I'm used to living off meagre portions but I know it's easier to labour on a well-fed stomach. I will accept your offer with pleasure,' Patrick said. 'Angelina, may I ask a question on a different subject?'

'Of course,' she acknowledged.

'I'd like to ask what materials you have on the scriptures.'

'We have a Bible in the library, for reference and a diary for pupils to book a reading time. There are a few codices of the Pentateuch, numerous of the gospels, and a few psalms in scrolls too.'

Patrick whistled through his lips. 'What a wealth.'

'Yes, we're well equipped. The generosity of donors and our own purchases, provide well for us. You are welcome to use the library yourself. Much of the resource is in demand when school is on but not everything.'

Patrick retired to bed that evening unable to believe his luck. *God sent me home this way, and I moaned when the merchant sold me to the quarry.*

* * *

At the end of the second day Domitius came to Patrick when all the workers had gone.

'How long then?' he asked.

'Two of us will need all of six weeks,' Patrick answered. 'But we only have material for four weeks of work.'

'I'll get the supplies; you get the job done. Six weeks it is.'

'I have a suggestion,' Patrick paused, looking for a nod. He received an angry glare instead, but continued because his suggestion made sense. Give me an extra man for half a day each day and we'll finish in three weeks. The saving is big.'

'And so is your nose. Keep it out of my business.'

'Yes, master,' Patrick replied. He backed off and made his way to the house.

Mid-morning the next day as Patrick was standing on the cart, hammering down a post; he saw a swift movement in the field beyond the stables. Two heads were bobbing in and out of sight. Patrick looked around for Domitius but he wasn't to be seen.

'Dig the next hole,' Patrick said to his helper as he grabbed a long stick and ran to the ridge.

There he saw two men running off with fence posts. Keeping out of sight in a shallow gulley, Patrick ran to catch up with the men who were carrying two posts each, on their shoulders. Once level, he ran at them. They saw him, dropped the posts, and fled.

The second man called to his friend in a Celtic brogue, 'This shouldn't happen.'

'Shut your mouth, idiot. He don't know that.' They cleared off. Patrick gathered the post, tied them in a line with twine and dragged them to his work place.

'Easy pickings at this place,' Patrick's helper laughed.

By day's end Patrick had realised a few things. He decided not to mention the occurrence to Domitius. His instinct was that Domitius would know of it, and Patrick's silence would draw him out.

The day's work finished and as Patrick was putting away the tools, Domitius was waiting for him.

'How many panels today?' Domitius asked but, not waiting for an answer, he punched Patrick in the gut. Patrick doubled over, feeling like he'd been kicked by a carthorse. A second hit landed near his side. Patrick used his elbows to protect himself from a kidney punch and defiantly stayed on his feet. After many more body blows Domitius backed off, smiling in satisfaction. There wasn't a bruise on Patrick's face, arms, or legs; all the evidence was on his torso. Patrick too was satisfied. He'd defended himself, but not struck back.

'Why did I give you a smack, young man?' Domitius taunted.

'I don't know,' Patrick answered.

'You didn't keep your nose clean.'

Domitius was looking mean, and Patrick understood what this was about.

'I still don't understand,' he feigned.

'I saw you leave your work to run in someone else's field.'

'Oh, that. It was just a couple of petty thieves trying to make-off with some fence posts. I chased them away.'

Domitius walked up to Patrick and child-slapped his face with the palm of his hand. 'I don't like your attitude.'

'And I don't like yours. If you are wise, master, you will stop the beating and let the fence be built. I want six weeks of work; payday, then I'll walk out of your life.'

Domitius laughed. 'Away with you, you don't know what a beating is. Go to your ladies.'

'I have your measure better than you have mine. You should think about my words.' Patrick turned away from Domitius and made his way to the house.

* * *

Sleep came slowly to Patrick that night. His dreams were lively as he relived the beating inflicted upon him by two sheep thieves in the hills of Voclut; the dream swirled into different places until the punches came from men in the fields.

'This shouldn't happen,' he said, kicking Patrick to the ground.

'He don't know,' the other one said, kicking Patrick's ribs. Patrick tried to separate the stories in his mind but they chased each other and he woke up. Patrick's ribs ached and pulsed and he remembered the last words of his dream.

'This shouldn't happen He don't know.'

Patrick lay awake, thinking over the events. The pilferers spoke in Gaelic, perhaps hoping I wouldn't understand. Patrick had found that people of high and low birth spoke Latin, in Gaul. The pilferers didn't expect to be challenged, which suggested they felt safe. Could there be a good reason? My intervention should not have provoked a wounded response from the simple thief.

As Patrick's mind churned, he heard a snort. It came again and this time he recognised the snort of a horse; one in distress or alarmed. Patrick listened carefully but heard no more. He dressed, left his room, and opened the back door. Maybe the pony was disturbed about something. Then he heard the snort again, clearly coming from the farmstead.

Patrick locked the back door, hid the key behind a bush and made his way to the stables. As he passed the farmhouse, he wondered where Domitius would be; sleeping perhaps? Or tending to the pony? Hearing low voices, Patrick crept to the stables and took a peep behind the storage building. There was Domitius supervising the loading of fence supplies. A man was carrying posts, two at a time, to a four-wheeled cart drawn by a horse. The driver was on the back of the cart, receiving and stacking the goods. Patrick watched. The man carrying the goods was out of Domitius's view for most of his trip to the cart, as the track veered behind dense bushes. He returned, collected and was out of sight again.

Having crept close to Domitius, who was leaning against a barrel, Patrick coughed. Domitius turned and met Patrick's palm, child-slapping him across his face. Domitius instinctively threw a punch, which Patrick dodged, and the big man hit the night air.

'Get my measure, if you can,' Patrick goaded, drawing Domitius round the corner.

Domitius punched again. He was fast for a man of his bulk but too slow to catch Patrick, who landed a thundering shot on the big man's belly. Domitius was unmoved. Patrick allowed himself to be backed into a corner to keep Domitius coming, until they were out of sight and earshot of the returning labourer. He then threw some quick punches to Domitius's face. Domitius raised his fists

369

in protection, exposing his breastbone briefly. Bang, bang. Two haymakers, delivered with power and speed, dropped Domitius to the ground like a sack of roots. Patrick laid him out, just as Guigan had done with him and, using twine, from the ample supplies hanging on the store wall, he bound his master to the wooden supports and removed a small knife from Domitius's belt. Patrick's instinct to catch the thieves was as active as it was when he was a shepherd. Taking a bundle of twine, Patrick made a wide detour, approaching the cart from behind; watching as more posts were fetched.

'Fat bastard's vanished,' said the carrier.

'He might have gone for a piss. Don't be calling him just yet. He's an awkward breed,' said the driver. The carrier headed back to the store.

In an instant Patrick's hand was over the driver's mouth and nose, as he pulled him roughly from the cart to the ground. Holding his man facedown, on the point of suffocation, Patrick whispered to him, 'Silent men live. Noisy men die.' He held the man till he stopped struggling. 'I want answers quickly. When I take my hand away, if you shout or make a noise, I will knock you out with a stone.' Patrick knocked a stone hard against the man's skull as a foretaste. The man nodded his understanding.

'Who owns the horse and cart?'

'Ephesus,' the man whispered.

Patrick smiled, relieved the driver was co-operating.

'Who is Ephesus?'

'Estate supplies.'

'Who do you work for?'

'Ephesus.'

'Has Ephesus sent you?'

'He has.'

Patrick stuffed the stone in the driver's mouth and, using his ankle bandage, gagged the man tight. He tied him to the cart; arms to the front wheel, ankles to the back.

Diving for cover Patrick looked out for the post carrier. He couldn't see him. Something was wrong. Patrick ran down the track and heard a voice calling 'Domitius'. Then he saw the carrier looking on the wrong side of the building. Patrick crept close to him. He gritted his foot to make a noise. The man turned, straight into a right-hander. He retreated, shook his head and came straight back at Patrick. They both took a boxing stance. The worker tried a couple of punches. Patrick dodged and landed some more punches at which point the worker put his hands up in surrender. Patrick threw two bundles of twine at him.

'Tie your ankles to that post,' Patrick commanded. The worker obeyed. 'Now lie on your back with arms outstretched.' He obliged. Patrick bound the man's wrists together and tied his outstretched arms to another post, then retied the man's ankles, surprised that the captive had made a good job of his own tethers.

'Who is paying you for tonight's work?' Patrick asked.

'Domitius.'

'I see you won't spill blood for him?'

'In a way I already do. He doesn't give me coin, but he will spill my blood and break my bones, if I don't work at night for him. Master, where is Domitius?'

Patrick smiled at the worker's reference to him as 'master', briefly reinstating Patrick's.

'I think he's lying down.'

Patrick left the scene, returned to the house, and raised the alarm as diplomatically as possible. Not knowing where the sisters slept, he remembered Angelina calling Mary by pulling a cord in the library. Guessing the room above might be Mary's, he pulled the cord. Mary arrived in a nightgown.

'Patricius, what is the matter?' Mary asked. Before he could answer Angelina arrived.

'Angelina, Mary, some disturbing events have taken place at the farm,' he said.

'What do you mean?' Angelina asked urgently.

'I heard the distressed snort of a horse so I dressed and went down to see if something was disturbing your pony. I came across an unexpected scene; thieves stealing your posts and rails.'

'Where is Domitius? Is he dealing with it?'

'In his own way. You should come to the scene and see things for yourself.'

'Wait for us, Patricius. We'll be as quick as we can.'

The women returned, dressed and cloaked; Angelina brought a lamp, though the night wasn't entirely dark.

As they approached the farmyard Patrick said, 'Over there is a four-wheeled cart, horse and driver.'

'What do you mean, is? Are they still there?' Angelina asked.

'I hope so,' Patrick answered then continued, 'there is someone at the stables you should see, before we go to the cart.'

'Patricius, you are going to tell me what has happened?' Angelina asked.

'Psalm and chapter, though I would like you to see the scenes for yourself without my comment; and when I am a suspect, I hope that you will question me last.'

Angelina thought for a moment, 'Yes, I'll do that.'

They approached the stables. The shackled man frowned on seeing Angelina. Patrick already had a feel for this man; he saw in his face no guilt or arrogance, but plenty of fear. Angelina walked up to the captive, squatted, and held her lamp close to him.

'I recognise you,' she said.

'Yes, ma'am, I work on the farm.'

'And why are you here, tied up, in the dark hours?'

'Your new fence-man caught me loading your supplies onto a wagon.'

'Why were you doing that?'

'I was told to.'

'Who told you?'

He anguished but didn't reply. Patrick felt for the man. He'll believe the truth won't answer. Angelina will be tested too.

'Who told you?' Angelina asked assertively.

'Ma'am, I'm already ruined. You can't believe me because I'm a servant, but I will lose my job for giving an honest answer.'

'I am your employer; you should trust me with your truthful answer.'

'Domitius, Domitius told me.'

Angelina was taken aback. 'You're asking me to believe Domitius told you to do this; my own manager?'

'No ma'am. I knew you couldn't believe me. I'm just answering your question.'

'Does he pay you to do this vile work?'

'No ma'am.'

'Then why do you do it?'

'Because he will beat me severely if I don't.'

She took a breath, 'Show me your bruises.'

'I don't have any ma'am. I co-operate to avoid getting them.'

'This is too easy for you, isn't it?' Angelina commented.

'Ma'am,' said Patrick, 'I cannot speak for this man, but let me show you something.'

Patrick stripped his tunic to his waist. Angelina saw his beaten body and was shocked; she stood closer, moved the lamp around and studied the bruises. She saw his ribs at the front were a melding colour of yellow, green, and blue, and the wheals on his sides showed four enlarged, circular, red, and purple imprints of a knuckled fist. Angelina's face showed anguish.

'Turn round.'

Patrick turned.

'These bruises are too fresh to be from the quarry. Has Domitius done this to you?' she asked.

'He has ma'am.'

Patrick looked across to the captive, who gave him an understated nod of gratitude.

'I have more to learn,' Angelina said to her employee, 'but I will judge you fairly.' She turned to Patrick, 'Lead me to the wagon, if it's still there.'

Patrick enjoyed her remark, and led the way. It was there. Patrick saw the gagged driver and quickly slit the mouth binding with his newly acquired knife. Angelina inspected the horse, the cart and finally the driver, recognising none of them.

'Who are you working for?' she asked.

Patrick looked on nervously, hoping the cart driver wouldn't change his story, or refuse to co-operate.

'Ephesus.'

Patrick breathed a sigh of relief.

'Are you from Estate Supplies?'

'I am; ma'am, cruel, isn't it?'

'What do you mean?'

'Well, you buy from him, run short because he steals from you, then you buy from him again.'

Angelina didn't reply. She turned to Mary and Patrick, 'Let's waken Domitius,' she said.

'You'll find him awake. He was stirring when I came to get you,' Patrick said, keeping a straight face.

As they came to the stables Angelina was about to turn to the farmhouse when Patrick said, 'He's behind the stables, Angelina.'

She cast a quizzical look Patrick's way and turned the corner to see her manager stretched out on his back, on the ground, arms and legs extended and bound.

'What on God's earth is this?' Angelina exclaimed. By now the big man had caught his breath and had prepared his case.

'Don't you believe anything he tells you,' Domitius declared angrily, nodding towards Patrick. Angelina drilled Domitius with her eyes. Suddenly he softened his tone.

'Ma'am, will you cut my bonds please?'

Ignoring his plea, Angelina leant over and looked him square in the face. 'You tell me what has happened,' she said, omitting the courtesy of addressing him by name.

'I heard noises and came out to look. I found your new fence builder organising the theft of your supplies. I tried to detain him, but he's young and fast. He overcame me,' Domitius explained.

'It was he who raised the alarm,' Angelina responded.

'He would, wouldn't he? I caught him in the act. He's trying to turn the table.'

'The dawn of his fifth day is not yet here. How could my fence builder organise a horse and cart, a driver and helper, as well as finding a customer?'

'Ma'am, you think you bought his freedom but it looks like the quarry set you up.'

Angelina paused thoughtfully. 'That is all for now,' but before she could turn, he appealed again.

'You are going to cut me free ma'am?'

'Not yet. I'm calling the night guards.'

'You'll have to tie him up as well.' He nodded to Patrick, resentment darkening his eyes.

'Domitius,' she squared with him, 'I know what I'm doing.'

Angelina, Mary and Patrick returned to the house in silence.

Inside the library, away from eyes and ears, Angelina said to Patrick, 'He thinks we bought you from the quarry, in which case his lie was plausible.'

'Indeed, and he doesn't know the men are captured,' Mary enthused. 'Shall I launch the flare?'

'Yes, Mary. I meant what I said to Domitius.'

Patrick looked puzzled as Mary took out a lighting set and left the room. Seeing his expression Angelina explained. 'It's how we call the night guards. The flare draws their attention, the colour identifies us.'

Mounted on the gable of the house was a flare, Mary lit the squibb and an orange shaft of light shot into the air, lingering about thirty feet above the buildings before the vitality faded into smoke and became the night air. Mary continued down the track to the gate, which she opened and returned to the library.

'You haven't questioned me, ma'am,' Patrick said.

'I didn't need to. The fact and the lies pointed to the truth, unless the night guards see things in a different way.'

Mary had barely sat down when the sound of horses' hooves arrived at the entrance. Mary leapt from her chair. Moments later she returned, the night guards with her. Angelina and Patrick were waiting.

'Good to see you both, impressively quick as well.' Angelina said.

'We were patrolling nearby, ma'am,' one replied.

Angelina nodded and continued. 'Time is short; I'll get straight to the problem. Meet Patricius, our new employee. His job is to improve our security. Over the last three months we've been losing things, in particular a large supply of wooden fencing supplies. Patricius has caught three men in the act of thieving. Two are my employees and one works for my fencing supplier. At least that is what we think. Officer, we would prefer to catch the organisers, so we called you.'

'I understand, ma'am. Patricius, tell me what happened.' After listening to Patrick's account, he then said, 'Ma'am, may I have a private word?'

'Of course,' Angelina showed the senior guard to the library and after speaking quietly, returned to the hallway. Patrick scrutinised the guard's face but there were no clues, as he addressed his assistant.

'The manager doesn't know the thieves have been caught. We should keep it this way.' He turned, 'Ladies, Patricius, take us to the scene.'

The guards interviewed the driver, a man they recognised from previous misbehaviour. They questioned the farm labourer and finally Domitius.

Out of sight of the culprits, the senior guard spoke to the women and Patrick.

'We believe your manager's account is false and will fare badly in front of a magistrate. We propose to scare the cart driver with the consequences of his actions and offer him a way out of trouble. We will mark the stolen goods and let him return to the company with the load, as though things went to plan. Later today, we will visit the company without warning. If the marks have been removed, we will prosecute the driver for his offence, as he is the only one at the company who knows the posts are marked. If they are there, we will question the management about the presence of stolen goods on their premises. Now ma'am, the farm labourer has probably been bullied into taking part. What are your intentions with him?'

'I will caution him, and ask him to report for work as usual.'

'Thank you. Would you do that right away, ma'am, meanwhile can Patricius come with me, to the cart?'

She nodded approval.

'Bring a small knife, Patricius,' the guard said. He then directed his assistant to bring his horse to the store.

Arriving at the cart, senior guard spoke to the driver, 'I believe you're a new father?'

'Yes, master.'

'How old is your baby?'

'Three months, master.'

Patrick was impressed with the night-guard's approach.

'And how are mother and baby?'

'Both are well, master.'

'So, this business comes at a bad time for you?'

The driver hung his head in shame and nodded, then found his voice, 'Master, you know better than I do. It's the bosses. My last offence was Ephesus. This one is Ephesus, but I'll get prison this time. Seriously, master, how can I, a servant, get a horse and cart.'

'We should have a chat then. Mark the wood, Patricius.'

The guard spent only a few minutes with the driver, by which time Patrick had marked most of the load.

'Show us the mark,' the senior guard said.

Patrick pointed to a small crucifix, cut into the end grain, and he watched the driver taking it in.

'Get on your way, young man. Hold your nerve and you'll get justice,' the night guard assured him.

As the horse and cart pulled away, the night guard and Patrick returned to Angelina. The senior guard put his thumb up to Angelina and his finger to his lips, to let her know the trap for Ephesus was set.

'Let's deal with Domitius. If you charge him now, we will take him with us and jail him till his date with the magistrate, or...'

'I don't need the alternative. Can I charge him? I mean, can I say the words to him in your presence?'

Patrick was impressed with Angelina's determination.

'Of course, you can.' He turned to his assistant, 'Get the hood ready.'

The delegation walked over to Domitius.

Angelina squatted and, looking him in the eye, said, 'Domitius, my heart is heavy. I trusted you. I gave you a career when you were fallen. How could such pettiness enter your heart? Patricius, show your bruises.'

The instruction caught him by surprise, but Patrick obeyed.

'You did this to my employee and friend, for no good reason. You are a brute. You stole from me when you had reason to be loyal. You are a low, contemptible scoundrel with a mean heart; therefore, I charge you, Domitius Dismas, with theft, brutalising a worker in your charge and dereliction of duty.'

'I'll save my words for the magistrate,' Domitius snarled at Angelina, confirming her judgement.

'Hoodwink him and strap him to your horse,' the chief night guard instructed his assistant. They watched the forlorn sight of a hooded Domitius, strapped belly down on a horse's backside, shifting up and down to the equine's gait, as the assistant guard led the way up the track.

At the house the chief guard climbed onto his mount and turned to Angelina, 'Good day, ma'am, one of us will call this evening.' He turned to Patrick, 'A question before we go; how did you capture all three of them?'

'One at a time,' Patrick answered.

'Very good,' he laughed. 'You've started well. Might I suggest you give some thought to keeping a guard dog?' He waved goodbye. 'I'll close the gate, Mary.'

Patrick's feelings were mixed. The night-guard's advice was sound, about a guard dog, but outsiders had not been the problem. He was glad not to have been a suspect, but wondered if Domitius would have means of taking revenge on him. Patrick was happy that Domitius was being taken into custody and that his punishment, when tried, would be custodial.

As Patrick watched the night guards and the dejected Domitius withdraw, he felt crestfallen; the affair had caused Patrick some disappointment. He'd been fighting again, and this time threw the first punch in all three cases. Should he have returned to his bedroom and just let it all happen?

They all waved then entered the house.

'What now?' Mary said, 'The sun will be up in two hours.'

'How about hot milk and honey?' Angelina suggested.

Patrick quickly thought of Cormac at Beltaine and the once a year treat of hot milk and honey mead.

'Perfect, I'll prepare it,' Mary said.

'We'll take it in the dining room.'

Angelina and Patricius took a seat at the table.

'What a dreadful night, Patricius, and your beating shocked me; I thought I was giving you a safe abode. The quarry could hardly have been worse.'

'No, Angelina. I like it here.'

'Thank you. What reason did Domitius give for hitting you?'

'Poking my nose into things that don't concern me, and leaving my job,' Patrick answered.

'You'll have to explain that to me, Patricius.'

'I saw two men running off with your fencing, so I chased them away and recovered four posts. That behaviour earned me a bruising. Living at the house was a source of amusement for him too. "Run along to the ladies," "Wash your hands and feet, nice and clean," and so on.'

'I had no idea,' Angelina insisted.

'It doesn't matter. I'm alright. More pressing is how are you going to handle the farm at sunrise?'

'There are two supervisors who know the routine. One of them was helping Domitius during the night.'

'How will he take your cautioning him?'

'He'll turn up for work, thankful I've been lenient, or I'll never see him again.'

'I think he'll return to work. My view is that he hated working against you.'

'I hope you're right,' Angelina said as Mary entered with the refreshment.

They each stirred honey into their mug of hot cow's milk. As Patrick enjoyed the taste of the drink, and, at the feel of the hot mug he thought of Bride and the hot broth she gave him one cold and wet night. He could think of Bride with contentment now. She was a treasured part of his life's journey.

'I'll get the workers started, are you organised for continuing the fence work, Patricius?'

'I am, but I should tell you something which I mentioned to Domitius on my second day. If you can provide one helper for half a day, every day, placing the materials where they are needed, we could finish the fence in three weeks.'

'I'm interested,' Angelina replied, 'What do you think, Mary?'

'I favour the quickest way; it's a good saving too,' Mary answered.

'I'll assign you a farmhand, Patricius,' Angelina declared.

'Thank you. Do you know that you are forty posts short, before counting last night's depletion of twelve?'

Angelina cringed at Patrick's words. 'He never said. Perhaps Domitius intended giving me an up-to-date count after tonight's thieving,' she shuddered.

'Patricius, you told the guard you rounded up the scoundrels one at a time. That isn't good enough for me and Angelina, we'd like the blow-by-blow account,' said Mary.

Patrick was charmed by the two women, who were at ease with each other, and could change from being business-like to frivolous in a breath.

'You can see we're not monastic; we like to talk, to laugh and we love stories.' Angelina laughed.

They passed time, listening to Patrick telling his story.

'You're quite a fighter, Patricius,' Angelina teased.

'I haven't fought in kingdom battles in the last two years. As a shepherd, scuffles and fights with rustlers and petty thieves have been few. I've grown in Christ and my desire to stop fighting has grown. However, I am fighting with myself. I lack the courage to turn the other cheek.' He saw Angelina and Mary listening and thinking. 'In the quarry I stood up to a bully who took my meal. He arranged two henchmen to tie me down, spread-eagled in a way he could rape me. One of the six prisoners in the cell came to my help. The two of us out-fought three as the other looked the other way. I was saved from a hideous experience.'

Mary sucked in a breath, as though horrified at the situation.

'Did I show a lack of faith when I fought back physically? Did God send me the man who helped me? Further tests of my understanding were to come. The bullies lost their privileged jobs, creating an opening for me and my helper, which in turn led to my escape on your cart.' Patrick, utterly conflicted, said no more.

'I can see your dilemma, but I don't think you are weak, unfaithful to God, or wrong, Patricius. I encourage you to keep on praying; maintain your faith and be patient. I believe the day will come when you find your resolution,' Angelina said with a humble air of wisdom.

'I think God is shaping you, Patricius,' Mary added.

'Thank you, Angelina. Thank you, Mary,' Patrick paused to lighten the discussion, 'I hear my job is to improve your security. Is that true?' he joked.

'Certainly, it's true,' Mary asserted, 'you're building a fence, aren't you?'

'And you caught some thieves. That's security, isn't it?' Angelina added.

* * *

The winter weeks passed enjoyably for Patrick. The crispy cold mornings and wintry days of Gaul were mild compared to the harsh and bitter clime of western Ireland. Patrick finished building the fence, to the immense satisfaction of the sisters and moved onto building repairs.

One day, as Patrick worked on the school roof, Domitius passed by pulling a two-wheeled handcart. He'd just collected his possessions from the farmhouse. Although in full sight of Patrick, Domitius pretended not to see him, but wore a bitter scowl nonetheless.

Patrick watched on, astounded at the pointless motivations of the big man. He'd lost his job and house, been fined a sum several times the value of the stolen materials, and his reputation locally had been ruined. His recent weeks had been spent in prison as punishment for brutality. Patrick wondered where Domitius would go now, right now, with his cart. How would he find a job? It occurred to Patrick that Domitius, having unwisely chosen a criminal path, whilst in respectable employment, would now have difficulty making a living legitimately. He could become trapped in crime.

Patrick found his own life so agreeable that he considered applying for the farm manager's position. Working and living in such a pleasant environment, with an hour of Bible study most evenings, was a God-given treat. Access to scriptural documents; the use of a private chapel, the enlightened company of the Cassian sisters, all heightened the temptation to change his life's path. But he wouldn't. His desire to go home was stronger. He would be leaving, with luck, in January. In the meantime, spending Advent and Christmas in the Cassian household was a delight to relish.

CHAPTER TWENTY-FOUR

Patrick's heart raced as he watched the horse and cart arrive at the front of the school. The driver, a monk dressed in an ankle-length, dark-brown robe, was helping two Virgin Marys from the cart. The women wore blue pallas over plain cream stolas, each with a draped, white, head covering. Angelina's groom was attending to the travelling cases, which he carried into the house. Patrick, returning to the school from the workshop, made his way to the back-door entrance and, once in his room, dropped to his knees in thanksgiving. His journey to home was about to resume. He washed thoroughly and changed into a clean tunic.

Arriving early at the dining room he decided to spend a few minutes in the chapel. As he knelt, a few students finished prayers and left silently. Patrick thought how the Sisters of Christ were being trained in the use of silence. John Cassian wasn't trying to create silent orders, he believed in speech for necessary communication within their community, and speech with visitors and the visited. Succinct expression was taught, including politeness by gesture and fewer words amongst peers. The use of silence was taught to create enhancements: concentration, awareness of God's presence and the development of continuous living prayer. Silence in deportment, care in handling cutlery and crockery, in picking things up and putting things down, including one's self when rising from a chair or settling in a seat; all things to serve serenity, allowing the awareness of Christ to the fore.

Patrick pondered his own prayer life as a shepherd. He could be immersed in prayer, yet freezing bodily while outside enduring a storm, or in a noisy bedroom with drunken soldiers. Patrick could appreciate the benefit of silence and serenity, though, and praying in the chapel felt especially enabling of the glorification of God. Patrick concluded his contemplation and made his way to the dining room.

Mary was in there, preparing the table for four.

'Ah, Patricius, Brother Barnabus will be joining us tonight. You will leave with him tomorrow, which is why Angelina wishes to speak with you privately before dinner. There will be little time in the morning. Would you go to the library, Angelina will meet you there?'

'Thank you, Mary, of course I will.'

As Patrick left the dining room, sisters were entering the hallway from all directions, making their way to the refectory. He lingered till the corridor cleared before entering the library. The room was empty of people. Patrick remained standing, idly looking at codices' titles and manuscript labels until Angelina arrived.

The door opened. 'Patricius, your visitor has arrived,' she announced.

'Angelina, I'm delighted, but I've so enjoyed my time with you. I...'

Angelina interrupted, 'We can talk over dinner, Patricius. For now, please take a seat,' she gestured to tall chairs at a table. 'We should discuss arrangements.' She passed him a small black purse, drawn together at the top with a leather thong. 'Here is a supply of coins. You will stay at five inns on your way to Autricum. The horse and cart have been paid for by the arriving women and the monastery does not require a contribution from you, for their driver. We expect you will need seven more inns and possibly a horse for your onward journey to Bononia. Finally, you will need a boat ride to the Britains. Mary and I have calculated the costs and the provision in this purse will get you to your homeland. Your work here has paid for your stay and the inns. We hope you consider this is fair payment.'

'Generosity beyond my dreams,' Patrick said, shaking his head in disbelief.

Angelina continued. 'However, exposing our corrupt manager and triggering the return of our stolen materials also is of great value to us. You may keep the clothing we have supplied to you. The abbot may require you to purchase a robe, and you can expect life to provide you with unexpected additional expenses. Mary and I have placed extra coins in your purse to ensure you make it to Dubrae.'

'I can't thank you enough, Angelina. I don't know how I can repay your generosity.'

'Patricius, we both think God is guiding you. However, when it comes to money, you can be sure you earned it. Let's join the others.'

The monk and Mary were standing behind their chairs when Angelina and Patrick entered.

'Brother Barnabus, Patricius, please be introduced.' Angelina gracefully swept her right hand and arm.

Patrick bowed his head reverently, saying, 'My pleasure to meet you, Brother Barnabus.'

'Thank you, Patricius, and may God bless you.'

Angelina said the blessings before the meal and they took their seats. Mary poured four dishes of tasty chicken broth, which proved to be an effective inducement to silence. Patrick decided he wouldn't speak until spoken to, except for passing compliments on Mary's cooking.

'You make a very tasty broth, Mary.'

'Perfect,' said the monk.

Angelina smiled and raised her thumb to Mary. After the broth, Mary served two wheat pancakes and a small pot of honey each. At this point Brother Barnabus pulled a bottle of mead from his deep-pocketed robe.

'Monastery mead,' he announced, 'home-brewed at Autricum.'

'Oh, thank you, Brother Barnabus, this is a treat,' Angelina enthused. She turned to Patrick. 'Patricius, you will find the brothers are such good winemakers.'

Mary pulled out the stopper and poured the wine.

'Patricius, have you been a monastery guest before?' Brother Barnabus enquired.

'I haven't, Brother Barnabus.'

'Let me explain a little. Our abbot will require you to wear a robe and to embrace the monastic life. There is a special programme for visitors. For example, the monks pray the hours, which is eight sessions. Visitors are asked to pray at least three of them. We eat twice a day. Visitors can eat three times. It is a working monastery and visitors will be given five hours of labour each day. Are these terms acceptable to you?'

'With all my heart, they are,' Patrick answered.

'Very well; we shall depart tomorrow at 6am.'

The precise time reference sounded comical to Patrick after years of dawn having no number.

Silence settled on them as they enjoyed their pancakes and honey. At the end of the meal Angelina called on Patricius. 'Would you lead us in thanksgiving after meals, please?'

'Of course,' Patrick replied, and with palms together and bowed head, he began, 'Merciful and compassionate Lord, thou hast given nourishment to we who fear you. We give thee thanks and praise. We beseech thee to give us in like manner, heavenly nourishment. Write in our hearts thy law. Sanctify our minds, our souls, and our bodies, through Jesus Christ Our Lord.' Four Amens followed in unison.

Brother Barnabus rose from his seat and, facing Patrick, said, 'A most sincere thanksgiving.' He turned to the sisters, 'Angelina, Mary, thank you for your hospitality. If you don't mind, I'd like to retire to my room.'

'Feel free. Your horse and cart will be ready at six. Goodnight, Brother Barnabus.'

'Good night, Angelina, goodnight, Mary, see you at six, Patricius,' Brother Barnabus glided gracefully from the room.

'He keeps a version of the eight hours even when travelling,' Angelina commented.

'I'm sure you will hear some chanting on your journey too,' Mary added.

Angelina picked up the mead bottle and filled all three glasses.

'Let's drink to a successful journey for Patricius. Salus Patricius,' Angelina toasted.

'To Angelina, Mary and the school, Prost,' Patrick responded. 'Which reminds me, have you considered giving the school a name?'

'Yes, we have. It's a question for John to answer. He wants the name to be honorific and says he will know when the right idea arrives. At a practical level, we fill the places available in the school with ease, so he is not in a hurry to find a name.'

Patrick nodded and turned the conversation to another matter. 'I'm worried about being robbed, now that I have coins in my possession,' Patrick explained to the sisters.

'From here to Autricum is a risk,' Angelina said, 'but monks are not usually a target. Stay close to each other when you stop to feed the horse. Don't get separated. You have a water tub, so don't stop at fords. This kind of robbery hasn't happened for a few years on this road, so you should be safe.'

'Patricius, we've enjoyed your company and it was a thrill to help you escape from the quarry. Adventure seems to follow you. You caught the fence thieves and Domitius,' Mary said.

'I pray for a quieter life, Mary,' Patrick added.

'You're a man of God, Patricius, and I think you were sent to us. We wish you success in fulfilling your dreams,' Angelina concluded.

'Thank you. Time for prayer and bed,' he said and left to go to the chapel.

The place was full. Only two kneeling stands were unoccupied. He took one and prayed deeply with his eyes closed for many minutes. When he opened them to look at the crucifix, he saw Brother Barnabus in the next stand. Patrick prayed for another hour and, when he left, Brother Barnabus, two pupils, and the Cassian sisters remained.

On returning to his room, Patrick found a dark-grey cloth shoulder bag on his bed with a little note attached, "Patricius, you may find this bag useful". The woollen bag had an outline of the school building embroidered onto the front. He was delighted with the gift which was practical, but the value as a memento was especially welcome. Inside he found an empty water bag. He counted his blessings and said thanks for a joyous experience at the Cassian school, and slept soundly, arising before dawn.

With his bag packed and strapped over his shoulder, he entered the chapel. Brother Barnabus was there, alone. Patrick knelt in the stand beside him. Brother Barnabus prayed his usual first hour ritual aloud and moved on to singing a chant. Patrick chanted with him as far as he could. They left the chapel together without a formal greeting of good morning.

Perhaps prayer together was sufficient acknowledgement, Patrick wondered as Mary entered the hall, 'Morning, Brother Barnabus, morning Patricius.'

They both bowed their head in greeting.

'I've put out oatcakes and juice for you in the dining room, and a pack of dates and cheese to take with you.'

'Thank you, Mary,' said Patrick, and the brother bowed graciously.

'Would you like me to fill your water skins?'

'Yes please,' Brother Barnabus replied.

Patrick nodded and handed over his skin, as did the monk. While Mary was away with the water bags the men ate their break of fast standing up. Mary returned with the filled water bags which the men packed in their bags along with the cheese and dates.

'Time to go,' Brother Barnabus declared. 'Is your sister here?'

'Yes, she's outside with the groom.'

They all made their way to the front of the house. A small barrel of water and a bag of grain for the horse were in place on the back of the cart; the whip was in its holder and the reins at the ready. The groom was stroking the horse's neck, as he made himself available for any last-minute instructions. Angelina and Mary stood together and Patrick gave them each a warm, two-handed, clasped handshake, saying, 'I hope our paths cross again, but if not, I shall never forget you.' Patrick turned to mount the cart.

'May God speed you on your way,' Angelina said.

Brother Barnabus stepped forward, 'Goodbye and thank you, ladies.'

Angelina passed a letter to Brother Barnabus, saying, 'Would you please hand this to Brother Abbot?'

'My pleasure,' he said, tucking it into his pocket. As this exchange took place, the groom said a few words to Patrick.

'I put something in the corn sack for you. You never know. The big man has a big shadow.'

Patrick was thrown a little. 'You're a good man. Look after your employers and they'll help you,' he said in reply.

Brother Barnabus took the driver's seat and gee'd the horse to his first steps. As the groom followed them down the track to close the gates behind them, Patrick stood up and looked back. He waved, smiling broadly then remembered, he hadn't said thank you for the bag and bottle. He held up the bag and ran his pointing finger around the house motif then raised his fist in triumph. His parting image of the Cassian sisters was their bubbling laughter and enthusiastic waving.

On the road, Brother Barnabus walked the horse mainly and gave him spells of trotting. During a walking spell he said to Patrick, 'I believe you are a relative of Martin?'

'Yes, but a little distant.'

'How distant?'

'Martin's mother and my grandmother were sisters.'

'So, you were first cousins once removed.'

'Exactly,' Patrick answered. 'Angelina referred to him as St. Martin of Tours. When was he made a Saint?'

'Five years ago, this summer,' the monk answered then returned to silence. This was agreeable to Patrick as he could see the quarry building and compound and knew from his own experience that some people were lawless in this territory. He stood up and watched out carefully for signs of danger. The miles passed and Patrick began to feel safer. Then he spotted a movement on the left, and next, a bobbing head on the right.

'Brother Barnabus, we are a hundred paces from an ambush. There are men on each side of the road.'

'What do you suggest?' Brother Barnabus replied with such calm that he seemed to be teasing.

'Run at them; get the horse moving fast,' Patrick said.

Brother Barnabus had already set the horse to trotting and cracking his whip in the air. The horse changed gait and ran at pace.

'I'll stop them pulling the horse down, you stop them getting on the cart,' the monk said as two men rose from the ditch, one on each side, and made straight for the horse.

Patrick quickly left the seat and jumped into the cart. He watched Brother Barnabus whip the man on the left and, with a continuous action, raise the whip over the horse and crack down on the attacker on the right. These determined men took their lashing and needed a second whipping each to prevent them from grabbing the bridle.

They changed their plan and began to mount the cart. One of the attackers had a two-handed grip on the cart cribs. Patrick ran to the attacker. Looking up at him, was the face of the merchant who'd sold him to the quarry. For one second Patrick had the upper hand. He should have prayed for the merchant, but he didn't. Patrick stepped on his adversary's fingers and took a moment's satisfaction from seeing him fall, face down on the ground. The merchant screamed in agony; more than the fall had called for and Patrick looked again to see why. The merchant's own dagger, unsheathed and hooked to his belt, was piercing his thigh as he rolled on the road. Patrick thought how the merchant had stolen Patrick himself and all his possessions; yet, with no plan in mind, vengeance had been exacted for Patrick, as a result of the merchant's own actions.

Dashing to the other side of the cart, the second attacker was over the crib and getting to his feet. A dagger hung from his belt. As Patrick made to push him over the edge, the man shoulder-charged Patrick in his midriff, sending him sprawling on his back. Patrick crashed into the water barrel and saw the open sack of corn. The groom put something in there for me, he remembered. Patrick pulled himself up to his feet with his right hand on the bag. He felt something wooden, standing upright in the corn, and grabbed it. He was too late, the man with the dagger was over him; but the attacker shrieked as Brother Barnabus gave him a good lash from behind. Patrick was on his feet now, armed with a two-foot-long wooden cosh. He swung at the dagger, sending it flying into the ditch. The right-hand knuckles of the assailant were shattered. He gaped at Patrick with cosh in hand, ready to strike again, then, glancing at the monk's whip hand, jumped off the cart. Patrick locked eyes with Brother Barnabus and laughed at the situation. The monk smiled back.

Brother Barnabus put a distance between them and the fallen attackers before slowing the horse to walking. Patrick felt sure this was not a random attack. He was the target. Patrick knew there was an association between the merchant and the quarry but how could the merchant know about this trip? He could only get to know through the quarry. Then it fell into place. Domitius has tipped-off the quarry so they can recapture me and grab a purse full of money. The groom probably had an inkling too, and hid a cosh in the grain for me. Whatever the speculation, Patrick decided to keep his thoughts to himself.

'You've done this before, Brother?' Patrick remarked.

'Yes, a few years ago,' the monk replied. 'Have you thought that you were the target?' the monk asked.

Patrick was surprised. How did Brother Barnabus get to this thought so quickly?

'Do you think so?' Patrick answered.

'Well, they didn't make a move against me?'

Patrick was relieved at the simpler explanation. 'Perhaps you were protected by the cloth?'

They travelled in silence for a few hours then Brother Barnabus asked, 'Are you comfortable on the reins, Patricius?'

'I am.'

'Then would you take over? I'd like to observe Terce.'

'My pleasure,' Patrick replied and as he reined the horse, the monk beside him prayed and chanted.

After that they swapped every three hours. The monk managed a good portion of his monastic timetable of prayer. Patrick, on the other hand was regularly serenaded with hymns and chants. There was only one rainy day out of five and their journey passed without further incident.

They returned the horse to a stabling establishment in the countryside, and walked for an hour to Autricum. The buildings there were made of stone with terracotta roof tiles. Shops selling bread, meat and candles surrounded a market square; a sight that made Patrick feel at home.

They passed through the town centre and came to a mundane church building called St. Paul's. Brother Barnabus led the way, along an adjacent path to a smallholding behind the church. Beside the agricultural land was a large rectangular field with a ladder stile for people and a wooden barred gate for animals. They climbed the stile and entered an enclave comprised of ten small square structures; stone built with thatched roofs, four down each perimeter wall left and right, and two across the bottom wall. On the right-hand side was an additional, more prominent looking building with a clay-tiled roof.

Brother Barnabus took Patrick to the front door of this large hall, and into a room that looked similar to a library. The walls were adorned with well stocked shelves containing codices, scrolls and supplies of writing materials. Tables and chairs were laid out for reading and writing. There were two doors along the long wall and Brother Barnabus knocked gently on one of them. The door opened; Brother Barnabus bowed his head. He turned to Patrick.

'Please wait a moment,' then he entered the room and closed the door behind him.

A few minutes later Brother Barnabus and a tall, brown-robed man appeared at the door. His robe was identical to the one Brother Barnabus wore, but the elliptical tonsure, identified him as the abbot.

'Patricius; meet Father Septus,' Brother Barnabus said.

'Father Septus,' Patrick repeated as he bowed his head.

Brother Barnabus bowed to Father Septus and departed.

'I'm pleased to meet you, Patricius,' Father Septus said, gesturing Patrick to take a seat in the room. They sat facing each other across the length of a table.

'Brother Barnabus delivered a letter from Angelina. You would like our help to get you to Bononia?'

'I would be grateful if you could, Father Septus.'

'Where do you live in Britanniae?'

'Near to Luguvalium.'

'When you reach Bononia, how will you travel for the remaining two thirds of your journey?'

'I'll walk.'

'And for accommodation?'

'I'll buy a sheepskin and sleep in the woods, caves, or any other outdoor shelter.'

Father Septus raised his eyebrows before continuing.

'We have experience of boat travel up and down the east coast of Britanniae. You could travel cheaply to Segedunum with a merchant boat from Dubrae. Boats return to Segedunum empty, having delivered their cargo. You'll save a week of footslogging. Keep back some of your Roman coins if you choose this option.'

'Thank you for your advice, Father.'

'The pleasure is mine. Let us speak about your time in the monastery. You are not trying to enter the brotherhood; you are a passing visitor. Therefore, we are accepting you into our community as a guest, on the strength of your excellent referral from the familial sisters of John Cassian, who is the founder of this monastery.'

Patrick thought of his good fortune. His connection with Martin of Tours transformed his acceptance by the Cassian sisters, and their reference in turn has opened doors to the monastery and the help of the Brothers.

'To be a guest you must agree to certain behaviours and rules; some you will have heard from Brother Barnabus which I shall expand upon and ask you for your agreement. You should wear a green robe, which marks you as a guest brother. You should partake in at least three of our liturgies of the hours. You should work five hours each day in the labour of the monastery. This could be on the farm, apiary, brewery, laundry, kitchen or workshop. Your speech should be quieter than civilian speech. Laughter as a spontaneous expression of joy is acceptable. You should not pursue laughter as entertainment or an end in itself. You should respect the general ethos of the monastery and its monks. Do you accept these conditions?'

Patrick knelt, and with palms together said, 'Father Abbot I accept these conditions.' He bowed his head and rose to his feet.

'I will speak to you after vespers regarding your onward journey. Finally, I can offer you accommodation in a solitary cell or with two brothers in a three-bed cell. What is your preference?' Father Septus asked.

'I'll take the shared accommodation please,' Patrick answered, wishing to engage as closely as possible with the monks and their lives.

Father Septus nodded and went to the door which he opened.

'Brother Barnabus, please take Brother Patricius to cell eight, and provide him with a guest robe, water bowl, soap and towel.' He beckoned Patrick to the door, bowed to him and Brother Barnabus and closed the door.

'Follow me,' Brother Barnabus said in an inviting tone. He appeared to walk slowly while moving at normal pace. Patrick followed as other monks crossed the quadrangle to enter their cells. The monk showed Patrick to his cell. On the wall opposite was a row of three beds, each with a small cabinet alongside. Against the left wall was a table and washing bowl. On the right, a plain table was positioned hard up to the wall, with chairs in place on the other three sides. A tall candlestick stood in the centre to facilitate reading and writing.

'This bed and cabinet are for you. I'll be back with your effects,' Brother Barnabus said.

Patrick unpacked his sandals, tunics, and underwear. The

brooch, pinned inside one of the tunics, could stay there, he decided, before folding his tunics neatly and placing them in his cupboard.

Two monks entered the cell. Patrick bowed his head in greeting, saying, 'My name is Patricius.'

'Andrew,' said one.

'Anthony,' said the other.

'Is this your first time in the Autricum Monastery?' Andrew asked.

'Yes,' Patrick answered.

'We wash hands and feet and enter the church for vespers, in order to go directly to the refectory after the service.'

'Thank you, Brother,' Patrick acknowledged as Brother Barnabus arrived with a new green robe and washing gear.

'Ah, you've met Brothers Andrew and Anthony already,' Brother Barnabus said, bowing his head to them both. 'They'll explain our routines to you. If you need any help, at any time, Patricius, I reside in cell eleven. Father Septus would like to speak to you after vespers, so keep an eye out for him.' He bowed to the three of them, and left.

'May I wash and change?' Patrick asked gesturing towards the jug and bowl.

'Yes, of course. The only individual privacy we have is in the bucket room,' Andrew said without a hint of a smile. Patrick nodded and set about his ablutions, finally donning his full-length green robe and sandals. The fit was good and he found the fabric impressively warm and comfortable.

While his cellmates were dressing, Patrick took to his knees giving thanks and praises.

'Time to go,' Brother Andrew said, and the three made their way to the church. Filing through a scripture room they each collected a book of psalms from the shelves and, with the rest of the monks, entered the church. The brothers filled the back three rows on both sides of the centre aisle, quickly and quietly. As Patrick flicked through the neatly handwritten psalms, produced here at Autricum, the public shuffled through the door continuously until the church was full. Patrick's spirits were high. He felt proud to be with the monks and to be called brother amongst the brothers.

The priest arrived and welcomed the congregation to the Lucernarium and the singing of the psalm. Patrick knew the Latin word Lucernarium, meaning lamp lighting, but had never heard of a church service by this name. The monks sang like a trained choir accompanied by laypeople who also were accomplished singers. Patrick enjoyed singing the psalms, this evening above all. He thought back to the hills of Ireland where he'd found God. With no scriptures or priests to assist him he'd organised his own prayer life. He'd arrived in Ireland in a serious state of sin and his first prayer had been for forgiveness. As he came through those miserable days, one day at a time, thanks became his second prayer. As he began to feel forgiven, and the days became joyous he went beyond thanksgiving and on to praise. He was thrilled with the message of the psalms and began to see in them a confirmation of his own approach to prayer.

As these thoughts bounced around in his mind the tone of the service became meditative, around receiving the message of the reading. Thereafter, the priest censed the altar. The burned and sweet aroma wafted through the church till all were inhaling. Then they were called to chant a canticle, the song of Mary. Patrick's eyes, though often closed in prayer, were being opened. He was experiencing a service: an ordinary sounding name for a routine and regular event. Yet he hadn't really understood the word service till now. The choir mastered musical complexity in order to raise the delivery of thanksgiving and praise, on behalf of all present. The priest, monks, choristers and congregation combined to create an enhancement of the sending and receiving of messages to and from the Lord.

Patrick came out of his reverie as the priest set off the Lord's Prayer and followed with a call for contemplation and the invocation of divine help. Patrick skimmed over the invocation and contemplated the role of the monks. Till now, Patrick had viewed ascetic monks as hermits, isolated from society with ideas and a manner of living too extreme to appeal to people in large numbers.

Here I am, on my first evening in the company of monks, seeing a bridge at work between the monastic community and the townsfolk. He was witnessing John Cassian's experiment with asceticism, in action. Cassian's idea of reining back on extreme personal deprivation and instead, feeding, clothing, and accommodating oneself, simply and without excess, was in practice. The development of self-sufficiency for food and services instead of reliance on the charity of local communities was under way. John Cassian was testing if the immensely spiritual gains of self-denial, structured prayer and contemplation could be achieved at a lower level of austerity, in a planned and cloistered environment. If it was possible, then monasticism could be brought to populated areas.

How lucky I have been to have climbed onto the cart of the Cassian sisters?

Patrick's enforced slavery at the quarry had made it possible, and yet the same experience had induced self-pity and the thought that God had forsaken him.

The priest closed the service and the monks began leaving.

'Brother Patrick, we can talk here,' Father Septus said, to a wide-eyed Patrick, whose mind was just returning to the present. Patrick bowed his head as the abbot sat next to him.

'One of our brothers will be leaving for Parisium in five days. He's a scribe, about to complete a project for them. If you walk together, I believe you both will be served well.'

'Thank you, Father. Much sooner than I expected but welcome news,' Patrick answered calmly though his heart beat faster than an excited sparrow's.

'Then I will assign you five hours a day of work for four days and you will leave on the morning of the fifth day. Brother Barnabus will explain your work schedule after prime tomorrow. Walk with me to the refectory, but first,' he said with his hand held out, 'we must return our psalms.' The abbot modestly returned both books to the shelf and they walked to, and entered, what appeared to be a banqueting hall. Brother Anthony stood up and beckoned Patrick to a seat that he'd kept for him.

'Brother Anthony seems to be looking after you,' said the abbot. 'Please feel free to approach me at any time, if I can help you further.'

Patrick thanked him and joined his cell brothers. Taking his place on a bench seat, he saw before him a mug and a wine glass and, at the side, a wooden spoon and spike. Set at intervals down the long, dark-oak tables, polished to a high sheen with beeswax, were plain reddish coloured amphorae labelled "ale" and "mead". Patrick looked at the room as a whole: I've never dined in a place with the atmosphere of a library.

A monk rose to his feet and gave thanks before the meal, after which the room filled with a gentle but unusual buzz of men enjoying food and drink. After fulfilment the brothers spoke sparingly and softly and the same monk rose again to deliver an after-dinner reading. The brothers remained in contemplation for a time and Patrick appreciated having the enjoyment of a communal meal without the tension and fear of altercation he'd experienced in the quarry. The monks began making their way to their cells whenever they were ready.

* * *

Patrick partook in all the liturgies, having been used to filling his days and evenings with prayer. He enjoyed the company of the brothers; the structured prayer, contemplation time and the access to reading materials. Through all this routine, he kept warm, sheltered and well fed. He was uplifted by the experience.

Brother Barnabus assigned Patrick to work in the laundry. Patrick learned the monks were issued two of every item of clothing. They slept in their daywear and in the morning robed afresh; as a result, the monastic laundry was a busy place. By chance, one shift, Patrick was washing underwear and was told to place the cleaned items in a cupboard. He discovered the monks wore underwear when travelling but not when based in the monastery. These items were handed in at the end of a journey, cleaned and stored, ready for issue to other travelling monks. Communal underwear, a sign, perhaps, that John Cassian had a sense of humour.

Patrick worked for two and a half hours, beginning directly after Terce. The working brothers stopped for a short session of prayer called Sext then it was lunchtime. Patrick waived his option as a guest brother, to have a three-course meal, and had two, the same as the monks. After lunch was a free period of half an hour to walk, nap or read. Patrick chose to read and discovered a supply of John Cassian's writings in the library.

He noticed Cassian's Latin was direct and simple, stripped of classical ornamentation. He'd written detailed rules and regulations for every facet of monastic life, both practical and spiritual. Patrick came across some interesting notes on Cassian's thoughts. His asceticism was rigorous and learned in the cells of Nitria, Kellia and Scetis in the Egyptian deserts, where Cassian spent seven years; some of them with Martin of Tours. Patrick recognised his own development in one of John Cassian's pronouncements: "Prayer and personal asceticism is essential in attaining salvation." Patrick found additional writings portraying Cassian's pragmatism, which fitted with the ideas that Angelina and Mary had explained. "Asceticism, as well as ministry are aspects of practical life." Cassian explained further with practical examples. "Hospitality should override ascetic routine, applicable to the most contemplative of orders." These principles appealed to Patrick. He was sorely tempted to abandon his plans to return to Britaniae and ask to become a novice, but the pull of home was stronger.

The day before his planned departure, Father Septus handed a letter to Patrick.

'Brother Patricius, hand this letter of introduction to the abbot. He doesn't know you are coming but he is expecting Brother Michael and the manuscripts as soon as they are ready. We always walk, in two's or more; never alone, which means he will be able to accommodate you at least for a short time.'

'Father, I have enjoyed my time here and I am grateful for your hospitality,' Patrick said with a degree of sadness. 'May I purchase the guest robe as a token of a most important time in my life?'

'Thank you for your kind words, Patrick. It is our pleasure to help. As a matter of fact, your walking with Brother Michael is a service to us. Please keep the robe for yourself with our thanks.'

'Thank you, Father Septus,' Patrick said as he bowed.

Patrick and Brother Michael, who carried a satchel of texts and manuscripts, observed Prime at the Autricum Monastery, and set off on foot shortly after sunrise. As they walked, the two held brief conversations, usually after prayers. Brother Michael asked Patrick if he had a favourite psalm. He replied Psalm 23; truthfully, not mentioning it was the only psalm that he knew. He'd heard many more psalms since leaving the Cassian School, but not enough times to have committed them to memory. Brother Michael mentioned his favourite, which meant nothing to Patrick, but Patrick kept the conversation going with a question.

'I read that John Cassian's favourite is Psalm 70?'

'Do you know the psalm?' Brother Michael asked.

'I'm sorry I don't,' Patrick answered.

'It's a short psalm. I'll sing it to you. "Make haste, O God, to deliver me, make haste to help me, O Lord".' When Brother Michael finished the psalm, Patrick walked in silence, taking in the words that seemed written for him. "Let them be turned backward that desire my hurt. Let all that seek thee rejoice."'

The weather was stormy, extending their journey by a night, however, Patrick and Michael made the best of it. By the time they reached their destination Patrick had doubled the number of psalms he knew from memory, and mastered a couple of chants too. He would never forget Brother Michael; there was something magical about walking and singing together in the rain.

* * *

They arrived at Parisium before sunset and reported to the abbot. Patrick handed over a letter, penned by Father Septus, and Brother Michael showed his satchel of scripts to the abbot who examined the documents with delight.

'Brother Michael, I thank you for the work and the speed of your response. Please take them to Brother Quillian, in the scriptorium. He will be pleased to see you.' As Brother Michael left the room the abbot turned to Patrick. 'Please take a seat,' he pointed to the table and taking a seat himself, opened the letter of introduction and read it. 'You've stayed with the Cassian sisters?'

'I have, Father.'

'How was the experience?'

'Uplifting; I believe God was guiding my path.'

'Perhaps he still is. I am advised you are returning to your home in Brittaniae?' the abbot asked.

Patrick nodded.

'I don't wish to rush you, Patricius, you are welcome as a guest for as long as is necessary but it happens that we are despatching a consignment of mead to a merchant in Bononia. The cart, two horses and two mounted guards arrive after prime tomorrow. If you wish to take the opportunity you can sit with the driver. There will be no charge for your travel but your lodgings, three nights, will be for your own purse. Would this arrangement be to your liking?'

Patrick didn't need words. He dropped to his knees and gave thanks.

* * *

Patrick, the only passenger, alighted with the eight-man crew onto the soil of Segedunum. The evening, dry and frosty, was cold enough to snap twigs. The captain and crew had delivered merchandise, including the monastery mead, from Bononia to Londinium. Their next job was to collect a consignment of corn from Segedunum and deliver it to Londinium. Patrick had gained a low-price passage on the outward leg, the dead leg of the journey; a technique advised by Father Septus, Abbot of Autricum.

The vessel hopped up the coast, stopping before sunset on three consecutive nights. The crew halved and took it in turns to visit an inn for ale and a hot meal. Patrick and the crew slept on board in a wooden enclosure and at sunrise the captain issued dates and cheese and a mug of drinking water for breakfast. Their routine was more austere than the Cassian monks.

Patrick lodged at the same inn as the crew in Segedunum, made possible because the vessel was moored in a secured harbour. He joined them for a stout meal of porridge, followed by fish and roots. There was merriment in the public room as the captain and crew celebrated a profitable trip and Patrick drank his ale feeling celebratory too. At last, he knew his homecoming was real.

The crew were lodged in a dormitory room and had asked Patrick to join them. He declined and booked his own room, thanks to the generous supply of Roman coins from Angelina and Mary. Anxious to think over his next few days in the hush of his room, Patrick left the party atmosphere early. His room consisted of a bed, two woollen blankets and a cupboard. There was no window or chair. Patrick sat on his bed, leant against the wall and thought.

Estimating a walk of around one hundred miles, he'd be in Banna Venta in four days if snow and gales kept away. By walking, avoiding the hire of horses, catching a lucky lift from Parisium to Bononia, and a gift from Londinium to Segedunum, he'd kept back enough coin to pay for lodgings all the way home. Three more inns and four good day's walking would see him at his parents' villa after almost seven years.

What changes will have happened in my parents' life? Would they be at home? Would it still be their home? Will they be in good health? Could they have been dispossessed since the Romans left? He'd heard say at the inn that successors of previous kings had repossessed successfully. Others told of Roman generals forming mercenary armies and taking lands by force. Some mercenaries had protected the status quo in return for their own security. Patrick was beginning to realise his parents' lives may have changed radically. His excitement was now tinged with fear and he braced himself for another bout of shattered dreams.

He thought of his worn-out boots: the only possession to survive the round trip. He felt the brooch in his pocket, which he purchased for his mother by exchange of goods, in his first season as a slave. He'd yearned for the moment he could give this gift to his mother and his largest obstacle, escaping Ireland and getting back, was almost behind him. His second problem had been keeping hold of the brooch, as he'd been robbed of all his possessions twice over. His time was coming and he laughed as a thought flashed through his mind. For all he'd learned about life, he was still taking his parents for granted, simply by expecting them to be there.

At dawn he rose to a breakfast of porridge and honey and took a chunk of bread and cheese for the journey. Paying the innkeeper, Patrick bade farewell and strode off for the Roman road heading west. Thankful for the warmth of his green robe and comfort of his tatty boots he climbed the road to the peak of the Peninus. The wind blew strong and Patrick pulled up his hood drawing the cord tight. The wind calmed as he descended into a valley where he filled his skin with fresh water from a fast-flowing stream. He came across a couple of workers unloading a cart of winter hay into a frost-bitten field, to the delight of a herd of hungry cows.

'How are you doing?' Patrick enquired.

'Doing alright,' one of the men said, bowing his head, thereby reminding Patrick that he was dressed as a man of the cloth.

'I've been away for a few years. What is it like, now the Romans have gone?' Patrick asked.

'We're alright. Doing alright,' said the talker.

Patrick was pleased to hear such a positive comment from the farm worker.

The talker's friend decided to say something.

'It's better since they gone. They don't take all our corn. Farmworkers is doing a bit better.' He looked pleased with himself.

'Thank you for that. I wish you both well,' said Patrick. He continued his journey till dusk, passing roundhouses with smoke spirals, fields of winter corn, and the occasional coming and going of people. Patrick was encouraged that the farming community, in this man's opinion were – he searched for the right words – doing alright.

That night he found lodgings high in the hills in a busy little town near to Vindolanda Fort. Chatting in the bar with locals and travellers he asked a merchant: 'How is Britain managing without the Romans?'

'It varies. Cities in the south are worst hit. Buildings are standing empty. Farming communities are faring well though, especially in the north.'

Patrick felt a little more optimistic going to bed. It was only pub-talk but news he wanted to hear.

The following day, on the way to Luguvalium, Patrick passed a couple of hillforts. One was clearly newly built, covering forty acres he estimated, and the uppermost perimeter mound was built like a castle rampart. The walls were guarded by men and dogs, safeguarding an entire village. These inland farmsteads were as far from the west coast as the east.

Who are they defending from? Could it be the Picts? Local defences of this type were not permitted under Roman rule. He wondered if the Alauna Fort would still be operational under local management. The wicus, where his parents lived, thrived half on the Roman presence and half on the local economy. Then Luguvalium came into sight, nestled in the foothills. One more night in lodgings, and one full day of walking and he would find out for himself if there was a home to go to.

His heart thumped an alternating beat of excitement and fear as he strode down the road into familiar territory.

CHAPTER TWENTY-FIVE
Home

The road south of Luguvalium was blessed with many inns. Patrick tried three and lodged at the third because they served a stout breakfast at sunrise and could provide him with a shaving set. Expecting a walk of ten to eleven hours next day, Patrick wanted to stride out early, on a full stomach.

In his room, he shaved around his beard with the sharp blade provided, watching his image in the polished plate mirror; and finished by trimming his whiskers with the clippers before settling to drink a mug of hot soup. Cormac, right now, would be drinking hot ewe's milk with honey in his room. Patrick prayed and fell asleep hoping his parents were in good health.

Half an hour before sunrise, Patrick was the only person in the breakfast room, except for the ins and outs of the young woman serving him. He downed his hot porridge and the servant returned with a platter containing two cooked eggs and a chunk of bread. The forgotten taste of honey and vinegar on his eggs was a pleasant surprise, after years of cracking eggs into a pot of unflavoured, water.

She collected his empty porridge bowl and asked with a polite smile, 'Would you like a wrapped meal for your journey?'

'I would, please,' Patrick answered, enjoying her local accent. 'Bread and cheese if you can and I'd like you to fill my skin with ale.' He passed her his empty pouch.

She returned, placed a filled skin and small packet on his table and left the room. Patrick peeked with satisfaction at the contents; fresh wholemeal bread and cheese. He tried the ale and found it to his liking, and having finished his breakfast, returned to his room.

Deciding to wear his monk's robe and the ragged, but still comfortable, leather boots, he packed all else in his Cassian bag and clipped the brooch inside his tunic pocket. Cormac's words, 'When were you thinking of giving this gift to your mother?' came back to him. Patrick had thought this time would never come and now it was imminent, excitement pumped his blood. He made his way downstairs. As he paid the innkeeper for his extra purchases, a question sprang to mind.

'Is the Alauna Fort in use these days?'

'No. It's not been active for a few years now.'

'Thank you and good day,' Patrick said, masking his sense of foreboding as he stepped outside. The fort was a part of his life. He learned boxing and stick-fighting there, before the bath house was built. Corn deliveries, which Patrick managed, were made to the fort and his father's stipends were paid from there. Striding directly onto the fort road which led to his parents' home in the wicus beyond; he worried what he would find.

The sky was white; daylight the only proof the sun had risen. Bitterly cold air, made worse by a westerly wind, proved Patrick's decision to wear the Cassian robe a sound one. The woollen cloth was heavy, though soft and warm, and Patrick used the hood, so biting was the wind around his ears. Being midwinter, farms were inactive but a small number of workers were visible, digging out ditches and repairing gates and fences.

By late morning the white of the sky had bunched up into clouds and the sun peeped through the gaps. Patrick passed homesteads with smoke curls rising and thought of all the homes he'd seen in Ireland, where the people couldn't afford to keep a fire burning; the sight was heart-warming.

Patrick stopped for a midday rest and, sitting on a low stone wall, he ate his bread and cheese between swigs of ale. After years of drinking fresh water from fast-flowing hill-streams in Ireland, Patrick was reluctant to drink water from sources he didn't know.

Refreshed, Patrick continued his journey, occasionally passing farm workers walking, others pulling carts. The Roman absence was striking. Even in winter there had always been regular traffic between Alauna fort and Luguvalium.

The sky turned grey and the clouds black. Struggling to carry their loads, they became sieves releasing millions of droplets, like a heavenly water disperser; for the wind to whip and drive, before they bounced into and off the ground. Patrick was soaked but the chill was mild compared to the bitterness of the weather in the hills of Mayo. The robe, efficient at keeping out the wind, was soon saturated. If only he had Bride's inspired waxed cover with him. Eventually the clouds broke up, as a watery sun lowered in the sky to sit on the distant hills, releasing little warmth as it slipped behind the horizon to end the day.

The Banna Venta coastline came into sight, reminding Patrick of his hasty departure. He felt a tinge of regret. The trades and craft area looked run-down, with many empty buildings in disrepair, inducing in Patrick a mood of despondency. As he neared the crossroads some of the businesses, from which he collected rents, had endured. Elijah the leather man was occupying extended buildings, clearly in good condition. Patrick's heart gladdened at the sight; some businesses were surviving the Roman withdrawal. Candles lit the workshop at the front. Elijah was probably in there working. *Should I knock on his door?* His answer came, as Elijah walked onto the street. Patrick smiled and dashed towards him. Elijah's face looked quizzical.

He doesn't recognise me. I'm not surprised. I'm wearing a monk's robe and half of my face is bearded.

'Good to see you, Elijah,' Patrick said, his words completely truthful.

'Patricius?' he asked, almost in disbelief, 'after all this time?'

Patrick hesitated. 'It's me,' he answered, caught by Elijah's level of shock.

'I didn't recognise you. It was your voice that told me.' Elijah extended his arm and they shook hands. Patrick held the greeting. 'Are you just back?' he asked, looking at Patrick warmly.

'I am. And I don't even know if I've got a home to go to.'

'I can tell you. You have. Your parents are both well and living in the same house.'

Patrick breathed out in relief and internally thanked God.

'Forgive me for saying, Patricius, but you look like an otter straight out of the river. Come into the house and warm up by the fire. Let's dry you off and smarten you up a bit for the homecoming.'

Patrick hesitated.

'It's been seven years, Patricius. Ten minutes won't spoil anything,' Elijah remarked, understanding Patrick was anxious to see his parents.

'You're right, Elijah.' Patrick had some news to tell them about their son Joshua, I'll tell him and his wife together, he thought.

Elijah locked up and led Patrick to an attractive, roundhouse, behind the workshop. He followed Elijah into a dimly lit room with a well stoked central fire. Elijah took a taper and lit a few candles, brightly illuminating the room.

'Is your wife at home?' Patrick asked, realising he had never learned her name.

'I'm afraid not,' Elijah answered with a tone of sadness. 'Eithne passed on a few years ago.'

'I'm sorry to hear it.' Patrick said.

Elijah put both hands up, 'I couldn't do anything about it.' He pointed to a stool by the fire. 'Take a seat, Patricius. How wet is your robe?'

Patrick squeezed the fabric at the hem. Water pooled on the rush-covered floor. 'That wet,' he answered.

'Have you got a change of clothing with you?' Elijah asked, taking a towel down from a shelf. 'Here, dry your hair with this.' He passed it to Patrick.

'Thanks.' Patrick enjoyed the feel of the warm towel and vigorously rubbed his hair till it was dry. 'I've got leggings and tunics in my bag,' he said and saw Elijah looking across the room at a divider.

'There's a screen over there if you'd like to change. Your robe isn't going to dry out quickly.'

'I'd like to, but I don't have a cloak and it's too raw out there to walk without one.'

How things had changed. Patrick would never have entered Elijah's house before his capture, let alone change clothes there. His past feeling of superiority seemed ridiculous to Patrick now.

Elijah lifted a few items off a peg. 'Here's a cloak. It's spare. You can give it back to me when you're passing. Now get yourself into some dry clothes. I'll make us a hot drink. After that you can be on your way.'

Patrick dived behind the screen and changed, putting both tunics on, and returned to the fireside where Elijah was now sitting.

'This'll warm you up,' Elijah handed a mug of hot milk to Patrick.

'Thanks, Elijah.' Patrick cupped his hands around the mug and took a sip. 'Did you ever hear from Joshua?'

'No. We've had no news at all. The merchants couldn't tell us anything.'

'Let me tell you what I know. I met Joshua the day after the raid, when a king called Miliucc bought both of us at a slave market. We walked together from the east coast of Ireland to the west.' Elijah listened intently. 'Joshua was sent to work in a craft village, under someone's supervision, but owned by the king.' Elijah nodded in relief on hearing the nature of Joshua's employment. 'Your son was strong mentally and took the shock of his situation as well as possible.' Tears of pride and sadness welled in Elijah's eyes.

'I travelled further west and slaved as a hill shepherd for King Miliucc. I found him to be a decent man. No one is lucky to be made a slave, but we had a master who was fair. I didn't see Joshua again until ten months ago when we both worked on the same project.' Patrick called the kingdom battle a project, to spare Elijah from worries.

We managed a snatch of conversation before going separate ways. He is well and is a successful craftsman. He's bought his freedom and earns wages, working for the king; he is married too, and they have a baby son.' Elijah cracked open and tears flowed. He couldn't speak but made a heart-breaking noise that might have been 'Oh!' and again 'Oh!'

They sat in silence, both digesting what they'd heard. Patrick witnessed the depth of pain and anguish that had been inflicted on Joshua's family. He saw the torn emotion, the joy in hearing Joshua was a freeman, married and with a firstborn, then the hurt, the pain of loss at being robbed of a living and loving experience.

Elijah found his voice.

'After Joshua was ripped out of our lives, Eithne was taken ill with the wasting disease. She never improved and died a year later. If she had known that Joshua would become free and have a full life, would she have lived? She might have. But she might not. When Joshua was taken, her heart was broken. She died of a broken heart.'

Tears welled in Patrick's eyes as he felt Elijah's suffering. Patrick had no words. He rose solemnly from the stool, quietly folded his soaked robe, relieved to be averting his eyes from Elijah's, and placed the garment in his bag. As he did so, he wondered about his own parents. How badly had they taken his disappearance? Patrick thought of others more readily these days but the visit to Elijah gave him an insight that he hadn't imagined. The consequence of his own capture was his parents' horror as much, possibly more, than his.

'Thanks, Elijah. I feel better for being dry. I'm sorry the news opened your wounds.'

'Don't be sorry, Patricius. I'm mighty pleased with the news.' He looked down at Patrick's boots as he handed the cloak to him, 'I'd say they're past their last mile.'

'You're right, but two more hours of service from these boots is all I need,' Patrick said.

'I'll make you another pair, Patricius. When you've settled in, come to the workshop; I'll measure you up.'

'Thanks,' Patrick smiled.

Elijah walked with Patrick to the road. 'Pass on my regards to your parents,' he said.

'Thank you, Elijah, I will. See you soon.' They waved.

Patrick came to the barn and thought of his last night in Banna Venta and the death of the lookout girl. He'd faced his sins before God and was at ease with himself, but wondered if he had more to come from the community. The beach was hidden behind the dunes but he saw the mile tower was in use, as a guard came into sight. It looks like they've improved the defences.

A couple of men carrying spades crossed the road. They looked Patrick's way, carefully, trying to make out who he was. Arriving at no conclusions, they continued down a track towards the roundhouses. Next Patrick saw his own villa. Weeds and un-tended shrubs gave the house an untidy look. There was clutter too; children's playthings and spare logs were strewn around.

Janus, his groom and Mary, the cook and housekeeper came to mind. He visualised Janus handing him the lamp on the night before his capture. A feeling of remorse crept over him. The death of the lookout girl gave him shivers. The event had been so unnecessary. Though forgiven by the highest, should there be questions to answer to the family and community, he would relive his regrets.

On the morning of the raid, Mary had served him fruit juice and prepared his clothing, including his boots and a cape. The idea now, of someone else doing these trivial things for him, seemed wrong. The shock of the raid came fresh to his mind; the disbelief that he'd been captured; the desperation as he realised that he'd been plucked from nobility to slavery. This too had been unnecessary. He'd steadfastly refused to live in the security of the walled town.

Snapping himself out of his teenage pain and misery, he wondered who lived at the villa. Would Mary and Janus still work there?

Patrick returned to a lively pace, gaining energy from the familiar surroundings and the knowledge that his long journey was almost over. The evening was dry and the wind had died. He thought of all the times he'd ridden this road with Shadow. Would the family still own Shadow? Would Shadow still be alive? He saw the fort, high on the hill and his excitement grew. As he walked closer, he could smell smoking chimneys puffing into the sky then he spotted guards on the fort ramparts.

The fort is intact and showing signs of life. Patrick felt the urge to run the last three miles, but restrained himself.

He passed the fort and arrived at the wicus, disappointed to see derelict buildings and open spaces where buildings had been demolished. The trade premises and the shops had gone. He came to the wall and gates of the old town; the gatekeeper called him to halt through his grilled window.

'What is your business here?'

'My name is Patricius Succat. I'm here to visit my parents.'

'Come closer.' The man peered. 'I'm sorry, I don't recognise you.'

'My father is a decurion called Calpurnius, and my mother's name is Conchessa.'

'I know them. Are you the son who was caught in a raid?'

'I am.'

'I remember you now. It's the beard that done it. You were a fresh-faced lad last I saw you.'

Relieved in the end to be recognised Patrick asked, 'And what is your name?' as the gate opened.

'I'm Wainwright.'

'Pleased to meet you, Wainwright,' Patrick said and held out his hand. Wainwright, caught by surprise for a moment, shook Patrick's hand then let him pass.

Beyond the gate things were different. Even in the semi-darkness Patrick could see that the businesses and shops were in good shape. There were a few people walking in the street. He came to an alehouse where customers were coming and going. Happy to see the evidence of normality he continued to the housing area and recognised his parents' home.

His stomach clenched with excitement as he approached their house. He wondered if his parents would still have a private groom and gatekeeper now the Romans had gone. Then he saw Wynnstan approaching.

'Whose there?' he called, not recognising the visitor.

'Wynnstan, It's Patricius.'

'On my oath, it is so, master,' he said and quickly opened the gate. 'Let me take your bag.'

'No thanks, Wynnstan. And please call me Patricius.'

About to close the gate, Wynnstan stood upright, 'If you don't mind me saying; it would feel strange me calling you Patricius.'

'I've been a slave for all these years. Believe me, Wynnstan, master feels strange to me. Please, it's Patricius.'

A horse whinnied and Patrick recognised the sound, 'Shadow?'

'Yes, master, sorry, Patricius.' Shadow whinnied again. 'The top door is open. He's heard you… Patricius.'

'I'll go to him,' Patrick said and they crossed the courtyard to the stables.

As Shadow saw Patrick approaching, he whinnied and tossed his head in excitement. Wynnstan opened the bottom door and Patrick entered. Shadow nuzzled Patrick with his head, and Patrick stroked Shadow's neck.

'I missed you, Shadow. I thought of you, and I'm glad you're still here.' He stroked Shadow and fussed him. Before parting Patrick whispered in the horse's ear, 'You're a good horse, Shadow, and you're my best friend. I'll see you tomorrow.'

Patrick turned to Wynnstan as he left the stable, 'Are my parents in good health?'

'Yes, they're doing well.'

'I think it's time to surprise them.'

'I'll announce your arrival; should I say Patricius, or a visitor?'

'Say a visitor, Wynnstan.'

Wynnstan knocked on the door and Patrick's mother arrived. Patrick was standing to the side.

'You have a visitor, ma'm, from foreign parts,' he added then retreated.

Patrick stepped forward. 'Mother, I'm back.'

'Patricius,' she froze for a second, then shrieked and ran at him, smothering him and knocking him backwards a stride. He hugged her in return.

'Oh, Mother, I missed you.' Patrick felt emotions rising in him, suppressed for years. He couldn't stop them. He didn't want to stop them. His tears flowed. His mother leant back and looked at him, soaking him in.

'It's been terrible, Patricius,' she sobbed as tears streamed down her cheeks too. Then she dived in again, for a longer hug. Eventually she released him and wiped her tears away on a hand kerchief. She passed it to Patricius and he dried his cheeks and dabbed his eyes.

'How are you? Are you well?' she asked.

'I'm well and happy, Mother.'

'Come inside, Patricius, I'll call your father.'

Patricius picked up his bag and followed her into the house. His father was already waiting in the hall.

'Patricius,' his father cried.

'I'm so glad to be back, Father.' They hugged. His father tousled Patrick's hair.

'I always believed you'd come home, Patricius. You took longer than I expected though,' his father teased.

'It is said no foreign slave ever escaped Ireland. In the end I managed it.'

His father nodded light-heartedly but Patrick saw his eyes narrow as he took in the meaning of the words.

'You must be hungry, Patricius. Would you like to eat?' His mother asked.

The name Patricius, spoken in familiar tones, reminded him of his earlier self, now that he was home. In Gaul it had been a convenient Roman name, spoken with a touch of foreign accent. Although he'd moved on and associated his new self with Patrick, his parents had given him the name Patricius and he wouldn't reject it. He liked being Patrick though, and decided to stay Patrick on the inside.

'Please; anything hot.'

'Steamed fish, perhaps?' his mother asked.

'That would be a treat.'

'We can't stand in the vestibulum all evening, let's move to the tablinum,' his mother said and led the way.

She took a small bell from her pocket and tinkled it to call the kitchen servant. Patrick observed the room. He liked it. The living room was smaller than he remembered; plainly decorated and without the opulence of the dining room. Three recliners formed a U shape around a low central table, close enough for all occupants to reach. They sat comfortably on the lounging chairs, with no one choosing to recline.

The servant arrived. 'Yes, madam,' she said to Conchessa.'

Patrick stood up as he recognised Mary. He was about to greet her but remembered and restrained himself.

'Welcome back, Master Patricius,' Mary greeted.

'I'm pleased to see you, Mary. In fact, the last time we spoke you had prepared my sturdy boots and a cape. Indeed, I'm standing in those boots now.'

Mary looked down, as did Patrick, at his tatty and dirty footwear.

'It seems they served you well, master.' She bowed and returned her attention to madam.

Conchessa addressed the men, 'Gentlemen, shall we start with a cup of hot milk and honey?'

'Most welcome.' Patrick said as his father nodded in agreement.

'Three cups of hot cow's milk with honey please, Mary.'

Mary bowed, 'Yes madam,' and left the room.

The thought of milk and honey made Patrick smile. His father caught the reflection.

'Share your thought with us, Patricius,' his father said.

'I will, and with pleasure. My supervisor in Ireland, Cormac, would give me a mug of milk and honey at Beltaine; reminding me of home. Now I'm home, my first drink with you is milk and honey, reminding me of Cormac in Ireland.'

'Good to hear. Though I think you will taste milk and honey more than once a year now,' his father responded.

'There is so much to talk about, Patricius, but first, how is your health, in body and mind,' his mother asked.

'I'm fit in both but a period of calmness would be welcome. I've experienced more ups and downs in the last five months than there are in the whole of the Peninus.'

Mary arrived with the milk and honey, served in cups of the finest Mediterranean ceramic. His father picked up first and toasted, 'Welcome home, Patricius,' he said. Conchessa raised her cup to concur.

Patrick raised his cup, 'Good to be home,' he responded and took a welcome mouthful.

'You're a healthy-looking man, Patricius, and your beard is strong; I'm still getting used to it,' his father said.

'Every man wears a beard in Ireland and shaving sets are scarce there.'

'You mentioned the last five months, Patricius.'

Patrick explained, 'From leaving my master in Ireland to arriving home this evening took five months. There are many stories, but not for now; first, how are you two?'

'We're both in good health,' his father replied, placing his cup on the table. 'Patricius, we have so much to say, it will take weeks. It might be a good time for you to wash and change clothes before you eat, which reminds me, the Roman bath house is a disused building now, which encouraged us to extend here and build a family bath house. You can have a hot wash in your room or a bath in the new rooms.'

Patrick had always enjoyed a hot bath and he knew the new extension would be something his father was proud of.

'The hot wash in my room has been overshadowed. I'll take a bath.'

His father beamed and his mother said, 'Where would you like your meal to be served?'

'This room please. I like the closeness. I want to be near to you at this time,' Patricius answered.

His mother smiled with lifted eyebrows, at the new Patricius, Patrick thought.

'Your room has been ready since the day you left. Come with me,' his mother said.

Patrick stood up. 'Father, I look forward to trying the bath room.' His father rose and Patrick went to him. They hugged and the eyes of both men glistened in the candle light.

Patrick followed his mother, noting the frescoes in the corridor as he passed them. They hadn't changed, but frescoes were only updated or renewed when new plaster was applied. His room was also unchanged. Laid out on his bed was a tunic, sandals, bath gown, towels, and a bag of toiletries. Mary must have prepared the finishing touches of her own accord because Mother has been with me all the time.

'What a welcome. Thank you, Mother.' He hugged her. She held tight and kissed him on both cheeks.

'I'll show you the bath room.' She led him along a short corridor leading into the new building. Entering through a generously wide door made of light oak, they came to an ante-room containing a bath tub for a single person. The floor and walls were mosaic tiled in white and light blue wave-shaped patterns.

'This is the tub for your ante-wash. Those are the taps,' she said, pointing to two large spouts and levers. 'The water gushes and the tub fills quickly. There are cleansing oils on the shelf there and towels and strigils for cleaning off. In the next chamber, we have a soaking bath. We keep it full and Graham changes the water once a week. Last of all you will find the drying and relaxing chamber at the end.' His mother pointed to a room containing two relaxing beds made of wooden slats with towels laid across. They faced a mosaic-tiled garden scene which adorned the entire wall.

Patrick applied the words of the optimistic farmhand to his parents' situation; they are doing alright.

'Mother, I have a robe in my bag which is saturated. I could do with drying it.'

'Ring the bell in your room, Patricius. Mary will take care of it for you,' his mother answered. 'I'll leave you to make yourself comfortable. We'll join you in the tablinum when you're ready.' She hugged him again, 'Welcome home, Patty.'

Patrick smiled at the memory of his baby-name for himself.

Returning to his room he emptied his bag, unclipping the brooch from his robe pocket he placed it in the pouch of the Roman-style tunic, which was laid out on his bed. Feeling the quality of the material made his slave's tunic in Ireland seem like sack cloth. He thought of the yellow colour, categorising the wearer as a slave, and was pleased to see the back of it. Then a thought crossed his mind; blue and cream was popular with the noble classes and was an identifier too.

He rang the bell and Mary came.

'Mary, I have a robe which I would ask you to wash but first I would like to speak with you.' Mary stood in deference, expecting a set of instructions. 'On the morning of the raid, when I was captured, what was your experience? How were you affected by the raid?'

Surprised, she took a moment to gather her thoughts.

'Master, shortly after you walked up the hill, I saw four men creeping stealthily towards the villa. Janus was outside the stables when two of the men attacked him from behind. They had him tied and hooded in seconds.'

Patrick understood the technique and speed, but was shocked to hear about Janus. The ordeal was tough on anyone, but for someone approaching their retirement years it would be a very harsh experience.

'I was scared and shaking with fear. I couldn't see the other two but I knew I was in danger. We have a cool pit in the kitchen store, where I hid. Within seconds I heard two men whispering.' Patrick nodded as he followed her story. 'They entered the store room, looked around quickly and moved on. I stayed in the pit, too frightened to come out lest I be caught. I shivered with cold but had no way of knowing when it would be safe. After an age, I heard horse's hooves arrive in the courtyard. The door banged open and I heard your father's desperate voice calling "Patricius, Patricius, are you here?"'

He came looking for me. Patrick imagined his father's terror.

'I crept out of hiding and saw your father stamping on the garden wall as he looked out to the sea.'

Mary stopped talking, her eyes were teary, disturbed by the memory. Patrick's eyes too were water-filled. He went to Mary and, holding her in his arms, spoke softly, 'I didn't see Janus here or in Ireland. There were so many captives; twenty boats in total.' He stepped back as he saw Mary's composure return.

'I lost some of my friends,' Mary added, 'but my brother and my parents live in Luguvalium which wasn't raided.'

'I'm pleased your family were spared, Mary, but I mustn't keep you. Here is the robe and the rest of my clothing.'

Mary thanked him, bowed her head, and left the room, smiling back briefly, before closing the door. Patrick caught her look and believed she was happy that the master had consoled her. He was aware that he'd engaged Mary in a conversation rather than an exchange of polite words. Putting his arms around Mary to comfort her was breaking with custom and Patrick was pleased to have shed the arms-length formality.

After undressing, he donned his robe and made his way to the bath room. As the water thundered from the taps, he examined the toiletries. Amongst them were two small horns with lids. One contained vinegar, the other almond oil. Tubs of body oil stood next to scrapers. A shaving set included a high-quality blade with a bone handle. Folded on the shelves were selections of palm, hand, and body towels.

Patrick oiled himself all over then scraped off with a strigil and towel before climbing into the tub. He washed his hair with vinegar, rinsed it off in the bath and applied the almond oil. Next, he washed his body using palm towels including rinsing out the almond oil from his blond mop. Using his fingers as a comb he removed the big knots from his hair, surprised at the ease of restoration after years of cold-water washing without cleansers or oils. Using a wide-tooth comb he removed all the remaining tangles, and amazed at the softness of his hair, he climbed out of the tub. Using a body towel, he cleaned any remaining oil from his skin and plunged into the bath in the next chamber.

He kept his soaking time short, dried off and robed, choosing to skip the relaxing room in favour of, prayer, food, and the company of his parents.

In his bedroom he knelt and gave thanks then rose, donned the Roman-style clothing provided and thought of the times before the raid ever happened. The comfortable, lavish and occasionally opulent evenings with his parents, came to mind. He'd taken them for granted. Selecting from the toiletries in his room he scented himself with a dab of musk behind his earlobes; applied as a courtesy to his parents, for the provision.

Taking out the brooch, he examined the item closely under a candle light, then returned the jewel to his pocket with a proud smile and made his way to the informal dining room, a larger version of the tablinum which accommodated a few extra tables for food and wine.

He arrived first but a small amphora of white Mediterranean wine and a cup was set before his place, next to a basket of breads and fine little dishes of oils. He poured a cup of wine and took a sip; the taste reminded him of that served by the Cassian sisters. Both wines probably both came from Massala.

His conversation with Mary was on his mind. Where would Janus be now? Patrick thought he'd made a mistake, being on the land so early in the day. Now it seemed he would have been dragged from the villa and captured all the same.

It really was my fate to be a slave. Did my misdemeanours deserve such severity? Is this part of a bigger fate?

Mary had seen the raiders coming and had responded quickly with a cool head, protecting herself with only seconds to spare. Had he been in the villa she might have taken a few seconds to warn him, resulting in both being captured? Was it Mary's fate to avoid slavery? Is the fate of everyone, somehow connected?

His parents arrived, dressed as before; his mother in a grey and blue stola. His father wore a long cream tunic with a thin purple edging.

'Patricius, you look clean and shiny,' his father remarked, taking his seat and propping himself against cushions.

His mother leant forward and kissed Patrick. 'Mmm, you smell nice too. Do you like the musk?' She asked, taking her seat.

'I do; it's almost seven years since I wore scent or even thought about it. I've been a hill shepherd throughout my absence.' He glanced his father's way. 'All the same, I enjoyed the bath room, Father.'

'I thought you would,' he replied as Mary arrived with a large tray. Patrick saw her hesitate, looking at his father before serving the dishes. His father nodded towards Patrick, indicating to Mary who she should serve first. She placed a fish dish with a selection of boiled roots before Patrick, followed by a bowl of liquamen and a serving spoon. Finally, Mary served a basket of breads and oils to his parents and retreated from the room.

'Enjoy your meal, Patricius then, if you can, we'd like to hear what happened to you,' his father said, dipping his bread in oil, savouring his light supper. His father, he noticed didn't observe the ritual of thanksgiving before his meal, so Patrick inwardly prayed his own thanks to God, then enjoyed the fish and the flavours of the herbs and the sauce.

'Excellent. So tasty,' Patrick exclaimed between bites. He started his tale at Banna Venta in front of the barn and broke out of the story to ask a question.

'I thought we were saved, Father. I was in one of the last three boats in the shallows when eighty soldiers ran towards us. How was that situation seen from the soldier's side?'

'I can tell you how I saw it. I was watching from the wall of your villa at the time, stamping the stones into dust with frustration. You might have been going on an outing with the soldiers waving goodbye.'

'Thank you, Father. We could have been saved and the leader

of the raid captured. Instead, we had to listen to the laughs of the raiders as their commander announced, "They're letting us go. They don't want to get their feet wet." I wanted to scream instructions at them, but we were all gagged.'

'I lost my temper in the defence committee,' his father explained. 'The Procurator Fiscal stood up and told me to find some respect or find new employment; I contained my anger thereafter.'

'How many deaths and injuries were there?' Patrick asked.

'We lost six soldiers, who killed three raiders. A farmhand and a tradesman were killed down at the craft sector and a farm-girl's body was found in the dunes. She had a broken neck. We calculated a loss of two hundred and twenty-eight workers taken captive.'

Patrick was completely thrown, his mouth open in surprise. This must be the girl from the barn.

'I'm not surprised you're stunned,' his father said. 'The loss was crippling to our businesses. The numbers of dead and wounded, however, was surprisingly low considering the size of the raid.' Patrick felt relieved when his father's interjection answered for his shock.

'I heard at the Irish side that twenty boats set out and twenty returned.' Patrick said. 'When I first saw the slave market I was knocked back by the size of the enterprise and the evidence of substantial planning; buyers, sellers, raiders and all the preparation for exchange of goods. The multitude involved was greater than a thousand.'

His mother shook her head in disbelief.

Patrick diverted back to eating. He wanted to think about the girl with the broken neck, without appearing distracted. Why would her body be placed on the beach? If her death was blamed on the raiders there would be no investigation involving the barn. The thieves would avoid punishment for stealing? It would keep the hidden panel secret. All this, made possible by my capture.

Mary entered to check the table.

'That was a delicious meal, Mary. Thank you,' Patrick said.

She acknowledged his compliment with a graceful bow and took his plate and utensils.

'I've learned much about the so-called barbarians in Ireland. They are behind us in some respects. For example, they don't have money; they buy things by exchange of goods.' His parents nodded knowingly. 'They don't have towns and main roads.'

'My mother never told me that,' Patrick's mother interjected.

'Travel is on farm tracks and cow paths inland. Wherever you travel, you are always on someone's land which makes it difficult for a foreign slave to travel freely. There are no public roads. No one reads or writes, including the kings, except for a few bards and settlers from overseas.'

'This is why they are barbarians,' his father added.

'Even so, the Irish are cleverer than we are told to believe. They can organise well. Their laws are fair and protect all classes. Slaves have a right in law to third-party assessment and judgement. Nobles must treat servants and slaves fairly and a lawyer called a brehon will judge them fairly.' His father's eyebrows lifted.

'How would a slave be able to pay a brehon?' he asked.

'They are provided by kings. No one pays a charge. And if a king should be judged then a neighbouring king's brehon has to be used.'

'I can't imagine the ruling classes allowing that sort of thing here,' his mother said.

'We were told the barbarians were no match for the Roman army. I can say they are brave and ferocious fighters on a battlefield and, in a raid, cunning and stealthy.'

'You are right, Patricius,' his father said. 'After the raid, we learned that not one soldier in Alauna fort had experienced battle. The experienced fighters were all on the mainland. We had a trainee army. Even the centurions had never led in a conflict.'

'How did life continue here, with so many workers taken?' Patrick asked.

'Sadness and fear had the worst effect,' his mother answered. 'The area felt to be in mourning. Families were hollowed out. People were scared to go to their places of work, especially the farm workers.'

Patrick's father added, 'We guarded the roads and fields with soldiers, to encourage people back to work. Recovery from the loss of workers was quick. People without employment came from a wider area; glad to find work.'

'I've heard the Romans have left Britain. When did that happen?' Patrick asked.

'By the law of the Britains, they still rule here but they have no military standing on the ground these days. For three years we've paid the Romans no taxes and delivered no grain. They struggled to press their demands on us for lack of soldiers, and in turn lost more soldiers when they couldn't pay their wages.'

Patrick could scarcely believe the speed of the changes.

'We councillors continued to collect the taxes and provided our own defences, but nationally they are insufficient. We're an open door to our enemies across the waters.'

His father's eyes twinkled, 'In Banna Venta, we fight them in the water, Patricius. We have fire bale boats and patrol boats. We brought to life all the coastal mile fortlets. We used your report as a basis for our defence strategy.'

Patrick breathed deep, nodding his satisfaction.

'I saw the wicus is looking derelict in places. Is the local economy struggling?' Patrick asked.

'The situation is mixed. Our local economy is down but recovering. However, the punishing levels of taxation have eased; we are keeping more of what we earn. We've learned to make things the Romans imported, creating new employment opportunities.'

As his father took a drink of wine, Patrick related to this point through Irish eyes: the skills of some of the raided slaves were learned and passed on.

'The dereliction you saw is not as bad as it looks. The fort stood empty before the council took ownership. We've made the fort into a small business district and many from the wicus have moved there for the greater security.'

'I've missed all the excitement,' Patrick said.

'It hasn't been fun,' his mother said, 'and if the Romans solve their problems closer to Rome they will return and want paying back. We could be swimming in deep waters.' She frowned.

Patrick decided to make his mother smile.

'Mother, I bought you a gift in Ireland. Keeping this out of the hands of thieves has been a challenge. At times I thought I'd never see you again, but I've made it home and I present it to you now.' Patrick passed her the cream-coloured, ceramic-coated brooch with a Celtic rope pattern framing a bright, ruby-red stone.

'Patricius, it's beautiful. It is my colour choice exactly.' She felt the brooch, running her finger around the edge, feeling the undulations. 'It's stylish. I've never seen such a pattern before. It's unique.' She leant across and kissed him.

Patrick's father looked on, delighted.

They stayed up late as Patrick recounted his boat journey, the slave market, the trek to the west with the king and his retinue and the shepherding with a kindly, sage of a man called Cormac. When he arrived at his first Beltaine, after describing the barter for the brooch, he moved on to explaining his life of prayer.

'Utterly fallen; l was broken in spirit. Stripped of all comforts I began to appreciate what you had done for me.' He looked at his father and mother in turn. 'I earned nothing for myself and yet I felt entitled. I was opinionated and in hindsight my opinions were mostly wrong. I rejected your advice to live within the town walls and paid the price.

'I was lazy, thinking it smart to work the least. I decided to reform; accept your challenge and show you what I could do. However, events overtook me before the sun rose. I have known from boyhood that I can achieve anything I'm minded to. I chose, however, to take life casually.'

'We both believed in you, Patricius. The challenge was intended to move you from being a carefree youth to becoming a responsible man,' his father said kindly.

'I turned my back against the church, not listening to the bishops, you, or Grandfather Potitus. My capture and fall were punishment for my own behaviour.'

His father's face was grave. His mother shook her head in contradiction.

'One beautifully sunny day in the hills with the sheep, I forgot my suicidal thoughts, and began to accept my situation as a slave. I prayed in thanks. I started enjoying my work, and as things improved, I felt forgiven.'

Patrick saw his father was listening in horror. He'd expected his father would be pleased, on hearing his son was prayerful.

'Patricius, I never wished to plant in you such guilt. Your mother and I were happy for you to be a carefree youth. All the things you didn't like in yourself are part of growing up. I was so pleased, even now, to hear that you had decided to accept our challenge and show us your worth.'

'You didn't plant the guilt in me, Father. The raid did that. Praying to God saved me.'

Patrick's mother glanced at her husband. Patrick read her face and wasn't sure why she was saddened. Could it be the extent of his guilt, or his belief that his fate was God's retribution? He looked his father's way. His face wasn't that of a deacon, delighted his son had found God; his face too was written with concern.

The hour was late, and Patrick was tiring but he couldn't retire with such gloom in the air.

'I met Elijah on my way here. He asked me to pass on his regards to both of you,' Patrick announced.

'Did you speak with him?' Patrick's father asked.

'I did. We spoke for a while. I gave him news about Joshua, who is a freeman, married with a baby boy. He was overjoyed but the news couldn't fill the hole in his life. He told me about his wife's death.'

'There is an example of the sadness I spoke of,' his mother interjected.

'I think Joshua's mother suffered worse than he did. On a different note, I was wearing the boots you gave me, Mother. I love those boots; I've worn them every day, but they're finished now.'

His mother cheered up a little. 'I've been on your mind, or on your feet, all this time?'

'Every day,' Patrick answered.

'You look tired, Patricius,' his father commented.

'I'm ready to rest my head,' Patrick answered.

'Break your fast whenever you are ready, Patricius. I'll rearrange my commitments for tomorrow. We can talk more in the morning and I'll take you round the neighbourhood and bring you abreast with local matters.' His father stood and extended his arm. 'Welcome home, son,' he said, shaking Patrick's hand warmly.

His mother stood and kissed him. 'On the best day of my life, you were born; and this day is its equal. Good night, Patricius.'

Patrick stepped slowly to the door and with tearful eyes turned to his parents and said, 'The nightmare is over.'

Acknowledgements

During an enjoyable social evening with a small group of friends, Noel Woodfine (RIP) told me the best book he'd ever read was, *How the Irish saved Civilisation* by Thomas Cahill. Knowing my interest, he suggested a section on St. Patrick, which I might find illuminating. He was right. The experience inspired me to write a biographical novel on the saint. Unfortunately, Noel passed away before I started writing but he'd already set me in motion.

I kept Noel's widow, Anne, informed of my progress and she was the first to read my finished manuscript. I thank Anne for her comments and encouragement after reading volume one, which helped me as I wrote part two.

I thank: Arvon – Totleigh Barton and authors Tiffany Murray and Richard Beard who were brilliant tutors; all in the Sheepwash Group, particularly Zoe Hackett for hosting the Isle of Wight retreat; Bill Ryan, via Bloomsbury London, for elevating workshops to a new level and for his unstinting personal attention; Tracey Iceton, author, and creative writing tutor, for being a great teacher, development editor and mentor.

I am grateful to Brother Robert Moore for bringing to my attention, and lending me, an out-of-print book by MacNeill – a learned analysis of historical books and manuscripts about St. Patrick – from the private St. John of God library.

It is not easy to ask experts to read your whole manuscript and give constructive feedback, but Fr Harry O'Reilly, PP St. Charles at Tudhoe and the Rt Reverend Séamus Cunningham, Bishop Emeritus, Hexham and Newcastle, obliged; a huge generosity for which I am grateful.

Thanks to Michelle Lavelle and Enda Geoghegan for accommodating me on a research trip, arranging a useful introduction and accompanying me around Ireland as I tried to walk in Patrick's footsteps, including literally sitting in Patrick's seat.

In October 2019 the historian Stephen Dunford received me at his home in Killala to discuss the local history of St. Patrick. He was generous with his time and knowledge, making useful suggestions for my research. Unfortunately, my acknowledgements in this book are posthumous, as this good and talented man left us too soon, in September 2021.

My thanks go to Barbara Ross, a friend and retired copywriter, who read my whole manuscript and gave me the benefit of her observations. Out of curiosity, her husband Don read the manuscript and enjoyed the experience.

And now we get to family: thanks go to my brother Clifford for his diligence as my beta reader; and the biggest thank you goes to my wife Kathleen, for her support in living without me whilst under the same roof, yet at times listening patiently as I gushed about an idea or read pieces out loud.